DAEMONSLAYER

'I HAVE COME to claim my blood debt, King Thangrim, as I said I would.'

The Bloodthirster's voice was like a brazen horn, and yet there was something in it that suggested the void, and a cold so chilly that it burned. It was as loud as thunder and yet so perfectly pitched that every word carried exactly the minutely calculated freight of hatred that the daemon intended it to. It was the voice of an angry and vengeful demi-god. Felix could tell that the daemon was not speaking in Reikspiel and yet he could still somehow understand its meaning perfectly, and not for a moment did he doubt that the same was true for the dwarfs.

'You have come to be cast into the pit once more,' King Thangrim said. His voice was clear and deep and resonant but, compared to the Bloodthirster, he sounded like a rebellious child shrieking defiance at an adult.

'I will tear out your heart and eat it before your still-living eyes, just as I promised,' the thing replied. 'And not all your little warriors will save you. For every moment of every hour of every day of every year of my waiting I have looked forward to this day, and now it has arrived.'

Also from the Black Library

GOTREK & FELIX: TROLLSLAYER
by William King

GOTREK & FELIX: SKAVENSLAYER
by William King

GAUNT'S GHOSTS: FIRST & ONLY
by Dan Abnett

INTO THE MAELSTROM
edited by Marc Gascoigne
& Andy Jones

A WARHAMMER NOVEL

Gotrek and Felix

DAEMONSLAYER

By William King

A BLACK LIBRARY PUBLICATION

Games Workshop Publishing
Willow Road, Lenton,
Nottingham, NG7 2WS, UK

First US edition, May 2000

10 9 8 7 6 5 4 3 2 1

Disitributed by Simon & Schuster
1230 Avenue of the Americas
New York, NY 10020

Cover illustration by John Gravato

ISBN 0-671-78389-0

Set in ITC Giovanni

Printed and bound in Great Britain by
Caledonian International Book Manufacturing Ltd, Glasgow, UK

See the Black Library on the Internet at
http://www.blacklibrary.co.uk

Find out more about Games Workshop
and the world of Warhammer at
http://www.games-workshop.com

'After the dire events in Nuln, we travelled northwards, for the most part following back roads, lest the Emperor's roadwardens come upon us. The arrival of the dwarf-borne letter had filled my companion with a strange anticipation. He seemed almost happy as we made our weary way to our goal. Neither all the long weeks of journeying, nor the threat of bandits or mutants or beastmen ever served to daunt him. He would barely stop for meat or, more unusually, drink, and would answer my questions only with muttered references to destiny, doom and old debts.

'For myself, I was filled with anxiety and recrimination. I wondered what had happened to Elissa and I was saddened by my parting with my brother. Little did I guess how long it would be before I would meet him again, and under what strange circumstances. And little, too, did I guess how far the journey which began in Nuln was to take us, and how dreadful our eventual destination was to be.'

— From *My Travels With Gotrek, Vol. III,*
by Herr Felix Jaeger (Altdorf Press, 2505)

ONE
THE MESSAGE

'You spilled my beer,' Gotrek Gurnisson said.

If the man who had just knocked over the flagon possessed any sense, Felix Jaeger thought, the menacing tone of the dwarf's flat gravelly voice would have caused him to back off immediately. But the mercenary was drunk, he had half a dozen rough-looking mates back at his table and a giggling tavern girl to impress. He was not going to back down from anybody who only came up to his shoulders, even if that person was nearly twice as broad as he.

'So? What are you going to do about it, stuntie?' the mercenary replied with a sneer.

The dwarf eyed the spreading puddle of ale on the table for a moment with a mixture of regret and annoyance. Then he turned in his seat to look at the mercenary and ran his hand through the huge crest of red-dyed hair which towered over his shaven and tattooed head. The gold chain that ran from his nose to his ear jingled. With the elaborate care of one very drunk, Gotrek rubbed the patch covering his left eye socket, interlocked his fingers, cracked his knuckles – then suddenly lashed out with his right hand.

It wasn't the best punch Felix had ever seen Gotrek throw. In truth, it was clumsy and unscientific. Still, the Trollslayer's fist was as large as a ham, and the arm that fist was attached to was as thick as a tree-trunk. Whatever it hit was going to suffer. There was a sickening crack as the man's nose broke. The mercenary went flying back towards his own table. He sprawled unconscious on the sawdust covered floor. Red blood gushed from his nostrils.

On considered reflection, Felix decided through his own drunken haze, as punches went it had certainly served its purpose. Given the amount of ale the Slayer had consumed it had been pretty good, in fact.

'Anybody else want a taste of fist?' Gotrek inquired, giving the mercenary's half-dozen comrades an evil glare. 'Or are you all as soft as you look?'

The soldier's comrades rose from their benches, spilling foaming ale onto the table and tavern wenches from their knees. Not waiting for them to come at him, the Slayer swayed to his feet and bounded towards them. He grabbed the nearest mercenary by the throat, pulled his head forward and headbutted him. The man went down like a pole-axed ox.

Felix took another sip of the inn's sour Tilean wine to aid his reflections. He was already several goblets south of sober, but so what? It had been a long, hard trek all the way here to Guntersbad. They had been moving constantly ever since Gotrek had received the mysterious letter summoning them to this tavern. For a moment, Felix considered reaching into the Slayer's pack and examining it again but he already knew that it would be a useless effort. The message had been penned in the strange runes favoured by dwarfs. By the standards of the Empire, Felix was a well-educated man but there was no way he could read that alien language. Foiled by his own ignorance, Felix stretched his long legs, yawned and gave his attention back to the brawl.

It has been brewing all night. Ever since they had entered the Dog and Donkey, the local hard boys had been staring at them. They had started by making nasty remarks about the Slayer's appearance. For once, Gotrek had paid not the slightest attention, which was very unusual. Usually he was as touchy as a penniless Tilean duke and as short-tempered as a wolverine with toothache. Since receiving the message, however, he had become withdrawn, oblivious to anything but his own excitement. All he had done all evening was watch the door as if expecting somebody he knew to arrive.

At first Felix had been quite worried by the prospect of a brawl but several flagons of the Tilean red had soon helped settle his nerves. He had doubted that anybody would be stupid enough to pick a fight with the Trollslayer. He had reckoned without the sheer native ignorance of the locals. After all, this was a small town on the road to Talabheim. How could they be expected to know what Gotrek was?

Even Felix, who had studied at the University of Altdorf, had never heard of the dwarfs' Cult of Slayers until the long-ago night when Gotrek had pulled him from under the hooves of the Emperor's elite cavalry during the Window Tax riots back in Altdorf. On the mad drunken spree which followed, he had discovered that Gotrek was sworn to seek death in combat with the fiercest of monsters to atone for some past crime. Felix had been so impressed by the Slayer's tale – and to tell the truth, so drunk – that he had sworn to accompany the dwarf and record his doom in an epic poem. The fact that Gotrek had not yet found his doom, despite some heroic efforts, had done nothing to reduce Felix's respect for his toughness.

Gotrek slammed a fist into another man's stomach. His opponent doubled over as the air whooshed out of his lungs. Gotrek took him by the hair and slammed his jaw down hard onto the table edge. Noticing that the mercenary still moved, the Slayer repeatedly banged his groaning victim's head on the table edge until he lay still, looking strangely rested, in a pool of blood, spittle, beer and broken teeth.

Two big burly warriors threw themselves forward, grabbing the Slayer by an arm each. Gotrek braced himself, roaring defiance, and hurled one of them to the ground. While he was down there, the Slayer planted his heavy boot into the man's groin. A high-pitched wailing shriek filled the tavern. Felix winced.

Gotrek turned his attention to the other warrior and they grappled. Slowly, even though the man was more than half-again Gotrek's height, the dwarf's enormous strength began to tell. He pushed his opponent onto the ground, straddled his chest, and then slowly and methodically punched his head until he was unconscious. The last mercenary scuttled for the door – but as he did so he slammed into another dwarf. The newcomer took a step back, then dropped him with one well-aimed punch.

Felix did a double-take, at first convinced he was hallucinating. It seemed unlikely that there could be another Slayer in this part of the world. But Gotrek was now looking at the stranger as well. The recent arrival was, if anything, bigger and more muscular than Gotrek. His head was shaved and his beard cropped short. He had no crest of hair; instead it looked for all the world like nails had been driven into his skull to make a crest and then painted in different colours. His nose had been broken so many times it was shapeless. One ear was cauliflowered; the other had actually been ripped clean away, leaving only a hole in the side of his head. A huge ring was set in his nose. Where his body was not criss-crossed with scars it was covered in tattoos. In one hand he held an enormous hammer and thrust in his belt was a short-hafted, broad-bladed axe.

Behind this new Slayer stood another dwarf, shorter, fatter and altogether more civilised looking. He was about half Felix's height, but very broad. His well-groomed beard reached almost to the ground. His wide eyes blinked owlishly from behind enormously thick glasses. In his ink-stained fingers he carried a large brass-bound book.

'Snorri Nosebiter, as I live and breathe!' Gotrek roared, his nasty smile revealing missing teeth. 'It's been awhile! What are you doing here?'

'Snorri's here for the same reason as you, Gotrek Gurnisson. Snorri got a letter from old Borek the Scholar, telling Snorri to come to the Lonely Tower.'

'Don't try and fool me. I know you can't read, Snorri. All the words were bashed out of your head when those nails were bashed in.'

'Hogan Longbeard translated it for Snorri,' Snorri said, looking as embarrassed as it was possible for such a hulking Trollslayer to look. He glanced around him, obviously wanting to change the subject.

'Snorri thinks he missed a good fight,' the dwarf said, eyeing the scene of terrible violence with the same sort of wistful regret that Gotrek had expended on his spilled ale. 'Snorri thinks he'd better have a beer then. Snorri has a bit of a thirst!'

'Ten beers for Snorri Nosebiter!' Gotrek roared. 'And better make that ten for me as well. Snorri hates to drink alone.'

An appalled silence filled the room. The other patrons looked at the scene of the battle then at the two dwarfs as if they were kegs of gunpowder with a burning fuse. Slowly, in ones and twos, they got up and left, until only Gotrek, Felix, Snorri and the other dwarf were left.

'First to ten?' Snorri enquired, knuckling his eye and looking up at Gotrek cunningly.

'First to ten,' Gotrek agreed.

The other dwarf waddled towards them and bowed, politely in the dwarfish fashion, raising his beard with one hand to keep it from dragging on the ground as he leaned forward.

'Varek Varigsson of the Clan Grimnar at your service,' he said in a mild, pleasant voice. 'I see you got my uncle's message.'

Snorri and Gotrek looked at him, seemingly astonished by his politeness, then began to laugh. Varek flushed with embarrassment.

'Better get this youth a beer as well!' Gotrek shouted. 'He looks like he could use being loosened up a little. Now stand aside, youngling, Snorri and I have a bet to settle.'

The landlord smiled ingratiatingly. A look of relief passed over his face. It looked like the dwarfs were set on more than making up for all the custom they had driven away.

THE LANDLORD LINED the beers up along the low counter. Ten sat in front of Gotrek, ten in front of Snorri. The dwarfs inspected them the way a man might inspect an opponent before a wrestling match. Snorri looked over at Gotrek, then looked back at the beer again. A swift lunge brought him within range of his chosen target. He grabbed the flagon, lifted it to his lips, tilted back his head and swallowed. Gotrek was a fraction slower to the draw. His jack of ale reached his lips a second after Snorri's. There was a long silence, broken only by the sound of dwarfs glugging, then Snorri slammed his flagon back on the table a fraction of a second before Gotrek slammed his. Felix looked over in astonishment. Both flagons had been drained to the last drop.

'First one's easiest,' Gotrek said. Snorri seized another flagon, grabbed a second with his other hand and repeated the performance. Gotrek did the same. He snatched up one in each hand, raised one to his lips, drained it, then drained the other. This time it was Gotrek who put down his beers fractionally before Snorri. Felix was staggered, particularly when he considered how much beer Gotrek had already drunk before Snorri had arrived. It looked like the two Slayers were entering into a well-practised ritual. Felix wondered if they really intended to drink all that beer.

'I'm embarrassed to be seen drinking with you, Snorri. A girly elf could do three in time it took you to down those,' Gotrek said.

Snorri gave him a disgusted look, reached for another ale and tipped it back so fast that suds erupted from his mouth and frothed over his beard. He wiped his mouth with the back of one tattooed forearm. This time he finished before Gotrek.

'At least all my beer went in my mouth,' Gotrek said, nodding his head until his nose chain jingled.

'Are you talking or drinking?' Snorri challenged.

Five, six, seven beers went down in quick succession. Gotrek looked at the ceiling, smacked his lips and let out an enormous cavernous belch. Snorri swiftly echoed it. Felix exchanged glances with Varek. The scholarly young dwarf looked back at him and shrugged his shoulders. In less than a minute the two Slayers had put back more beer than Felix would normally drink in one night. Gotrek blinked and his eyes looked slightly glassy, but this was the only sign he gave of the enormous amount of alcohol he had just consumed. Snorri looked not the slightest worse for wear, but then he had not been drinking all night already.

Gotrek reached out and downed number eight, but by that time Snorri was already half way through number nine. As he set down the flagon, he said, 'Looks like you'll be paying for the beer.'

Gotrek didn't answer. He picked up two flagons at once, one in each hand, tilted back his head, opened his gullet and poured. There was no sound of gulping. He was not swallowing, just letting the beer run straight down his throat. Snorri was so impressed by the feat that he forgot to pick up his own last pint before Gotrek had finished.

Gotrek stood there swaying slightly. He belched, hiccuped and sat down on his stool.

'The day you can out-drink me, Snorri Nosebiter, is the day Hell freezes over.'

'That will be the day after the day you pay for a beer, Gotrek Gurnisson,' Snorri said, sitting down beside his fellow Trollslayer.

'Well, so much for starters,' he continued. 'Let's get down to some serious drinking then. Looks like Snorri has some catching up to do.'

'IS THAT PROPER World's Edge tabac you have there, Snorri?' Gotrek asked, looking hungrily at the stuff Snorri was tamping into his pipe. They had all settled down by the roaring fire in the best seats in the house.

'Aye, 'tis old Mouldy Leaf. Snorri picked it up in the mountains afore coming here.'

'Give some here!'

Snorri tossed the pouch over to Gotrek, who produced a pipe and started filling it. The Slayer glared over at the scholarly young dwarf with his one good eye.

'So, youth,' Gotrek growled 'What is the mighty doom your Uncle Borek has promised me? And why is old Snorri here?'

Felix leaned forward interestedly. He wanted to know more about this himself. He was intrigued by the thought of a summons which could excite even the normally morose and taciturn Slayer.

Varek looked at Felix warningly. Gotrek shook his head and took a sip of beer. He leaned forward, lighted a spill of wood in the fire then lit his pipe. Once the pipe was burning well, he leaned back in his chair and spoke earnestly.

'Anything you want to say to me, you can say in front of the manling. He is a Dwarf Friend and an Oathkeeper.'

Snorri looked up at Felix. Surprise and something like respect showed in his dull, brutish eyes. Varek's smile showed sincere interest and he turned to Felix and bowed once more, almost falling out of his chair.

'I'm sure there is a tale there,' he said. 'I'd be most interested in hearing it.'

'Don't try and change the subject,' Gotrek said. 'What is this doom your kinsman has promised me? His letter dragged me halfway across the Empire and I want to hear about it.'

'I wasn't trying to change the subject, Herr Gurnisson. I simply wanted to get the information for my book.'

'There will be time enough for that later. Now speak!'

Varek sighed, leaned back in his chair and steepled his fingers over his ample stomach. 'I can tell you little enough. My uncle has all the facts and will share you with them in his own time and fashion. What I can tell you is this is possibly the mightiest quest since the time of Sigmar Hammerbearer – and it concerns Karag Dum.'

'The Lost Dwarfhold of the North!' Gotrek roared drunkenly, then suddenly fell silent. He looked around, as if fearing that spies might have overheard him.

'The very same!'

'Then your Uncle has found a way to get there! I thought he was mad when he claimed he would.' Felix had never heard such an undercurrent of excitement in the dwarf's voice. It was contagious. Gotrek looked over at Felix.

It was Snorri who interrupted. 'Call Snorri stupid if you like, but even Snorri knows Karag Dum was lost in the Chaos Wastes.' He looked directly at Gotrek and shivered. 'Remember the last time!'

'Be that as it may, my uncle has found a way of getting there.'

A sudden trepidation filled Felix. Finding the location of the place was one thing. Having a method of getting there was another. It meant that this wasn't simply a fascinating academic exercise but a possible journey. He had a terrible sinking feeling that he knew where all this was going to end up, and he knew that he wanted no part of it.

'There is no way across the Wastes,' Gotrek said. Something more than mere caution was in his voice. 'I have been there. So has Snorri. So has your uncle. It is insanity to attempt to cross them. Madness and mutation wait for those who would go there. Hell has touched the world in that accursed place.'

Felix looked at Gotrek with new respect. Few people had ever travelled so far and returned to tell the tale. To him, as to all folk of the Empire, the Chaos Wastes were but a dire rumour, a hellish land in the far north, from which the terrible armies of the four Ruinous Powers of Chaos emerged to reave and plunder and slay. He had never heard the dwarf speak of having been there, but then he knew little of the Slayer's adventures in the days before they had met. Gotrek did not speak of his past. He seemed ashamed of it. If anything, the dwarf's obvious fear made the place seem even more daunting. There was little enough in this world which dismayed the Slayer, as Felix well knew, so anything that did was to be feared indeed.

'Nonetheless I believe that is where my uncle wants to go, and he wants you to with him. He has need of your axe.'

Gotrek fell silent for long moments. ''Tis certainly a deed worthy of a Slayer.'

It sounds like absolute madness, Felix thought. Somehow he managed to keep his mouth shut.

'Snorri thinks so too.'

Then Snorri is an even bigger idiot than he appears to be, thought Felix, and the words almost burst forth from his lips.

'Then you will accompany me to the Lonely Tower?' Varek asked.

'For the prospect of such a doom, I would follow you to the mouth of Hell,' Gotrek said.

That's good, Felix thought, because it sounds like that's exactly where you're going. Then he shook his head. The dwarf's madness was beginning to infect him. Was he actually taking all this talk of journeys to the Chaos Wastes seriously? Surely this was just tavern talk and the fit of madness would pass by morning...

'Excellent,' Varek said. 'I knew you'd come.'

TWO
MARK OF THE SKAVEN

THE BOUNCING of the wagon did nothing for Felix's hangover. Every time a wheel hit one of the deep ruts in the road, his stomach gave a troubled lurch and threatened to send its contents arcing out onto the roadside hedges. The inside of his mouth felt furry. Pressure was building up inside his skull like steam within a kettle. Oddest of all, now he had a terrible craving for fried food. Visions of fried eggs and bacon sizzled through his mind. Now he regretted not having taken breakfast earlier with the Trollslayers, but at the time the sight of them throwing back piled plates of ham and egg and chomping on great hunks of black bread had been enough to turn his stomach. But now he was almost prepared to commit murder for the same food.

It was some consolation to him that the Slayers were more or less silent, save for grumbles in dwarfish which he assumed concerned the awfulness of their hangovers or just how plain dreadful human beer was. Only young Varek seemed cheerful and bright-eyed, but then he ought to. Much to the disgust of the other two, he had stopped drinking after three ales, claiming that he had enough. Now he guided the mules with sure tugs of the reins and whistled a happy tune, oblivious to the dagger-like looks his companions aimed at his back. At that moment, Felix hated him with a passion which could be explained only by the intensity of his hangover.

To distract himself from that, and from thoughts of the awful adventure that was surely to come, Felix gave his attention to their surroundings. It was indeed a beautiful day. The sun was shining brightly. This part of the Empire looked particularly productive and cheerful. Huge half-timbered houses rose from the surrounding hilltops. Thatch-roofed cottages, the homes of the peasant labourers, surrounded them. Big splotch-sided cows grazed in enclosures, bells tinkling cheerfully on their necks. Each bell had a different tone, which Felix deduced was to enable the herdsmen to track each individual cow by sound alone.

Alongside them a peasant drove a gaggle of geese along the dusty track for a while. Later, a pretty peasant girl looked up from the hay she was forking into a stack and gave Felix a dazzling smile. He tried to muster the energy to smile back but couldn't. He felt like he was a hundred years old. He kept his eyes on her until she disappeared around a bend in the road though.

The wagon hit another rut and bounced higher.

'Watch where you're going!' Gotrek growled. 'Can't you see Snorri Nosebiter has a hangover?'

'Snorri doesn't feel too good,' the other Slayer confirmed and gave an awful muffled gurgle. 'It must have been that goat and potato stew we had last night. Snorri thinks it tasted a bit off.'

More likely it was the thirty or so jacks of ale you threw back, Felix thought sourly. He almost said this out loud, but even through the misery of his hangover a certain prudent caution stopped him. He had no wish to be cured of his hangover by having his head chopped off. Well, maybe, he thought, as the wagon and his stomach gave another lurch.

Felix gave his attention back to the hard-packed stony earth of the road that jarred and juddered along beneath them, trying to focus his mind on anything except the awful churning in his stomach. He could see the individual rocks jutting out of the ground, any one of which looked like it could break the wagon's wooden wheels if hit at the wrong angle.

A fly landed softly, ticklingly, on the back of his hand and he swatted at it miserably. It eluded the blow with contemptuous ease and proceeded to buzz around Felix's head. His initial effort had exhausted him and Felix gave up the attempt to strike the insect, only shaking his head when it came too close to his eyes. He closed his eyes and focused his willpower on the creature, urging it to die, but it refused to oblige. There were occasionally times when Felix wished that he was a sorcerer and this was one of them. He bet that they didn't have to put up with hangovers and the disturbances created by fat-bodied buzzing flies.

Suddenly it got darker and slightly cooler on his face, and he looked up to see that they were passing through a copse of trees which had overgrown the road. He glanced around quickly – more from habit than fear, because these were the sort of woods that bandits liked to frequent, and bandits were not uncommon in the Empire. He wasn't sure what sort of fools would attack a wagon which contained two hungover Trollslayers, but you could never tell. Stranger things had happened to him on his travels. Maybe those mercenaries from the night before would come back seeking revenge. And there were always beastmen and mutants to be found in these dark times. In his time Felix had encountered enough of them to be something of an expert on that subject.

To tell the truth, Felix thought, he would almost welcome taking an axe blow from a beastman the way he felt right now. At least it would put him out of his misery. It was strange, though, how his eyes were playing tricks. He was almost sure he could see something small and pink-eyed skulking amongst the undergrowth a little way back from the track. It was only there for a second and then it was gone. Felix almost called Gotrek's attention to it but decided against doing so, because interrupting the Slayer's recovery from a hangover was never a good idea.

And it really probably was nothing after all, just some small furry animal scuttling for safety as travellers moved by on the road. Still, there was something familiar about the shape of the head that nagged at Felix's numb brain. He couldn't quite place it just yet but if he thought about it long enough he was sure it would come back to him. Another great lurch by the cart almost threw him off. He fought to keep last night's goat and potato stew within his stomach. It was a long fight and he only won it when the stew had battled halfway up his throat.

'Where are we heading?' he asked Varek to distract himself from his misery. Not for the first time he swore that he would never touch another drop of beer. It sometimes seemed that most of the troubles in his life had somehow begun in taverns. It was amazing, really, that he had not had the sense to realise this before.

'The Lonely Tower,' Varek said cheerfully. Felix fought down the urge to punch him, more because he couldn't summon the energy to do it, than from any other reason.

'Sounds... interesting,' Felix managed to say eventually. What it really sounded was ominous, like so many other places he had visited in his sorry career as the Slayer's henchman. Any place called the Lonely Tower to be found anywhere in the Empire was most likely to be the sort of place no one in their right mind would visit. Fortifications in the middle of nowhere had a habit of being overwhelmed by orcs, goblins and other worse things.

'Oh, it's an interesting place all right. Built on top of an old coal mine. Uncle Borek took it over and renovated it. Good sound dwarfish workmanship. Looks like new. Better in fact, because the original work, human, – no offence – was a bit slipshod. It was abandoned for several hundred years till we came along, except for the skaven. Of course, we had to clear out them out first, and there might still be a few lurking down in the mine.'

'Good,' Gotrek grunted. 'Can't beat a spot of skaven-slaughtering for sport. Clears up a hangover better than pint of Bugman's.'

Personally Felix could think of dozens more appealing ways of spending the time than hunting for vicious rat-like monsters in an abandoned and doubtless unsafe mine but he did not communicate this information to Gotrek.

Varek looked back over his shoulder to where his passengers huddled alongside their gear. They must have made a pitiful sight, for Snorri wasn't any better equipped than Gotrek or Felix. His pack was as empty as a sailor's purse after a spree in port. He didn't appear to own a cloak or even a blanket. Felix was glad that he had his red Sudenland wool cloak to huddle under. He did not doubt that the nights would get pretty cold. He did not look forward to the prospect of a night on cold ground.

'How long till we get there?' he asked.

'We're making good time. If we take the short path through the Bone Hills, we'll be there in two, three days at most.'

'I've heard bad things about the Bone Hills,' Felix said. It was true. Then again, there were few places beyond the cities and towns of the Empire that he had not heard bad things about. At once Gotrek and Snorri looked up, interest written all over their faces. It never ceased to amaze Felix that the worse things sounded, the happier a Slayer looked.

'The skaven from the mine used to haunt them, and attack travellers. They'd come down and raid the farms as well. Nothing to worry about now though. We've seen them off,' Varek said. 'Snorri and I came all the way down here in the cart by ourselves, never sniffed a hint of trouble.'

The two Slayers slumped back into apathetic contemplation of their hangovers. Somehow Felix was not reassured. In his experience, trips through the wilderness never went smoothly. And something about the mere mention of skaven caused that rat-like shape he had noticed back in the wood to begin niggling worryingly at the back of his mind.

'You came all the way here yourselves?' Felix asked.

'Snorri was with me.'

'Are you armed?' Felix asked, making sure that his own longsword was within easy reach.

'I have my knife.'

'You have your knife! Oh good! I'm sure that will be very useful if skaven attack you.'

'Never saw any skaven. Just heard a little scuttling some nights. Whatever it was, I think Snorri's snoring scared it away. Anyway, if something attacked I have my bombs.'

'Bombs?'

Varek fumbled inside his robe and produced a smooth black sphere. A strange metal device appeared to have been glued to the top. He handed it to Felix who inspected it closely. It looked like if you pulled the clip on top it would come free.

'Be careful with that,' Varek said. 'It's a detonator. You pull that, it tugs the flint striker which lights the fuse which sets off the explosive. You've got about four heartbeats to throw it, then – boom!'

Felix looked at it warily, half-expecting the thing to explode in his hand.

'Boom?'

'It explodes. Shrapnel everywhere. That's assuming the fuse fires. It sometimes doesn't. About half the time, actually, but it's very ingenious. And of course, very, very occasionally they go off for no reason at all. Almost never happens. Mind you, Blorri lost a hand that way. Had to have it replaced with a hook.'

Felix swiftly handed the bomb back to Varek who tucked it back inside the pocket of his robes. He was beginning to think this mild-mannered young dwarf was crazier than he looked. Perhaps all dwarfs were.

'Makaisson made it, you know. He's good at that sort of thing.'

'Makaisson. Malakai Makaisson?' Gotrek asked. 'That maniac!'

Felix looked at the Slayer in open-mouthed astonishment. He wasn't sure he wanted to meet this Makaisson. Anyone who Gotrek could describe as a maniac must be crazed indeed. Could probably win prizes for their madness, in fact. Gotrek caught Felix's look.

'Makaisson believes in heavier-than-air flight. Thinks he can make things fly.'

'Gyrocopters fly,' Snorri piped in. 'Snorri been up in one. Fell out. Landed on head. No damage.'

'Not gyrocopters. Big things! And he builds ships! Ships! That's an unnatural interest for a dwarf. I hate ships almost as much as I hate elves!'

'He built the biggest steamship ever,' Varek said conversationally. 'The *Unsinkable*. Was two hundred paces long. Weighed five hundred tons. It had steam-powered gatling turrets. It had a crew of over three hundred dwarfs and thirty engineers. It could sail at three leagues an hour. Such an impressive sight it was, with its paddles churning the sea to foam and its pennons flying in the breeze.'

It certainly sounded impressive, Felix thought, suddenly realising how far the dwarfs had taken this strange magic they called 'engineering'. Like everybody else in the Empire, Felix knew about steam-tanks, the armoured vehicles which were the spearhead of the realm's mighty armies. This thing sounded like it made the steam-tank look like a child's toy. Still, if it was so impressive, he wondered, why had he never heard of it?

'What happened to the *Unsinkable*? Where is it now?'

There was a brief embarrassed silence from the dwarfs.

'Err... it sank,' Varek said eventually.

'Hit a rock on its first trip out,' Snorri added.

'Some people claim the boiler exploded,' Varek said.

'Lost with all hands,' Snorri added with the almost happy expression with which dwarfs always seemed to confront the worst news.

'Except Makaisson. He was picked up later by human ship. He was thrown clear by the explosion and clung to a wooden spar.'

'Then he built a flying ship,' Gotrek said, savage irony evident in his voice.

'That's right. Makaisson built a flying ship,' Snorri said.

'The *Indestructible,*' Varek said.

Felix tried to imagine a ship flying. In the abstract he could manage it. In his mind's eye, he saw something like the old river barges on the Reik, their sails filled, their sweeps tugging. It was powerful sorcery indeed that could do that.

'Amazing thing it was,' Varek said. 'Big as a sailing ship. Wrought iron cupola. Fuselage almost hundred paces long. It could fly at ten leagues an hour – with the wind behind it, of course.'

'What happened to it?' Felix asked, a sinking feeling hinting that he already knew the answer.

'It crashed,' Snorri said.

'Crosswinds and some liftgas leaks,' Varek said. 'Big explosion.'

'Killed everybody aboard.'

'Except Makaisson,' Varek said, as if this made a big difference. He seemed to think this was an important point. 'He was thrown clear and landed in some treetops. They broke his fall along with both his legs. Had to use crutches for the next two years. Anyway, the *Indestructible* had a few teething problems. What do you expect? It was the first of its kind. But Makaisson has sorted them now.'

'Teething problems?' Gotrek said. 'Twenty good dwarf engineers killed, including Under-Guildmaster Ulli and you call that "teething problems"? Makaisson should have shaved his head.'

'He did,' Varek said. 'After he was drummed out of the guild. He couldn't face the shame, you know. They did the Trouser

Legs Ritual to him. Pity. My uncle says he's the best engineer who ever lived. He says Makaisson is a genius.'

'A genius at getting other dwarfs killed.'

Felix was thinking about what Gotrek had said about Makaisson shaving his head. 'Do you mean Makaisson became a Trollslayer?' he asked Varek.

'Yes. Of course. He still does engineering work though. Says he'll prove his theories work or die trying.'

'I'll bet he will,' Gotrek muttered darkly.

Felix wasn't listening. He was wrestling with another, far more troubling concept. Counting Gotrek and Snorri, that would make three Trollslayers in one place. What was Varek's uncle up to? A mission which required three Slayers didn't sound good. In fact, it sounded positively suicidal. Suddenly something that Varek had said earlier came sharply into focus in Felix's mind, cutting through even the awful fog of his hangover.

'You said earlier you heard scuttling,' Felix said, thinking of the small shape he had seen in the undergrowth. He was starting to have an awful suspicion about that. 'On your way to meet Gotrek and myself.'

Varek nodded. 'Only at night, when we made camp.'

'You've no idea what made the scuttling?'

'No. A fox, maybe.'

'Foxes don't scuttle.'

'A big rat.'

'A big rat...' Felix nodded his head. That was exactly what he hadn't wanted to hear. He looked over at Gotrek to see if the Slayer was thinking what he was thinking, but the dwarf had his head thrown back and was staring blankly into space. He appeared to be lost in his own thoughts and was paying not the slightest bit of attention to the conversation.

Rats made Felix think of only one thing, and that thing scared him. They made him think of skaven. Could it be possible that the foul rat-men had tracked him even here?

It was not a comforting thought.

FELIX SAT BESIDE the fire and listened to the tremulous whickering of the mules. The darkness and the occasional distant howls of the wolves made them nervous. Felix rose and ran his hand over the nearest one's flanks in an effort to calm it and then returned to the fire where the others were sleeping.

All day the track had risen into the Bone Hills, which had turned out to be as bleak and unprepossessing as their name suggested. There were no trees around them, only lichen covered rocks and sharp hills covered by short stunted grass. It was fortunate that Varek had thought to bring firewood with them or they would have spent an even more uncomfortable night camped out. It was cold in the hills, despite the summer heat of the day.

Supper had consisted of some bread bought at the inn back in Guntersbad and hunks of hard dwarf cheese. Afterwards they had sat round the fire and all three dwarfs had lit their pipes. For entertainment they had the distant howling of the wolves. Felix found this marginally less depressing than dwarfish conversation which always seemed to rotate around ancient grudges, tales of misery long endured and epic drinking bouts. And horrifying as the howling was, it at least drowned out the sound of dwarfish snoring. Felix had drawn the short straw and won the dubious privilege of taking the first watch.

He tried not to stare into the fire and kept his eyes turned in the direction of the darkness so that he would not ruin his night vision. He was worried. He kept thinking about skaven and the thought of those ferocious Chaos-spawned rat-men appalled him. He remembered encountering them in the Battle of Nuln. It had been like a scene from a nightmare, battling in the dark with man-sized humanoid rats who walked upright and fought with weapons just as humans did. The memory of their hideous chittering language and the way their red eyes glittered in the darkness came back to him and made him shudder.

The most awful thing about the skaven was that they were organised in a hideous parody of human civilisation. They had their own culture, their own fiendish technologies. They had armies and sophisticated weapons that were in some ways more advanced than anything humanity had ever produced. Felix had seen them when they had erupted from the sewers to invade Nuln. He could still picture that monstrous horde rushing through the burning buildings, spearing anything that got in their way. Vividly he remembered the green flames of their warpfire throwers illuminating the night and the sizzle of human flesh as it was eaten away by the blazing jets.

The skaven were the implacable enemies of humanity, of all the civilised races but there were those who sided with them for pay. Felix himself had killed their agent, Fritz von Halstadt, who had risen to become the chief of the Elector Countess Emmanuelle's secret police. He wondered how many other agents the rat-men had in high places. He did not want to think about it now in this lonely spot. He pushed thoughts of the skaven aside and tried to turn his mind to other things.

He let his thoughts drift back into the past. The howling reminded him of the terrible last nights of Fort von Diehl down in the Border Princes, where he watched his first great love Kirsten die, murdered by Manfred von Diehl, and seen most of the population slaughtered by goblin wolf riders let in by Manfred's treachery. It was strange, but he could still remember Kirsten's gaunt face and her soft voice. He wondered if there was anything he could have done to make things turn out differently. It was a thought that tormented him sometimes in the quiet watches of the night. It was an event that still caused him pain although of late he had felt it less often and knew that it was fading. He could even consider other women now. Back in Nuln, there had been the tavern girl, Elissa, but she had left in the end.

The picture of the smiling peasant girl in the field came back to him very vividly. He wondered what she was doing right now. He resigned himself to the fact that he would never even know her name, just as she would never know his. There were so many encounters in the world like that. Chances that never turned out right. Romances which died stillborn before ever they had a chance to live. He wondered whether he would ever meet another woman who touched him as much as Kirsten had.

So engrossed was he in these thoughts that it took some time for him to realise that he was hearing scuttling, the soft sounds of claws scrabbling on flinty rock. He kept himself low to the ground and then glanced around, carefully, suddenly fearing that at any moment he might feel the searing pain of a poisoned knife driven into his back. As he moved, however, the scuttling sounds stopped.

He kept still and held his breath for a long moment and it started again. There. The sound came from off to his right. As he watched, he could see the glitter of red eyes, and dark silhouettes creeping ever closer over the ridge top. He slid his sword from its scabbard. The magical blade which he had acquired from the dead Templar Aldred felt light in his hand. He was about to shout a warning to the others when an enormous howling battle-cry erupted. He recognised the voice as Gotrek's.

A strange musky scent that Felix had smelled before filled the air. The rat-like shapes turned and fled immediately. The Slayer dashed past into the darkness, the runes on his huge axe glowing in the night, swiftly followed by Snorri Nosebiter. Felix would have raced after them himself, but his human eyes could not see in the gloom like a dwarf's. He flinched as Varek moved up beside him, one of his sinister black bombs in his hands. The firelight reflected off the young dwarf's spectacles and turned his eyes into circles of fire.

They stood side by side for long tense moments, waiting to hear the sounds of battle, expecting to see the sudden rush of a horde of rat-men. The only sound they heard was the stomping of boots as Gotrek and Snorri returned.

'Skaven,' Gotrek spat contemptuously.

'They ran away,' Snorri said in a disappointed tone. Treating the event as if nothing untoward happened, they returned to their places by the fire and cast themselves down to sleep. Felix envied them. He knew that even once his watch had ended there would be no sleep for him this night.

Skaven, he thought, and shuddered.

THREE
THE LONELY TOWER

FELIX LOOKED DOWN into the mouth of the long valley and was overcome with awe. From where he stood, he could see machines, hundreds of them. Enormous steam engines rose along the valley sides like monsters in riveted iron armour. The pistons of huge pumps went up and down with the regularity of a giant's heartbeat. Steam hissed from enormous rusting pipes which ran between massive red brick buildings. Huge chimneys belched vast clouds of sooty smoke into the air. The air echoed with the clanging of a hundred hammers. The infernal glow of forges illuminated the shadowy interior of workshops. Dozens of dwarfs moved backwards and forwards through the heat and noise and misty clouds.

For a second the fog cleared as the cold hill wind cut through the valley. Felix could see that one vast structure dominated the length of the dale. It was built from rusting, riveted metal with a corrugated iron roof. It was perhaps three hundred strides long and twenty high. At one end was a massive cast-iron tower, the like of which Felix had never seen before. It was constructed from metal girders, with an observation point and what looked like a monstrous lantern at its very tip.

High over the far end of the valley loomed a monstrous squat fortress. Moss clung to its eroded stonework. Felix could make out the gleaming muzzles of cannons high among the battlements. From the middle of the structure loomed a single stone tower. On the face nearest the roof was a monstrous clock, whose hands showed that it was almost the seventh hour after noon. On the roof, an equally gigantic telescope pointed towards the sky. Even as Felix watched, the hand reached seven o'clock and a bell tolled deafeningly, its echoes filling the valley with sound.

The eerie wail of what could only have been a steam whistle – Felix had heard something like it once at the College of Engineering in Nuln – filled the air. There was a chugging of pistons and the clatter of iron wheels on rails as a small steam-wagon emerged from the mine-head. It moved along iron tracks, carrying heaps and heaps of coal into some great central smelting works.

The noise was deafening. The smell was overwhelming. The sight was at once monstrous and fascinating, like looking at the innards of some vast and intricate clockwork toy. Felix felt like he was looking down upon a scene of strange sorcery of a kind which, if truly unleashed, might change the world. He had not realised what the dwarfs were capable of, what power their arcane knowledge gave them. He was filled with a wonder so strong that, for a moment, it overcame the fear which had been nagging at the back of his mind all day.

Then the thought came back to him, and he remembered the tracks he had seen this morning mingled with the hob-nailed boot prints of the Slayers. There could be no doubt that they belonged to skaven, quite a strong force at that. Felix knew that fearsome as the Slayers were, the rat-men had not fled out of terror. They had retreated because they had other things to do, and getting into a fight with his companions might have slowed them down in the performance of that mission. It was the only possible explanation for why so strong a party of skaven had fled from so few.

Looking at this place now, he understood what the probable objective of the skaven force was. Here was a thing which the followers of the Horned Rat would want to capture – or destroy. Felix had no idea what was taking place down in that valley but he was certain that it was important, because so much industry, energy and intelligence were being expended, and Felix knew that dwarfs did nothing without a purpose.

Once more, though, he felt his heart start to race. Here was industry on a scale that he had not imagined possible. It had a sordid magnificence and implied a terrifying understanding of things beyond the knowledge of human civilisation. In that moment Felix understood just how much his people had yet to learn from the dwarfs. From beside him he heard a sharp intake of breath.

'If the Engineers Guild ever finds out about this,' Gotrek rumbled, 'heads will roll!'

'We'd better get down there and tell them about the skaven.' Felix replied.

Gotrek looked at him with something like pride showing in his one mad eye. 'What could those people down there have to fear from a bunch of scabby ratlings?'

Tempted as he was to agree, Felix kept quiet. He was sure that he could think of something, given long enough. After all, the skaven had given him plenty of reasons for terror in the past.

Somewhere off to their right something glinted, like a mirror catching a beam of sunlight. Felix wondered briefly what it was and then dismissed it from his mind as being some part of the wondrous technology he saw being deployed all around him.

'Let's go tell them anyway,' he said, wondering why the dwarfs had put something that glittered so brightly amongst a clump of bushes.

GREY SEER THANQUOL peered down at the scene through the periscope. The device was yet another magnificent skaven invention, combining the best features of a telescope and a series of mirrors, thus allowing him to watch those unsuspecting fools below unobserved from within the cover of this clump of bushes. Only the lens at the mechanism's tip was visible and he doubted that the dwarfs would notice even that. They were so slow-witted and stupid.

Still, even the grey seer had to admit that there was something magnificent about what the dwarfs had built down there. He wasn't sure what it was but even he, in his secret ratty heart, was impressed. It was fascinating to look at, like one of the mazes he kept for humans back home in Skavenblight. There was so much going on that the eye did not quite know where to look. There was so much activity that he just knew that something important was happening down there – something that might well redound to his credit with the Council of Thirteen once he had seized it.

Yet again he congratulated himself on his foresight and his intelligence. How many other grey seers would have responded to the reports of a bunch of skavenslaves who had been driven out of the old coal mines beneath the Lonely Tower?

None of his rivals had paused to consider that there must be something important going on when the dwarfs sent an army to reclaim an old coal mine in these desolate hills. Of course, he had to admit, none of them had had the chance because Thanquol had executed most of the survivors before they had a chance to tell anybody else. After all, secrecy was one of the greatest weapons in the skaven arsenal and none knew this better than he. Was he not pre-eminent among grey seers, the feared and potent skaven magicians who ranked just below the Council of Thirteen themselves? And given time even that would change as well. Thanquol knew that it was his destiny to take his rightful place on one of the Council's ancient thrones some day.

As soon as he was certain the report was true he had journeyed here with his bodyguards. And as soon as he had seen the size of the dwarf encampment, he had sent a summons to the nearest skaven garrison, invoking the name of the Horned Rat and enjoining the strictest secrecy of its commander, on pain of a long, protracted and incredibly agonising death. Now the valley was all but surrounded by a mighty skaven force, and whatever it was that the dwarfs sought to protect would soon be his. This very night he would give the command that would send his invincible furry legions surging forward to inevitable victory.

A flicker of movement attracted Thanquol's attention for a moment, a flutter of red in the breeze which reminded him vaguely of something ominous he had seen in the past. He ignored it and tracked the periscope along the side of the hill, inspecting the potent dwarf-built engines. Greed and a lust to possess them filled him; ignorance of their purpose did nothing to discourage him. He knew that they simply must be worth having. Anything which could make so much noise and create so much smoke was in and of itself a thing to make any skaven's heart beat faster.

Something about that fluttering scrap of red nagged at his mind but he dismissed it. He began to draw up a plan of attack, studying all the lines of approach along the valley edges. He wished he could summon a huge cloud of poison wind and send it blowing down the valley, killing the dwarfs and leaving their machine intact. The simple beauty of the idea struck him. Perhaps he should sell it to the warp engineers of Clan Skryre the next time he was negotiating with them. Certainly a device which could pump out gas the way those chimneys pumped out smoke would...

Wait a moment! The strange familiarity of that flapping scarlet cloak sunk into his forebrain. He suddenly remembered where he'd seen its like before. He remembered a hated human who wore something very similar. But surely... it couldn't be possible that *he* was here.

Hastily Thanquol twisted the periscope on its collapsible frame. He heard a grunt of pain from the skavenslave to whose back it was strapped, but what did he care? The pain of a slave meant less to him than the fur he shed each morning.

With a flick of his paws he brought the lenses into focus on the source of his unease. For a shocked instant he fought down an almost overwhelming urge to squirt the musk of fear. He stopped himself only by reminding himself that there was no way that the hairless ape could see him.

Thanquol flinched and ducked his horned head down, even though his mighty intelligence told him that he was already out of sight. He looked around to see if his two lackeys, Lurk and Grotz, had noticed his unease. Their blank faces looked up at him placidly and he was reassured that he had not lost face in front of his underlings. He took a pinch of warpstone snuff to calm his shaking nerves, then offered up something which could have been a prayer, or might conceivably have been construed as a curse to the Horned Rat.

He could not believe it. He simply could not believe it! As plain as the snout on his face, he had seen the human, Felix Jaeger, when he looked through the periscope. He leaned forward and snatched another glance just to be sure. No – there was no mistake. There he stood, as plain as day. Felix Jaeger, the hated human who had done so much to thwart Thanquol's mighty plans, and who mere months before had almost succeeded, beyond all reason, in disgracing him before the Council of Thirteen!

Justifiable hatred warred with the rational instinct of self-preservation which dominated Thanquol's soul. His first thought was that somehow Jaeger had sought him out and had come all this way to thwart his schemes of glory again. The cold light of logic told him that this could not be the case. Nothing so simple could possibly be true. There was no way that Jaeger could know where to find him. Not even if Thanquol's masters on the Council of Thirteen knew his current location. He had cloaked his departure from Skavenblight in the utmost secrecy.

Then the terrifying thought struck Thanquol that perhaps one of his many enemies far away, back in the City of the Horned Rat, had by some arcane means located him, and was feeding the information to the human. It would not be the first time that wicked rat-men had betrayed the righteous skaven cause for their own gain or revenge on those they envied.

The more he thought of it, the more likely this explanation seemed to Thanquol. Rage bubbled through his veins along with the powdered warpstone. He would find this traitor and crush him like the treacherous worm he was! Already he could think of half a dozen culprits who would be deserving of his inevitable vengeance.

Then another thought struck the grey seer, one which very nearly sent the musk of fear squirting despite all of his efforts at self-control. If Jaeger was present it meant that the other one was most likely there as well. Yes, it meant that most likely the only other being on the planet who Thanquol hated and feared more than Felix Jaeger was there too. He did not doubt, and nor was he mistaken, that when he next looked through the periscope, that he would see the Trollslayer, Gotrek Gurnisson.

It was all he could do to suppress the mighty squeak of rage and terror that threatened to burst from his lips. He knew he was going to have to think about this.

THE BUSTLING ACTIVITY of the place became even more evident to Felix as the wagon descended into the valley. All around them groups of dwarfs moved purposefully. Leather aprons protected their burly chests. Sweat ran down their soot-smudged faces.

Dozens of odd-looking implements – which reminded Felix of instruments of torture – hung from loops on their belts. Some of the dwarfs wore strange-looking armoured suits; others were mounted in small steam-wagons with forked lifting tines on the front. These machines carried heavy crates and packages along the iron rails between the workshops and the central metal structure.

All around the factory complex a shanty town had sprung up where the dwarfs apparently lived. The buildings were of wood and drystone, with sloping roofs of corrugated metal. They seemed empty, all their occupants were out at work.

Felix looked at Gotrek. 'What is going on here?'

There was silence for a long moment as Gotrek appeared to consider whether he should even answer at all. Eventually he spoke in a slow, solemn voice.

'Manling, you are looking on something I had never thought to see, that perhaps only you of all your people will ever see the like of. It reminds me of the great shipyards of Barak Varr but... So many forbidden Guild secrets are being used here that I cannot begin to number them.'

'All of this is forbidden, you say?'

'Dwarfs are a very conservative people. We do not care much for new ideas,' Varek said suddenly. 'Our engineers are more conservative than most. If you try something and it fails, like poor Makaisson did, then you are ridiculed and there is nothing worse than that to a dwarf. Few are even willing to risk it. And of course some things have been tested and because the tests failed so... spectacularly... they were forbidden to be used, by the guild. There are things here which we have known of in theory for centuries, but which only here have we dared put into practice. I know that what my uncle wants to do is considered so important that many talented young dwarfs were prepared to take the risk, to work here in secret on our great project. They think it is worth the attempt.'

'And the expense,' Gotrek said, with something like awe in his voice. 'Somebody spent a pretty penny here, and no mistake.'

'Well, and that too,' Varek said, flushing red to the roots of his beard for no reason that Felix could understand.

Gotrek glanced around with a critical eye. 'Not very well fortified, is it?'

Varek gave an apologetic shrug. 'Things were built so fast, we didn't have time. We've only been here just over a year. And anyway, who would possibly think to attack such of an out of the way place as this?'

GREY SEER THANQUOL scuttled back down the slopes to where his army had mustered in the gathering gloom. Clawleaders Grotz and Snitchtongue were already in position at the heads of their respective forces. Both looked at him with the expression of brute submissiveness which he had come to expect from lackeys. The communication amulets he had hammered into their foreheads glittered with the fire of trapped warpstone.

He looked down on a seething sea of shadowy, rat-like faces, each one set with fierce determination to conquer or die. He felt his tail stiffen with pride as he looked upon this mighty horde of chittering warriors. He could see black armoured stormvermin where they loomed over the lesser clanrat warriors, the masked and heavily muffled warpfire thrower teams, and his own mighty bodyguard, Boneripper, the second rat-ogre to bear that name.

It was not the most formidable force he had ever commanded. In truth, it was a mere fraction of the size of the force he had led to attack the human city of Nuln. There were no plague monks present, none of the mighty war engines that were the pride of his race. He would have liked a doomwheel or a screaming bell, but there had not been time to drag them here through the tunnels or over the rugged hills to this remote place. Still he was certain that the hundreds of fine troops standing before him would be enough for his purposes. Particularly attacking at night, and with the benefit of surprise.

And yet… A spasm of doubt shuddered through him and made his fur bristle. The dwarf and Jaeger were present down there and that was a bad omen. Their presence never seemed to augur well for Thanquol's plans. Had they not managed to somehow thwart his invasion of Nuln, and in some not-as-yet-understood way destroyed an entire skaven army? Had they not forced the grey seer himself to beat a hasty but prudent tactical withdrawal through the sewers, while the streets above ran black with skaven blood?

Thanquol dribbled some more warpstone snuff onto the back of his paw from the manskin pouch he always carried. He stuck his snout into it and sniffed, and felt anger and confidence surge back into his brain. Visions of death, mutilation and other wonderful things flooded through his soaring mind. Now he felt sure that victory would be his. How could anything resist his mighty powers? Nothing could stand in the way of the supreme skaven sorcery he commanded!

His hidden enemies back in Skavenblight had overreached themselves when they sent Jaeger and Gurnisson here. They thought to strike a blow against Thanquol by using his bitterest enemies to smite him! Well, he would show them that what they believed was cunning was merely sorely misguided folly! All they had succeeded in doing was placing the two fools he most wanted to humble within the grasp of his mighty paw. They had provided him with the opportunity to take a most terrible vengeance on his two most hated foes, while at the same time covering himself with glory by seizing the machinery the dwarfs had built in this place!

Surely, he thought as the foul stuff bubbled like molten Chaos through his veins, this would be his greatest triumph, his finest hour! For a millennium, skaven would speak in hushed whispers about Grey Seer Thanquol's cunning, ruthlessness and awesome intelligence. He could almost taste victory already.

He raised his paw and gave the signal for silence. As one, the entire horde laid off its chittering. Hundreds of red eyes looked at him expectantly. Whiskers twitched in anticipation of his words.

'Now we will smashcrush the dwarfs like beetle-bugs!' he squeaked in his most impressive, oratorical tones. 'We will roll over the valley from both sides and nothing will stop us. Forward, brave skaven, to inevitable victory!'

The horde's squeaking rose in volume until it filled his ears. He knew that tonight victory would certainly be his.

FELIX SHIVERED as he walked. A sense of foreboding filled his mind. Instinctively, he threw his cloak back over his right shoulder to free his sword arm. His hand strayed to the hilt of his sword, and he felt a sudden urge to pull it free and be ready to fight.

The castle loomed high above them, and he could see from this close that it was not quite as formidable as it looked from a distance. The walls were cracked and weakened; in some places the stone had crumbled away entirely. Despite what Varek had claimed, the work of the dwarfs did not in any way appear to have increased the defensibility of the place. Although Felix was no expert, he could see that Gotrek's claim that the place was not particularly well fortified was true. If they were to be attacked, this whole valley would turn out to be one big death-trap.

They were almost at the castle now. Their road had led all the way to the foot of the cliffs on top of which the castle sat. Despite the gathering gloom, Felix could spy an old dwarf with an enormously long beard who had emerged onto a turreted balcony above the castle portcullis. The ancient waved. Felix was about to wave back when he realised that dwarf was greeting Gotrek. The Slayer looked up, gave a sullen grunt and raised his ham-like fist up a few inches in greeting.

'Gotrek Gurnisson,' the old dwarf called. 'I never thought I would see you again!'

'Nor did I,' Gotrek muttered. He sounded almost embarrassed.

LURK SNITCHTONGUE felt his heart beat faster with pride, excitement – and a certain justifiable caution. Grey Seer Thanquol had chosen him to lead the attack, while the skaven mage observed the battle site from the slopes to the rear. It was the proudest moment of Lurk's life and he felt an emotion which could almost have been described as gratitude to Thanquol, had gratitude not been a weak, foolish, un-skaven emotion. He had not been so happy since he had recovered from the plague which had threatened his life back in Nuln. It appeared he had been forgiven for his part in the failure in that great human warren. Once again he was Grey Seer Thanquol's favoured emissary. Of course, if Grey Seer Thanquol ever found out how Lurk had conspired with his enemies during the Nuln fiasco...

Lurk pushed that thought aside. He knew that if this attack succeeded he would be well rewarded with breeders, warptokens and promotion within the ranks of his clan. More than that, he would gain a great deal of prestige, which to a skaven like him was worth more than any of the other things. Those siblings who had sneered at him, mocked and ridiculed him behind his back would be silenced. They would know that Lurk had led his mighty horde to victory over the dwarfs.

The thought sidled sideways into his mind that it might even be possible to eliminate Thanquol and claim credit for this operation himself. He dismissed the idea as absurd immediately, fearing that the mage might even now might be reading his thoughts through the amulet on his brow, but somehow the wicked notion stayed put, leaping into his consciousness despite all his attempts to suppress it.

He cast around for something to distract himself, and felt his heart race with anxiety. They had almost reached the crest of the hill and still they had not been spotted. Soon would come the moment of truth. As they broached the hilltop they would become visible to the dwarfs below unless their advance was concealed by the night and smoke. He raised his claw in the sign for silence. All around him, his stormvermin stalked near-silently forward, save only for the occasional clanking of sheath against armour that most likely would not be noticed by their dull-witted opponents.

It was not the slight noises of the stormvermin which worried Lurk. It was the racket that those stupid clan rat warriors and skaven slaves were making! Lacking the imperial discipline of the Stormvermin, and the long hours of training, they were making a great deal of noise. Some of them were even chittering among themselves, trying to keep their morale up in the traditional skaven way – by boasting to each other about what torments they would inflict on their prisoners.

Much as Lurk sympathised with their sentiments, he swore that he would have those chatterers' lips sewn shut after his inevitable victory. Since he could not see who was talking at this distance, he decided that he would just have to pull out a few clanrats at random and make an example of them.

By now he knew that Clawleader Grotz was most likely in position on the other side of the valley. With typical skaven precision, they would be in place ready to sweep down on both sides of the valley, taking the surprised stunties from two sides and drowning them under a furry wave of unstoppable skaven might!

He looked around him and offered a silent prayer in hope that the warriors remembered his last feverish instructions – no burning of buildings, no taking of loot. Grey Seer Thanquol wanted everything left in one piece so that they could sell it to the warp engineers. He froze for a moment, almost hesitant to give the order to attack. Then the thought that Grotz might already be sweeping down on the valley and seizing all the glory took hold of him and swept away what remained of his caution. He crawled up the slope and looked down into the valley, driven on by the comforting smell of the mass of skaven around him.

The dwarfish settlement stretched out below him. By night it was even more impressive than by day. The flames of the foundries and the fires within the smokestacks illuminated the place with an eerie glow which was reminiscent of the great city of Skavenblight. The buildings bulked vast and shadowy in the gloom.

Lurk hoped there were no unpleasant surprises waiting down there, but then realised that it was impossible for there to be. Had not the great Grey Seer Thanquol himself planned this attack?

VOLGAR VOLGARSSON stared out into the gathering darkness and tugged his beard distractedly. He was getting mightily hungry, and the thought of the ale and stew which the others would be tucking into down in the Great Hall made his mouth water. He patted his belly just to make sure it was still there. After all he hadn't eaten a morsel in over four hours. Except, of course, for that loaf of bread and hunk of cheese, but that hardly counted at all, not by Volgar's standards.

By Grungni, he hoped that Morkin would hurry up and relieve him. It was cold and uncomfortable up here in this sentry post and Volgar was a dwarf who valued his comforts. Of course, he was proud in his way to be part of the great work going on here, but there was a limit. He knew he wasn't smart enough to be an engineer and he was too clumsy to help in the manufacturing, so he did what he could, acting as a guard and sentry, spending long lonely hours with nary a morsel of food in this chill, damp place, keeping a look-out for anyone or anything creeping up on the valley.

He knew his position was a good one. The sentry's pillbox was set in the ground, with only an observation slot looking out on the far side of the valley. There were similar such posts on the other side and looking down on the road. All he had to do was keep an eye open for trouble and if he spotted anything nasty sound the horn. Simple really.

And in a way it was actually a good posting. What trouble could there possible be in this gods-forsaken spot? Ever since they had kicked the skaven out, there had not been the slightest hint of a problem. Now there had been a good fight, Volgar told himself, taking a long pull from his hip flask, just to keep the chill away, of course. They'd helped settle the score for a few grudges against the rat-men there. Over a hundred of the furry little buggers killed and barely a dwarf scratched. He belched loudly to show his appreciation.

It had been so quiet that Volgar had even managed a quick nap this afternoon. He was sure he had missed nothing. That was the one good thing about the settlement being so undermanned. There was no troublesome fellow sentry to keep you awake with their talk about ale and the grudges they would settle when they got back to Karaz-a-Karak. Volgar liked a good natter about score-settling as much as the next dwarf but he preferred his kip more. Couldn't beat a good snooze right after luncheon. It helped set you up proper for the rest of the day.

And now, well, his dwarfish eyes were good at night, and his dwarfish ears, attuned to listening to the warning hints concealed within the sounds of subsidence in the depths of the earth, were more than capable of alerting him to any trouble. If there was anything out of the ordinary – like that faint scuttling sound – or even something which sounded like the clink of weapon on weapon – like the noise he had just heard, in fact – he would notice it in an instant, and be ready to respond.

Volgar shook his head. Was he hearing things? No, there it was again, and there was a faint high-pitched chittering as well. It sounded just like skaven. He rubbed his eyes to clear them of any obscuring film and peered out through the observation slot into the darkness. His eyes were not deceiving him. A tide of shadowy rat-like shapes were flowing up the hill all around him. Their beady red eyes glittered in the darkness.

His hand almost shook as he grasped the sentry horn. He knew that if he kept quiet, the skaven would most likely pass him by. They obviously hadn't spotted his concealed outpost. If instead he gave the signal, then he was going to die. He would give away his position to the horde which surrounded him and they would swarm over it like flies on carrion. The door behind him was strongly barred but it would not hold them forever, and then there was the poison gas and the flame-throwers, and all the other strange skaven weapons he had heard of. One poison globe through the observation slot and that would be the end for old Volgar.

On the other hand, if he did not give the signal, his companions would be overwhelmed by the rat-men, and would most likely die in his stead. The great work they were embarked on would fail and it would all be his fault. If he lived, he would have to live with the shame that he had brought on not only himself but on his ancestors.

Volgar was a dwarf, and for all his flaws he had a dwarf's pride. He took a last long pull from his flask, wasted a second on a final regretful thought of the dinner he was never going to have, took a deep breath, put the horn to his lips and blew.

THE LONELY BELLOW of the horn filled the valley. It seemed to come from below the earth itself. Felix looked around wildly.

'What was that?' he asked.

'Trouble,' Gotrek responded cheerfully, pointing at the vast horde of skaven swarming over the brow of the hill and into the valley.

FOUR
THE SKAVEN ATTACK

FELIX WATCHED IN abject horror as the dark tide of skaven flowed down the hill towards him. He was unsure how many there were but it looked like hundreds, maybe thousands – it was hard to tell in the darkness. He whirled to investigate as a great clamour arose behind him. Looking up he saw yet more skaven entering the valley from the other side. The jaws of a huge trap were closing.

Felix fought down a surge of panic. Somehow, no matter how many times he had been in situations like this – and he had been in many – it never got any easier. He felt a sick feeling spread in the pit of his stomach, a tenseness in his muscles, and somehow a strange light-headedness too. His mouth was dry and his own heartbeat sounded loud in his ears. Just for once he would have liked to have been calm and relaxed in the face of danger, or filled with furious berserker rage like all those heroes in the storybooks. As always, it didn't happen.

All around him, dwarfs were downing tools and snatching up weapons. Horns sounded, each one with a different tone, their long notes like the wails of souls in torment, adding to the cacophony all around. Felix turned again and was about to make a sprint for the portal of the castle when he realised that no one else was doing that. All around him dwarfs raced through the gloom towards the enemy.

Were they all mad, Felix wondered? Why did they not make a dash for the safety of the castle? Unsound as its walls appeared, they would doubtless have a better chance within them. It would almost certainly be safer inside the keep but these crazy dwarfs paid no attention.

He froze momentarily, overcome with curiosity and apprehension. The thought struck him that perhaps there was some good reason why they weren't going into the keep... and perhaps finding out that reason for himself was not such a good idea.

Slowly it percolated into Felix's panicking brain that the dwarfs were not going to leave their machines in the hands of the skaven. They were prepared to fight and, if need be, die in defence of these monstrous smoke-belching mechanisms. It showed a determination that was either truly impressive or monumentally stupid, Felix could not decide which.

While he was still making up his mind, an ominous clanking sound started up from behind him, followed by the ring of metal on stone. He turned just in time to see the keep's portcullis slam down. From inside he heard the grinding of gears and the whistling of a steam engine's boiler, then the enormous chains which held the drawbridge in place tightened and begin to raise the wooden structure. Suddenly there was a deep ditch between him and the castle. At least someone inside was showing some sense, Felix thought, even if they had trapped him outside in what promised to be a mad melee.

A thunderous roar erupted from the castle above. A huge cloud of smoke belched above his head and the acrid smell of ignited gunpowder filled the air. Felix realised that someone above had wit enough to bring one of the cannons to bear. There was a whistling sound and then an explosion ripped through the darkness. A dozen of the charging skaven were thrown into the air. Limbs flew in one direction, torsos in another. The dwarfs let out a loud cheer; the skaven emitted what sounded like a long hiss of hatred.

All around him dwarfs raced into battle positions. Deep voices bawled out harsh guttural words in the ancient dwarf language. Felix felt lost and alone in the midst of this maelstrom of furious and yet somehow ordered activity. He could see that from the mad whirl of shouting and running dwarfs a coherent pattern was starting to emerge. The engineers and warriors were taking up their places beside their brethren in the line. Felix felt that he was the only one here who did not seem to have some idea where he was supposed to go.

They were all rallying around the horns, Felix suddenly realised, and now the different notes made sense. They were like those individual bells he had seen on the cattle a few days before. They identified their owners, gave his comrades a point to rally to, a nucleus around which a hard armoured shell could form.

Felix could see now that this was a tactic which had long been drilled into the dwarfs, until they had it down perfectly. Where a few moments ago there had been a mass of disorganised souls just begging to be massacred, now there were well-disciplined ranks of dwarf warriors, wheeling to face their foes, marching with a discipline that would have shamed imperial pike-men. Perhaps whoever was in charge here knew what he was doing, Felix thought. Perhaps this was not going to be the utter bloody slaughter he had feared only a few moments ago.

He wasn't sure it would be enough, judging by the size of the skaven force tearing down the hill, picking up speed like a juggernaut, gathering what looked like irresistible momentum for its charge. The seething furry horde was so close now that he could see individual skaven, make out their foam-covered lips, the rabid fanaticism in their eyes. Some of them were larger, more muscular, and better armoured than others. He had fought such beasts in the past and knew that they would be the toughest. He kept his eyes peeled for any of those clumsy, awkward and yet oh-so-deadly field weapons the skaven loved, but mercifully could see none present.

Suddenly Felix felt very alone. He was not part of any of those hastily assembled dwarfish units. There was no one beside him to watch his back. Perhaps in the darkness the dwarfs might even take him for a foe. There was only one place for him here. He looked around for Gotrek but overcome with battle-lust he and Snorri had raced off to get closer to the foe.

Felix spat out a curse and clambered hastily onto the wagon, to get a better view of his surroundings. He noticed that Varek was sitting there, peering interestedly out into the gloom, occasionally laying the bomb he held in his hand down on the seat beside him, and scratching a note in the book before him with what looked like some strange mechanical pen. His eyes glittered feverishly behind his glasses.

'Isn't this exciting, Felix?' he asked. 'A real battle! This is the first one I've ever been in.'

'Pray it isn't your last...' Felix muttered, taking a few practice sweeps with his sword, hoping to loosen his tense muscles before the horde smashed into the dwarf line. He took a quick glance around hoping that he would be able to pick out Gotrek.

The Slayer was nowhere in sight.

FROM HIS PERCH on the hill high above the battle, Grey Seer Thanquol peered down at his seeing stone. It lay blank and dormant before him. Within its depths there was perhaps a tiny flicker of warpfire, undetectable save to an eye as keen and all-seeing as Thanquol's.

Indeed, to the untrained skaven eye it looked merely like a large multi-faceted piece of coloured glass inscribed with the Thirteen Most Sacred Symbols. Thanquol knew enough about the race of man to know that, to a human eye, it would look like some tawdry gewgaw used by a sideshow fakir. He was also wise enough to know that the human eye would be mightily deceived, for this was a most potent artefact indeed.

At least, he hoped so. The raw moon-crystal had cost Thanquol many warptokens. The carving of those runes, each one inscribed on a different moonless night, had cost Thanquol much lost sleep. The embedding of potent spells within the crystal had been paid for in blood and pain, some of it the grey seer's.

Now was the moment to find out whether it had all been worth it. It was time, thought Thanquol, to begin to use his new toy. Hastily he scratched runes in the hard earth around him, making the Thirteen Sacred Signs of the Horned Rat with practised ease. Next he put his thumb into his muzzle and bit hard. His sharp teeth drew blood, though he hardly felt a thing through the haze of powdered warpstone snuff and the seething sorcerous energies which filled his brain.

Black blood dripped from the wound. He held his thumb out over the first rune. A droplet impacted in the centre of the symbol and as it did so Thanquol spoke a word of power, a secret name of the Horned Rat. Immediately the fluid vaporised into a puff of acrid smoke, forming a small skull-like mushroom cloud over the rune. The symbol flared to life, lines of green fire illuminating its outline brilliantly before fading down into a less lurid yet still visible glow.

Quickly and expertly Thanquol repeated the procedure with every rune and, once that was completed, he carefully dribbled three final droplets of his own precious blood onto the seeing stone itself. Instantly a dim picture flickered into life. He could make out the scene of chaos and imminent carnage in the valley below as if looking down on it from a great height, then the picture flickered and a cloud of static filled the stone. Thanquol administered an irritated thump to the side of the crystal and the picture cleared and settled. The sight of the battle came into view as clear as day. Well almost – there was a faint greenish tinge to the picture that would not go away, no matter how many gentle taps and thumps of adjustment Thanquol administered.

No matter! Thanquol felt like the master of some vast and secret game. All those skaven below were now but pieces for him to command. Pawns to be moved by his mighty paw. Tokens to be placed on the board and guided by his titanic intelligence. He took another pinch of warpstone snuff and almost howled with glee. He felt his power to be infinite. There was nothing like it, this sensation of control, of mastery. Best of all, he could exercise his power from well out of sight and personal danger. Not that he feared danger, of course, it was merely sensible to keep himself out of the way of unnecessary risks. It was every grey seer's greatest dream come true!

Thanquol allowed himself to gloat for a long moment, then gave his attention to the battle, trying to decide in exactly which spectacular way he would seize victory and immortal fame among skavenkind.

FELIX SPLAYED HIS feet wider, trying to find his balance on the back of the wagon. The vehicle rocked slightly on its suspension and he wondered whether it was wise to stand here. On the one hand, the footing was unsure and he was a conspicuous target standing upright on the wagon's back. On the other hand, at least up here he had the advantage of being on somewhat higher ground and having partial cover from the wagon's sides. He decided to remain where he was for the moment – and to jump to the ground at the first sign of missile fire. That was the logical thing to do. Besides, it looked like someone would have to stay here and look after Varek.

The unworldly young dwarf was scribbling away for all he was worth in his book. Felix was amazed that he could see to write. He knew from his long association with Gotrek that dwarfs could see in the dark better than humans, but here was astonishing proof of the fact. By the flickering furnace light, which showed Felix only the barest of outlines of objects, the young dwarf was writing for all the world like a scribe copying a manuscript by candlelight. If nothing else, it was an amazing feat of concentration. To tell the truth Felix would have been happier if Varek paid more attention to the mules. The animals were showing distinct signs of distress as the skaven raced ever closer.

Felix glanced nervously about them, wondering if any of those nasty skaven assassins with poison blades were skulking around. It was unlike the rat-men to go for a simple frontal assault without springing some nasty, sneaky surprises. He knew from bitter experience what they were capable of. He nudged Varek gently with the tip of his boot.

'Best pay attention to the mules,' he said. 'They look restless.'

Varek nodded amiably, put his pen back in his capacious pockets, snapped his book shut and picked up his bomb.

Somehow Felix was not reassured.

THANQUOL GLARED into the seeing stone with furious concentration. He placed a paw on either side of it and chittered frantic invocations, trying to keep control of his point of view. It was not nearly as easy to control as he would have liked.

He raised his right claw and the point of view swung up and to the right. He clenched his paw into a fist and punched it forward, and the viewpoint shifted until he had a panoramic view of the battlefield. He saw the skaven loping down the hillside towards the hastily marshalling dwarfs. He saw the great furry spearheads of stormvermin aimed directly at the centre of the assembling dwarf host. He saw the flanking forces of clanrats and skavenslaves running somewhat less enthusiastically by their sides. He saw his bodyguard, Boneripper, running along beside Lurk Snitchtongue.

The keep above the valley looked like a ratchild's toy when viewed from this height, and the whole vast intricate structure of the dwarf camp looked suspiciously ordered and patterned, almost as if every building, pipe and chimney were the component of one vast machine. It was all very fascinating and he had to fight to keep his attention on the upcoming conflict. One of the side-effects of warpstone snuff was that the user could become enthralled by the most trivial things, losing himself in contemplation of the majesty of his toenails while all around cities burned. Thanquol was an experienced enough sorcerer to be aware of this, but sometimes even he forgot for a moment. And it was such a tantalising scene, so... He wrenched his thoughts back to the battle and willed his point of view to shift, zooming in like the eyes of a bird on the centre of the dwarf lines, to the wagon on which Felix Jaeger stood, sword in hand, looking tense and justifiably afraid.

A simple but brilliant plan struck the grey seer. He had some doubts as to whether this Boneripper could handle the Slayer any better than his predecessor had, but he had no doubts whatsoever that the monster could slaughter that Jaeger. He had some special instructions for the rat-ogre concerning the human and he knew that the fierce, loyal and stupid brute would obey them to the death. In a glorious rush, he knew that Felix Jaeger's painful death was assured.

Having located his intended victim, Thanquol sent his sorcerous gaze questing back in search of Boneripper. When he found the monstrous hybrid of rat and ogre, he muttered another spell which would allow his thoughts to communicate with those of his henchling.

He felt a sudden dizziness and the blast furnace of hunger, rage and brute stupidity that was the rat-ogre's consciousness. Swiftly he placed the image of Jaeger's position in the monster's mind and gave his instructions: *Go, Boneripper, kill!! Kill! Kill!*

FELIX SHIVERED. He knew someone was watching him. He could almost feel the burning eyes boring into his back. He glanced around, certain that he would see some malevolent skaven ready to plunge a knife between his shoulder blades, but when he did so no one was there.

Slowly the eerie feeling passed from him, to be replaced by a more immediate worry. The skaven were almost upon them! He could hear their chittering, and their crude weapons clashing terrifyingly on their shields. With a great rushing hiss, a flight of bolts flashed overhead from the castle battlements. Dwarf crossbowmen were at work firing into the nearest and largest skaven. A few of them fell, but not enough to slow the skaven advance. Their fellows simply ran on, trampling their fallen comrades into the dirt, in their frantic haste to enter combat.

An enormous roar filled Felix's ears, the deep basso rumbling of a creature far larger than a human. The mules whinnied and reared in terror, fear foam frothing from their lips. Felix shifted his weight to keep his balance as the wagon shifted. He turned his head, gripped his sword tightly and turned to look at the monster he knew was behind him.

This time his premonition was correct.

LURK FOUGHT THE fear which filled him, threatening to overwhelm his ratty frame. It was a sensation that he was used to. It nagged at his mind and told him to scamper from the fray, chittering with fright. With the mass of his fellows around him, he knew he could not do that without being trampled so instead, as he knew it would, the fear turned inward and like a dammed river flowed in a new direction.

Suddenly he wanted desperately to get into combat, to face the source of his terror – to rend it with his weapons, stamp on its recumbent corpse, to bury his muzzle in its dead flesh and tear out its still warm entrails. Only by doing this could he slow his racing heart, fight down the urge to void his musk glands, and end this anxiety which was almost too terrible to be borne.

'Quick-quick! Follow me!' he chittered and, racing forward, hurled himself at a burly leather-aproned dwarf armed with an axe.

FELIX DOUBTED THAT he had ever come face to face with a humanoid creature quite so big. Even the monsters he had fought in the streets of Nuln were small by comparison. This thing was huge, immense. Its monstrous head, a distorted parody of that of a rat, was level with his own, despite the fact that he was standing high atop the back of a wagon. Its shoulders were almost as broad as the wagon itself, and its long muscular arms reached almost to the ground. Its vast hands ended in wicked curving claws that looked capable of shredding mailed armour. Enormous pus-filled boils erupted through its thin and mangy fur. A long hairless tail lashed the air angrily. Red eyes, filled with insane bestial hatred, glared into his own.

Felix's heart sank. The beast had come for him, he just knew it. There was a look of feral recognition in its malevolent eyes, and something oddly familiar in the way that it tilted its head to one side. A pink tongue flickered over its lips, suggesting an obscene and all-consuming hunger for human flesh. Sharp rending teeth, each as long as a dagger, showed themselves in its mouth. The creature let out another triumphant bellow – and reached for him.

It was all too much for the mules. Frenzied with fear, they reared and fled. The wagon lurched forward, almost tipping as the terrified beasts turned just in time to avoid the ditch around the keep. The wagon hit a rock and bounced, sending Felix sprawling in the back. He had just enough presence of mind to hold on to his sword.

The rat-ogre behind them gaped at him in stupid astonishment and then lurched forward in pursuit.

'NO!' THANQUOL SHRIEKED, seeing Jaeger slip from Boneripper's grasp. The power of the seeing stone let him view the scene from close up. He had gloated in delight at the look of horror and apprehension on the man's face, felt a thrill of anticipation as Boneripper prepared to reach out, pull off his arm and eat it in front of Jaeger's horror-struck eyes – and been appalled when the mules had pulled the wagon into motion.

It was all so unfair.

And yet somehow it was typical of the human's luck that, just as he was about to receive his well-merited doom, those dumb brute creatures should save him. It was galling that the man should still be alive and unharmed, instead of writhing in agony. Briefly and bitterly Thanquol wondered whether Jaeger had been born simply to thwart him, and then pushed the notion aside. He sent another thought arcing towards Boneripper: *What are you waiting for, idiotfool beast? Get after him! Follow quick-quick! Kill! Kill! Kill!*

* * *

FELIX ROLLED ABOUT in the back of the wagon, instinctively trying to get his footing. He could hear Varek calling to the mules, trying to calm them and bring them under control. Briefly Felix wondered whether this was wise. At the speed they were currently moving they were at least keeping ahead of the rat-ogre… weren't they?

He managed to get his hands underneath him at last, and pushed himself up onto his knees. As he stuck his head above the level of the wagon's tailboard, he saw that the monster was pursuing them and closing the distance with appalling speed. Its long stride was covering the ground as fast as any charger. Its yellow fangs gleamed in the light of the furnaces. Its long tongue lolled out. It brandished its claws furiously. Felix knew beyond a shadow of a doubt that if ever he got within range of those talons he was going to die.

He heard something metallic rolling about on the floor of the wagon, then felt something cold and hard brush against his leg. He reached down and found that it was one of Varek's bombs. It must have rolled off the wagon seat when the animals shied. He almost dropped the thing in fright. He felt like any moment it might explode; in truth, he was surprised that it hadn't done so already. He was tempted simply to lob it from him as fast and as far as he dared, when the thought struck him that that was exactly what he should do.

He fumbled the orb up in front of his face, fighting to hold onto it as the wagon lurched again, throwing him painfully against the wooden side wall. In the half-light, he could see the firing pin in the top and the complex cumbersome mechanism below. He frantically tried to remember how it worked. Let's see: you pull the pin, then you've got five – no! – four heartbeats in which to throw it. Yes, that was it.

He dared to glance up again. The rat-ogre was closer. It seemed like it was almost on top of them. In mere moments it was going to leap into the back of the wagon and shred his flesh with those awful claws and fangs. Felix decided he could wait no longer. He pulled the pin.

He felt resistance as the pin came free, and something long and soft whipped into his hand. As he did so he noticed sparks coming from the top of the bomb. It seemed that there was a string attached to the pin, and the string was attached to some sort of mechanical flint-striker. When you pulled the pin, the flint struck, lighting the fuse. All of these thoughts flickered idly through his head as he rapidly counted up to three.

One. The rat-ogre was only a few strides away, moving impossibly fast, a look of awful hunger distorting its face. From behind him, he could hear Varek beginning to shout *'Whoa–'*

Two. The monster was so close now that Felix could almost count its monstrous tusk-sized teeth. He was uncomfortably aware of the huge claws reaching out to grasp him. He knew that he wasn't going to make it. Perhaps he should just throw the bomb now. Varek called *'–oa–'*

Three. Felix lobbed the bomb. It arced towards the creature, its fizzling fuse leaving a trail of sparks spraying behind it. The rat-ogre opened its mouth to bellow in triumph – and the bomb went in. Another lurch of the wagon threw Felix flat, slamming painfully on to the wooden boards. Varek finished shrieking *'–aaaa!'*

Timed seemed to stretch out for a hour. Felix lay on the floor gasping hard, remembering what Varek said about these bombs often not working, expecting at any second to feel the great razor-like claws burying themselves in his neck and to be hefted from the back of the wagon. Then he heard a dull crump, and something horribly moist and jelly-like splattered onto his hair and face. It took a few moments for Felix to realise that he was covered in blood and brains.

THANQUOL WATCHED Boneripper's head explode and cursed the stupid brute long and loudly. It was true, he thought: if you want a bone gnawed properly, you had to gnaw it yourself. The foul and unreliable monster had been so close. Jaeger had been almost within his grasp. If the dumb brute had not swallowed the bomb, the human would now be writhing in pain. It was almost as if Boneripper had done it deliberately just to frustrate him. Perhaps the creature had been in league with his hidden enemies. Perhaps its idiot brain had been tampered with during its creation. Stranger things had happened.

Thanquol chewed his tail with frustration for a moment and expended a hundred furious curses on Boneripper, Felix Jaeger and every rival in skavendom he could think of. If pure malevolent wishes had been enough, their bones would have been filled with molten lead, their heads would have exploded and their guts turned to rotting pus in that singular moment.

Unfortunately, such fine things were beyond even Thanquol's sorcerous powers at this range. Eventually he calmed, and contented himself with the thought that there was more than one way to skin a baby. He sent his point of view soaring over the larger battlefield once more.

Fortunately here things were going better. At a glance Thanquol saw that most of the dwarfish units had formed up in squares ready to resist the two-pronged skaven attack. The initial skaven rush has reached the dwarfish line. It had broken against it like the sea crashing down on a rock but the stormvermin, at least, were still fighting. As more clanrats and slaves poured into the melee, slowly the weight of numbers was starting to tell. Even as he watched, one closely packed dwarf unit started to break up and the melee became close and general. Under such circumstances, the greater number of skaven was a considerable advantage.

Thanquol saw one dwarf warrior bludgeon a stormvermin with his hammer, only to be leap on from behind by a skavenslave. While the dwarf frantically tried to dislodge his clinging foe, he was dragged down like a deer surrounded by hounds by the rat-man's fellows. As he disappeared under the pile of skaven bodies, he managed a last blow with his hammer, smashing a clanrat's skull and sending blood and fragments of brain and bone everywhere. Thanquol felt no pity for the dead skaven. He would gladly make such a trade for a dwarf life with every heartbeat. There were always plenty more stupid warriors where those had come from. Thanquol knew that out of all skaven, only he was truly irreplaceable.

Thanquol watched happily as the green blaze flung from a warpfire thrower incinerated a clutch of dwarfs, melting their armour, causing their beards to ignite, reducing them first to skeletons and then to wind-blown dust within mere heartbeats. He was considering rewarding the weapon team when they themselves vanished in an enormous green fireball, killed by their own malfunctioning weapon. Still, thought Thanquol, at least they served the greater purpose... his purpose.

Slowly but surely, across the whole battlefield the tide was turning in favour of the skaven. The dwarfs were well-disciplined and brave in their foolish way, but they had been caught unprepared. Many of them were unarmoured and equipped only with the hammers they had been using to work with. They were inflicting incredible casualties on the skaven but these were meaningless. Thanquol did not care if they slaughtered his entire force, just so long as the dwarfs were all dead by the end of the evening. So far, he congratulated himself heartily, things were going just exactly as he planned – except on one corner of the battlefield.

Swift as thought, he sent his view arcing towards the disturbance. Somehow he was not surprised to find two burly shaven-headed figures hewing a path of bloody carnage through his troops. One of them he recognised instantly as the hated figure of Gotrek Gurnisson. The other was new to Thanquol, but just as fearsome in his own way. Where Gurnisson fought armed only with that appallingly powerful axe, the second Slayer fought with a smaller axe in one hand and large hammer in the other.

The slaughter the pair wreaked was immense. With every blow at least one skaven fell. Sometimes Gurnisson would drive his axe through several bodies at once, hewing through skaven flesh and bone as if it were matchwood. At that moment Thanquol would have given anything for the presence of some jezzail teams. He would have ordered those cunning skaven snipers to pick off the gruesome pair from a distance. Still, there was no point in wishing for what you could not have. He would just have to do something about the pair himself.

His initial gambit was to send tendrils of his thought out to the leaders of two of his units, drawing them away from the main melee and into combat with the Slayers. It was regrettable that this would relieve pressure on the embattled dwarfs, but also necessary. Thanquol knew that he could not take the chance of leaving those two free to slaughter at will. It was sound good sense, as well as gratifying to his personal desire that Gotrek Gurnisson and his comrade should die.

LURK LOOKED UP in disbelief as the voice spoke within his head. *Take your squad to your left and slaughter those two Slayers.*

He recognised the voice at once as belonging to Grey Seer Thanquol. A vivid picture of his route through the melee towards the tattooed dwarfs appeared in his mind. For a moment he considered the fact that he might be hallucinating but the voice spoke again in the familiar imperious chittering style which Lurk knew so well. *What are you waiting for, fool-scum? Go now-now or I will eat your heart!*

Lurk decided that it would be best to obey. 'At once, most superlative of sorcerers,' he muttered. He shrieked for his troops to follow him and raced off in the direction he had been ordered.

DRAWN BY THE panicked mules, the wagon raced through the melee out of control. Hastily dwarfs and skaven threw themselves aside to avoid the creatures flailing hooves. Felix rolled about in the back, trying frantically to regain his balance. He could hear Varek alternately shouting at the mules to stop and laughing maniacally as he tossed bombs into onrushing groups of skaven. It did not seem to have occurred to him that every time the tired mules appeared about to slow down, he spooked them some more by lobbing another of his explosive devices. It did not surprise Felix in the least that the poor mules were terrified. The bombs had that effect on him too. Every moment he half-feared that one of the devices would explode in Varek's hand, destroying the wagon and sending the dwarf and Felix straight to the grave.

Every so often he managed to pull himself above the level of the wagons sides and he caught glimpses of sights that he knew would be burned into his memory forever. Some of the buildings had caught fire and the blaze was spreading. Clouds of sparks and soot floated on the wind. Perhaps other dwarfs had used bombs like Varek, perhaps it was the effect of some dread skaven weapon or sorcery, but Felix did not doubt that the conflagration would consume the entire complex. Already flames gouted from the great chimneys, fitfully illuminating the battle to produce a selection of scenes from some lunatic vision of hell.

He saw a skaven burst out from one the foundry buildings, its entire body in flames, burning hair trailing from its body like a comet's tail. The horrible but tantalising smell of scorched flesh filled the air. The creature's agonised squeaks were shrill and audible even above the roar of the battle. As he watched, the dying rat-man threw itself on a dwarf warrior and held on like grim death. The flames from its body lapped around its victim and the dwarf's clothing began to smoulder, even as he put the creature out of its death agony with a swift blow of his axe.

The wagon shuddered and bounced over the ground. Something cracked and there was hideous sensation of snapping and grinding. Looking backwards Felix could see they had run over the corpse of a dwarf. The wheel had squashed its chest, and blood and pulped flesh oozed from its mouth and beard.

Steam blinded him, and his skin felt momentarily scorched. Condensation gathered on his blade and brow, and he had a horrible feeling that this must be what it would be like to be boiled alive. After a brief, agonising moment they emerged from the cloud of steam. He saw then that one of the great pipes was broken, steam spraying freely across the battlefield. As he watched, a dwarf and two skaven rolled free of the cloud, hands still locked around each other's throats. The dwarf's face was lobster red and great patches of skin had blistered and come away from the heat. The skaven's fur looked horribly wet and sticky.

The wagon thundered into the centre of a great melee. Bodies were packed so close that there was no chance of anyone avoiding the mules' hooves. Skulls cracked and bones splintered as the wagon rolled through the ruck like a war-chariot. Those who fell were crushed beneath the iron-shod wheels. As the vehicle slowed, Felix managed to sway to his feet, and take a look around. Varek had stopped tossing his bombs. To do so now would be to cause indiscriminate carnage. The dwarfs and skaven were now too intermingled to provide any easy targets.

The mules reared and struck out with their hooves. As they did so the wagon started to unbalance. There were tides and currents in this vast ruck just like those in the sea. The press of bodies from one side began to tip the overbalancing wagon. Felix grabbed Varek by the shoulder and indicated that they should jump. Varek looked up at him and smiled. He paused only to snatch up his book, then leapt out into the throng.

From the corner of his eye, Felix thought that he saw two squat, tattooed figures hacking their way through a horde of skaven. From his high vantage point he could see a new force of rat-men emerging from the gap between two buildings and bearing down on the Slayers. Pausing only to fix the direction in his mind, Felix leapt down from the wagon, sword swinging. Even before he hit the ground, his blade was cleaving skaven flesh.

* * *

Lurk halted for a moment and let his warriors sweep past him. He pointed to the two dwarfs he had been sent to kill and barked an order: 'Quick-quick! Slay-slay!'

Heartened by the fact that they outnumbered their foes twenty-to-one, his brave stormvermin swept forward, frothing with eagerness to be in at the kill, to claim the credit and the glory. Lurk was tempted to join them but just the look of these two dwarfs made the fur near the base of his tail stand on end, and sent shivers of justifiable caution running up his spine.

He was not quite sure what it was about them. Certainly they were big for dwarfs, and certainly they looked fierce with their bristling beards, outlandish tattoos and their gore-caked weapons, but that was not it. There was something about the way they stood, their complete lack of fear, the suggestion that they might even being enjoying the fact that they faced hopeless odds which gave him pause. It seemed certain that they were quite insane, and that in itself was cause to give them a wide berth. Then he recognised one of them from the battle of Nuln, and he wanted no part in fighting that one. Was it possible that Gotrek Gurnisson was really here, of all places?

His forebodings became certainties as the first stormvermin reached the two. He knew the skaven: it was Underleader Vrishat, a pushy, fierce foolish skaven who all to obviously wanted to challenge Lurk for the position of clawleader. A fool, but a fierce warrior and one who would doubtless make short work of their stunted foes – although the dwarfs gave no sign of any concern. The familiar one, the one with a huge crest of dyed hair rising above his furless scalp, lashed out with his monstrously large axe, and parted Vrishat's head from his shoulders. He didn't wait for the following skaven to come to him either but charged forward, axe swinging, roaring and bellowing outlandish challenges in his own brutish and uncivilised tongue.

Lurk fully expected to see the dwarf go down, overwhelmed by a tidal wave of skaven but no – he wasn't even slowed. He came on like a ship of steel crashing through a storm-tossed sea, massive axe whirling, ham-like fist lashing out, breaking bones, severing limbs, killing anything that got in his path.

The other one was no better. His mad laughter roared out over the battlefield as he struck out with a weapon in each hand, killing just as dextrously with either, his appalling strength displayed by the way his hammer reduced helmeted skulls to jelly, and his axe buried itself happily within thickly armoured stormvermin breasts.

As Lurk watched, one smaller, more cunning skaven managed to circle behind the Slayer and leapt at his back, fangs bared, bright blade gleaming in the light of the blazing buildings. Without pause, somehow aware of the skaven presence without even seeing him, the dwarf whirled and chopped down his foe with his axe, then for good measure broke his neck with the hammer – all the while laughing out loud like a maniac and calling: 'Snorri kill loads!'

Was the dwarf's hearing so good that he could not be snuck up on? Had he felt the merest presence of the skaven's shadow fall across his own in the half-light? Lurk could not guess but the lightning quickness with which he had turned and lashed out told Lurk that he himself wanted to get nowhere near those weapons, at least until their owners were tired and severely wounded. This was not a thought he decided to share with his followers. He booted the nearest towards the fray.

'Hurry quick. Weakening they are! The kill is yours.'

The warrior looked back at him somewhat dubiously. Lurk revealed his fangs and lashed his tail menacingly and was gratified to see the skaven charge, somehow more afraid of his clawleader than of the foe. Lurk pushed another two forward, shrieking: 'Swift swift. Outnumber them you do. Good their hearts will taste.'

This reminder of superior numbers was all it took to encourage the rest of the claw to advance into the fray. Such a sign of superiority always heartened bold skaven warriors. Lurk only hoped he didn't run out of minions before the dwarfs tired.

THANQUOL CURSED once more. What fool had set light to the buildings? Thanquol swore that if it was one of his incompetent lackeys he would eat the fool's raw heart before his very eyes. If those buildings were destroyed, this great victory would count for almost naught. He wanted them taken whole and intact so that they could be inspected by the warp engineers, their secrets snatched and improved on by superior skaven technology. He did not want the whole complex burned to the ground before then. Right at this moment he could see nothing that he could do except order all of his clawleaders to take more care.

At least he would see the accursed Trollslayer destroyed, he consoled himself.

THE AGONISED SCREAMS of the dying. The night pierced by the flickering light of burning buildings, the light dimmed further by the thick clouds of scalding steam. The press of hairy bodies. The shock of blade on bone. The sticky feel of warm black blood flowing over his hand. The look of sick hatred in the dimming eyes of the dying skaven. All of it, the whole infernal scene, seared itself into Felix Jaeger's memory. For a brief breathless moment time seemed to stop and he was alone and calm in the centre of this howling, turbulent maelstrom. His mind cleared of fear and horror. He was aware of his surroundings in a way that a man can only be when he knows each breath he draws may be his last.

Close by him, two burly dwarfs fought back to back against a pack of howling skaven. The dwarfs' beards bristled. Their hammers were caked with gore. Their leather aprons were soaked with glistening black blood. The rat-men were thin, stringy, underfed, with the gaunt feral look of winter wolves. Bloody froth foamed from their lips where they had bitten their tongues and the inside of their cheeks in their battle-frenzy. Their swords were nicked and rusty. Filthy rags covered their scabby hides. Their eyes glittered with reflected firelight. One of them bounded forward, clambering over his fellows in hasty rush to get at his prey. It reminded Felix of the seething advance of a pack of rats he had once witnessed in the streets of Nuln. Despite their humanoid forms, at that moment there was nothing human whatsoever about the skaven. They were unmistakably beasts in man's image and their resemblance to humanity only made them all the more horrifying.

A terrible shriek from his right grabbed Felix's attention and he looked around to see a wounded dwarf warrior being dragged down by a pack of rat-men. There was a look of stoic endurance in the dwarf's eyes.

'Avenge me,' he croaked with his dying breath.

Something about the way the skaven fell to fighting over scraps of the still-warm corpse sickened Felix. He leapt over to where it lay and plunged his sword into the back of a skaven slave. The glowing blade passed right through the scrawny body and into the neck of a skaven below. A kick sent another skaven flying backwards. Felix ripped his weapon free and brought it down again, driving it with full force into the bodies below him. The shock of the impact flexed the blade until he feared it would break. Driven by his hatred, Felix rotated the hilt, opening the wound with a hideous sucking sound, then he stepped back with barely enough time to parry the stroke of the huge skaven who leapt at him.

He had passed beyond fear now. He was driven only by the instinct to kill. Knowing there was no way to avoid fighting, he was driven to do so as best he could. It made him an awful opponent. He lashed out with his foot, catching the skaven a crunching blow to the knee. As it hopped backward shrieking in agony, he drove the point of his sword into its throat, turning his head to avoid the blood which sprayed from the severed artery. Now was no time to be blinded.

In the distance he heard a familiar bull-like voice bellowing battle-cry. He recognised it instantly as Gotrek's and began to move towards it, hewing to left and right as he went, not caring whether he killed his foes, merely intending to clear them from his path. The skaven gave way before his furious rush and in ten heartbeats he came upon a scene of the most appalling carnage. Snorri and Gotrek stood atop a great heap of skaven bodies, hewing all around them with their terrible weapons. Gotrek's axe rose and fell with the monotonous regularity of a butcher's cleaver, and every time it descended more skaven lives ended. Snorri moved like a dervish, whirling this way and that, the foam of berserker rage bubbling from his lips as he lashed out with axe and hammer, pausing occasionally only to head-butt any rat-men which had got within his guard.

All around the pair flowed a tidal wave of huge black-armoured rat warriors better armed than most. The hideous emblem of the Horned Rat was emblazoned upon their shields. There must have been two score of these elite skaven warriors and it seemed all but impossible that anything could survive their furious charge. Even as Felix watched, the press of bodies obscured Snorri and Gotrek from view. It seemed like they must surely be dragged down by sheer weight of numbers. Felix stood frozen for a moment, unable to decide whether he was too late to be of assistance, then he saw Gotrek's axe pass through a skaven body, chopping the armoured figure in two despite its mail. In an instant the area around the Trollslayers was cleared. It seemed like nothing could live within the circle of that unstoppable axe. The skaven backed off and regrouped, trying to gather enough courage for a second rush.

Felix charged down into the fray, striking right and left, shouting at the top of his lungs, trying to make it sound like there was more than just the one of him. Gotrek and Snorri moved to meet him, killing as they came. It was all too much for the skaven, who turned tail and tried to flee into the night.

Felix found himself face to face with the Slayer, who paused for a moment to inspect the mound of dead and dying he had left in his wake. Blood caked the Slayer's entire form, and he himself bled from dozens of nicks and scratches.

'Good killing,' he said. 'Reckon I got about fifty of them.'

'Snorri reckons he got fifty-two,' Snorri said.

'Don't give me that,' grumbled Gotrek. 'I know you can't count above five.'

'Can too,' Snorri muttered. 'One. Two. Three. Four. Five. Er, seven. Twelve.'

Felix looked on in astonishment. The two maniacs looked almost happy in this midst of this scene of incredible destruction.

'Well, best get going. Plenty more to slaughter before this night is over.'

THANQUOL BIT HIS tail with a raging fury. He could not believe it. Those incompetent fools had failed to kill the Slayers despite their overwhelming advantage in numbers and superior skaven ferocity. Not for the first time, he suspected some hidden enemy was sabotaging his efforts by sending him inferior pawns. Doubtless it was the same wicked conspirators who had dispatched Jaeger and Gurnisson to this distant location in the first place. Well there would be a reckoning, he would see to that!

Right now, though he did not have time to worry about it. This was the moment to inspect the battlefield and see how his forces were doing. He pulled both hands backwards and upwards away from the seeing stone, and his point of view retracted until it seemed that he hovered over the battlefield like some enormous bat. Below him he could see the burning buildings – curse those incompetent fools! – and the signs of the savage struggle.

Here and there, huge clumps of warriors still battled it out. Weapon clashed with weapon. Sparks flew where skaven sword hit dwarf-forged axe blade. Blood gouted from fresh wounds. Headless corpses writhed in the dust, still spending the last of their life blood in a spasm of furious energy. Sparks rose, driven skywards by the night wind. On the walls of the keep, a group of sweating dwarfs struggled to push a multi-barrelled organ gun into position.

It was obvious that this was the moment of crisis. Everything hung in the balance. It was equally obvious to the grey seer that his skaven were going to win. They had overwhelmed the dwarfs from both sides and the sheer weight of their numbers had ground down their ill-equipped opponents. Thanquol's frustration at the escape of his two deadliest enemies started to be replaced with the warm glow of imminent triumph.

FELIX KNEW THAT he was going to die. Wearily he parried the blow of a skaven scimitar. His aching muscles turned his arms and sent a counter-blow arcing towards his foe. The huge black-furred thing sprang backwards, lithely avoiding the stroke. Its tail lashed out, entangling Felix's legs, trying to trip the human by tugging him off his feet. A spark of exhausted triumph flickered feebly in Felix's mind. He had seen this trick before and knew how to respond instantly. He lashed out with his sword, severing the tail near its root, but only just managed to get his blade back into guard position in time to block the downward sweep of the rusting scimitar.

The shock of the impact almost numbed his hand, and reflexively he clutched tighter on the hilt of his sword to prevent it from slithering from his sweaty grasp. The skaven shrieked in horror and swished the stump of its tail. It made the mistake of looking down to inspect the flow of blood. As its eyes left him, Felix took advantage of its distraction to launch his sorcerous blade into its stomach. Warm entrails tumbled over his hand. He fought down a feeling of disgust as he stepped back. Clutching its stomach with both paws, an almost human look of disbelief on its face, the skaven tumbled forward. Felix drove his blade through the back of its neck, severing the vertebrae just to make sure that it was dead. He had seen many warriors dragged down to death by foes they thought they had killed, and he was determined never to make that mistake himself.

For an instant all was calm. He looked around and saw Gotrek and Snorri and a whole group of battered and fierce looking dwarfs. They all looked bone-tired, even the Slayers. It seemed like they had been killing for hours, yet for every foe that fell another two strode forward to take its place. The skaven came on in seemingly inexhaustible waves. In the distance Felix could hear the clamour of weapon on weapon, so he knew somewhere others still fought on but even as they listened an ominous silence fell, and then there was a roar that seemed to have been torn simultaneously from a hundred bestial throats. The dwarfs exchanged glances that told Felix that they were all thinking the same thing as him. Perhaps they were the very last dwarfs left alive outside the keep.

That wasn't going to last. Looking around them, Felix could see that they were ringed by fierce skaven warriors. Hundreds of reddish eyes glittered in the darkness. The light of the burning buildings reflected off a similar number of glistening blades. The skaven had pulled back momentarily to regroup for what he knew would be their final rush. They moved with a strange precision as if being organised by some swift, evil and unseen intelligence. In that moment Felix knew that he was definitely going to die, right here.

He took advantage of the momentarily lull to wipe the sweat from his brow. His breath came raggedly from his lungs. His gulped in air as greedily as a drowning man. All his muscles were on fire. His blade weighed a ton or more. He felt sure that he could not raise it again, even to save his life, but was thankful that he had enough experience to know how false that feeling was. When the time came there was always a little more strength with which to fight. Not that it made much difference now, looking out onto those rows and rows of silent rat-like faces.

'Form up there,' he thought he heard someone say behind him. 'Get ready to repel the charge. Let's give those verminous scum a taste of true dwarf steel!'

Felix wondered at the sheer stubborn courage of the dwarfs. The sergeant who spoke must know it was thoroughly hopeless, yet he was heartening his troops to sell their lives dearly.

Felix prepared to do the same but only because he had no choice in the matter. If he could have seen a way out of here to live to fight another day, he would have taken it.

Somewhere in the distance he thought he heard a droning as of some monstrous insect – or an engine. What was going on? Was this some new infernal device that the skaven were launching at their foes. Oddly enough, it seemed to be coming from the direction of the castle. A faint hope stirred in Felix's breast. Perhaps the dwarfs had a surprise waiting for their attackers. Although it seemed unlikely they could do anything before the skaven overwhelmed their current position, perhaps they might be avenged.

The skaven leaders seemed to be grunting orders to their teeming followers. Slowly, almost reluctantly, as if they feared to be first to spend their lives against the living wall of their grim foes, the skaven began to advance. As they took their first faltering steps they seemed to gain in confidence and their advance picked up speed and momentum at a terrifying rate. The strange thrumming noise grew much louder. It seemed to be coming from overhead. Felix wanted to look up but couldn't tear his eyes from the rush of the rat-men.

'Come on and die!' Gotrek roared and the skaven looked prepared to take him at his word as they charged forward ever faster, brandishing their weapons, chittering their evil sounding war-cries, swishing their tails in fury. Felix braced himself for the impact and then fought the urge to throw himself flat as some outlandish shape roared close overhead. This time he did look up, and he saw a great flight of bizarre machines passing above them. Trails of fire leaked from their boilers as they blazed across the night. Enormous rotor blades whirled near-invisibly over their hulls.

'Gyrocopters!' he heard somebody roar and realised that he was witnessing the night flight of some of the legendary dwarfish aircraft.

Blazing sparkles of light descended from the machines and landed in the middle of the oncoming skaven. It was only when they began to explode in the rat-men's midst that Felix realised that they must have been the fizzling fuses of dwarf bombs.

The skaven rush slowed as the bombs tore their targets limb from limb. Their apoplectic leaders tried frantically to rally them, but as they did so one of the copters descended almost to head height and sent a wide jet of scalding, super-heated steam into their midst. Yelping with unutterable terror a huge group of the rat-men turned tail and fled. The panic was contagious. Within moments the charge had become a rout. The dwarfs around Felix watched with almost numbed disbelief, too weary even to chase after the fleeing foe.

FIVE
THE GREAT PLAN

FELIX SLUMPED DOWN against the broken wreckage of the wagon and inspected the blade of his sword. It had seen a lot of use in this battle but somehow it wasn't notched. The edge was still as keen as ever, even after all the hacking and chopping he had done. The ancient enchantment on the weapon obviously still held good.

Somewhere off to his right, the wall of a burned-out shed, unable to support its own weight any more, came down with a crash. Overhead a gyrocopter moved with the sinister grace of an enormous insect, pausing for a moment to hover over a blazing building. Its nose swivelled downwards and with a hiss like an angry serpent a jet of steam emerged. Felix wondered what the pilot hoped to achieve.

The steam met the fire and the flickering flames changed colour, becoming a duller yellow with perhaps a hint of blue. As the jet continued to play, the fire slowly died down, smothered by the vapour and condensation like a small rainstorm. Even as Felix watched, the gyrocopter swung around on the spot and moved towards the next nearest blaze.

He suddenly felt enormously tired, drained of all energy by the conflict. He was bruised and battered, bleeding from dozens of small nicks and cuts which he had not noticed during the frenzy of combat. His right shoulder, the shoulder of his sword arm, ached horribly. He was almost convinced that the repeated swinging of the sword had dislocated it. It was an illusion he was familiar with, having survived many other battles. He wanted to lie down and sleep for a hundred years.

Looking around him, he wondered where the dwarfs got their energy. Already they were starting to clear up the debris of the battle. Bodies of fallen dwarfs were being gathered for burial in the sacred earth. Skaven corpses, meanwhile, were being lugged into a huge pile for burning. Fully armoured sentinels had descended from the keep and kept watch, just in case the skaven should return.

Felix doubted that they would tonight. In his experience it took the skaven longer than a human army to recover and reassemble after a defeat. They did not seem to like to return so swiftly to the scene of a defeat, and for this he was profoundly glad. At this moment he doubted he could move a muscle, even if the rat-ogre was to rise from the dead and come looking for him. He pushed that evil thought from his mind and searched for a happier topic.

He found one: at least he was still alive. He was beginning to believe again that he just might live. Sometimes before and during a battle, when fear threatened to overwhelm his reason, he had this terrible sensation that he was certain to die. It settled on him like a curse, this certainty of his own mortality. Now it amazed him that he was still here, that his heart still beat, that breath still moved in and out of his lungs. Looking around he could see plenty of evidence that this could easily not have been the case.

Blood-covered corpses were everywhere, being pulled like sacks of dead meat through the thoroughfares by bone-weary, grumbling dwarfs. The sightless eyes of the dead stared at the sky. Despite his earlier imaginings, he knew they would not get up again. They would never laugh or cry or sing or eat or breath. The thought filled him with a profound melancholy. Yet at the same time, he knew with certainty that he still lived, that he could do all those things, and for that he should therefore rejoice. Life is all too brief and fragile, he told himself, so enjoy it while you can.

He began to laugh softly, filled with a quiet joy which felt strangely like sorrow. After a moment he limped painfully off into the night to see if he could find Gotrek or Snorri or anybody else he might know amidst this vast shambles.

THANQUOL COULD not believe it. How could it all have gone so wrong so quickly? One moment, victory was within his grasp. His brilliance seemed to have assured triumph. In the next, it had vanished as quick as a skavenslave turning tail in battle. It was a sickening, dizzying sensation. It took long, bitter moments of reflection to convince the grey seer that even the most brilliant of schemes could be foiled by the incompetence of underlings. Through no fault of his own, his lazy, cowardly and stupid minions had let him down once more.

Reassured by this brilliant insight, he considered his options. Fortunately he had a contingency plan, devised for just such an unlikely eventuality as this. Lurk was still alive and still reachable though his speaking stone. With any luck, he could be left in place, ready to report on the secrets the unscrupulous dwarfs had tried to conceal here.

Thanquol looked into the seeing stone once more and sent his mind questing for contact.

FELIX FELT A TUG on his sleeve. Looking down he saw Varek. The young dwarf's blue robes were soiled with mud and blood. The sleeve of his robe had come away, ripped at the seams to reveal a ripped and tattered white linen shirtsleeve. His glasses were broken; a crazy web of cracks marked their lenses. In one hand he clutched a small warhammer. The other held his leatherbound book tightly against his chest. Felix was surprised by how large Varek's hands were, how white the knuckles seemed. There was a mad feverish gleam in the youth's eyes.

'That was the most amazing experience of my life, Felix,' he said. 'I have never seen anything so exciting, have you?'

'It's the type of excitement I could cheerfully live without,' Felix said sourly.

'You don't mean that. I saw you fighting back there. It was like watching a hero from the days of Sigmar. I never knew humans could fight so well!'

Varek blushed, seeming to realise just what he had said. It was a dwarfish fault, being blunt about what they considered to be the inferior abilities of the younger races.

Felix laughed softly. 'I was only trying to stay alive.

'And I hate skaven,' he added as an afterthought. He considered that fact and felt slightly appalled. He did not consider himself to be a particularly violent or vengeful man, but the skaven made his flesh crawl. He was slightly shocked by the idea that he took pleasure in killing them but inspecting his feelings now he was honest enough to admit that it was true.

'Everybody hates the skaven,' Varek agreed. 'Even other skaven, most likely.'

LURK SNITCHTONGUE moved stealthily through the burned-out ruins. Fear filled his heart and warred with his hatred of Thanquol. His musk glands felt tight and he fought down the urge to squirt the fear scent, for it might give away his presence to the dwarfs all around him. Right now, away from the comforting scent and furry mass of his brethren, he felt terribly alone and exposed. He wanted to run swiftly into the night and find the other survivors of the battle. The thought goaded him intolerably.

Still, fear of the grey seer was uppermost in his mind. Staying here most probably meant death, but defying one of the Chosen of the Horned Rat meant an inevitable, agonising doom. There were worse things than a swift blow from a dwarf axe, as Lurk well knew. Not that he wanted one of those either.

Turn right, the nagging voice said inside his head.

'Yes, most magnificent of masters,' Lurk whispered. He followed orders, moving down a long, quiet alley towards the monstrous structure which dominated the centre of the dwarf settlement. He flinched, wondering whether Thanquol could read his thoughts. He certainly hoped not, after some of the things he had been ruminating on.

His paw toyed idly with the amulet and briefly he considered what would happen if he tore it from his flesh and threw it away. Something nasty, he was sure. It would be just like a grey seer to have some intricate curse woven into the device. He did not doubt that digging it from his skull would most likely kill him, or cause him severe pain at the very least, and Lurk was no keener on pain than most skaven.

Again he flinched, hoping that thought had not gone over the link to Thanquol. He hoped not; he was only supposed to be able to send when he touched the stone and concentrated. He supposed it would take a lot of effort to drive his thoughts through the ether. He didn't know that for sure, not having tried it, but right at this moment he actually hoped it was the case.

Stop! came the imperious command. He did so at once, automatically and instinctively. A moment after he did so, he heard the sound of booted dwarfish feet ahead of him. A moment after that, a small squad of dwarfs stomped past the alley mouth. Lurk shivered instinctively when he saw that they were dragging skaven corpses off to be burned. His whiskers twitched. He had already recognised the foul scent of scorching skaven flesh earlier.

Now – run quickly across the street. Hurry-scurry while the way is clear.

He steeled himself and leapt forward into the wide exposed space between the buildings, risking a quick glance right and left as he did so, and seeing that the way was indeed clear save for the backs of the departing dwarfs. He had to admit that, whatever else he might be, Thanquol was a mighty sorcerer. He had no idea how the grey seer was able to guide him so well, but so far he had made no mistakes.

Lurk dove into the cover of the alleyway opposite and hurried on. Directly in front of him now was the huge dwarfish building. Its metal roof gleamed in the moonlight. He saw that vast and powerful steam engines were attached to its side. His skaven curiosity was piqued. He wondered what could possibly be stored within so huge a structure.

Quick-quick – head right till you find the entrance or swift death will be yours.

Lurk hastened to obey. He slid through the entrance arch and halted – and stared upwards in wide-eyed wonder. A gasp of pure amazement was torn from his uncomprehending lips.

FELIX WANDERED through the burning night, Varek by his side. Things look worse than they are, he told himself, hoping against hope that it was true. It was evident that both sides had taken enormous casualties. Many dwarfs had fallen in the conflict and each and every one of them seemed to have taken at least two skaven with him. The stink of burning rat-man flesh was well-nigh unbearable. Felix pulled his cloak across the lower half of his face to keep out the smell. No one else seemed at all bothered.

It looked like the vast complex had taken a lot of damage. Felix wondered whether it would be enough to set back whatever project the dwarfs had been working on, and realised that he was in no position to hazard a guess. He simply did not have enough knowledge of what was going on here.

'What is this all in aid of?' he asked Varek suddenly. The young dwarf stopped polishing his broken glasses on the hem of his tunic and looked up at him. He breathed on the lenses as if wanting time to gather his thoughts, then started to polish again, not noticing that a shard of glass had broken free.

'What is what in aid of, exactly?'

'All this machinery,' Felix said.

'Er – perhaps I should leave that for my uncle to explain. He is in charge here.'

'That's very discreet of you. Where can I find your uncle?'

'In the keep, along with the others.'

Before he could ask another question, a gyrocopter whizzed low overhead. Standing on the strut of the landing gear was a burly figure with a shaven head. He held a monstrous multi-barrelled musket. Something about the way he stood set Felix's senses to prickling. The dwarf turned a crank on the side of the musket and a hail of shot churned up the earth at Felix's feet. Felix pushed Varek to one side and threw himself flat, turning to track the gyrocopter, wondering what madness had possessed the demented dwarf. Surely he had not mistaken Felix for a skaven? Then from behind him Felix heard a chorus of agonised squeaks.

It was only as he turned his head that Felix saw the group of skaven who had been advancing noiselessly behind him, blades bared. Felix recognised them as gutter runners, the dread skaven assassins he had fought in the Blind Pig tavern back in Nuln. The dwarf on the gyrocopter had cut the things down with his strange weapon. He had most likely saved their lives, even if his lack of accuracy had almost killed them both.

The gyrocopter swept backwards and slewed down to a not-quite perfect landing. The musket-toting figure leapt down from its side, and hurried away from the flying machine in a low crouch designed to stop the swiftly rotating blades separating his head from his shoulders. The downdraft from the machine flattened the enormous crest of red dyed hair which rose above his head. The gale sent Felix's cloak flapping in the wind and the dust the machine stirred up brought tears to his eyes. Varek was forced to squint through the lenses of his broken glasses. He had covered his mouth with his book to prevent himself from breathing in the dust. The strange chemical smell of the vehicle's exhaust reached Felix's nostrils even through the wool of his cloak.

The newcomer was short and incredibly broad. His chest was bare, revealing amazing muscular definition. Twin bandoleers of what must have been ammunition were looped over his shoulders. A red scarf was tied round his forehead. He wore high leather boots with a large dagger scabbarded on the right boot. A monstrous silver skull buckled the belt which held up his green britches. His white beard was cut short almost to his jaw. A two-headed Empire eagle was tattooed on his right shoulder. Strange thick optical lenses covered his eyes. Felix could see that they were engraved with some sort of cross hairs. Judging from his appearance, Felix decided that this had to be another Trollslayer. The stranger clumped over to him and looked him up and down, then he spat on the corpse of one of the skaven.

'Nasty, evil wee creatures, skaven!' he said by way of a greeting. 'Never liked them. Never liked their machinery.'

He turned to Felix and executed a formal dwarfish bow. 'Malakai Makaisson, at your service and your clan's.'

Felix returned the bow with that of an Imperial courtier. He used the movement to cover up his expression of astonishment. So this was the famous mad engineer of which Gotrek and Varek had talked. He did not look that crazed. 'Felix Jaeger, at your service.'

The dwarf turned the crank on his musket again. The barrels spun. Shot tore into the skaven corpses. Black blood spurted as fur and flesh tore.

'Ye cannae be too careful with these beasties. They're awfae sleekit, ye ken.'

'He means they are very cunning,' Varek translated.

'Ach, awae wi' ye! Ah'm sure Herr Jaeger kens exactly what ah mean, don't ye, Herr Jaeger?'

'I think I follow you,' Felix said non-committally.

'Well, there ye go then. Best be gettin' up tae the castle. Auld Borek will be wantin' tae talk tae ye and the others. I suppose ye'll be wantin' tae ken what this is ah aboot.'

'That would be excellent,' Felix said.

'Well, just wait till they lower the brig then – unless ye want a wee lift back the noo. Ah think the copter will tek an extra body.'

It took Felix a few moments to work out that this maniac was offering him a ride on the landing gear of the gyrocopter. He tried to force a pleasant smile onto his face as he said, 'I think I'll just wait for the gate to open, if it's all the same to you.'

'Fine by me. See ye later then.'

Makaisson clambered back on to the landing gear of the gyrocopter and shouted something to the helmeted and goggled pilot. The engine roared and the machine lurched skyward – leaving Felix wondering whether the meeting had ever actually happened at all.

'Do all your engineers talk like that?' Felix asked Varek. The young dwarf shook his head.

'Makaisson's clan comes from the Dwimmerdim Vale, way up north. It's an isolated place. Even other dwarfs find their manner of speech strange.'

Felix shrugged. He could hear the creaking of huge chains as the drawbridge into the keep was lowered. He paced rapidly in the direction of the gate, suddenly aware of exactly how tired he was and hoping to find a place to lie down for the night.

FELIX WOKE FROM a nightmare of insane violence, in which a great rat-ogre chased him round a burning town while the gigantic figure of an enormous pale-skinned skaven leered down from the sky. Sometimes the city was the dwarfish community around the Lonely Tower; sometimes he ran through the cobbled streets of Nuln; sometimes he was in his home city of Altdorf, the Imperial capital. It was one of those dreams where his foes' blades were bright and terribly sharp and his own blade simply bounced off unarmoured flesh. He ran and ran while mangy, flea-infested skaven-things clutched at his arms and legs, slowing him, and all the time his monstrous pursuer came ever closer.

His eyes snapped open and he found himself staring at the ceiling of an unfamiliar room, an awakening which always disoriented him, even after many years of wandering.

He found that he was lying in a bed designed for a much shorter and broader person, and that even though he was lying diagonally his feet still protruded over the bottom. He was sweating from the heavy blankets entangling his limbs and he began to see where the feeling of being dragged down in his dream might have stemmed from. He had vague memories of entering the castle the night before, being introduced to various dwarfs and being shown to this chamber. He could remember casting himself on the bed, and after that nothing – except his fast-fading bad dreams.

He had not even taken off his clothes. Blotches of blood and dirt stained the sheets. He sat upright and shook his head wearily, aware of all the aches in his muscles left behind by his participation in last night's battle. Still he felt a sense of exhilaration. He had survived to see a new dawn, and that was the main thing. There was no feeling quite like it, knowing that you were one of the lucky ones after a battle. He pulled himself off the bed and stood up, half-expecting to need to duck his head and therefore rather surprised to find that the castle had been built on a human scale.

He moved to one of the narrow arrowslit windows and gazed out into the valley. Clouds of smoke rose from below and with them came the stench of burning skaven flesh. He wondered how much of the obscuring vapours came from the machines down there and how much from the funeral pyres, and then he realised that he didn't care.

He was suddenly very hungry. There was a knock on the door and he realised the sounds of his awakening had been noticed.

'Come in!' he shouted.

Varek entered. 'Glad to see you're up. Uncle Borek wants to see you. You're to come to breakfast in his study. Hungry?'

'I could eat a horse.'

'I don't think it will come to that,' Varek said.

Felix laughed – then from the expression on the dwarf's face he realised that Varek wasn't joking.

IT WAS A COMFORTABLE room, which reminded Felix of his father's study. Books lined three walls, embossed spines showing Reikspiel script and dwarfish runes. Scroll racks filled some shelves. A huge map of the northern Old World, covered in pins and small flags, draped all of the fourth wall. The northernmost parts of the world showed symbols for cities and mountains and rivers in an area that Felix had never seen shown on any human map, and which he realised must have been long swallowed by the Chaos Wastes. A massive desk in the centre of the study was drowning beneath a sea of letters and scrolls and maps and paperweights.

Behind the desk sat the oldest dwarf Felix had ever seen. His huge, long beard was forked and reached all the way to the floor before being looped back up into his belt. The crown of his head was bald. Wings of snowy white hair framed his face, which was lined with deep furrows of age in the tough leathery skin. The eyes that peered out from behind the thick pince nez glasses twinkled like those of a youth, and at once Felix discerned a family resemblance to Varek.

'Borek Forkbeard, of the line of Grimnar, at your service and your clan's,' the dwarf said, advancing from behind the desk. Felix saw that he was so bowed as to be almost hunch-backed and walked only with the aid of a stout, iron-shod staff. 'Excuse me if I don't bow. I am not as flexible as I once was.'

Felix bowed and introduced himself.

'I must thank you for your aid in the battle last night,' Borek said, 'and for saving my nephew.'

Felix was going to say that he had only fought to save himself, but somehow that did not seem very appropriate.

'I only did what any man would under the circumstances,' he managed to force himself to say.

Borek laughed. 'I think not, my young friend. Few of Sigmar's people remember the old debts and the old bonds these days. And few indeed can fight like you do, if my nephew is to be believed.'

'Perhaps; he exaggerates.'

'Few dwarfs speak anything but the truth, Herr Jaeger. You are making a serious accusation when you say such a thing.'

'I... I did not mean to say...' Felix stammered, then realised from the look in the old dwarf's eye that he was teasing him. 'I simply meant that...'

'Do not worry. I will not mention this to my nephew. Now you must be hungry. Why do you not join the others to eat? After that there are serious matters to be discussed. Very serious matters indeed.'

BREAKFAST LAY SPREAD across the table in the adjoining chamber. Huge ham hocks lay on plates of wrought steel.

Monstrous slabs of cheese formed monuments to gluttony. Massive loaves of dwarf waybread, dark and yeasty, made mountain ranges across the middle of the spread. The smell of beer filled the air from the barrel that already been broached. It came as no surprise to Felix, to see Gotrek and Snorri squatting down by the massive fire, swilling ale and cramming food into their mouths like they had just heard news of an imminent famine.

Varek watched them as if they were about to perform new prodigies of valour at any moment. His leather-bound book lay close at hand just in case he needed to record them. He wore new glasses of a style Felix now realised had been copied from his uncle's.

Another dwarf was also present, one whom Felix did not recognise and who did not immediately move forward to make his introductions in the dwarfish fashion. He glared at Felix suspiciously, as if expecting him to steal the cutlery. Ignoring his glares, Felix walked up to the table and helped himself to food. It was among the best he had ever tasted, and he wasted no time in saying so.

'Best wash it down with some ale, young Felix,' Snorri suggested. 'It tastes even better then.'

'It's a bit early in the day for that,' Felix said.

'It's after noon,' Gotrek corrected.

'You've slept through two watches, young Felix,' Snorri said.

'A minute wasted is like a copper spent,' grumbled the dwarf Felix did not recognise. He turned to regard him. He saw a dwarf shorter than most, and broader than most too. His beard was long and black; his hair was close cut and parted in the middle. His eyes were keen and piercing. His severe black tunic and britches while obviously well made were old and threadbare. His high boots looked old but well-polished. Metal segs protected the heels from wear and tear. He was portly and there was a fleshiness about his face which reminded Felix of his father and other rich merchants he had known. There was a suggestion to it of large meals eaten in well-appointed guildhalls where serious business was discussed. The dwarf's hands flexed at his belt as if constantly checking to see whether his rather flat purse was still there.

Felix bowed to him. 'Felix Jaeger at your service, and your clan's,' he said.

'Olger Olgersson at yours,' the dwarf said before bowing back. 'You wouldn't be connected with the Jaegers of Altdorf, by any chance would you, young man?'

Felix felt momentarily embarrassed. He was the black sheep of the family after all, and had left the family home under a cloud after killing a man in a duel. He forced himself to meet Olgersson's gaze calmly and said, 'My father owns the house.'

'I have done good business with them in the past. Your father has a good head for business – for a human.'

The near contempt in the dwarf's tone made Felix bristle but he kept calm, reminding himself that he was a stranger here. It would not do simply to take offence in a keep full of touchy dwarfs who may all be this stranger's kin.

'He'd have to be, if he made any money dealing with you, Olger Goldgrabber,' Gotrek said unexpectedly.

'Olger is a famous miser,' Snorri said cheerfully. 'Snorri knows that when he takes a coin from his purse the king's head blinks.'

The two Slayers cackled uproariously at this ancient joke. Felix wondered how much they had already drunk. Olgersson's face went red. He looked as if he would like to take offence but did not dare. Obviously neither Gotrek or Snorri cared about his wealth, his influence or his kin.

'No one ever got rich by spending money,' he said huffily and turned and stalked back into the other room.

'You should be kinder to Herr Olgersson,' Varek said. 'He is the one funding this expedition.'

Gotrek sputtered out a mouthful of beer in astonishment. His head swivelled to inspect the young scholar as if he had just claimed that gold grew on trees. 'The greatest tightfist in the dwarf kingdom is giving you gold. Tell me more about this!'

'My uncle will, in just a few moments.'

FELIX FELT A mixture of trepidation and curiosity as they filed into Borek Forkbeard's study. He was curious to hear what had drawn all these disparate dwarfs to this out-of-the-way place. He was worried by the prospect of where this whole thing might lead. Looking out the window at those mighty industrial structures, recalling the ferocity of the skaven's attempt to take possession of them, and seeing the huge assemblage of craftsmanship and skill which had been put into place here made it difficult for him to imagine that the dwarfs were not serious about their mysterious purpose. It was all too easy to imagine how Gotrek and himself might be drawn into it.

Borek looked up at him with twinkling eyes. Olger stood in the far corner, swivelling a globe of the world with his hands, his back ostentatiously turned to the party. The old scholar grinned at them, and bade them all take a seat. Since the dwarf armchairs were too close to the ground for Felix he remained standing.

There was a moment's silence while Borek consulted some of the papers on his desk and made an annotation in runic with a quill pen. Then he coughed to clear his throat just like Felix's lecturers used to back at the University of Altdorf and began to speak.

'I am going to find the lost citadel of Karag Dum,' he said without preamble. There was a challenging look in his eye when he glanced over at Gotrek.

'You cannot,' Gotrek said flintily. There was a hint of bitterness in his voice. 'We tried all those years ago. We failed. The Wastes are impassable. Nothing can survive there sane and unchanged. You know that as well as I do. '

'I believe we have found a way.'

Gotrek snorted then shook his head in disbelief. 'There is no way. We tried to force a passage with the best armed and equipped expedition ever assembled for the purpose. You know how many of us survived. You, me, Snorri, maybe a handful of others. Mostly dead now or mad. I tell you it cannot be done. And you know how many died in the expeditions before ours.'

'You did not always think that way, Gotrek, son of Gurni.'

'I had not then seen the Chaos Wastes.'

'Then you will not even listen to what I have to say?'

'No, no. I will listen, old one. Go ahead, tell me what crazy scheme you have in mind. Perhaps it will give me a good laugh.'

There was a shocked silence in the room. Felix suspected that dwarfs were not used to hearing venerable loremasters spoken to in that way. To break the tension, he dared to ask, 'Why do you want to go to this place? What's so special about it?'

All eyes in the room turned to him. Eventually Borek spoke: 'Karag Dum was one of the greatest cities of our people, the mightiest in all the northern lands. It was lost over two centuries ago during the last great incursion of Chaos, just before the reign of the one you call Magnus the Pious. In the great Book of Grudges, on page three thousand, five hundred and forty-two of volume four hundred and sixty-nine, you will find a record of the debt of blood we owe to the foul followers of the Dark Powers. In the ancillary codicils, we find records of all the names of those who fell, of all the clans which were wiped out. The last message we had was that Thangrim Firebeard had led his brave hosts in a doomed defence of the citadel against a mighty host which came from the north as the Chaos Wastes advanced. Since then, there has been no word from Karag Dum, nor has any dwarf from our lands been able to reach the place.'

'Why?' Felix asked.

'For the Chaos Wastes advanced and swallowed all the lands between Karag Dum and the Blackblood Pass.'

'How can you know where to find it then?'

'It was I who brought the last message from Karag Dum,' Borek said, bowing his head sadly. 'The city was once my home, Herr Jaeger. I am kin to King Thangrim himself. During those last dreadful days, our foes had summoned a mighty daemon, and our need for aid was great. We drew lots to see who would carry the word of our need to our kinfolk. I and my brothers were chosen. We left the citadel by secret routes, known to but a few. Only myself and my brother, Vareg, Varek's father, made it through the Wastes. It was a hard trek and not one I wish to recall at this moment. When we reached the south, we found that war raged there too and no aid was to be had. Then we found there was no way back.'

Was it possible that this dwarf was so old, Felix thought? He certainly looked ancient and Felix knew that dwarfs lived longer than men. Even so, it was an astonishing idea that this dwarf was at least ten times his age, perhaps more. Then another thought struck him.

'If the Wastes are so deadly, how could you make it through and then not get back?' Felix asked.

' I see you are a sceptic, Herr Jaeger. I must convince you. Well, let me just say that in the days of our escape, the Wastes had only just advanced and the influence of Chaos was not so strong. By the time we tried to return, the fell power of Chaos had grown great indeed and the land was impassable. Now, if I have your permission to continue...'

Felix realised that he was interrupting the old dwarf, and making him go over ground that everybody else present seemed familiar with. He suddenly felt embarrassed. 'Of course. Forgive me,' he said.

'Tell us of the treasure that was lost,' Olgersson cut in.

Borek looked less than pleased by the second interruption. He cast a quick glare at the merchant. Felix caught the glint which had appeared in the miser's eye. It was something akin to madness and Felix knew enough about dwarfs now to recognise it for what it was: gold fever. Suddenly it was no mystery why Olger was putting up money to fund this quest. He was in the throes of the near-insane thirst for gold which sometimes overtook even the sanest of dwarfs.

'Yes, the huge hoard of Karag Dum was lost when the city fell, and all the treasure was lost. And of all the treasures that were lost, the most precious were the Hammer of Fate, the mighty weapon born by King Thangrim himself, and the Axe of the Runemasters.'

At this point, Borek turned and looked at Felix. 'We are talking of such things that it is moot only for a dwarf or a Dwarf Friend to know, Felix Jaeger. Gotrek, son of Gurni, has spoken for you, but now I must ask you for your word that you will speak of nothing discussed here with any but a dwarf of the true blood or with another Dwarf Friend. If you feel that you cannot give your word on this, we will understand, but we must ask you to leave this gathering.'

As if a light had been shone upon him, Felix suddenly felt that he had reached a boundary, one which if he crossed would significantly change his life. He felt that if he agreed to stay he was in some way, tacitly committing himself to whatever mad scheme these dwarfs were undertaking. At the same time, he had to admit to a fascination with what was being discussed, with this tale of lost cities, ancient battles, old grudges and vast treasures. He certainly was curious – and surely there could be no harm in simply listening.

'You have my word,' he said, almost before he realised he had spoken.

'Very good. Then I will continue.' Somehow Felix had expected something more. He had expected to be asked to swear an oath or maybe seal the bond in blood as he had done with Gotrek during that epic drinking bout. This simple taking of his word at face value seemed altogether too casual for one about to be initiated into the lost secrets of an Elder Race. Something of his astonishment must have shown in his face, for Borek smiled at him.

'Your given word is enough for us, Felix Jaeger. Among our people, a warrior's word is a sacred thing, stronger than stone, more enduring than mountains. We ask for nothing more. If you will not hold to it, what use are written contracts, oaths sworn before altars or anything else?'

Felix realised that disagreement would only reflect badly on him, so he kept quiet while the old scholar continued to speak.

'Yes, the Hammer of Fate and the Runemaster's Axe, perhaps the most potent of the artefacts bequeathed to us by the Ancestor-Gods were lost to us, and with it a mighty portion of our ancient power and heritage. When Karag Dum fell we believed it lost forever. The howling Chaos Wastes flowed over the ancient lands like a sea of corruption and buried the ancient peaks, and we wailed and gnashed our teeth in dismay and resigned itself to our loss. We thought them lost forever, and so it seemed for these two centuries.'

'And they remain lost,' Gotrek said grimly. 'And always will be. I repeat that there is no way through the Wastes.'

'Perhaps. Perhaps not. After we failed in our last attempt, Gotrek, I renewed my search through the lorehalls and libraries. In the master lorehall of Karaz-a-Karak I searched through the oldest galleries, pulled dust-encrusted tomes from shelves where they had lain mouldering for millennia. I recorded every tale and mention of survivors who claimed to have visited the Wastes. I gained access to the forbidden vaults of the Temple of Sigmar in Altdorf. In their records, taken from the confessions of wracked heretics across the centuries. I found references to runes, spells and talismans that would protect against the influence of Chaos. I was determined to succeed this time. And I believe I have found the man who can make them.'

'And who would that be?' The note of mockery had diminished somewhat in the Slayer's voice.

'The man you will meet soon enough, Gotrek. He has convinced me that his enchantments work. I give you my sworn word that I believe they will shield us.'

'For how long can you protect those who travel in the Chaos Wastes from madness and mutation?'

'Weeks, maybe. Certainly days.'

'Not long enough. It would take months to cross those wastelands to Karag Dum.'

'Aye, Gotrek – on foot, or in armoured wagons as we tried to use last time. But there is another way. Makaisson's way.'

'By airship?'

'Yes, by airship.'

'You are mad!'

'No – not at all. Listen to me. I have studied the phenomenon of the Chaos Wastes extensively. I know much more now than we did then. Most of the mutations are caused by warpstone dust contaminating the food and the water or being breathed into unprotected lungs. It is that which drives folk mad and twists their shapes and forms.'

'Aye, and it is present in the very sands of the Waste and in the clouds which rise from it. It is in the dust and the sandstorms and in the wells.'

'But what if we were to fly above the clouds?'

Gotrek paused for a moment and appeared to consider this. 'You would have to descend to take bearings, to check landmarks.'

'The airship will be sealed with screens of fine mesh. There will be portholes and filters of the type you see on the submersibles of our fleets.'

'The airship might be forced down by storms, or winds or mechanical failure.'

'The amulets would protect the crew until repairs could be effected or the storm cleared.'

'Perhaps repair would be impossible?'

'A risk, certainly, but an acceptable one. The amulets would allow survivors to at least attempt a march home.'

'No airship could carry enough coal for its engines to make the journey without stopping.'

'Makaisson has developed a new engine. It uses the black water instead of coal. It has the power to propel the airship and the fuel is light enough to make the journey.'

As quickly as his objections were overcome, the Slayer seemed to find new ones. He seemed to be frantic to find a hole in the loremaster's arguments.

'What about food and water?'

'The airship would carry enough of both to make the trip.'

'It would be impossible to build an airship large enough to do this.'

'On the contrary, we have already done so. It is what we have been building here.'

'It will never fly.'

'We've already made trial flights.'

Gotrek played his final card: 'Makaisson built it. It's bound to crash.'

'Maybe. Maybe not. But we're going to try it anyway. Will you come with us, Gotrek, son of Gurni?'

'You would have to kill me to stop me!'

'That is what I hoped you would say.'

'The airship – is that what the skaven were seeking?'

'Most likely.'

'Then you will need to move fast before they can amass another army.'

Felix paused for a moment, his mind reeling from what he had heard. It seemed that Gotrek was taking very seriously indeed all this lunatic talk of flying to the Chaos Wastes in an untried and highly dangerous machine, designed by a known maniac. And he did not doubt that he would be expected to come along for the ride. Then there was the fact that there was most likely some great foul daemon waiting for them at the end of the journey.

Worse yet, it appeared that the skaven knew all about this new machine and would stop at nothing to get their hands on it. What hellish sorcery had they used to find out about something so new and well concealed? Or had they secrete traitorous agents in place even among these dwarfs? Felix's respect for the long reach and fiendish intelligence of the ratmen was raised another notch by this evidence of their foresight and planning ability.

AS HE HEARD the dwarfs approach, Lurk quickly scurried into cover. He had spent most of the night gnawing his way through the back of a packing crate and had finally broken through just in time. He wriggled into its innards just before it was picked up by one of the strange, steam-powered lifting machines. He seemed to going up some sort of ramp.

His mind was still reeling from what he had seen last night. Within the huge hangar a massive sleek thing like an enormous shark had hovered overhead, apparently unsupported by any girders. The thing had bobbed up and down like an angry beast. The resemblance had been increased by the fact that the dwarfs had seen fit to tether it with steel hawsers. The sight of the monster had caused Lurk to spurt the musk of fear, but he felt not the slightest sense of shame at having done so. He did not doubt that any other skaven would have done just the same under similar circumstances, even the great Grey Seer Thanquol.

It had taken him long moments of observation, during which he thought his pounding heart would fight its way out of his breast, before he had realised that the creature was not actually alive and was in fact a machine. Something very like wonder had filled his mind as he contemplated the scale of the thing. It was several hundred skaven tails long, larger and more impressive than any other piece of machinery Lurk had seen in Skavenblight or in this dwarf town.

He was amazed by the sorcery which could keep such a huge seeming thing airborne. The skaven warrior in him turned over the possibilities in his mind. With such a machine, a skaven army could fly over human cities and drop poison wind globes, plague sacks and all manner of other weapons, without ever being attacked by the defenders below. It was every skaven leader's dream come true: a means of attack against which there might be no sure defence! For surely such a large armoured vessel must be proof against anything, short of an attack by dragons. And even then, judging by the size of it, and were those – yes, they were! – weapons cupolas embedded in the thing's fuselage, the vessel would have a good chance of surviving. This vessel would provide an awesome weapon in the paws of any skaven intelligent enough to understand the possibilities it offered.

At that moment, he guessed that Grey Seer Thanquol had come to much the same conclusion, for a mighty voice had squeaked inside his head. *Yes-yes, this flymachine must be mine-mine!*

Perhaps Lurk realised he would soon have a chance to seize it, for the crate in which he was hiding was surely being raised on high into the very bowels of the mighty airship.

SIX
DEPARTURE

FELIX STARED OUT from the battlements of the keep. Below him the dwarf township filled the entire valley, but his eyes were glued to the huge central building, the one he now knew contained the airship. Beside him Gotrek leaned against the battlements. His massive head rested on his arms, which were folded atop the parapet. His axe lay near at hand.

Below them Felix could see long lines of dwarfs assembling in ranks before the great doors of the central hangar. Small but powerful steam-engines moved along the rails to the entrance. He picked up the telescope that Varek had lent him and placed it against his eye. A twist of his hands brought the scene into focus. He made out Snorri, Olger and Varek far below. They stood at the head of the line of dwarfs, almost like troops at attention.

Flags fluttered from the struts of the enormous steel tower which loomed over the hangar. It was an imposing structure, more like a spider web of girders than a fortification. At the very top of the tower was what appeared to be a small hut or an observation post with a balconied veranda running all the way around it.

Somewhere in the distance a steam whistle sounded its long lonely cry. By the side of the hangar one of the engineers pulled a huge lever. Pistons rose and fell mightily. Great cogwheels turned. Steam leaked from the monstrous pipes that had been hastily patched after the previous day's battle. Slowly, but surely, the top of the hangar opened. The roof itself slid apart, folding down the sides of the building. Eventually, an enormous structure rose into view, like a gigantic butterfly emerging from a monstrous chrysalis.

Felix knew at once that, as long as he lived, he would never forget his first sight of the airship. It was the most impressive thing he had ever seen. With painful slowness great hawsers were paid out and, like an enormous balloon, the airship rose into view. At first Felix saw only a tiny cupola raised on the top of the vehicle, and towards the rear an enormous fin-like tail. Then, like a whale of the northern seas breaking surface, the gleaming expanse of the airship rose from below.

It was like watching the birth of a new volcanic island in the midst of the trackless ocean. The vast body of the vehicle was almost as long as the hangar and it sloped smoothly downwards like the beaches of an island running down to the sea. As the great craft continued to rise, Felix saw that this first impression was wrong, for, having reached its widest point, the hull curled inwards again, a smoothly curved cylinder. At the stern of the vessel were four massive fins, like the flights of a crossbow bolt.

Dangling from below its belly was a smaller cylindrical structure constructed from riveted metal. In this smaller structure were portholes, and from it protruded cannons and rotors and other mechanical devices whose purpose Felix could only guess at. He focused the telescope on it and could see that this smaller structure resembled the hull of a ship. Right at the front of the airship was a huge glass window. Through this he could see Malakai Makaisson, standing at the controls. Around him were many engineers.

Slowly a strange thought occurred to Felix. Was it possible, he asked himself, that the real ship was the smaller vessel dangling beneath the mighty structure, that somehow the larger structure was something like the sail of a ship or the gasbag of a hot air balloon, huge and necessary for locomotion but not part of the living or working quarters below it? He did not know but he found himself at once repelled and fascinated by the idea, and he knew beyond a shadow of a doubt that, even if he only did so once in his life, he had to get aboard that craft. It was a thought which filled him with fear and curiosity. He glanced over at Gotrek, who was watching with equally rapt attention.

'Are you seriously considering going across the Chaos Wastes in this thing?' Felix asked.

'Yes, manling.'

'And you expect me to come with you?'

'No. That choice is yours alone.'

Felix looked over at the dwarf. Gotrek had not mentioned the oath that Felix had sworn, perhaps because he had felt that no reminder of it was needed – or perhaps because he was genuinely offering Felix the choice. Even after all this time Felix found it difficult to read the Slayer's moods.

'You have tried to cross the Wastes before, with Borek, and others.'

'Yes.'

Felix drummed his fingers on the cold stone of the battlements. For long moments there was silence and then, just when Felix thought the dwarf was not going to say any more, Gotrek spoke again.

'I was younger then, and foolish. There were many of us, young dwarfs, full of ourselves. We listened to Borek's tales of Karag Dum and the Lost Weapons and how it would make our people great again if we found them. Others warned us that the quest was madness, that no good would come of it, that it was impossible. We would not listen. We knew better than them.

'Even if we failed, we told ourselves, we would fail gloriously, seeking to restore the pride of our people. If we died, we would give our lives in a worthy cause, and not have to witness the long slow years of attrition which ate away at our kingdom and our kin. Like I said, we were fools, with the confidence only fools have. We had no idea of what we were letting ourselves in for. It was a mad quest but we were desperate for some of the glory that Borek promised.'

'The Hammer of Fate – what is it?'

'It is a great warhammer, about the length of your forearm but weighing much more. The head is made from smooth, impervious rock, inscribed deeply with runes that…'

'I meant, why is it so important to your people?' If Felix had not known better he would have suspected that Gotrek was trying to avoid the subject.

'It is a sacred object. The Ancestor Gods inscribed it with master runes when the world was young. Some think that it contains the luck of our people, that by losing it we brought a curse upon ourselves that we can only remove by recovering it. Certainly since the hammer was lost, things have not gone well for our race.'

'Do you really believe that bringing it back will change things?'

Gotrek shook his head slowly. 'Perhaps. Perhaps not. It may be that recovering the hammer will bring new heart to a people who have lost much over the past centuries. It may be that the weapon itself will unleash its magic to aid us once more. Or it may not. Even if not, the Hammer of Fate is said to be an awesome weapon, able to unleash lightning bolts and slay the most powerful foes. I do not know, manling. I do know that it is a mighty quest, and a worthy doom to fall on such a quest. If we can find Karag Dum. If we can cross the Wastes.'

'And the axe?'

'Of that I know even less. It is as ancient as the hammer, but few have ever looked upon it. It was always kept in a secret holy place and brought forth only in times of greatest danger, wielded by the High Runemaster of Karag Dum. In three millennia it was carried into battle less than a dozen times. Some whisper that it was the lost Axe of Grimnir himself. Only the High Runemaster of Karag Dum would know the truth of that for certain and he is dead, lost when the Wastes swallowed that place.'

'Are the Wastes so bad?'

'More terrible than you can imagine. Much more terrible. Some claim they are the entrance to Hell. Some claim they are the place where Hell and Earth touch. I can believe it. In all my days I have never seen a more foul place.'

'And yet you would go back!'

'What choice have I, manling? I am sworn to seek my doom. How could I remain behind when old Borek and Snorri and even that young pup Varek will go? If I remain behind I will be remembered as the Slayer who refused to accompany Borek on his quest.'

It seemed strange to hear Gotrek express doubts or admit that he was considering accompanying the loremaster only because of the way others would remember him. He was usually so terrible and full of certainty that most of the time Felix had come to look upon him as something more than human, more like an elemental force. On the other hand, the Slayer was also a dwarf, and his good name meant far more to him that it could mean to even the proudest human. In this the Elder Race seemed truly alien to Felix.

'If we succeed, our names will live in legend for as long as dwarfs mine the under-mountains. If we fail…'

'You can but die,' Felix said ironically.

'Oh no, manling. Not in the Chaos Wastes. There, you really can find fates far worse than death.'

With this Gotrek fell silent and it was obvious that he would speak no more.

'Come on,' Felix said. 'If we're going we'd better get down there and join the others.'

THE AIRSHIP HAD emerged fully from the hangar now. It was moored, like a galleon at anchor, to the top of the great steel tower. It was only when he stood below it, and looked up at the tower's enormous metallic height that Felix truly appreciated the sheer size of the thing. It seemed as large as a cloudbank, big enough to block out the sun. It was larger than any ship Felix had ever seen, and he came from Altdorf, where ocean-going traders sometimes moored, sailing up the Reik all the way from Marienburg.

He had changed into clean clothes. His red woollen cloak flapped in the breeze. His pack was slung over his shoulder. He thought that he was packed and ready to go but now, for the first time, standing in the shadow of the immense metal tower with Gotrek and Snorri, he had some inkling of what he was really letting himself in for.

A metal cage descended from the heights, supported by great metal hawsers unwinding from a drum at the structure's base. The drum was powered by one of the dwarf's steam engines. As it moved it reeled the cable in and out and raised and lowered the cage as needed. It seemed like a mechanical marvel to Felix but Gotrek had remained unimpressed, insisting that such things existed in dwarf mines throughout the World's Edge Mountains.

The cage stopped next to them and its barred door was opened by one of the engineers. He bowed and gestured for them to enter. Felix felt a surge of trepidation, wondering whether the cable was strong enough to hold the combined weight of all three of them and the cage, wondering what would happen if it snapped, or something went wrong with the mechanism.

'Heh! Heh!' Snorri cackled. 'Snorri likes cages. Snorri's been going up and down in this one all day. Better than riding a steam-wagon it is. Goes much higher!'

He leapt in like a child given an unexpected treat. Gotrek followed him in showing no emotion whatsoever, his enormous axe slung lightly over his shoulder. Felix stepped tentatively inside and felt the metal floor flex under his feet. It was not a reassuring feeling. The engineer slammed the cage door shut and suddenly Felix felt like a prisoner in a cell. Then another engineer pulled a lever and the engine's pistons started to rise and fall.

Felix's stomach gave a lurch as the cage began to move and the ground fell away beneath them. Instinctively he reached out to grab one of the bars and steady himself. He gulped in air as nervous as he had been before the battle with the skaven. He noticed that he could see the ground through the small holes in the floor beneath his feet.

'Whee!' went Snorri happily. The faces of the dwarfs on the ground shrank beneath him. Soon the machines were small as child's toys and the vast bulk of the airship swelled ever larger above them. Looking down gave Felix a very unsettling feeling. It wasn't as if they were really going that much higher than the topmost battlement of the castle, it just felt so much further.

Perhaps it was something to do with the motion, or the wind whistling past through the bars of the cage but Felix felt very much afraid. There seemed to be something unnatural about just standing there with all your muscles rigid and your knuckles white from gripping cold metal while the girders of the metal tower glided past. His heart almost stopped as the cage came to rest and all motion ceased save for the slight swaying of the cage on its hawsers.

'You can let go now, manling,' Gotrek said sarcastically. 'We've reached the top.'

Felix pried his grip loose to allow the engineer at the top to open the cage. He stepped through the opening and out onto a balcony. It was a structure of metal struts that ran around the top of the metal tower. The chill wind whipped his cloak and brought tears to his eyes. He felt suddenly frozen with fear when he saw how high he was above the ground. He could now no longer see all of the airship. It was too large for all of it to fit within his field of vision. A metal gangplank ran between the top of the tower and a door in the lower part of the airship's side. On the far side of it he could see Varek and Borek and the others waiting for him.

For a moment he could not make himself move. The ground was at least three hundred paces below him and that metal gangplank could not be that firmly attached to the airship or the tower. What if it gave way below him and he fell? There would be no chance of surviving a drop of this magnitude. The pounding of his heart sounded loud in his ears.

'What is Felix waiting for?' he heard Snorri ask.

'Move, manling,' he heard Gotrek say and then a powerful shove sent him stumbling forwards. 'Just don't look down.'

Felix felt the fragile metal bridge strain under his weight and for a moment thought that it was going to give way. He virtually bounded forward on to the deck of the airship.

'Welcome aboard the *Spirit of Grungni*,' he heard Borek say.

Varek grabbed him and pulled him further past. 'Makaisson wanted to call this ship the *Unstoppable*,' the dwarf whispered, 'but for some reason my uncle wouldn't let him.'

FELIX SLUMPED BESIDE Makaisson at the helm of the airship. He had been forced to duck as he came below. The airship had been designed with dwarfs in mind and so the ceilings were lower and the doors wider than they would have been for humans.

The engineer was dressed differently today. He wore a short leather jerkin with a massive sheepskin collar raised against the cold. A leather cap with long earflaps covered his head. There was another flap cut in the top for Makaisson's crest of hair. Goggles covered the dwarf's eyes, presumably as some protection against the wind if the front window was to shatter. Heavy leather gauntlets enclosed the dwarf's large hands. Makaisson turned and looked up at Felix, beaming with all the pride a father might show when pointing out the achievements of a favourite child.

As far as Felix could tell, some of the controls resembled those of an ocean-going ship. There was an enormous steering wheel which looked rather like a cartwheel, except that it had handgrips around the rim at strategic intervals to allow the pilot a comfortable grip. Felix imagined that by swinging the wheel the pilot could alter the direction of the craft. Beside the wheel were set a group of levers and a square metal box bearing all manner of strange and alarming gauges. Unlike with a ship, the pilot stood at the bow of the craft behind a shield of glass so that he could see where he was going. Looking out the window over the prow Felix could see there was a figurehead, some bearded and roaring dwarf god, which Felix presumed was the dwarf god, Grungni.

'Ah can tell ye're impressed,' Makaisson said, glancing over at Felix. 'An so ye should be – this is the biggest and best airship ever built. Actually, as far as ah ken it's only the second one ever built.'

'You're certain that this thing will fly?' Felix asked nervously.

'As certain as ah am that ah had ham fur breakfast. The balloon, that big thing above yer heed, is full of liftgas cells. There's enough o' the stuff up there to keep twice oor weight airborne.'

'Liftgas?'

'Och, ye ken, it's stuff that's lighter than air. It naturally wants to rise skyward, and as it does it taks us way it.'

'How did you manage to collect the stuff if it's lighter than air. Wouldn't it just float away?'

'A sensible enough question, laddie, an' one that shows ye hay the makin' o' an engineer. Aye, it's naturally rarer than hen's teeth but we make the stuff oorselves doon there in the toon. At least oor alchemist dae. Then we pipe it intae the balloon above us.'

'The balloon.' The thought worried Felix even more. It made him think of the tiny hot air balloons he had made of paper as a child. It seemed inconceivable that such a thing could lift a weight of solid metal, and he said so.

'Aye well, is a lot stronger than hot air and the balloon above ye heed is no made o' metal, nae metter what it looks like. It's made of mare resilient stuff. Alchemists made that as weel.'

'What if the gas leaks out?'

'Och, it woudnae dae a thing like that! Ye see inside that big balloon are hunnerds o' wee balloons. We call them gasbags or cells. If yin bursts it disnae metter much, we'll still hae plenty o' lift. Ivver half they wee balloons would hae tae burst before we lost altitude and even then it would be gradual. It just woudnae be natural for them tae aw burst at yince.'

Felix could see the sense of this arrangement. If the balloon above held thousands of smaller balloons, it was indeed unlikely that they could all be burst at once – even if they were attacked with hundreds of arrows, only the gasbags on the outside would be punctured, if arrows could even penetrate the outer structure of the balloon. Clearly Makaisson had given considerable thought to the safety of his creation.

Somewhere at the rear of the ship a bell rang out. Felix looked around to see that the gangplank had been slid into place and a railing had been swung back round to cover the gap. He felt marginally safer.

'That's the sign that we're supposed to be awa',' Makaisson said. He pulled one of the smaller levers close to hand and a steam-whistle sounded. Suddenly engineers swarmed across the ship to take up positions all around. From the ground below Felix heard cheering.

'Brace yersel!' shouted Makaisson and tugged another lever. From somewhere below the ship came the sound of engines starting up. Their roar was almost deafening. At the sides of the ship the dwarfs were starting to reel in the hawsers on great drums, for all the world like a horde of sailors weighing anchor. Slowly Felix began to sense movement. Currents of air stroked his face. The airship began to rise and to move forward. Almost unwilling he moved to the side of the ship and looked out through the porthole. The ground was starting to slip away below them, and the Lonely Tower complex fall away behind. The tiny figures of the dwarfs on the ground waved up at them and on impulse Felix waved back. Then he was overwhelmed by a sickening sense of vertigo and had to step back from the window.

For the first time it came home to him that he really was on a flying ship heading out for parts unknown. Then he started to wonder how they were ever going to land again. There were no hangars and no great steel towers that he knew of out in the Chaos Wastes.

* * *

VAREK LED HIM down a metal stepladder which had been welded into the structure of the airship. Felix was glad to be off the command deck, away from the mass of excited dwarfs. The drone of the engine was audible even through the thick steel of the vehicle's hull, and occasionally for no reason that Felix could detect the floor flexed beneath his feet.

Suddenly the whole vessel lurched to one side. Instinctively Felix reached out with his hand to steady himself against the wall. His heart leapt into his mouth and for a moment he was convinced that they were about to plummet to their doom. He realised that he was sweating, in spite of the chill.

'What was that?' he asked nervously.

'Probably just a crosswind,' Varek said cheerfully. Seeing Felix's confusion, he began to explain: 'The part of the ship we're in is called the gondola. Its not rigidly attached to the balloon above us. We're actually dangling from hawsers. Sometimes the wind catches us from one side and the whole gondola starts to swing in that direction. Nothing to worry about. Makaisson designed the airship so that it could fly through a gale if need be – or so he claims.'

'I hope he did,' Felix said, finding the nerve to put one foot in front of the other once more.

'Isn't this exciting, Felix?' Varek asked. 'Uncle says we're probably the first people ever to fly at this altitude in a machine!'

'That just means we have further to fall,' Felix muttered.

FELIX LAY ON the short dwarfish bed and stared at the riveted steel ceiling of his stateroom. He found it difficult to relax with the thought of the long drop below him and the occasional motion of the vessel. He was pleased to discover that the cramped bunk had been bolted to the floor of the chamber to prevent it from moving about. The same was true of the metal storage chest in which he had thrown his gear. It was a good design and showed that the dwarfs had thought of things that he never would have. Which he admitted was typical; as a people, they were if nothing else thorough.

He turned on his stomach and pressed his face against the porthole, a small circle of very thick glass set in the airship's side. A chill communicated itself almost immediately to the tip of his nose and his breath misted the pane. He wiped it away and saw that they had risen still higher and that below them lay clouds in a near-endless rolling sea of white.

It was a view which Felix had imagined that only gods and sorcerers had ever seen before, and it sent a thrill of fear and excitement coursing through his whole body. Through a sudden gap in the clouds he could see a patchwork quilt of fields and woods spread out far below. They were so high that, for a moment, he could read the surface of the world like a map, glancing from peasant village to peasant village with a turn of his head. He could follow the course of streams and rivers as if they were the pen-strokes of some divine cartographer. Then the cloud closed again, to lie below him like a snow field. Above them the sky was an incomparable blue.

Felix felt privileged to be given even a glimpse from such heights. Perhaps this is what the Emperor himself felt like when he looked down from the saddle of his royal pegasus, he thought, and took in all the kingdoms of his domain, stretching off into the distance as far as his regal eyes could see.

The gondola of the *Spirit of Grungni* was very impressive, in a cramped, claustrophobic sort of way, Felix decided. It was as big as a river barge and certainly a lot more comfortable. En route to his state room they had passed many other chambers. There was a small but well stocked kitchen, complete with some sort of portable stove. There was a ship's mess with enough space for thirty dwarfs to dine at a sitting. There was a map room filled with charts and tables and a small library of volumes. There was even a huge cargo hold packed with wooden crates which Varek had assured him were full of all the food and gear they would require further north. The thought reminded Felix that when they next stopped – if they next stopped – he would have to pick up some winter clothing and equipment. He did not imagine that it was going to get any warmer the further north they got.

Felix wondered to himself whether this meant he was committing himself to going with the dwarfs. He wasn't certain. In its way, it was an exciting prospect, making such a journey in this mighty airship, to visit a place that no man had seen for three thousand years. If only they had been going any place other than the Chaos Wastes, Felix was certain that he would have chanced it in an instant.

He was not a particularly brave man but neither, he knew without false modesty, was he a coward. The thought of what this vessel was capable of excited him. Mountains and seas would prove no obstacle to a machine which could simply float over them, and this airship was capable of speeds far greater than the fastest ship. According to Varek it could average over two hundred leagues a day, a stupendous velocity.

By Felix's best reckoning it had taken him and the Slayer over a month to cover a similar distance on foot and cart. This vessel was capable of making passage to Araby or Far Cathay in under a week, journeys which took many months. Assuming the vehicle didn't crash or get blown from the sky by a storm or attacked by a dragon, it was capable of amazing feats of locomotion. The commercial possibilities were enormous. It could be used to move small precious perishable cargoes at speed between distant cities. It could do the work of a hundred couriers or stagecoaches. He was sure that there were those who would pay simply to be given a glimpse of the stupendous views he had witnessed through the gap in the clouds. Felix smiled ironically, realising that he was thinking as his father would under the circumstances.

But of course, having created this amazing vehicle, what did those crazed short-legged idiots propose to do with it? Nothing less than fly directly into the deadliest wilderness on the planet, a place which Felix had been brought up to believe was the haunt of daemons and monsters and those who had sold their souls to the Dark Powers – a belief that Gotrek had practically confirmed was true.

Felix wondered at that. Was there some strange compulsion lodged in the dwarfish mind to always seek destruction and defeat? Certainly they seemed to relish tales of disaster and woe the way humans relished epics of triumph and heroism. They seemed to enjoy brooding on their failures and recording their grudges against the world. Felix doubted that any such cult as the Slayer cult could attract worshippers in the Empire and then pulled himself up short. That was most likely not true. Even the incredibly evil Chaos Gods had found worshippers amongst his people, so there would probably be no shortage of human Slayers if they were offered the chance.

He dismissed this line of speculation as pointless, and realised that he did not have to come to any decisions right now about whether he would accompany the dwarfs. He could always decide when they stopped.

If they stopped, he corrected himself.

LURK FLEXED MUSCLES long cramped from inaction. He wondered where he was. He wondered what he was supposed to do. For many hours now, he had heard no communication from Grey Seer Thanquol. For many hours now, he had felt a sense of isolation that was quite new in his experience, and in a way terrifying.

He had been born in the great warrens of Skavenblight, eldest of an average sized litter of twenty. He reached full growth surrounded by his siblings and all the others in the cramped burrow. He had lived in a city filled to bursting point with his fellow skaven, hundreds of thousands of them. When he had left that city it had always been on military duties, as part of a mighty unit of skaven. Even in the smallest guard posts there had been hundreds. He had lived and ate, defecated and slept always within squeaking distance of his kind. There had never been an hour of his short life when he had not been surrounded by the scent of their musk and their droppings, or the sound of their constant stealthy movements.

For the first time in his life he felt that absence like a sharp pain, as a man newly blinded might feel the absence of light. Certainly, all his fellows had been his rivals for the favour of his superiors. Certainly, they would all have stabbed him in the back for a copper token, just as he would them. But always they had been there. There had been something reassuring about their massed presence, for it was a world full of danger, of lesser races who hated the mighty skaven breed and envied their superiority, and in numbers there was safety from any threat. Now he was isolated and hungry and filled with the urge to squirt the musk of fear although there were no fellow skaven around to heed its warning. Now it was all he could do to simply listen to his racing heart and not bury his head in his paws in paralysed terror. In that horrible moment, he realised that he even missed the presence of Grey Seer Thanquol in his mind. It came as a terrible revelation.

At that exact moment, the whole ship began to shake.

FELIX OPENED HIS eyes in alarm. He realised that he must have dozed off. What was that banging sound? Why were the walls shaking. Why was his bed moving? Slowly it came to his puzzled mind that he was on the dwarf airship and it looked like something had gone terribly wrong. The floor was bucking and he could feel the vibration through his mattress. He rolled off the bed, sprang to his feet and banged his head painfully on the ceiling.

He fought down a feeling of claustrophobic terror as the whole airship thumped, creaked and vibrated round about him. In his mind's eye he pictured the ship breaking up and everyone in it plunging to their doom. Why had he ever allowed himself to set foot on this terrible machine, he asked himself as he opened the door. Why had he ever agreed to accompany these dwarf maniacs even this far?

Expecting something terrible to happen at any moment, he threw open his door and shuffled out into the corridor, praying frantically to Sigmar to get him out of this mess, and hoping against hope that he lived long enough to find out what was going on.

SEVEN
EN ROUTE

THE ROCKING OF the airship threw Felix headlong into the corridor. Stars flashed before his eyes and pain seared through his head as his skull struck one of the metal walls. He started to pull himself upright again, realised that he was simply begging to have his head cracked on the ceiling and instead stayed down and started to crawl along the corridor.

Of all the terrors he had ever faced, this was quite possibly the worst. Any second he expected the hull to shatter, the wind to snatch him up and then a long fall to his death. It occurred to him that, for all he knew, the gondola may already had parted from the balloon and be plunging to its doom. Impact with the solid earth might happen at any second.

It wasn't so much the fear that was appalling. It was the sense of helplessness. There was simply nothing he could do to alter his predicament. Even if he managed to get to the control room, he did not know how to steer the craft. Even if he found his way to an exit they were thousands of feet above the ground. Never before had he known a sensation quite like it. Even in the midst of battle, surrounded by enemies, he had always felt like he was in charge of his own destiny and could fight his way clear by virtue of his own skill and ferocity. On a tempest-tossed ship he might have been able to do something; if it sank, he could dive into the sea and swim for his life. His chances in either case might be slim but at least there was something that he could do. Here and now there was nothing to be done except crawl along this claustrophobic walkway, with the vibrating steel walls pressing in, and pray to Sigmar that he would be spared.

For a moment, something like blind panic threatened to overwhelm him, and he fought down an overwhelming urge to simply curl up in a ball and do nothing. He forced himself to breathe normally as he pushed these thoughts aside. He was not going to do anything to shame himself in front of these dwarfs. If death came he would face it standing, or at least crouching. He forced himself upright and slowly made for the control chamber.

Just as he was congratulating himself on his determination, the airship rose then fell mightily, like a ship breasting an enormous wave. For a long moment, he was convinced that the end had come and he stood there waiting to greet his gods. It took several heartbeats for him to realise that he was not dead, and several more before he could gather the nerve to put one foot in front of the other and continue.

ON THE COMMAND DECK no one showed any signs of panic. Tense-looking engineers strode backwards and forwards, checking gauges and pulling levers. Makaisson stood straining at the wheel, his enormous muscles swollen under his leather tunic, his crest bristling through his helmet. All the dwarfs stood with their legs wide apart, maintaining perfect balance. Unlike Felix they were not having any trouble standing upright. Envy filled him. Maybe it was because they were smaller, broader and heavier, he thought. Lower centre of gravity. Whatever it was, he wished he had it.

The only one showing any discomfort was Varek, who had turned a nasty shade of green and had covered his hand with his mouth.

'What's going on?' Felix asked. He was proud that he managed to keep his voice level.

'Nithin tae worry aboot!' Makaisson bellowed. 'Joost a wee bit o' turbulence!'

'Turbulence?'

'Aye! The air beneath us is a wee bit disturbed. It's just like waves in water. Dinna worry! It'll settle itself doon in a minute. Ah've seen this before.'

'I'm not worried,' Felix lied.

'Guid! That's the spirit! This auld ship was built for far worse than this! Trust me! Ah should ken – I built the bloody thing!'

'That's what I'm worried about,' Felix muttered beneath his breath.

'Ah still wish they'd called her the *Unstoppable*! Cannae understand why they didnae.'

LURK SQUIRTED THE musk of fear again. The inside of the packing case stank of it. His fur was matted with fine droplets. He wished he could stop but he couldn't. The banging and shaking of the dwarf airship had him convinced that he was going to die. He knew he should stop, that the reek of the musk was only likely to draw attention to him but that thought just scared him more and kept him squirting the bitter acrid stench. It was only when his glands were empty and sore that he stopped. Bitterly he cursed Thanquol and the machinations that had placed him in this position of jeopardy. What was the grey seer doing now, he wondered?

THANQUOL SAT hunched in the desolate cave high in the mountains, pondering how he was going to get in touch with Lurk and find out the location of the airship. He had watched its departure, his heart filled with a lust to possess the thing such as he had never in all his life felt before. He finally understood what the dwarfs had been working on, and what it represented.

The military possibilities were endless. Judging by the speed with which the vehicle had gained height and flown off it was capable of moving from one end of the Old World to the other in less than a week. The vision of a great fleet of such ships carrying the invincible skaven legions to inevitable victory filled his mind. The sky would be darkened by mighty vessels bearing the banner of the Horned Rat and Thanquol, his most favoured servant. Armies could be moved behind the lines of bewildered enemies before they realised what was happening. Cities could be brought to their knees by bombs, gas globes and plague spores dropped from above.

When he looked at that airship, Thanquol had known that he looked upon the very pinnacle of technological achievement in the Old World and that it was the destiny of the skaven race to possess it and improve on it in their own inimitable way. Refitted with superior skaven engines and weapons, the airship would become better, faster and more powerful than its creators could ever imagine. Thanquol knew that it was his duty to his people and to his own destiny as one of their leaders, to acquire that airship, whatever the cost, however long it took. Only a skaven of his brilliance could understand its true potential. He must have it!

But right now the first problem was to find out where the thing was. He had lost contact with Lurk when his lieutenant had passed out of the range of the speaking stones. Thanquol knew he would have to extend himself to re-establish contact by sorcerous means. The link between his stone and his lackey's still existed but there was just not enough power in the spell. He believed he could compensate for that himself, given the opportunity.

He swiftly glanced round the cave. It was a propitious spot, one of the entrances to the great web of tunnels that linked the Under-Empire, the place where the survivors of his attack on the Lonely Tower had mustered beyond reach of dwarfish vengeance. It had been a long, tiring scuttle through the night to reach this place and Thanquol was weary as he had not been in many a year. Still, he was not about to let fatigue stop him from gaining possession of the airship.

He touched the amulet with the slender talon that tipped one of his long delicate fingers. He sensed the surge of warpstone energies trapped within the talisman. Patiently he sent his thoughts questing down the tenuous ectoplasmic link which streamed from the amulet. It was reassuring to know that it still existed in some form, even though it was stretched far beyond any distance he had ever envisioned. Slowly the grey seer gathered his power and sent his mind stretching out further. He closed his eyes to aid his concentration, feeling like one stretching further and further out over some abyss.

It was no use. He could not make contact over this distance, not unaided. He reached into his pouch and took a generous pinch of warpstone snuff, snorting it hungrily. The power aided him, bringing him the strength he required. Far, far off, at enormous range, he sensed the dim, frightened presence of the wretched Lurk. A smile of triumph revealed Thanquol's fangs. He knew instantly the distance and direction in which the airship flew. He could find it again when required. Now he needed more specific information.

Lurk, listen to me! Here are your orders!

Yes, mightiest of masters! the reply came back.

FELIX LOOKED OUT through the window of the command deck in astonishment. The turbulence had ended. Night had come. Below him he could see countless lights which marked the presence of taverns and villages spread across the hills and plains of the Empire. Some that moved marked the presence of coaches hastening through the darkness to inns or other refuges. Off to the left he caught the glitter of moonlight on a river and patches of denser shadow which marked a forest. It was a scene of strange and eerie beauty, and something that Felix knew few men had ever seen.

They had passed through the turbulence of the storm and everything seemed to be going smoothly. The droning of the engines was regular. None of the dwarfs showed the faintest signs of alarm. Even Varek had lost some of his greenness and headed off to his cabin to rest. All was peaceful in the control deck.

They had been aloft now for many hours and at last Felix was starting to believe that this ship really could fly. It had survived the shaking and bucking earlier. Aside from a bruise on his forehead there was no sign of any trouble. Incredible as it had seemed just a few hours ago, he was starting to enjoy the sensation of being airborne, of travelling at astonishing height at god-like speed.

He glanced around. By the soft lamplight he could see the skeleton crew on the command deck. Most of the dwarfs had gone off to rest. Makaisson was slumped in a padded command chair while another engineer took the wheel. His eyes were shut but a maniacal grin of justified triumph spread across his face. Behind him, with his back to Felix, Borek leaned on his staff and gazed out the window. Thighs burning from maintaining his unnatural crouch, Felix shuffled over to him.

'Where are we headed?' Felix asked quietly.

'Middenheim, Herr Jaeger. We're going to pick up some fuel and supplies and a few more passengers, then we'll be heading north-east to Kislev and the Troll Country. Makaisson says we lost some time against the head winds but we should reach the city on the spire by dawn tomorrow.'

'Dawn! But it must be scores of leagues from the Lonely Tower to the City of the White Wolf.'

'Aye. This is a fast ship, is it not?'

Intellectually Felix had already grasped this point but now he realised that emotionally he had not. Nor would he, really, until he saw the narrow, winding streets of Middenheim below him. It was all very well calculating in your head just how fast the airship was moving. It was another thing entirely experiencing it.

'It is one of the wonders of the age,' Felix said with feeling.

Borek stroked his beard with gnarled fingers and limped over to a seat. It was a huge, padded leather armchair, built to accommodate dwarfs. It was fixed to a short column, atop of which it swivelled, and there was a harness for strapping the occupant in which at the moment lay loose on the floor. Gratefully the old dwarf slumped into his seat, took out his pipe and lit it. He fixed Felix with one bright eye. 'That it is! Let us hope that it is good enough for our purposes. For if it fails, there will most likely never be another.'

LURK LEVERED OPEN the packing case and steeled his courage to the sticking point. Slowly, stealthily, he clambered out onto the mass of packing cases. He realised at once that the Horned Rat had smiled upon him. If the case in which he had taken refuge had been on the bottom of this mass, he would never have been able to get free. The weight of all the other cases packed above him would have left him trapped to die of slow starvation.

He paused, nose twitching and sniffed the air. He could detect no scents of anyone close to him. His eyes probed the darkness. They were well adapted for this task. The skaven were a race of tunnel dwellers. Although their vision was poorer than that of human eyes in full daylight, they could see much better in the gloom. There was no sign of anybody in the hold either. To most people the cargo space would have been in total darkness. Lurk guessed this most likely meant that it would be night outside.

The first thing he needed to do was shift his refuge. If any dwarf looked into the case, they would find it suspiciously empty and stinking of his musk and droppings. It would not take them long to work out that they had a stowaway aboard ship and start a search. The very thought made Lurk's musk glands tighten.

As it turned out, the empty case was light enough and he had little difficulty lifting it and placing it further back in the rows of similar cases. Perhaps he should look for something to put in it, so that anyone lifting it would not notice its suspicious lightness. For the life of him he could not think how to do this, though, so he abandoned consideration of the problem and gave thought to something else. He was hungry!

Fortunately he could smell food. Nearby were sacks of grain. He gnawed the corner of one and plunged his muzzle in deep, chewing and swallowing frantically to assuage his hunger. In the far corner he now noticed hundreds of cured hams hung from a steel rack. Surely no one would miss one, and he knew that meat would satisfy his stomach far better than grain. He grabbed a haunch of meat and gobbled half of it greedily. It was just too bad it wasn't fresh and raw, but then he supposed you couldn't expect the Horned Rat to provide everything. He stuffed the rest of the joint inside his tunic for later. Now it was time to set about his mission for the grey seer, to carry out Thanquol's orders and search the ship.

Slowly, using all the stealth he had learned in long years of ambushes and sneak attacks, he stalked forward. His natural posture caused him to slouch forward and he had little difficulty moving on all four paws. Actually, had the floors not been metal and had he not been surrounded by the presence of his enemies, he would have felt quite at home here. These low wide corridors reminded him oddly of a skaven burrow.

He fought down feelings of nostalgia. Ahead of him was a metal ladder fixed into the walls. He scampered up it easily and prowled on down a long corridor. All around him he heard the sound of snoring, from where the unsuspecting dwarfs lay asleep. If only he had a squad of his stormvermin now, he thought, he could take the entire ship. Unfortunately he did not, so he scurried on.

Ahead of him he heard the sound of pistons moving up and down and dwarfish voices shouting above the din. Slowly, heart pounding, he poked his head through a doorway and looked within. Fortunately the chamber's occupants had their backs to him. He glanced around. The room was filled with huge machines. Cogs turned, pistons pumped and two enormous crankshafts ran out through the walls, rotating as they went. Some buried instinct told Lurk that he had found the engine room. If only he could sabotage this machine he could bring the whole ship to a halt. He had no idea what good this would do him, but he felt that he'd best report the fact to Grey Seer Thanquol.

Not wanting to push his luck, he ducked backwards and scampered along his scent trail back towards the hold. He still had not found what he was looking for and from portholes along the side of the ship he could see the sun was starting to peak over the horizon. He wanted to be back in his hiding place before the crew came fully awake.

Glancing out through the porthole, he suddenly realised he had the answer to the grey seer's question. In the distance he could see a mighty peak rising out of the forest. That peak was crowned with the towers of a human city. He knew that city.

For long years he had been part of the skaven garrison which dwelt in the tunnels below the peak ready at a moment's notice to infiltrate the metropolis of their hated enemies. The airship was heading for the place humans called Middenheim, the City of the White Wolf.

FELIX'S EYES snapped open. He had fallen asleep in one of the armchairs in the control room. He noticed at once that the sound of the engines had altered and that the craft was juddering slightly as it lost height. He rose up, and only at the last second remembered to stoop before he banged his head on the ceiling. He shuffled slowly over to the window and saw distant towers silhouetted against the rising sun. It was a sight of considerable beauty, for the buildings rose out of a mighty fortress that occupied the heights of a great peak. They had reached Middenheim more or less on schedule.

Even as he watched he saw a large creature starting to rise from within the citadel and fly towards the airship. He fervently hoped that it had no hostile intent.

EIGHT
MIDDENHEIM

AS FELIX WATCHED in rapt fascination, he could see that the creature was a winged horse, one of the fabled pegasii. Its rider wore the long robes and intricate headpiece of a sorcerer. A globe of fire encased one hand, and Felix knew that the mysterious rider could unleash it with a gesture. He had seen the wizards of the Empire on the field of battle and knew the awesome power they wielded.

The wizard directed his great flying steed alongside the airship. Its mighty pinions moved rhythmically, keeping the creature abreast of the airship with ease. The mage looked over and Borek rose from his chair and hobbled over to the window. He waved to the man, who answered him with a look of recognition. He applied spurs to his steed and hurtled forward, gesturing for them to follow.

Makaisson took over the wheel and began to make minute adjustments to their course. The airship moved in response, losing speed and altitude swiftly as they moved towards the spires of the city.

Looking down, Felix could see that the cobbled streets were full of people. They stared upwards in amazement, craning their necks for a better view of the vessel passing overhead. On some faces was written wonder, on others merely fear. In a way, Felix realised, whether they knew it or not, those people down there were looking on the passing of their way of life.

For thousands of years their city had rested secure and impregnable in its rocky eyrie. The only approach was up a long, narrow, spiralling path in the cliff-side or via a cableway that ran from the villages below. In its entire existence, no invader had ever managed to conquer this place. It was a location where ten men could easily hold off a thousand, and often had. There were relatively few pegasii, wyverns or other flying steeds – and certainly no great armies of them.

The *Spirit of Grungni* changed everything. It could carry an entire company of soldiers in its hold. A fleet of such ships could deliver an army on to this spire. The odd-looking cannons he had noticed in the ship's side could bombard those cobbled streets and shale roofs from afar in a way no besieger could ever have managed before. In an odd way, today was the beginning of a new era, and he wondered if anybody except he himself realised it.

THEY PASSED OVER the steep and winding streets. The tall narrow tenements of the city rose towards the central heights of the peak which were dominated by the twin masses of the Elector Count's Palace and the mighty Temple of Ulric, Lord of Wolves. The two enormous structures glared at each other across the highest square of the city and it was over this open space, with a clear view of the maze of rooftops and chimneys spread out beneath them, that the airship came to rest.

For the past few minutes Felix had wondered how this operation was going to be achieved and now he watched in fascination as it was revealed to him. Clearly they were expected. A group of dwarfs had mustered in the square, where great metal rings had already been driven into the stones of the plaza. Makaisson threw one of his control levers backwards and the noise of the engines altered.

'Reverse engines,' he called. 'Brace yersels!'

Felix had a few moments to realise what he meant before the airship slowed to a stop. Makaisson then moved the lever to a neutral position and the noise of the engines died almost completely.

'Anchors awa'!'

A group of engineers stood by the hawser cables. They hit release catches and the cables spun out dropping their attached lines. When the cables dropped like anchors, the dwarfs below were ready. They grabbed the lines and swiftly attached them to the hooks. In a matter of moments, the airship was made fast. Felix was still not sure how they themselves were going to get down, though. His curiosity on this point was soon satisfied.

IT WAS A long way down. They were in the very bottom level of the gondola, looking at a massive hatch that an engineer had just thrown open. As Felix watched, a rope ladder was unrolled and dropped through the hatch. Still unfurling as it fell, it soon reached the ground below. One of the dwarfs in the square grabbed it and attempted to brace it but, for his pains, began to swing backwards and forwards.

Gotrek looked down through the hatch, grabbed the rope and swung himself out into space. He began the long descent, as agile as an ape. He used only one hand, fearlessly clutching his enormous axe in the other.

'After you, Felix,' Snorri said.

Felix looked down. It was a long drop but if he ever wanted to get his feet on solid earth again he was going to have to use the ladder. He swung himself outwards and down, feeling a moment of sick fear as his feet kicked in empty air before contacting the rope. Next he grabbed the top rung with his hands and began his descent, clinging on desperately as the wind tore at his cloak and brought tears to his eyes.

The rope ladder was not at all stable. It swung back and forwards in the breeze. Felix wished he had worn gloves, for the rope was digging into his fingers painfully. He forced himself to put one foot down and then the other. Having learned from his experiences when boarding the airship he did his best not to look down. At the level of the rooftops he was surprised to see people hanging out the windows and waving to him. In the distance he could hear cheering.

A dizzying sense of vertigo overtook him as he glanced down for the source. He saw that the square was surrounded by a throng of people being held back only by the count's elite guard of Knights of the White Wolf. It slowly dawned on him that the people were cheering for him. He was the first and only human to have descended from this airship and they assumed that he was some kind of hero. So as not to disappoint them he waved. Losing his grip almost overbalanced him and the ladder lurched to the right, nearly sending him tumbling to the cobblestones below. Hastily he gripped the ladder once more and continued his descent.

He doubted there was ever a man happier than he was when his boots touched the ground.

A GROUP OF heavily armoured and richly-dressed men strode out of the palace to greet them. Their robes were of the finest cloth, their heavy fur cloaks of mink and sable pelt. On their tabards was the wolf-head emblem of the Elector Count of Middenheim. They presented a sight that was at once redolent of wealth and strangely barbaric. Felix knew this was in keeping with the reputation of the city of their origin, for, in many ways, the Middenheimers were a people apart. The dominant faith in this city was the cult of the berserker god Ulric, and the priesthood of Sigmar, patron deity of the Empire, was more tolerated than revered. It was a source of abiding tension within the Empire but such was the wealth and military might of this powerful city-state that it was free to carve out its own path. Felix knew that this was a rare thing in a land where religious dissent had often been the cause of bloody civil strife.

It seemed that these men had been sent to welcome the dwarfs and usher them into the presence of Elector Count Stephan. Felix noticed that they were looking at him with something like surprise in their eyes. Quite obviously, whatever else they had been expecting, having a human descend from the great airship had not been included. Nonetheless they bowed to him in a courtly manner and informed him that the count requested his company. Felix returned their bows and allowed himself to be led into the palace, not quite sure whether he was a prisoner or a guest.

THE PALACE WAS old and sumptuous. Great tapestries covered the walls, depicting scenes from the city-state's long, proud history. As he walked Felix recognised scenes from the Battle of Hel Fen, and the wars with the vampire counts of Sylvania. He saw wolfskin-cloaked warriors engaged in battle with green-skinned orcs. And depictions of the hideous hordes of Chaos, which had besieged the city two hundred years ago during the time of Magnus the Pious.

The palace was huge, carved from the same stone as the peak by craftsmen who had obviously been stupendously skilled. Above each doorjamb, gargoyle heads leered down and the arches themselves were carved with the most intricate of frescoes. Carpets from Tilea, Araby and distant Cathay covered the heavy flagstones. In each hall a massive fire burned, keeping the chill of the heights at bay. Even in the daytime, lanterns burned in those halls furthest from the light, shining out in the gloom.

Here and there massive burly palace guards moved around on missions for their master, and every so often richly garbed councillors paused to gape at the dwarfs and those that accompanied them. So it was, spreading a strange silence in their wake, that Felix and his companions entered the throne room of the Elector Count of Middenheim, and confronted the lean, powerful figure sitting erect on the Wolf Throne.

Felix could see others grouped around the throne. Most were old, bearded men who he assumed were councillors, but two figures stood out. One leaned forward and whispered something in the count's ear. He was a tall and slender man, garbed in robes of sumptuous purple. The robes were trimmed with gold cloth inscribed with symbols which Felix had come to recognise as mystical signs. An ornate headpiece rested on his brow, of all things it resembled most a tall, conical elvish helm, only fashioned from felt and cloth-of-gold. Rings containing precious stones glittered on the man's fingers. An intangible aura of power hung over him, and made Felix uneasy. It was the pegasus-riding wizard and in the past his dealings with wizards had rarely been pleasant.

The other figure was equally intriguing. She stood just below the count's dais, a tall woman and perhaps a lovely one, but it was difficult to tell. Felix guessed that she was almost his height. She was not dressed in a court gown as the other ladies present were. She wore a sleeveless jerkin of leather over a white linen shirt. Her leather britches were cinched at the waist with a studded leather belt. High riding boots encased the thighs of her long legs. Her ash-blonde hair was cropped short almost to the scalp. Two swords were sheathed at her narrow waist. She stood straight-backed, with her chin tilted back.

There was an air about her of far lands and distant places. Feeling his eyes upon her, she turned and glanced back in his direction.

The dwarfs bowed before the count's throne and began making florid introductions. Count Stephan cut them short politely enough, but with the manner of a military man who had no time for long-winded speeches. Felix was brought forward to stand beside Gotrek and Snorri and gave the best courtly bow he knew how. He saw interest flicker in the eyes of the count when he noticed a human in the dwarf party, before the ruler returned his full attention to Borek.

'Our chancellors have prepared the substances you requested for transfer to your vessel,' Count Stephan said.

By the look on Olger's face, Felix guessed that whatever those substances were, they must have cost a pretty penny. The miser looked as pale and miserable as a man who had undergone amputation.

'I thank you, noble lord, and welcome this affirmation of the ancient friendship among our people.'

The count smiled as if he and Borek were old friends and he had only been too pleased to make the gift. Felix looked up and was startled to find himself looking directly into the blue eyes of the woman on the dais. She was about the same age as he was, he realised. Unlike the noblewomen, her face was tanned. She had high cheekbones and wide lips, which lent her a decidedly exotic beauty. Felix guessed that she was not from anywhere within the Empire. She cocked her head to one side and examined him. Felix was unused to such direct and appraising scrutiny from a woman but he forced himself to hold her gaze. She smiled at him challengingly.

'Now you must tell me of your unique vessel and your mission,' Elector Count Stephan was saying.

Borek looked around the chamber meaningfully. 'Gladly, your Excellency, but some things are best discussed in private.'

The count surveyed the vast audience hall, the crowds of lackeys, guards and hangers-on. He nodded to show he understood and clapped his hands.

'Chamberlain, I would speak to noble Borek in private. Have food and wine brought to my apartments.'

The chamberlain bowed and without further ceremony Count Stephan rose, descended from his dais and offered

Borek his arm to lean upon. Before Felix had even realised it, the audience chamber began to clear. In moments, he and the remaining dwarfs were left alone in the suddenly empty chamber.

Felix turned to Varek. The young dwarf shrugged.

'Who were the wizard and the girl?' Felix asked.

'I think they might be our passengers,' Varek replied.

'Passengers?'

'I'm sure either they or my uncle will tell you more when you need to know.' Varek seemed to realise that he had said more than he ought to and scuttled swiftly out, leaving Felix alone with Gotrek, Snorri, Olger and Makaisson.

'I'll be leaving the expedition here,' Olger said suddenly. 'Much as I would like to stay with you, I have clan business to transact here in Middenheim. Good luck and bring back the gold.'

He bowed and stumped away.

'Good riddance,' Gotrek jeered.

'Snorri thinks the old skinflint is scared,' Snorri said.

And why shouldn't he be, thought Felix? He was beginning to suspect that the miser was the most sensible dwarf of all he had ever encountered.

'Let's find some beer,' Gotrek said.

FELIX STOPPED TO purchase a pastry from a street vendor. He paused and looked around the street, happy to be in a human city once more, enjoying the teeming throngs all around him. Overhead the tall tenements of Middenheim loomed. People filled the narrow winding streets. Jugglers tossed multi-coloured balls. Acrobats tumbled. Gaudily garbed men on stilts towered over the crowd. Drums beat. Pipers played. Ragged beggars stuck out grubby hands. The smells of roasting chicken, cooked pies and night soil filled the air.

Felix kept one hand on his purse and the other on the hilt of his sword, for he was familiar with the perils and predators of urban life. Thieves, cut-purses and armed robbers were all too common. Dirty-faced children watched him with predatory eyes. Here and there warriors in the tabards of guardsmen moved through the crowds.

'Hello, handsome. Want a good time?' A painted women waved to him from the doorways of shabby houses. She jiggled her hips in a parody of lust. From the narrow windows above, others blew him kisses. Felix turned his eyes away and pushed on past. Briefly he wondered about the woman he had seen back in the palace. but he pushed the thought aside. There would be time enough to get to know her as their journey continued.

A drunk staggered from the door of a tavern and reeled against Felix. Felix smelled the man's beer soaked breath and then felt fingers fumbling for his purse. He brought up his knee, jabbed it into the would-be pickpocket's groin. The man collapsed, groaning.

'Quickly, this poor fellow has been taken ill,' shouted Felix and stepped over the prostrate body. Like wolves on a sickly deer, the street people descended on the fake drunkard. Felix vanished swiftly into the crowd before the guards noticed the disturbance.

He smiled. It felt good to be back in civilisation, surrounded by his own people. It felt good to have some time to himself. He was glad that he had been given the day off while Borek talked with the duke, and the dwarf engineers loaded the barrels of black stuff aboard the airship. Gotrek and Snorri had headed off to a tavern in the lower levels but Felix was in no mood for an all day drinking session. The memory of his last appalling hangover was still too fresh in his mind. Instead he had decided to take a wander round the city and meet up with the Slayers later. He was sure that the Wolf and Vulture tavern would be an easy one to find. He did not have to return to the airship until dawn tomorrow. There would be plenty of time for carousing later, if he decided that was what he wanted to do.

Felix shook his head ruefully. Somewhere, somehow, during the flight to Middenheim he had obviously made up his mind to accompany the dwarfs. He was not entirely sure why, for it was certain to be dangerous. On the other hand, perhaps that was the reason. If he had wanted a calm, safe life he would doubtless now be working in the counting house of his father's business back in Altdorf. At some point during his wanderings with Gotrek he had come to enjoy the life of the wandering mercenary adventure, and he doubted now that he could return to his old life even if he wanted to.

This quest was taking on a momentum of its own. There was an excitement about simply being aboard the airship which genuinely thrilled him. By daylight, in this teeming city, even the prospect of the Chaos Wastes was not so daunting. In fact it represented a chance to see a place which few sane men had ever visited and returned to tell the tale. And of course, there was his oath to accompany Gotrek and record his doom as well.

Of course, he knew he was kidding himself. He could pinpoint exactly where his decision to remain with the airship had taken place. And it had nothing to do with oaths or adventure or the thrill of travel. He had made up his mind to go on when he had discovered that the woman in the throne room was also going to be a passenger.

And there was nothing wrong with that, he told himself. Providing it didn't result in his death.

FROM THE EDGE of the city, Felix looked down on the forest below. He had followed the winding alleyways all the way down to the great outer walls, where a short climb had taken him up to the battlements. From here he could see the cableway that brought merchants and their goods up from the small township below. As he watched, the last carriage of the day crawled up the cables towards its terminus in the walls.

Looking further afield he saw the woods and the river stretching away to the horizon, and he appreciated the fact that the inhabitants of Middenheim had almost as good a view as the one he had got through the portholes of the airship. He wondered at the ingenuity and determination that kept this vast city supplied. According to the books of legend that he had read, the City of the White Wolf had started life as a fortress, its heights giving shelter to those who fled the constant tide of warfare that flowed below.

Down through the long centuries a fair-sized community had grown up on the heights, clustered around the fortress and the monastic temple of Ulric. The township had begun as home to the nobility and their garrisons, but had grown to include the merchants who provided them with luxuries. Of course, all food and goods were more expensive here, for they had to be hauled up the cables from below, but the nobles controlled vast estates out there in the hinterland and were not short of a gold piece or two. The cost was more than made up for by the increased security they enjoyed on their lofty perch.

And, of course, there were the mines below the peak, a source of much wealth.

And other darker things besides. Felix had heard Gotrek talk of those mines and of a vast labyrinth of tunnels which extended below the peak. The mines were patrolled by dwarf soldiers and human guards, for it was rumoured that skaven had established a lair down there. Felix cursed suddenly, wondering if he was ever going to be out of reach of the accursed rat-men. Probably not. Somehow he knew that if the airship turned its nose towards the steaming jungles of legendary Lustria, they would arrived to find skaven already scuttling through the undergrowth.

The sun was starting to set. A bloody glow spread across the clouds as it descended below the horizon. Lanterns flickered to life on the watchtowers along the walls, and looking back Felix could see lights appearing in the windows of the tenements and taverns of the city. Soon he knew the lamplighters would be emerging and lantern-toting watchmen would start tolling the hours in the streets.

He knew it was time to go back. He had taken the last glimpse of Imperial society that he might ever have, and he felt strangely relaxed and contented, as if by making his decision to accompany the dwarfs on their quest, he had somehow absolved himself of all fear and doubt. It was better to have the thing decided, he thought, than to writhe in an agony of uncertainty. His way was clear now and he was relieved to find that he was not unhappy about it. He turned and started back up the long, cobbled path towards the palace, wondering whether he was imagining things when he thought he heard scurrying over the rooftops behind him.

NINE
BEYOND THE SEA OF CLAWS

As THE AIRSHIP cast off, the crowds stared up in awe. Makaisson turned the wheel and pulled the levers to alter their course a fraction. Narrowly avoiding the great spire of the Temple of Ulric, they set off northwards.

Felix relaxed in one of the armchairs on the command deck. There was plenty of room. Most of the dwarfs were sleeping off hangovers, leaving only a skeleton crew to man the bridge. To tell the truth, Makaisson himself looked a little worse for wear. The little groans he emitted from time to time, combined with the way he squinted at the horizon through sore eyes, were not reassuring. Felix was not at all sure that he should be flying the ship.

'Can I help you?' he asked the chief engineer.

'What dae ye mean, young Felix?'

'Perhaps I can take the controls while you rest.'

'Ah dinnae ken. It's a highly technical job.'

'I could try. It might prove useful to have somebody else on board who can fly the ship, in case anything should happen to you. I mean you are a Slayer, you know.'

'The other engineers ken hoo to dae it... still, ah suppose ye hae a point. It woudnae dae onnie herm to hae an extra pilot – just in case.'

'Does that mean you'll do it.'

'Ah shouldnae really. It's against guild regulations tae teach onybody but a dwarf hoo to dae these things, but then again, this whole bloody thing is against guild regs, so whar's the herm, ah ask ye?'

He beckoned for Felix to come over and stand where he was standing. 'Tak the wheel, Herr Jaeger.'

Felix had to bend his knees to stand at the same height as the dwarf and he found the position fairly uncomfortable. The wheel felt heavy in his hands. He did his best to hold it steady but it felt like it had a life of its own, exerting pressure first this way and then that, so that Felix had to constantly fight to hold his position.

'That's the air currents,' Makaisson said. 'They tug at the rudder and the ailerons. Take's a while tae get used to it. Ye got it?'

Felix nodded nervously.

'Look doon a wee bit and tae yer left. Ye'll see a wee gadget there. It's a compass.'

Felix did so. He could see a compass that swung on a complex arrangement of gimbals so that the needle in its centre always pointed north.

'Ye'll notice that we're heading north-north-east at the moment. That's oor course. If ye turn the wheel a wee bit, we'll shift the course. Joost jink aroond a wee bit and bring the course back to north-north-east,'

Felix did as he was told and moved the wheel as gently as he could. Outside the window, the horizon seemed to spin slowly. He moved the wheel the opposite way and they spun back onto the correct heading.

'Weel din! Nithin' tae it, eh?'

Felix found that he was grinning back at Makaisson. There was something exhilarating in being in control of so massive and swift a thing as the airship.

'What next?' he asked.

'See that row o' levers next tae yer right hand?'

'Yes.'

'OK the first yin is fur speed. Dinna dae onything till ah tell ye tae, right, but when ye push it forward the engines pick up speed. When ye pull it back the engines lose speed. When ye pull it ah the way back, ye gan backwards, intae reverse. Ye follow me?'

Felix nodded again.

'Noo there's a dial in front ye, marked in increments. Ye'll see that it's marked in different colours as weel.'

Felix saw the indicated gauge beside the compass. Right now the needle was in the green zone at the tenth increment. It was about five increments short of the red zone.

'While the needle is in the green, ye're fine. That's the zone o' tolerance for the engine. Move it forward – but keep the needle in the green.'

Felix leaned forward on the lever. It resisted his efforts, so he pushed harder than he had originally intended. As he did so the needle moved forward and the drone of the engine altered to a higher pitch. The ground seemed to unreel faster below them, and the clouds drifted by more quickly on either side. Suddenly Felix felt Makaisson's hard hand on top of his. Fingers like steel bands closed and he found the lever was being pulled back.

'Ah said keep it in the green, ye unnerstan? The red is for emergencies only. Ye run the engine in the red and ye'll gaun much faster but ye'll burn it oot after awhile, maybe even explode it. That's no such a guid thing at this height.'

Felix saw that he had accidentally run the needle into the red zone. He tried to pull his hand away but Makaisson's held it in place for a moment. 'Dinnae tak yer hand of the controls until ah tell ye. Keep yer hand on the speed stick the noo, alright?'

Felix nodded and the engineer freed his hand. 'Dinnae worry. Ye're no daein' too bad. So, the next stick on the right controls the fins. Try tae no get the two sticks mixed up, it could be messy!'

Felix was beginning to wish he had never suggested that he might learn this. It seemed that there were many possibilities for disaster that he had never thought of. 'In what way?'

'Well, the fins control oor height above the ground. When ye pull that lever back the fins on the tail change attitude and we gaun up. When ye push it forward we gaun doon. That's all ye really need tae ken. The actual reasons are a wee bit technical and ah doobt ye'd understand them.'

'I'll take your word for it.'

'Right, pull the lever back. Gently! We dinna want to wake onybody up. Now ye'll notice a wee gadget next tae the speed gauge. That's yer altitude. The higher the increment, the higher we are. Yince mare, dinna gaun intae the red zone for ony reason. That could be fatal because we'll be flying too high. An' try no to lay the thing get doon to zero either, coz that means we'll hae hit the ground. Now, slide the lever back to the neutral position. ye'll feel a wee click when ye dae. That means we'll hae levelled off.'

Felix did as he was told. There was an odd buzzing in his ears, which vanished when he swallowed. He took his hand off the altitude lever and pointed to a smaller row of stubby levers attached to a panel at the height of his left hand. 'What do these do?'

'Dinna ouch ony of them. They control different functions like ballast, fuel and ither stuff. I'll tell ye aboot them anither time. Right noo, ye ken ah ye need to fly the ship. Noo, keep headin' north-north-east. An' see that clock there? In two hours' time wake me up. Ah'm ganne hae a wee kip. Ma heed's a bit sare fae ah the booze yesterday.'

'What if something goes wrong?'

'Joost gae me a shout. Ah'll be in this chair here.'

So saying, Makaisson sat himself down in the chair, and soon his snores filled the bridge of the airship.

FOR THE FIRST few minutes Felix felt a certain nervousness guiding the craft but as time wore on he gained confidence that nothing was going to go wrong. As time went on, some of the engineers came onto the bridge. Some glanced at him in amazement but seeing Makaisson slumbering nearby let him be. After a while, it became quite relaxing to watch the land and the clouds unroll beneath them.

'Are you the pilot then?' The soft voice stirred Felix from his reverie. It was a woman's voice, husky and with more than a trace of a foreign accent in it. At a guess he would have said Kislevite.

Felix shook his head but did not turn to look at the woman. He kept his attention focused on where they were going, just in case anything unexpected came their way. 'No. But you could say I am training to be one.'

A soft laugh. 'A useful skill.'

'I don't know. I doubt that I can base a career on it. There are not too many vessels like this in the world.'

'Only this one, I think. And given its mission, I doubt there will be another.'

'You know where we are going, then?'

'I know where you are going, and I do not envy you.'

Felix had to fight to keep his eyes fixed ahead and not to look round at her. He remembered what he had sworn to Borek back at the Lonely Tower. He did not really know this woman, and it was possible she was quizzing him for information.

'You know where we are bound?'

'I know you are headed out into the Wastes and that is enough for any sensible body to know. I do not think you will be coming back.'

Felix was discouraged to hear an assessment which so closely concurred with his own. He was also disappointed to learn that the woman had no intention of coming with them on their quest.

'I take it you are familiar with the place then?'

'As familiar as anybody can be who is not sworn to the Ruinous Powers. My family estates border the Troll Country which is as close as any mortal dare dwell to the accursed lands. My father is the March Warden there. We have spent much time battling the followers of Chaos when they try to infiltrate the lands of men.'

'It must be an interesting life,' Felix said ironically.

'You could say that. I doubt that it is any more interesting than yours though. What brings you aboard this vessel? I must admit I was astonished to see a human, and a good-looking one, where I expected only to find Borek and his people.'

Felix smiled. It had been a long time since anyone, particularly an attractive woman, had told him he was handsome. He did not let his guard down though. 'I am a friend.'

'You are a Dwarf Friend? You must have performed some epic deeds then. Ulric knows there have been few enough of those in history.'

Felix wondered whether this was true. He had always assumed that it was simply a polite form of address. Now it appeared that it might actually be some form of title. He was about to reply when Makaisson interrupted from behind them.

'Och, the lad has stood beside Gotrek Gurnisson on many an occasion, lassie. And he had a hand in cleansing of the Sacred Tombs of Karak Eight Peaks. If that is nae grounds for namin' him a Dwarf Friend ah dinna ken what is! Onyway, noo that ye've woke me up wi yer chatter, ye may as well gimme that wheel. Ah'll tak iver noo.'

Makaisson stumped over and elbowed Felix from his position at the controls. He gave Felix a broad wink. 'Noo you and the lassie can talk tae yer heart's content.'

Felix shrugged and turned to smile at the woman. 'Felix Jaeger,' he said, bowing.

'Ulrika Magdova,' she said, smiling back. 'I am pleased to make your acquaintance.'

There was a formality about the way she spoke the words which showed she was unaccustomed to them. They were like a polite formula she had been taught for dealing with people from the Empire. He thought that in her own land the greeting would be somewhat different.

'Please, take a seat,' he said, feeling a certain stupid formality he wished he could have avoided. They both slumped down with their legs stretched out in the overstuffed dwarfish chairs. Felix could see that his earlier guess was correct and she was almost as tall as he. Looking at her face, he revised his earlier opinion of her appearance. It went from merely beautiful up to stunningly beautiful. His mouth felt suddenly dry.

'So what are you doing on this craft?' he asked, just for something to say. She gave him a glance of languid amusement, as if she could read his thoughts exactly.

'I am travelling home to my father's estates.'

'I cannot imagine Borek simply letting somebody on to this ship as a passenger for no reason.'

She raised her right hand to her mouth and stroked her lip with its forefinger. Felix could see that the fingers were callused like a swordsman's, the nails pared very short. 'My father and Borek are old friends. They fought together on many occasions in my father's youth. He helped guide Borek's last expedition to the edge of the Wastes. He looked after him and your friend Gotrek when they staggered back with the survivors. He was not surprised. He had warned them not to go. They would not listen.'

Felix stared at her. He had not imagined that any humans had been involved in that last expedition. 'That does not surprise me,' Felix said ruefully. He possessed considerable experience of just how stubborn dwarfs could be.

'Some things about it surprised even my father. He had not expected anybody to return from that doomed mission. Few indeed, save the followers of Chaos, ever do.'

'How long ago was this mission?'

'Before I was born. Over twenty winters ago.'

'They have waited a long time to go back then.'

'So it would seem. It also seems that they have prepared well. Indeed it was a message from my father to say that he had done what they asked which brought me to Middenheim.'

'What do you mean?'

'Borek asked my father to make certain preparations on our estate. To collect the black water. To build a tower. To stockpile certain supplies. At that the time, they did not make sense, but now that I have seen this ship I think I understand.'

'The dwarfs have built a base, a way-station, on your father's land.'

'Aye. And paid for it in good dwarfish steel.'

Seeing Felix's quizzical look she smiled at him, and unsheathed one of her swords, pulling it part way from its scabbard. Felix noticed dwarf runes along the blade. 'We have little use for gold along the Marches of Chaos. Weapons suit us better and the dwarfs are the finest armourers in the world.'

'You came a long way from Kislev to Middenheim. That is far for a beautiful young woman travelling on her own.'

'Better, Herr Jaeger! I had despaired of ever getting a compliment from you. Men are more forward about such things in Kislev.'

'Women too, it seems,' Felix said in mild surprise.

'Life is short and winter is long, as they say.'

'What does that mean?'

'Are you so obtuse?'

Felix could not help but feel that this conversation was moving out of his control. He had never quite met a woman like this Kislevite before and he wasn't quite sure he liked it. Imperial women did not behave in quite this way, except perhaps for camp followers and tavern girls, and Ulrika Magdova certainly did not have the manner of either. Or perhaps, he was simply misunderstanding her manner. Maybe this was just the way women behaved in Kislev.

She spoke to fill the silence. 'I did not travel to Middenheim on my own – although I could have. I came with a bodyguard of my father's lancers. They departed northward and I waited to return with Borek.'

For the first time, she did not meet his gaze. He sensed that she was hiding something and he was not sure what. Certainly there was more going on here than met the eye. Also, for the first time, he started to suspect that she was not quite as confident as her beauty and her boldness had led him to believe. That suddenly made her more approachable and, in a way, more attractive. He smiled at her again and she smiled back, a little ruefully this time. Then she glanced over his shoulder, smoothed her britches with both her hands, and rose to her feet, all the while keeping him fixed with that dazzling smile.

Felix looked over in the direction of her gaze and saw that their other passenger, the sorcerer, had just entered the bridge area. He was looking at them in a puzzled, and Felix thought, perhaps resentful manner. If that was the case, he soon regained control of himself. A look of languid amusement passed over his lean handsome features and he advanced into the room. Ulrika Magdova sauntered past him, pausing only to give him a mildly disdainful glance.

'Good day, Herr Schreiber. A pleasure talking to you, Felix.'

'Good day,' Felix said weakly, rising just as she vanished from view. The magician threw himself down in the chair she had left.

'So,' he said, 'you've met the fair Ulrika. What do you think, eh?'

It was an impertinent question from a complete stranger, thought Felix, but then he had heard magicians could be somewhat odd. Then he noticed that the man was smiling and shaking his head like someone enjoying a private joke. White teeth showed against his tanned skin, the animated expression taking years off the wizard's age. Felix guessed that the mage could not be more than ten years older than himself. Suddenly, impulsively, the man stuck out his hand.

'Maximilian Schreiber, at your service. My friends call me Max.'

'Felix Jaeger at yours.'

'Felix Jaeger. That's a name I've heard before. There was quite a promising poet of that name. Are you any relation? I read some of his verses in Gottlieb's anthology several years before. Rather liked them, actually.'

Felix was pleasantly surprised to find that the stranger had heard of him. He cast his mind back to his student days when he had written verse and contributed to various anthologies. That all seemed to have happened to someone else, a long time ago.

'I wrote those,' he said.

'Excellent. A pleasant surprise. Why did you stop writing? Gottlieb's chapbook must be at least three years ago.'

'I ran into some problems with the law.'

'What were those?'

Something about the mage's smooth manner was starting to set Felix's teeth on edge. 'I was expelled from the university for killing a man in a duel. Then there were the Window Tax Riots.'

'Oh yes, the riots. So, in addition to being the poet Felix Jaeger, you are also the notorious outlaw Felix Jaeger, henchman to the infamous Gotrek Gurnisson.'

Felix went white with shock. It had been a long time since he had encountered anyone who had put those two facts together or even known he was an outlaw. The Empire was big and news travelled very slowly. It had been such a long time since he had been anywhere near Altdorf, the scene of that terrible slaughter during the riots. The wizard obviously noticed his expression. His smile became a grin.

'Don't worry. I am not about to turn you over to the law. I always thought it was an unjust and foolish tax myself. And to tell the truth, I sympathise with your predicament at the university. I was booted out of the Imperial College of Magicians myself, albeit a few years before you began your career of insurrection.'

'You were?'

'Oh yes. My tutors believed that I showed an unhealthy interest in the subject of Chaos.'

'I would have to agree with them, I think. It's a subject in which any interest is unhealthy.'

A gleam had come into the wizard's eyes and he leaned forward eagerly in his seat. 'I cannot believe that you think that way, Herr Jaeger. That's the kind of short-sightedness I would expect from the wizened greybeards at the college but not from an adventurer like yourself.'

Felix felt compelled to defend his point of view.

'I believe I know something of the subject. I have had more experience of fighting Chaos than most.'

'Exactly! I, too, have fought against the Dark Powers, my friend, and I have found its minions in some unlikely places. I do not think that I am wrong when I say that it is the greatest single threat to our nation, nay, our world, that currently exists.'

'I would agree with you there.'

'And that being the case, can it be wrong to study the subject? In order to fight such a powerful foe we must understand it. We must know its strengths and its weaknesses, its goals and its fears.'

'Yes, but the study of Chaos corrupts those who engage in it! Many have started down that path with the finest of intentions, only to find themselves enthralled by that thing they sought to fight.'

'Now you really do sound like my old tutors! Has it occurred to you that, if you were a servant of Chaos, you would use exactly that argument to discourage any investigation into your works?'

'You're not seriously suggesting that your tutors at the Imperial College were–'

'Of course not! I am just saying that the servants of Chaos are subtle. You have no idea how subtle they can be. All they would need to do was put the idea into books, spread the rumour, encourage its belief. And, of course, Chaos does corrupt. If you work with warpstone, it will change you. If you perform dark rituals, your soul will be tarnished. I admit there is some truth to this line of argument. However I don't think that this should stop us from examining Chaos, trying to find ways to prevent its spread, to detect its followers, to blunt its terrifying power. There is a conspiracy of silence which permeates our entire society. It encourages ignorance. It gives our enemies shadows in which to hide, places in which to lurk and plot.'

Felix had to admit there was something in what Schreiber was saying. To tell the truth, he had often had similar thoughts himself. 'You might be right.'

'Might be? Come now, Felix, you know I am right. And so do many other people. Unfortunately, I made the mistake of publishing my opinions in a small pamphlet. The authorities decided that it was heretical and…'

'You too became an outlaw.'

'That more or less sums it up.'

'Why are you aboard this ship?'

'Because I continued my researches. I moved from place to place fighting against Chaos where I could, compiling information when I found it, hunting down wicked sorcerers. I have made myself into something of an expert on this subject, and in the end found a refuge at the court of Count Stephan. He is more far-sighted than many of our nobles.

'He and the Knights of the White Wolf have helped fund my researches. Five years ago I met your friend Borek when he visited the library in the temple. He was most interested when he found out that I believed I had found a way to protect against the worst affects of Chaos. He enlisted me to help protect his airship on its voyage.'

Suddenly Felix began to understand the scale of the planning which had gone into their quest. It was of an order of magnitude that he had never encountered before. Not only had Borek overseen the building of the vast industrial complex at the Lonely Tower, he had employed Ulrika's father to build an advance base and discovered and engaged this wizard to ward them against Chaos. The old dwarf had not been exaggerating when he claimed this was his life's work. Felix began to wonder what other feats of planning would be revealed as the trip progressed. Still, he was not entirely convinced by Schreiber's claims.

'You have found a way of protecting this airship against the effects of Chaos?'

'There are a number of them ranging from simple runes, to protective enchantments, to basic precautions such as ensuring an adequate supply of uncontaminated food and water. Believe me, Felix, I would not have agreed to aid you unless I believed that there was a good chance that you would be safe.'

'You are not coming with us then?'

'Only to Kislev. Not all the way to Karag Dum.'

Felix looked at the wizard in surprise.

'I told you, Felix, I am a scholar. This is my field. I have studied all I could find on this subject. I was quite capable of working out for myself why an expedition of this magnitude is being prepared by a dwarf like Borek. It came as no surprise to me when he told me his goal.'

Schreiber rose from the chair. 'Speaking of that long-bearded scholar, I must go and discuss some things with him now. But I hope to have a chance to talk more with you before this voyage is complete.'

He bowed and walked away, but at the doorway he turned. 'I'm glad there is an educated man aboard. I thought I might have to spend this voyage simply chasing the delectable Ulrika. It will be nice to have some enlightened conversation as well.'

Felix wasn't sure why he found this remark so offensive. Perhaps, he told himself, he was simply jealous. And then he wondered, why did he already feel that way about a woman he had only just met?

TEN
KISLEV

THANQUOL'S PALANQUIN hustled northward along the great tunnel of the Underways. This section of the mighty road that ran beneath the spine of the World's Edge Mountains was almost totally empty. Normally Thanquol would have been nervous, travelling these dangerous corridors with his much reduced bodyguard. He could easily be attacked by orcs, goblins or dwarfish raiding parties, trying to reclaim some part of their ancient domain. However at this moment the grey seer was too upset to be nervous.

He gnawed his tail in despair. He knew from his lackey, Lurk, that the airship had departed from Middenheim and headed north-eastwards. The snivelling wretch had managed to report that they had passed over water, before making landfall again, and that the land below them was starting to look emptier and bleaker all the time. Fortunately for Thanquol, he was a far-travelled skaven of considerable knowledge, and he recognised that the airship's destination could only be the land known to humans as Kislev.

He had no idea what those foolish dwarfs could possibly want in that barbarous place. Perhaps they had heard rumours of gold or ancient treasure. Although dwarfs were not the race he had made his deepest studies of, Thanquol knew enough about them to guess that this was their most likely goal. Unfortunately he had no idea where this might eventually take them, and he also knew that the airship had travelled much further and much faster than he was capable of pursuing by normal means.

He was almost tempted to order Lurk to find some means of sabotaging the airship to give him time to catch up. Only one thing prevented him from doing this. In his considerable experience, a doltish lackey like Lurk would do something wrong and either get himself killed or destroy the very airship that Thanquol so desperately wanted to possess. No – giving such an order was the option of last resort, and Thanquol decided that he would have to be desperate indeed to try it. Before then, he would exhaust every other avenue open to him.

He considered his options. Perhaps he could contact the Lords of Clan Moulder. Their mighty fortress, Hell Pit, was located in northern Kislev and was the nearest skaven stronghold to the airship's probable destination. To a lesser intellect than Thanquol's, this might have seemed like a wise plan. Potent as he undoubtedly was, even the grey seer was forced to admit capturing the airship single-pawed was almost certainly beyond him. He was going to need help, even if it meant going with downcast tail to the Beastmasters of Clan Moulder. But the thought had also occurred to him that it might not be wise to give them all the details of his scheme, for they might try to seize the airship by themselves. Being the blundering fools they were, they too would doubtless fail without his guidance.

No, he decided, the best he could do was to scurry north as quickly as possible and hope that something would arise to delay the dwarfs until his arrival. He leaned out the palanquin's window and chittered at his bearers to redouble their efforts. Fearing their master's righteous wrath, they scuttled along more quickly, groaning beneath the weight of their burden and all his sorcerous equipment.

FELIX HAD ALWAYS thought of Kislev as a land of ice and snow, where winter never lifted, and the folk wandered around constantly wrapped in furs. The land below contradicted this impression quite mightily. It consisted of rolling plains of long grass set amidst thick forests of pine. A moment's consideration told him that this had to be so, for Kislev was a land famed for its horsemen, and it would be difficult for them to be that way if they lived amid endless snowdrifts.

Felix had to admit that, if anything, the sun shone even more brightly than it did on the Empire at the moment. The Kislevite summer might be brief but it was also intense. Felix wondered if this, too, was part of Borek's plan, to come northward before the stormy winds of winter could threaten the airship's progress. It would not have surprised him to discover that this was the case. The ingenuity and skill with which this expedition had been planned was a far cry from his haphazard wanderings with Gotrek. During their travels they had simply decided to go as the whim took them, with only whatever they happened to be carrying at the time to aid them. Obviously that this was not typical dwarfish behaviour, except perhaps where Slayers were concerned.

Below the airship he could see a herd of caribou, startled by the airship's vast shadow begin to bound away. Hunters rose from their crouches and shaded their eyes to peer up in wonder in the passing vehicle. One of them, braver or more frightened than the rest, cast his spear up at them but it fell a long way short of the vessel and fell point first to stand quivering amidst the long grass.

They were flying beneath the clouds for a good reason. Watchers peered from every porthole and through the large windows of the command deck. They were nearing their destination and all of them had been ordered to keep their eyes peeled for Ulrika's father's mansion. Makaisson's navigation had brought them to the general area. Now they quartered the landscape seeking the exact spot where they would make their final landfall before heading into the Chaos Wastes.

So far all they had seen was the occasional hunter and the odd village where smoke drifted lazily skyward from holes in the turfed roofs of the peasants' log huts. Their presence had sent the villagers scurrying away from their harvests to huddle within the village walls, doubtless convinced that the airship was some new manifestation of Chaos come to trouble their land.

Felix was still amazed at how swiftly they had made the trip. A journey that would have taken months overland looked like it was going to take them only a few days at most, and much of that time had been spent searching for the Boyar's mansion in this sea of grass. Truly this engineering of the dwarfs was a most potent form of magic.

'There!' he heard Ulrika shout and turned to see her pointing to something in the distance. It lay in the shadows of a distant range of dark and threatening mountains. Felix realised her eyes must be keen. All he could see was a vague smudge of smoke.

Makaisson's hands shifted on the wheel, and the nose of the airship swung around in the direction the woman had indicated. He pushed the altitude lever and they swung down lower and faster, sending flocks of startled birds flapping out of the long grass. As the mountains approached Felix kept his eyes pinned to the direction Ulrika had indicated. Slowly he saw a large, long hall come into view. To his surprise, beside the mansion house, within the compounds massive walls was a tall tower, a smaller wooden version of the steel monstrosity which had loomed over the Lonely Tower.

This then was the place where they were going to land. This might well be the last human habitation he would ever see.

ULRIKA'S FATHER was huge, a head taller than Felix and burly as a bear. His beard was long and white, but his head was shaved except for a single topknot. His eyes were the same startling blue as his daughter's; his teeth were yellow. A thick leather tunic encased his torso. Coarse cloth trousers covered his lower body, except where high riding boots covered his legs. A longsword and a shortsword hung from his thick leather belt. A dozen amulets jingled on the iron chains around his neck.

He strode out to where the dwarfs waited at the foot of the tower. Behind him a row of warriors presented their weapons with ritual formality. He loomed over Ulrika and clasped her to his mighty chest then swept her off her feet and whirled her round and round as if she were a child.

'Welcome home, daughter of my heart!' he bellowed.

'It is good to be here, father. Now put me down and greet your guests.'

The old man's gusty laughter boomed out and he stomped over to where the crew of the airship stood waiting. He stopped short of embracing the dwarfs. Instead he bowed low in the dwarfish fashion, showing surprising flexibility for a man of his age and enormous girth.

'Borek Forkbeard! It is good to see you. I trust you will find all as you requested it.'

'I trust I will,' the old dwarf said, bowing just as low.

'Gotrek Gurnisson, I bid you welcome also. It has been a long time since you honoured my hall with your presence. I am pleased to see you still carry that axe.'

'I am pleased to return, Ivan Mikelovitch Straghov,' Gotrek said in his least surly manner. Felix guessed that the Slayer was almost pleased to see the Kislevite.

'And who is this? Snorri Nosebiter? I must see that a bucket of vodka is left at your table. Welcome!'

'Snorri thinks that would be a good idea.' One by one all the dwarfs were greeted or introduced and then Ulrika led her father over to where Felix and the wizard stood waiting.

'And, father, this is Felix Jaeger of Altdorf.'

'Pleased to make your acquaintance,' Felix said, extending his hand. Straghov ignored it as he loomed over Felix, hugged him in welcome and then kissed him once on each cheek. 'Welcome! Welcome!' he bellowed in Felix's ear, loud enough to threaten deafness. Before Felix could respond, he had been dropped and the old man was doing the same to Schreiber.

'I thank you for the enthusiasm of your welcome, sir,' the wizard said when he had regained his breath.

Felix exchanged glances with Ulrika, then looked in wonder over at the row of warriors who lined their way to the hall. Ivan Straghov might look and behave like a barbarian but there could be no doubt that he was a mighty warlord in his own land. A hundred riders stood by as an honour guard. All had hard faces and cold eyes, and all looked like they could use the well-honed weapons they presented to the dwarfs. According to Ulrika there were nine hundred more of these fierce riders who had sworn allegiance to her father. Being March Boyar was obviously an important post. Since it commanded the first line of defence against the hordes of Chaos, Felix guessed that it ought to be.

'Now we eat!' boomed Straghov. 'And drink!'

HUGE TABLES HAD been set up inside the mansion's walls. Minor functionaries from all around had been invited to feast and marvel at the dwarfish airship. Caribou had been roasted on spits over great fire-pits. Plates were heaped with coarse black bread and cheese. Great flasks of fiery spirit which Snorri identified as vodka were put beside each plate. As promised, a bucket of the stuff was put beside Snorri.

Felix followed the example of the locals and tossed back his tumbler in one swift gulp. It felt like he was swallowing molten metal. A cloud of something acidic seemed to burn the lining of his throat and make its way up to his nostrils, bringing tears to his eyes. He felt like he ought to be breathing fire and it was all he could do to keep himself from spluttering. He guessed that such behaviour would not be good form here however. He was glad that he had not done so when he noticed that all eyes watched him to see how he reacted to his first taste of the spirit.

'You drink like a true winged lancer!' Straghov bellowed and all the table banged their glasses on the table in agreement. Their host insisted that everyone fill their glasses, then shouted: 'To Felix Jaeger, who comes from the land of our allies, the Empire!'

Of course, Felix could do nothing less than pledge a return toast to the ancient friendship between his folk and the folk of Kislev. Before long, the dwarfs were joining in too. Felix noticed that a pleasant warmth had settled in his stomach and that his fingers felt slightly numb. The vodka certainly got easier to drink the more glasses he tossed back, and soon he ceased to feel like it was burning his throat.

Great mounds of food were devoured. Toast after toast was made. Great speeches of welcome and friendship were spoken until darkness fell. Somewhere during the course of the afternoon, Felix lost track of events. His head swimming from the vodka, he was only dimly aware of eating far too much, drinking far too much and joining in the singing of songs whose words he did not know. Some time during the evening he was sure he danced with Ulrika, before she whirled away to dance with Schreiber, and then sometime after that he wandered off to be sick beside the stables.

After that his mind blanked completely and great chunks of memory were lost to the vodka and Kislevite hospitality. For the rest of his life he was not sure quite who he spoke to or what he said or how he got to the chamber that was allocated to him. Forever afterwards, however, he was grateful that he did.

* * *

FELIX AWOKE THE next day feeling like a horse had kicked him in the head. Perhaps one had, he thought; he checked his face for bruises but could find none. He looked around the room and saw that the floor was of packed earth. The mattress was filled with straw and someone had thrown a thick quilt over him. During the night he had drooled on his pillow and a patch of wetness was evident where his head had been. At least, he hoped it was just drool.

He pulled himself to his feet, and wondered whether at some point during the previous evening he really had challenged Snorri Nosebiter to a wrestling match. He seemed to have a vague recollection of some such thing, or maybe he had just dreamt it. His limbs certainly felt twisted enough for him to have engaged in such a foolish pursuit. Maybe he had. That was the worst thing about a really hard drinking session. You could never quite remember what you had said, who you had insulted and to whom you had issued foolish challenges. You simply engaged in insane behaviour. At that moment, he wondered if perhaps it was true that alcohol was a gift from the Dark Gods of Chaos intended to make men mad, as some of the temperance minded cults in the Empire claimed. Right now he didn't care. He just knew that he never, ever intended to drink again.

A knock sounded on the door. Felix threw it open and blinked out into the harsh daylight.

'Amazing,' Ulrika said by way of a greeting. 'You are on your feet. I would not have thought it possible after the amount of vodka you consumed last night.'

'That impressive, eh?'

'All were impressed. Particularly by the way you climbed the airship tower while reciting one of your poems.'

'I did what?'

'I am only joking. You only climbed the tower. Most people thought you would fall and break your neck, but no...'

'I really climbed the tower?'

'Of course, don't you remember? You bet Snorri Nosebiter a gold piece that you could. At one point you were going to do it blind-folded but Snorri thought that was an unfair advantage because you would not be able to see the ground and would not be quite so afraid. That was just after you'd lost a silver piece arm wrestling him.'

Felix groaned. 'What else did I do?'

'When we were dancing, you told me I was the most beautiful woman you had ever seen.'

'What? I'm sorry.'

'Don't be! You were very flattering.'

Felix felt himself starting to blush. It was one thing flattering a pretty woman. It was another having no memory of having done so.

'Anything else?'

'Is that not enough for one night?' she smiled.

'I suppose so.'

'So you are ready to go riding then?'

'Eh?'

'You told me that you were a great horseman, and you agreed to go riding with me this morning. I was going to show you round the estate. You were very enthusiastic about it last night.'

Felix pictured himself drunk and talking with this extremely pretty woman. He guessed that if she had offered to show him her father's pig-sties in his inebriated condition he would have shown a creditable amount of enthusiasm for it. Actually, he was certain he would have managed to be enthusiastic about it in any condition except his present one. His hangover made even Ulrika Magdova look less ravishing than the prospect of going back to sleep.

'I am looking forward to seeing you on horseback. It should be quite an impressive sight.'

'I might have exaggerated about my horsemanship.'

'You can ride?'

'Er-yes.'

'Last night you told me you could ride as well as any Kislevite.'

Felix groaned again. Had some daemon taken over his tongue while he was under the influence of the vodka? What else had he said? And why had he drunk so much?

'Ready to go then?'

Felix nodded. 'Just let me have a wash first.'

He strode out into the courtyard. Snorri Nosebiter lay, still slumped over the table, his head encased in a bucket. Gotrek lay snoring by the smouldering remains of one of the fire-pits, his axe clutched comfortingly in his hands. Felix walked over to the water pump, put his head below it and began to work the lever. The cold stream sent a shock jarring along his spine. He puffed and blew and continued to pump, hoping to drive the hangover away by inflicting still greater pain on himself.

Had he really said all those things or was Ulrika Magdova kidding him? He found it all too easy to believe that he had told her she was beautiful. He had thought it often enough over the past few days. He knew how much he had a tendency to run off at the mouth when he was really drunk. On the other hand, it scarcely seemed possible that he had climbed the airship tower while so drunk he could not remember it. It was an act of mad recklessness. No, he decided it was simply not possible. She had to be joking.

Snorri took his head from the bucket. He looked blearily over at Felix. 'About that gold piece Snorri owes you?'

'Yes,' said Felix uneasily.

'Snorri will pay you when we get back from the Chaos Wastes.'

'That seems reasonable,' Felix said and hurried off towards the stables.

FELIX LEANED BACK in the saddle and rolled his head around to clear the stiffness out of his neck. He looked down from the top of the rise to where the small streams cut across the rolling plain. The land was somewhat marshy down there, and bright birds flickered in and out of the reeds. He thought he saw some frogs splashing into the water. Dragonflies flickered past his face, as did other larger insects which he did not recognise. Some of them had bright metallic coloured carapaces, far more striking than those of any insect he had ever seen before. Was this perhaps some evidence of the nearness of the Wastes, he wondered?

He looked over at his companion and smiled, glad at long last to be here. At first the ride had seemed like a peculiarly refined form of torture, with the motion of the horse sending spasms of protest through Felix's queasy stomach. He had cursed the woman, his mount, the fresh air and the bright sun, in roughly that order. But the exercise and the sunlight seemed to have at long last worked their spell on him, and sent his hangover back into the dim, dark recesses of his skull. He had found himself beginning to take an interest in the landscape, and even to enjoy the sensation of speed, of the wind on his face and the sun on his skin.

Ulrika rode easily, as if born in the saddle. She was a Kislevite noble, so of course she had been riding virtually since she could walk. She had not said a word since they had set out, seemingly content to race along beneath the vast, empty sky until at last they had reached this small hillock and by wordless agreement come to a halt.

Beyond the stream, in the distance, the dark mountains marched threateningly towards the horizon. Their huge bulk seemingly carved from the bleak bones of the earth. They looked more desolate than any place he had ever been. No snow marked those rugged peaks, but there was a hint of something else, of an oil-like film whose colours shifted and shimmered in the light of the sun. There was a sinister, threatening air about the mountains, hinting at the fact that beyond them lay the outriders of the Chaos Wastes.

'What is that pass?' Felix said, pointing north to the enormous gap which looked as if it had been hacked out of the mountain barrier by some giant's axe.

'That's Blackblood Pass,' Ulrika said quietly. 'It's one of the major routes down from the Wastes, and the reason why the Tzarina has placed this outpost here.'

'Do the Dark Ones pass this way often?'

'You can never tell when they will come or even what they will be. Sometimes they are huge riders in black plate mail. Sometimes they are beastmen, with the heads of animals and the weapons of men, but sometimes other twisted deformed things that are even worse. There seems to be no rhyme or reason to it. It does not matter whether it's high summer or the depth of winter; they can come at any time.'

'I have never been able to fathom the way Chaos works. Perhaps you should talk to Herr Schreiber about it.'

'Perhaps but I doubt that even Max's theories could explain it. Best just to keep weapons sharp and the beacons manned, and be ready to fight at any time.'

'Beacons?'

'Aye, there is a system of beacons stretching back from the pass. When they're lit all the villagers know to flee to their villages and lock the gates, and all the lancers know to muster at my father's house.'

'Smoke by day, fire by night,' Felix murmured.

'Yes.'

'You live in a frightening land, Ulrika.'

'Aye, but it is also beautiful, is it not?'

He looked at her and the land beyond and nodded his head. He noticed that her pupils were large in her eyes, and that her lips were slightly parted. She was leaning slightly towards him. Felix knew a cue when he heard one.

'That it is. As are you.' He leaned towards her. Their hands met and fingers interlaced. Their lips touched. It was as if an electric shock had passed through Felix, and almost as quickly as it had happened, it was over. Ulrika broke away, and reined her horse about.

'It's getting late. I will race you back to the mansion,' she said and turned her mount suddenly and took flight. Feeling more than a little frustrated, Felix set off in pursuit.

LURK SCURRIED ALONG the top of the gondola. He was happier than he had been in a long time. It was dark and the skeleton crew left on the airship were mostly asleep, except for the dwarf on the command deck. The others were down below, drinking and laughing and singing their foolish human songs. There was plenty of food in the hold, and so far no indication that his presence had been noticed. Now that he was starting to feel more relaxed he could indulge the curiosity which was another Skaven trait. He had slunk around the airship, exploring all the nooks and crannies and he had discovered some very interesting things.

There was a flexible metal tunnel that ran up into the big balloon overhead. It passed right through the body of the gasbag and came out on a small observation deck on top. There was a hatch which led out onto the top of the gasbag, The whole thing was covered in webbing to which you could cling.

At the very rear of the airship was a chamber containing one of the small flying machines which had helped rout the skaven force during the Battle of the Lonely Tower. There was a huge doorway and a ramp that looked like they were designed to let the flying machine out. If only he knew enough to fly the thing, he could have stolen it and made his way back to Skavenblight a hero. The urge to get behind the controls and start flicking switches and pulling levers had been almost irresistible. He had given the notion serious consideration – but the grey seer had been very specific during their last communication.

Lurk was to do nothing and touch nothing without Thanquol's express instructions. The grey seer's words had been quite insulting, implying that Lurk was an idiot who would most likely do something disastrously wrong without Thanquol's guidance. It was just as well for Thanquol that he was who he was, Lurk decided. Only a sorcerer of Thanquol's ability could get away with talking to Lurk that way.

No, he was just going to have to sit tight and do nothing until he got his orders. There was nothing more to do except wait.

ELEVEN
NORTHWARD

FELIX JOINED THE crowd of peasants in the courtyard and stared up at the airship. Provisions were being placed aboard the craft, a reminder of the grim fact that all too soon they must leave this place.

From the courtyard of the mansion he could see crates, cases and large leather sacks being winched up the tower and then heaved across the gangplank and into the vessel. It looked like the dwarfs intended to take plenty of vodka aboard to supplement their casks of ale, for, as Snorri had pointed out, you could never be too careful about such things. Mostly, though, the provisions were of a more basic nature: smoked and sun-dried caribou meat, hundreds of loaves of black bread, and as many huge round cheeses. Whatever else might happen, Felix doubted that they would starve, unless they spent a very long time in the Chaos Wastes. Of course, starvation was the least of his worries.

He had noticed the dwarfs were making modifications to their craft. Fine mesh screens had been fitted over the ventilation holes that allowed air to enter the cupola. This was supposed to filter out the mutating dust which rose from the deserts of the Chaos Wastes. Dwarfs in elaborate cat's cradles hung over the side of the airship and made last minute modifications to the engines and rotors.

Other preparations were being made. For the past three days, Max Schreiber had retired to a small tower near the mansion and engaged in some arcane ritual. By night, Felix could sometimes see an eerie glow illuminating the tower windows, and feel the strange prickling of the hairs on the back of his neck that told him magic was being worked. If this bothered any of the others they did not show it. Presumably, Borek had told them it was the wizard's role to help them ward off the evil influence of Chaos, and he appeared to be doing just that. Schreiber himself had told him that this had been left until the last moment because the magic lost its potency over time. The nearer to their final goal he cast the spell, the more time it would last over the Wastes. Felix saw no reason to doubt the magician's expertise in this.

Even as Felix looked up, he could see the engineers clambering along the meshwork on the side of the huge balloon, attaching things that must be jewelled amulets judging by the way they sometimes glittered when the light caught them. He knew that the eyes of the figurehead had been replaced with two oddly glowing gems for he had been up on the bridge of the *Spirit of Grungni* once or twice to take more lessons from Makaisson in how to fly the airship.

Felix had come to enjoy these lessons and he believed that in an emergency he could most likely pilot the vast airship, although he was still uncertain whether he could land the thing if he was forced to. The banks of smaller levers had turned out to fulfil a multitude of purposes. One of them would release ballast, causing the ship to rise swiftly at need. Another sounded the horns which alerted the crew to some upcoming danger. A third would jettison all the black stuff in the fuel tanks in case of a fire, an eventuality that Makaisson assured him would be just about the worst thing that could happen to the airship.

He had found himself gaining a great respect for the chief engineer. Makaisson might well be as crazy as Gotrek claimed, but he obviously knew and loved his subject and he had supplied Felix with simple answers to even his most technical questions. He now knew that the airship flew because the gasbags were filled with a substance that was lighter than air, and had a natural tendency to lift up. He knew that black stuff was highly inflammable and might even explode if lit, and that was why it would have to be vented in an emergency.

Still for the most part life on the Boyar's estate in these warm summer days had been idyllic, and there had been times when he could almost forget the danger which awaited them on their departure. Almost.

A hand fell on his shoulder and a low laugh sounded in his ear.

'There you are. Tell me, can you use that sword, Herr Jaeger?' It was Ulrika.

'Yes,' he said. 'I've had some practice.'

'Perhaps you would care to give me a lesson.'

'When and where?'

'Outside the walls, now.'

'You're on.'

FELIX WAS NOT quite sure what he expected when he got outside. Ulrika had already unsheathed a blade and was making a few practice cuts in the air. Felix cocked his head to one side and watched her. She moved well, feet wide apart, right foot forward. keeping her balance as she advanced. The sabre gleamed brightly in the sun as she slashed at some imaginary foe.

He stripped off his cloak and jerkin, and unslung his own blade. It was a longsword, and it had greater length and weight than her weapon. It hissed through the air as he made some practice swipes. Felix moved confidently forward. He was good with a blade and he knew it. In his youth he had excelled in his fencing lessons, and as an adult he had survived many fights. And the Templar's blade he used was the best and lightest he had ever handled.

'Not with that, fool! With that,' she said, nodding in the direction of another blade, which lay in a wooden case by the wall.

Felix strode over to where the other sword lay against the wall. He unsheathed it from its scabbard and inspected it. It was another sabre, long and slightly curved. The cutting edge had been dulled which made sense if this was a practice weapon. He tested the weight and balance. It was lighter than his own sword but the grip felt unfamiliar in his hand. He tried a few experimental passes with it.

'Not what I'm used to,' he said.

'Excuses, excuses, Herr Jaeger. My father always said in a fight, you must be able to use whatever weapon comes to hand.'

'He is correct. But usually I make sure that the first weapon that comes to hand is my own sword.'

She merely smiled at him mockingly, head tilted back, lips slightly open. He shrugged and moved over towards her, the blade held negligently in his right hand.

'Are you sure you want to do this?' he asked, staring directly into her eyes, and wondering exactly why they were doing this. A few of the guards must be thinking the same thing he guessed, for a small crowd had gathered to watch them from the walls.

'Why do you ask?'

'People can get hurt.'

'These are practice blades, deliberately blunted.'

'Accidents can still happen.'

'Are you afraid to fight me?'

'No.' He was going to say he was afraid that he might hurt her, but something told him that this would be the wrong thing to say.

'You should know that in Kislev we fight to first blood. Usually the loser comes away with a scar.'

'I already have many.'

'You must show me them some time,' she smiled.

While Felix was still wondering what she meant by this, she lunged. Felix barely managed to leap aside, as it was a slice was taken out of his shirt. Reflex action let him parry the next blow, and before he could even think about it, the action sent his counter hurtling back towards her. She blocked the blow easily, and suddenly their blades were flickering backwards and forwards almost faster than the eye could follow.

After a few moments they sprang apart. Neither was breathing hard. Felix realised that the woman was very, very good. Realistically, with his own blade in his hand, he was probably the better swordsman. But fighting at these speeds was mostly a matter of reflex, of a trained response which had been drilled into the fighter so often as to be automatic. In this kind of lightning-fast combat, things happened too quickly for any conscious response. The lighter curved blade was throwing his timing off and giving her the advantage. And that was the last chance he had to think about it for a while, as Ulrika pressed forward with her attack. The guards on the wall cheered her on.

'Did I tell you I have beaten all my father's guards at sabre practice,' she said, as he just managed to get his guard up in time to block her swipe. She wasn't kidding about fighting to first blood either. This was not like the sporting duels of his youth, where you fought to display your skills. This was much more like real combat. He supposed it made sense in a way. In a place as deadly as Kislev you did not want to acquire reflexes that would cause you to pull your blows. He knew, for it had taken him many real fights to completely overcome that conditioning.

'If you had, we wouldn't be doing this,' he muttered, slashing back at her wildly.

'And I have beaten all the local's noblemen as well.' Her blow ripped the chest of his shirt and severed a button. Felix wondered if she was playing with him. The guards above jeered at him. 'Since I was fifteen no man has beaten me with the sabre.'

Felix very much doubted that they had let her win simply to curry favour with her father either. He had fought many men, and she was a lot better than most. His face was flushed and he was panting with effort. He was starting to feel a little angry about the way the guards were applauding his humiliation. He forced himself to concentrate, to keep his breathing easy, to keep to his stance as he had been taught.

He realised now that he faced another disadvantage. Most of the fighting he had done had very little to do with this formalised style of combat. It had all been in the rough and tumble of melee combat, where you killed your foe in any way that you could and style counted for nothing.

Realising that he would inevitably lose if he continued to fight in this manner, he decided to change his tactics. He blocked her next blow and pushed forward. As they were face to face, he reached forward and grabbed her left arm with his. Using all his strength he jerked hard, and pulled her around. As she went off-balance, he managed to strike her blade from her hand. He let her go and she fell backwards and he brought his blade down so that the point was against her throat.

'There's a first time for everything,' he said. The slightest drop of blood trickled down her throat.

'So it would seem, Herr Jaeger. Best of three, perhaps?' He saw that she was laughing, and he laughed too.

FELIX LAY DOWN by the stream near the mansion, looking out across the rolling grasslands, lost in reverie, wondering what was going on between himself and Ulrika. The woman herself stood nearby, holding a short Kislevite composite bow. She stood for a moment, with the bow tensed, in a posture which could not help but reveal her excellent figure, then sent another arrow flashing one hundred strides into the direct centre of the target. It was her third bulls-eye.

'Well done,' Felix said.

She looked over at him. 'This is easy. It would be a far more difficult shot from the back of a galloping horse.'

Felix wondered if she was trying to impress him. It was hard to tell. She was very different from the other women he had known. She was more forward, more accomplished in the arts of war, more direct. Of course, this was Kislev, where noblewomen often fought alongside their menfolk in battle. He supposed they had to be able to, for this was wild frontier country with the Darkness to the north and wild untamed lands full of orcs to the east. This was a harsh country where every blade was needed. She seemed interested in him, in the way men and women always are interested in each other, but whenever he had pressed his suit she had backed away. It was most frustrating. He felt like the more he saw of the woman, the less he actually understood her.

A shadow fell across him and a hand tapped him lightly on the shoulder. Felix looked up, his train of thought disturbed. Varek stood there, peering short-sightedly into the distance towards Ulrika.

'What is it?' Felix asked.

'My uncle asked me to tell you that our preparations are complete. We will leave tomorrow at dawn.'

Felix nodded to show his understanding. Varek bowed low to Ulrika and then backed away.

'What was that?' she asked.

Felix told her. A cloud passed across her face.

'So soon,' she said softly and reached out to touch his face, as if to reassure herself that he was still there.

* * *

THE SUN SANK beneath the horizon. In the darkness, Felix stood on the wall and looked towards the distant mountains. It was still early and a warm breeze blew across the grasslands. The two moons had yet to rise. A strange shimmering glow was visible beyond the northern peaks. The sky was filled with dancing lights, the colour of gold, silver and blood. It was a strange sight at once captivating and frightening.

From below came the sound of musicians tuning their instruments, and cooks bellowing to each other as they prepared the evening feast. Judging from the number of cattle slaughtered and flasks of vodka being produced, Straghov was preparing to give them a right royal send-off.

A slight noise to his left attracted Felix's attention and he realised that he was not alone on the battlements. Gotrek stood there too, gazing into the distance. He seemed rapt and a look of concentration creased his face.

'That glow – is it the light of Chaos?' Felix asked at last.

'Aye, manling, that it is.'

'From here it looks almost beautiful.'

'You might think now so but if you went through Blackblood Pass and marched under that sky you would think differently.'

'Is it really so bad?'

'Worse than I can make it sound. The sands of the deserts are all of strange colours, and the bones of huge animals gleam in the light. The wells are poisonous, the rivers are not of water but other stuff like blood or mucous. The winds drive the dust everywhere. There are ruins that once were the cities of men, elf and dwarf. There are monsters and enemies without number, and they are not troubled by fear or by sanity.'

'You lost a lot of people, the last time you were there.'

'Aye.'

'What are our chances then?' Felix wanted to add 'of surviving', but he knew that would be a meaningless question to ask a Slayer. 'Of reaching Karag Dum?'

Gotrek was silent for a long time. From behind them rose the sound of singing. From the grass beyond the manor house came the sound of night insects. It was so tranquil that Felix found it hard to believe that this was a land on the frontier of an endless war, and that tomorrow they would be passing over the Chaos Wastes, through a country from which they might never return. Standing here in the warm night air, Felix felt like he was going to live forever.

'In truth, manling, I cannot say. If we went on foot, there would be no chance whatsoever, of that I am certain. With this airship of Makaisson's we might be able to make it.'

He shook his head ruefully. 'I do not know. It depends on how accurate Borek's maps are, and how potent Schreiber's spells prove, and whether the engines break down or we run out of fuel or food, or warpstorms…'

'Warpstorms?'

'Monstrous tempests filled with the power of the Darkness. They can make stone flow like water and turn men into beasts or mutants.'

'Why do you want to go back?' Felix turned to lean against the battlements so that he could get a view of the courtyard behind them.

'Because we might get to Karag Dum, manling. And if we do, our names will live forever. And if we fail, well, it will be a mighty death.'

After that Felix asked no more questions. Looking down into the courtyard and catching sight of Ulrika in a long bright dress, he did not want to believe that it was possible that he could die.

FELIX MADE HIS way to the edge of the courtyard. Behind him he could hear the sounds of drinking and dancing. Pipers tootled on instruments which resembled miniature bagpipes; other musicians banged away rhythmically on their hide-covered wooden drums. The smell of roasting meat filled his nostrils, warring with the sharp acrid taint of vodka. From somewhere outside came shouting and grunting and cries of encouragement as the warriors egged on two wrestlers.

He was not hungry and he was stone cold sober, for he had decided that he could not face another night of drinking, even if it was to be his last night on earth. He was looking for Ulrika but she had vanished earlier, accompanied by two of the peasant women who appeared to be either her maids or her friends, he was not sure which. It was all a bit anti-climactic. Here he was, dressed in his freshly washed and mended clothes, his hair combed and his body washed – and he could not even find her to steal a kiss. He felt surly and miserable, and more than a little confused. Didn't the girl even care that he was leaving tomorrow? Wouldn't she even talk to him? He was in no mood for the gaiety behind him. He was going to return to his room and sulk. He smiled bitterly as he went, knowing he was being childish and not wanting to do anything about it.

At the half-open door he paused. His chamber was dark and there was a quiet sound from within. Felix's hand reached for his sword, wondering if this was a robber or some servant of the powers of Chaos which had slithered in from the night under the cover of the merrymaking.

'Felix, is that you?' asked a voice that he recognised.

'Yes,' he said in a voice suddenly so thick that he had difficulty forcing the words out of his mouth. A light flickered and a lantern was lit. Felix could see a bare arm protruding from beneath the coverlet.

'I thought you were never going to show up,' Ulrika said and threw the quilt aside to reveal her long, naked body. Felix rushed to join her on the bed. The scent of her filled his nostrils. Their lips met in a long kiss and this time she did not break away.

THE LIGHT OF dawn and the crowing of the cockerels woke Felix. He opened his eyes to see that Ulrika lay beside him, propped up on one elbow, studying his face. When she saw that he was awake she smiled a little sadly. He reached up and ran his hand across her cheek, feeling the soft skin of her face beneath his fingers. She caught his hand, and turned it over to kiss the palm of his hand. He laughed and reached out. He drew her down to him, feeling the warmth of her body, happy to be there, happy to be holding her and feeling her heart beat against his naked flesh. He laughed from sheer pleasure, but she shuddered and turned away from him as if she was about to cry.

'What's wrong?' he asked.

'You must go,' she said.

'I'll be back,' he blurted foolishly.

'No, you will not. No man ever returns from the Wastes. Not sane. Not untouched by Chaos.'

He realised then why their lovemaking of the previous evening had possessed such desperate urgency. It was a one night thing, a gift from a woman to a warrior she thought she would never see again. He wondered if that happened a lot here. His happiness vanished but he held her anyway, stroking her hair.

A heavy knock sounded on the door.

'Time to be away, manling,' came Gotrek's voice, and it sounded like the voice of doom.

TWELVE
THE CHAOS WASTES

Felix felt sadness settle on him like a cloak as he watched the Straghov mansion fall away below the airship. The tiny waving figures slowly receded into the distance and then faded from view entirely as the *Spirit of Grungni* picked up speed. The mansion dwindled until it was lost in the endless immensity of the rolling grass-covered plains. Felix paced the metal deck restlessly.

He wondered if he would ever see Ulrika again. She plainly didn't think so, and she was in a better position to know about these things than he was, having lived on the borders of the Chaos Wastes all of her life. It was odd but already he missed her, strange considering he had never even met the woman until a few days before.

For a swift, dreadful moment, he felt like going to Makaisson and asking him to turn the airship around. He wanted to say that there had been a terrible mistake and he did not want to leave. He found himself wishing he had stayed behind with her, but things had happened so quickly and he had been swept up suddenly once more by the momentum of the dwarfs' quest. Everyone, including her, had seemed to believe he was going, and so he had gone, despite having no real inclination to do so.

It was typical of how things went in his world. Small events took on a life of their own, and before he knew it, he was caught up in wildly unlikely occurrences far beyond his control. He wondered if everybody's lives were like that and not just his. Did everyone pile tiny decisions upon tiny decisions like a child piling pebbles, only to realise at the last moment that they had built a shifting unstable mountain beneath themselves, and that there was no way off without causing an avalanche?

He knew that he could not go to the chief engineer and ask him to turn back for a number of reasons. The first and simplest was that Makaisson might not do it, and he would forfeit the respect and goodwill of the crew without gaining anything. The second reason was that he had no idea what reception he would get even if he did turn back. Perhaps what had attracted Ulrika to him was the belief that there was something heroic about his part in the quest, and abandoning it now would mark him as a coward. He knew that the people of this harsh land would want no truck with cowards.

And maybe, he was forced to admit, part of him wanted to go on anyway, to see this new place, to find out how it would all end, to measure his courage against a wilderness that caused dismay even to Gotrek. Maybe the way he felt other people might judge him was the way he judged himself. If he abandoned the *Spirit of Grungni* he would be abandoning his heroic view of himself and retreating into being just like everybody else. Maybe part of him really wanted the fame that the dwarfs aboard the airship craved. He did not know. There were times when his motives confused even himself. They seemed to vary with his moods or his hangovers.

He just knew that he felt terrible right now – and that he wanted to see Ulrika again. The mood of gloom seemed to have infected the whole airship. All the dwarfs were quiet and their expressions were pained. Perhaps they felt this unaccountable sadness as well. Or maybe they were simply hungover, for last night every last one of them had drunk like a Marienburg sailor on a spree or, to be nastily exact, dwarfs confronted by a lake of free booze. Felix had to admit that the airship was currently no place for those with a hangover. The deck vibrated visibly and occasionally the whole gondola shook as they passed through clouds and patches of turbulence.

He pushed his way towards the command deck and saw that it was mostly empty, save for the basic crew needed to fly the ship. He paced moodily over to stand beside Makaisson and looked out the window. The vast stone bulk of the mountains loomed ever closer. He could see that they were headed for Blackblood Pass. It yawned in front of them like the mouth of some great daemon.

Soon they were in the pass itself with the mountains looming all around them, and the lowest of the strange glittering peaks level with the airship. Felix studied them but the glowing, shimmering substance that capped them seemed strangely hard to look at. The eye slid along it like a man tumbling on ice, and he found that he could not really focus on the peaks close up. It was his first indication of how strange Chaos could be. He was sure that it would not be his last.

The pass itself was rocky and bleak. Here and there oddly shaped boulders had been placed alongside the track, and Felix felt sure that strange, outlandish runes had been carved into them. Noticing that some of them gleamed white, he borrowed a telescope from Makaisson and focused it on them. To his horror he saw that what he had taken to be a chalked symbol was in fact a deformed skeleton chained to the rock. Were they human sacrifices left here by warriors of Chaos, he wondered, or warning markers left by the Kislevites? Either seemed perfectly possible.

Varek appeared beside Felix and maintained an awe-struck silence for a few minutes. Felix knew that the young dwarf shared his mood.

'Schreiber thinks these mountains shield all of Kislev,' Varek said eventually.

'What do you mean?'

'I talked with him back at the manor house. He has a theory that says that if it wasn't for this range of mountains, the wind would blow all the warpstone dust down from the Chaos Wastes and infect the population with mutation. He says that they would all change and become deformed and subject to the mad whims of the Dark Gods.'

'I thought there already were mutants in Kislev. Sigmar knows, I've fought enough of them in the Empire. There cannot be fewer here!'

Varek looked at Felix and smiled sadly. 'In Kislev they kill anyone who shows the slightest stigmata of mutation – even babies.'

'They do the same in the Empire,' Felix said, but he knew that wasn't really true. Many parents hid their mutant children and people shielded their mutant relatives. He had encountered such cases in his wanderings. Mutants were not bad people, he thought; they were just suffering from an illness. He shook his head bitterly, knowing that no dwarf and most likely no Kislevite would agree with that conclusion. It was indeed a terrible world.

'Schreiber claims it would be much worse without these mountains, that they are a natural barrier which prevents most of the dust reaching the lands of men. He says that the strange stuff on the peaks is congealed Dark Magic, the pure stuff of Chaos.'

'He has many interesting theories, Herr Schreiber,' Felix said sourly.

'He says these are not just theories. He has conducted experiments on animals using warpstone dust.'

'Then he is mad. Warpstone is an evil substance. It drives men mad. I have seen it.'

'He says he is very careful and shields himself with magic, and all manner of protective substances. My uncle believes his theories. It is one reason why there is a layer of lead foil within the hull of this airship.'

'I think no good will come to Herr Schreiber in the end.'

'I am inclined to agree, Felix, but all the same he could be right. My uncle says it fits with dwarfish lore. Some claim that our people first started building their cities underground during the first great Chaos incursions long ages ago and that the rock shielded us from the taint of Chaos which has affected all other races.'

He seemed embarrassed as he said this, as if unsure how Felix would respond to the accusation that his folk were touched by Chaos. From his own experience of travel within the Empire and beyond, however, Felix found it only too easy to believe that it was the case. Humankind gave itself over all too easily to the worship of the Darkness. It was a depressing thought.

'When we pass beyond these mountains we will be on the very edge of the Realm of Chaos,' Varek muttered darkly.

'Do you think that the spells Schreiber wove around the airship will protect us?' Felix asked.

'I know nothing of magic, Felix. It is not a subject that many dwarfs know about. My uncle believes that it will, and he is considered wise in these matters.'

'A strange man, Herr Schreiber. You know, he asked me to record my impressions of the Wastes in case we made it back.'

'Me too. He says it will help with his researches.'

'Let us hope then that we return to present him with useful material.'

Varek smiled. 'Indeed, let us hope so.'

LURK WAS WORRIED. Ever since the human wizard had come aboard the airship and begun casting his spells, he had been unable to contact Grey Seer Thanquol. It was a terrible thing, for he knew the skaven sorcerer would blame him for it, whatever the real cause. He wanted to do something, but he knew nothing about sorcery. A feeling of helplessness surged in him. With it came a desire to rend and tear, to exorcise his fears by killing something, preferably something weak and helpless.

Unfortunately there had been no likely candidates for his fury. The airship was full of well-armed and equipped dwarfs, and Lurk did not have a dozen of his packmates with him to encourage his righteous skaven wrath.

He had known that he needed to find this outlet for his pent-up energies. He had found it in exploring the airship while most of the dwarfs slept. Once again he had found himself at the promising tunnel opening in the topmost level of the gondola.

Slowly, carefully, he turned the massive handle and felt the lock click open. He pushed upwards with all his strength and saw a ladder running upwards. Wind tugged his fur for a moment and he realised he stood atop the gondola. Looking up he saw the ladder disappeared into a circular opening in the fabric of the gasbag. He pulled himself up through the opening and was immediately surrounded by what appeared to be a mass of monstrous balloons. They were fixed in long rows within the gasbag by fine wires.

Quickly he scurried up the ladder, leaping upwards with the natural agility of a skaven, reassured by the pressing closeness of the gasbags all around him. His keen nostrils twitched and his whiskers bristled. He recognised a faint acrid tang to the air that no human or dwarf would have noticed. He recognised this scent! He had caught hints of it down below in the gondola but that was not where he knew the smell from. No, he had encountered it in the great marshes around Skavenblight where the ratfolk factories poured their chemical by-products into the mud and quicksand. Sometimes huge bubbles would form where the effluent was piped, and when those bubbles broke the surface and popped this particular smell was emitted.

Was it possible that the dwarfs had trapped this gas in these thin balloon-like sacks, and that it was these thousands of sacks which lifted this vessel into the sky? Could it be that the means to create airships was already within skaven paws? Should he tell Grey Seer Thanquol of his suspicions?

He considered the thought for a moment and then decided against it. It was a ludicrous theory! Surely only the most powerful of sorceries could keep this vessel aloft. That must have been what the human sorcerer was doing back at the human surface-burrow! He must have been recharging the spells that let the airship fly. These gasbags must serve some other purpose. Perhaps they were weapons, like poison gas globes. That, too, seemed unlikely, however, for he had never heard of the marsh gases giving anybody anything worse than a bad headache.

He scampered all the way to the top of the ladder, noting that various rope walkways ran through the massive balloon to allow access to its innards. This would make a good hiding place if he had to abandon the cargo hold below. When he reached the top of the ladder he emerged into an open crow's nest atop the ship. It seemed to be a kind of observation deck, about the size of a rowing boat. Various strange meters and gauges were set into a large metal box. Heeding Thanquol's words, he did not dare touch them. Standing on a large tripod beside them was a telescope, mounted above a large, multi-barrelled weapon which reminded Lurk of the organ guns he had faced in his battles with humans and dwarfs. Doubtless the weapon was meant to protect the airship in case of attack from above.

Overhead he had a perfect view of the sky. The chill wind whipped his fur, and he sniffed the air. By the Horned Rat! It contained the faintest hint of warpstone! Lurk's fur bristled. If he could find a source of that fabled substance he would be rich beyond his wildest dreams of avarice – provided Thanquol let him keep some. Perhaps best not to mention the precious Chaos rock to the grey seer before it was absolutely necessary. After all, he could be wrong.

A walkway ran away along the top of this massive structure to other crow's nests at the front and rear of the ship. He realised that he was looking at a row of defensive emplacements similar to this one. It looked like the dwarfs were taking no chances. Was it possible that those rope walkways within the balloon itself led to other weapons in the sides of the airship? He would have to investigate.

He looked through the eyepiece of the telescope and scanned his surroundings, taking careful note of the enormous mountains with their glittering peaks, and the odd traces of colour in the northern sky. He suddenly felt enormously exposed. This was not the place for a tunnel-dweller like himself. There was too much sky, too much fresh air and the horizon was too far away. He had best return below.

There you are! The thought was so powerful it truly startled him. Lurk shot bolt upright and his tail stretched to its fullest extent. *Where have you been?*

Nowhere, most understanding of Overlords. Lurk thought carefully. *In the airship, as you commanded.*

Then our foe-fiends have shielded their ship with sorcery. Incompetent fool-slave, they must have detected your presence!

It was a terrifying thought, which Lurk prayed most devoutly was not true. He swiftly explained to the mighty voice thundering in his head about the presence of the human sorcerer on the ship, and about how he had enshrouded the cupola in mysterious spells. The silence which followed was so long that Lurk started to believe that Thanquol had lost contact. Just as he was offering up his thanks to the Horned Rat, though, the commanding voice spoke again.

The man-wizard must have put shieldspells on the shipcraft to protect it from something. The spells are only on the vessel below not where you are. Come to where you are now at the same time each day and I will contact you.

Yes, most potent of potentates, Lurk thought back.

Lurk hastily scampered back down the ladder. Only on his way back down did he wonder whether the grey seer understood the danger. Perhaps the crows nest would be occupied. Perhaps he would be unable to carry out this order. It was a frightening thought. Lurk wished he had a few underlings present to bully and relieve his frustrations. On the way back down he settled for slashing a few balloons with his claws. They burst, sending rushes of foul but familiar gas into his nostrils.

Only when he was safely back in his crate did Lurk start to worry what would happen to him if any of the dwarfs noticed the balloons he had burst. Perhaps they would suspect his presence. On the other paw, his natural skaven curiosity also made him wonder what would happen if he burst all of the balloons.

FELIX CONTINUED to survey the ground beneath them, as he had done for hours. They had reached the very beginnings of the Chaos Wastes now. Below them he could see the first dunes of odd, multicoloured sand beginning to mingle with the bleak rocky plain. The sky ahead was turbulent, filled with shifting clouds of unusual metallic shades. The sun was rarely visible and when it showed its face it looked larger, and redder. It was as if they were not only crossing into a new land, but into an entirely new world. The gems in the eyes of the ship's figurehead glowed brightly, as if whatever spell had been placed upon them was now fully activated.

Once again the sheer speed of the airship filled Felix with appalled wonder. In the past few hours they had passed over towering mountains, then rolling plains. Those plains had not looked too different from the grasslands of Kislev – except that when you looked more closely you could see charred ruins where the stones had apparently flowed like water into new and bizarre shapes, and the ponds and lakes shimmered with odd pinks and blues as if tainted by strange chemicals.

After the plains had come marshland and then the tundra. The temperature had dropped noticeably and sometimes flurries of crimson snow had battered against the windows, before melting and running down the glass in red droplets which reminded Felix uncomfortably of blood.

Eventually these bleak lands had also given way, to a place where nothing grew, a stony plain littered with towering boulders that reminded Felix of ancient menhirs. It seemed to him unlikely that these could have been raised by men, but then you never knew. Sometimes they had passed over small bands of beastmen who had beat their chests and bellowed challenges up at them. On other occasions they had flown above clusters of foraging men, who scattered at their approach. Through the telescope Felix saw that all of them bore the stigmata of mutation. How did they survive in this unhealthy land, he wondered – trying not to consider the dark tales of cannibalism and necrophagy that were told of the cults of Chaos.

Now they had left even those bleak lands far behind them and were looking down on the shimmering desert. Felix heard the click of Borek's stick on the stone floor as the old dwarf approached, then felt the touch of a leathery hand on his sleeve.

'Take this amulet and put it on,' Borek said. 'We have entered the Chaos Wastes proper now, and it will shield you against their influence. Try to keep it at all times against your flesh for that will transfer its power to you and ward you against the warping emanations of the Dark Magic.'

Felix accepted the amulet and held it up to the light. A silver chain and casing held a gem the exact shape and colour of a piece of ice, the sort of frozen stalactite he had often seen in winter hanging from the eaves of his father's house. It was a crystal of a type he had never seen before, and as he looked within it he thought that he caught sight of a faint glow. He touched the stone, half-expecting it to be frozen, but if anything it felt slightly warm.

He cocked his head suspiciously and looked down at the old dwarf.

'This was made for you by Herr Schreiber, wasn't it?'

Borek beamed gnomishly up at him. 'You do not trust him, do you, Herr Jaeger?'

Felix shook his head. 'I trust no wizard who has dealings with Chaos.'

'That is commendable, I suppose, but also a little foolish.'

'I have had some experience of magic and of Chaos.'

Borek glanced out the windows and smiled ruefully. 'As have I. And let me tell you I trust Maximilian Schreiber with my life.'

'Good! Because it seems to me that is exactly what you're doing.'

'You are stubborn. We dwarfs find that an admirable quality. Yet you are wrong about the wizard. I have known him many years. I have talked with him and travelled with him. I have saved his life and he has saved mine. There is no taint in him.'

The quiet tone of authority in the loremaster's voice was more convincing than his words. He felt that the dwarf was probably right, but still... Felix had grown up in a land where magic and Chaos had often been regarded with horror, and he had some terrible experiences at the hands of sorcerers. It was hard to put aside a lifetime of prejudices. He said as much.

The loremaster shrugged and then gestured at the gondola that surrounded him. 'Even dwarfs can change, Herr Jaeger, and if anything we are far more bound by tradition and by prejudice than you. This whole airship goes against the traditions of one of our strongest guilds. Yet we have put aside our prejudices because our need is great.'

'And you think my need for this amulet is great.'

'I think it will be your best protection against Chaos, Herr Jaeger, while its magic lasts. And believe me, you will need protection against Chaos.'

He turned and shouted something in rapid dwarfish to Makaisson. It came as a shock to Felix to hear him speaking that harsh guttural tongue. During their travels together all of the dwarfs around him had spoken Reikspiel. At first Felix had thought it was out of politeness, because he was a foreigner and could not understand, but later he had come to realise that it was really down to the peculiarly suspicious dwarfish mind. Yes, they were being polite, but they also regarded their tongue as sacred and secret, and did not want outsiders to learn it unless they were completely trustworthy. Of all the humans he knew, only the higher ranks of the priesthood of Sigmar were proficient in the language and they taught it only to their own priests after ordination. Felix guessed that Borek's decision to speak now meant that he had crossed some barrier and that the old dwarf trusted him. He felt obscurely pleased.

'I was just telling the pilot to take the craft down towards those ruins. I thought I recognised them,' Borek said.

Felix followed the direction indicated by the loremaster's pointed finger. There were tumbled down buildings and other things among them. He raised the telescope to his eye and saw that they resembled wagons of metal, totally enclosed with only crystal window slots out of which drivers could see, and four more slots in the side through which weapons could be poked. There was a peculiar arrangement of funnels at the back and no yokes to which any beast of burden might be harnessed. Something about them reminded him of Imperial war wagons that had been completely roofed over, and also of the Imperial steam-tanks he had once seen in Nuln.

'This was our last expedition's first campsite in the Wastes,' Borek said. 'See where those rusting hulks are? Those were our vehicles. We were attacked here by an enemy warband and drove them off only with great losses. Those cairns there were raised over our dead.'

Felix realised that the airship had come to a halt over the ruins and that the other dwarfs were crowding the windows and portholes to gaze down on it. They looked down at it with the sort of awe that Felix had seen human pilgrims display when they entered a shrine. In a way, it was worrying evidence of the dangers of the Wastes. In another, it was reassuring, in that it showed that people had come this way before, and that things were not a complete unknown here.

He looked down on the abandoned vehicles and the empty tombs, and his earlier sadness returned redoubled. Those things had stood there for nearly twenty years and the only other eyes that had looked upon them were those of Chaos worshippers and monsters. He truly wished that he had not come here.

'Near here are the caves where Gotrek found his axe,' Borek said softly.

'Is that so? Was the failure of your expedition the reason why Gotrek became a Slayer?'

'No. That happened later...'

Borek smiled sadly then looked at him, opened his mouth as if to speak, and then, as if realising that he had already said too much, closed it again. Felix wanted to ask more but it came to him that if the old dwarf didn't want to speak there was no way to make him do so.

Felix noticed that he still held the amulet negligently in his hand. The thought struck him that it was undoubtedly true that the old dwarf knew more about these things than he did, and that perhaps he should heed the loremaster's words. He looped the silver chain around his neck and let the stone dangle down inside his shirt. Where it touched his flesh he felt a strange tingling. A shiver passed through him and then was gone, leaving only a warm glow that in no way reassured him.

Borek patted him on the back. 'Good,' he said. 'Now you are better protected than we ever were in the old days.'

Felix looked up towards the horizon and offered up a prayer to Sigmar for the souls of the dwarfs down there, and for his own safety. A sudden premonition of doom came to him and did not leave, even after the airship's engines roared to life once more and they began to move forwards, deeper into the Chaos Wastes.

THIRTEEN
WARPSTORM

FELIX PRESSED HIS nose against the cold glass of the window and for the first time felt truly terrified. The horns calling the crew to battle stations had just sounded, and all the dwarves ran to take up their positions at the guns and engines, leaving Felix to stand idly by, a helpless spectator in this time of fear. He looked down on the eerie landscape below.

The desert had a wild and terrible beauty. Enormous rock formations towered over the glittering sand like wind eroded statues of monsters. An emerald lake glittered greenly under the crimson sky. By its shores two enormous armies marched towards each other in a tide of flesh and metal.

Felix wondered at his fear. The warriors of Chaos advancing below seemed not at all concerned with the airship overhead. They were far too intent on each other. Only occasionally would a beastman or a Chaos warrior look up at the sky and brandish a weapon. None of the missile weapons they carried appeared to have the range to hit the airship. Makaisson had sounded the alert just to be on the safe side, however, and Felix could not blame him. The numbers and the insane ferocity of the crowd below them were terrifying.

These were both mighty forces, perhaps the largest armies he had ever seen. Thousands of beastmen surged below, like a sea of hoofed and horned animals grown upright into twisted parodies of men. Felix had fought these followers of Darkness before, but now something about the sheer numbers here made them seem far more terrifying than ever before. Huge banners rose from the midst of the forces, each a twisted parody of the heraldic emblems of his distant homeland. Monstrous men garbed in incredibly ornate black armour marched at the head of each force or rode at its flanks on mutated steeds which dwarfed even the largest of human war-horses.

There were thousands upon thousands of warriors present. Felix wondered at that. How could this barren landscape support such vast regiments? Obviously there was sorcery at work here. Looking down on these immense armies he recalled the descriptions he had read of the previous incursions of Chaos, during the time of Magnus the Pious, when Praag had been besieged and it seemed like the forces of the Dark Gods were about to sweep away the entire civilised world. They had always seemed faintly unreal to him, with their lurid depictions of daemons, and their enormous hordes of twisted feral things but those armies down there made those hellish visions seem all too plausible. He could easily see those mighty forces crashing through Blackblood Pass and smashing through the lands of men. For the first time he started to truly understand the power of Chaos, and he wondered why it had not yet devoured the world.

With a roar Felix could hear even above the racket of the airship's engines, the armies closed the distance between them. Felix trained the telescope, focusing on those distant figures, turning them from tiny marionettes into living breathing warriors.

A huge figure garbed in armour of black iron, on which was inscribed redly glowing runes charged his barded war-horse towards a mob of beastmen. This foul knight brandished an enormous battleaxe in each hand. The horse's trappings were fantastically ornate. Its head was shielded by a moulded mask that gave it the features of a daemonic dragon. The armour on its body was segmented like that of a centipede and on each section were numerous discs, carved in the shape of leering daemon masks. The mounted warrior rode full pelt into a band of beastmen. His axe decapitated a foe with each swing. His horse's hooves dashed out the brains of another, and it continued onwards trampling the bodies of the slain into bloody mush. Behind the knight his fellows charged with maniacal fervour towards packs of beastmen that outnumbered them more than twenty to one. They seemed fearless and uncaring of whether they lived or died.

In another part of the battlefield, monstrous minotaurs armed with axes the size of small trees hacked their way through all that opposed them. They towered over the beastmen the way adults tower over small children, and it seemed to Felix that a beastman had about as much chance of overcoming one as a child had of overcoming a full grown man. Even as Felix watched, one of the bull-headed giants caught a goat-headed thing on its horns and lifted it kicking and screaming from the ground. With a shake of its head, the monster sent its gored victim flying twenty paces to land atop its comrades. The impact sent half a dozen of them sprawling onto the bloody sand. But then, even as Felix watched, the rest of beastmen swarmed over the minotaur, striking with spears, clambering up its legs, harrying it the way a pack of wild dogs would savage a bear. The massive creature fell and disappeared in a cloud of dust, to be trampled under the beastmen's hooves and impaled on their spears.

Winged humanoids with daemonic features rose like a flock of hideous bats and wheeled over the battlefield. At first Felix feared that they were going to attack the airship and his hands reached for the hilt of his sword but then the hellish flock gave out a hideous, ear-piercing shriek and descended down onto the beastmen hordes. They lashed out with taloned claws and ripped their victims limb from limb with a strength that seemed supernatural, before being lopped into pieces themselves by their frenzied foes.

In the centre of all this howling madness loomed a gigantic figure clad in the most fantastically ornate armour Felix had ever seen. Every piece of it appeared to moulded with grinning skulls and leering gargoyle faces. The warrior was mounted on a skeletal steed which seemed barely able to sustain its great weight and yet moved with a speed like the wind. In his right hand, the Chaos champion held an enormous scythe; in his left, a banner depicting a throne of skulls whose empty eye-sockets wept tears of blood. The warlord gave instructions to his followers with great sweeping gestures of the scythe and hordes of lesser, black armoured warriors leapt to obey, running to their deaths or to dispatch their foe with a strange savage joy.

Felix had to admit that they were terrifying. He watched aghast at the sheer frenzy with which the combat was fought. He had never seen such insane hatred as these two forces seemed to possess for each other, and suddenly it came to him that here was the reason why the followers of Darkness had yet to overwhelm the world. They were as divided amongst themselves as the nations of men were; more so, in truth. Perhaps then the rumours of rivalry between the Ruinous Powers were true. For this Felix was profoundly grateful, for here was a force that inspired respect and fear.

There was something disturbing about all this as well. What if the powers were somehow to put aside their rivalry and turn their faces towards the world? What if some mighty warlord was to arise among the forces of Chaos and unite them in one invincible horde? Then the uncountable hosts would march down on Kislev and the lands beyond. Suddenly Straghov's fortress and his thousand lancers seemed pitifully few.

In a matter of minutes the airship swept over the battle and it dwindled away behind them, lost in the enormous immensity of the endless desert. No matter how vast the warring armies were, this landscape could reduce them to less than the significance of ants. A vast dark gloom, obscuring the northern horizon. The very sight of it filled him with foreboding. Felix let out his breath in a long sigh and returned to his cabin to sleep.

THE SHAKING OF the airship woke Felix unhappily from a dream of Ulrika. He pulled himself upright just as an enormous crash echoed through the steel corridors, and the whole vessel vibrated as if struck with an enormous hammer. His stomach lurched as the lantern on his wall swung, sending shadows flickering across his chamber. In that brief instant he felt certain he was going to die.

He pulled himself upright and glanced through the porthole. Outside all was roiling murk. Then there was a flash of incredible green lightning, multiple forks flickering down from above and losing themselves in the gloom. After a few seconds the voice of thunder spoke and the whole ship shook once more. The vibrations cast Felix from his bed and sent him rolling to the floor. As he leapt upright, he banged his head against the low ceiling. The pain sent lights dancing before his eyes and he reached a hand out to grasp the wall and help keep his balance. To his surprise it felt warm.

Struggling to keep his balance on the rocking floor, he shuffled out into the corridor and headed towards the control room. His ears rang with the sound of thunder, and he could barely control the terror which clawed at his guts. This was far worse than any earlier turbulence. It was as if a giant had grasped the airship in its enormous hand and was trying to wrestle it to the ground. He could hear the roar of titanic winds hurtling past the hull. Any moment he thought the vessel would be split like a ripe melon hit by a hammer, and he and everybody else in the vessel would fall tumbling through a thousand strides of storm-tossed air to splatter on the ground below.

It was the sense of helplessness that was so frightening, the knowledge that there was nothing he could do to prevent any of this happening. There was no way off the *Spirit of Grungni* except clambering out through the hatches in the roof and leaping to certain death. At least in battle he could do something, wield a sword, smite a foe. Here and now he could do nothing save pray to Sigmar, and he doubted very much, given where they were currently located, that there was anything the God of the Hammer could do to save them. The twenty strides to the control room seemed to take a lifetime and Felix confidently believed that each step might be his last.

Arriving at the control room at last, he saw the dwarfs clutching at their control stations like it was their last hope of life. Gotrek stood in the centre, his axe held negligently in one hand, looking almost relaxed, riding the rolling deck with slight adjustments of his stance. No fear showed on his face, just a fixed grin of the sort he normally only revealed in combat. Felix noticed that the runes on his axe-blade were glowing redly. Makaisson wrestled with the control wheel, his enormous muscles straining, huge sinews standing out like cables beneath his tattooed flesh. Old Borek was strapped into one of the armchairs, while Varek huddled behind him, a look somewhere between fear and wonderment inscribed on his face. Snorri was nowhere to be seen.

'What's going on?' Felix shouted, struggling to make himself heard over the echoes of thunder, the roar of the wind and the scream of the engines. The whole ship shook once more and there was sickening sensation of being dropped, as if the airship had suddenly lost buoyancy and was falling like a stone towards the earth.

'Warpstorm, manling!' Gotrek bellowed. 'The worst I've seen!'

Eerie green lightning flickered once more, the flash illuminated the whole cabin intensely, elongated Makaisson's shadow until it filled the floor, then vanished. The bolt appeared to have flickered only a few hundred yards away. Felix noticed that in its aftermath particles of shimmering dust, like a cloud of strangely coloured fireflies, filled their field of vision as far as the eye could see. Then the blast of thunder almost deafened him and the ship began to drop once more. After a moment the sensation of falling stopped and the airship righted itself like a ship cresting a wave.

Felix scrambled over to the window and looked downwards. Through a gap in the clouds, in the flickering of the lightning, he thought he caught sight of the ground below. It was only a few hundred paces beneath them, dunes of glittering sand rising and tumbling, being driven before the titanic winds like foaming breakers on a storm-tossed sea. The wind shook the huge airship like a terrier shaking a rat. Felix knew that in a few dozen more heartbeats they were going to be driven into the ground, and the vessel was going to buckle and break like a toy boat thrown against a wall by a vicious child.

'Malakai! We're going to crash!' he shouted. 'We're almost at the ground!'

'Then come ivver here and gae us a hand, laddie. Pull on that altitude stick for all ye're worth. An' keep yer eyes peeled. The instruments hae stopped workin' in this storm.'

Felix rushed over to stand beside the engineer and pulled on the lever. Normally it would have moved easily but now it appeared to be stuck. Felix braced both his legs and heaved with all his might but still it would not move. The cold metal refused to be shifted. A vision of the airship impacting on the rocky desert below filled Felix's mind and he pulled once more, putting all the strength of fear into his efforts. Sweat ran down his brow. His muscles felt like they were going to erupt through his skin, and he knew that if he kept this up much longer he would burst a blood vessel. It was no use; still the cursed lever would not move.

'I can't shift it!' he called.

''Tis the wind on the ailerons, laddie. It's fightin' ye. Keep trying'. Dinna gae up!'

Felix kept tugging and still nothing happened. He knew they must be mere seconds from disaster and still there was nothing he could do. He offered up a prayer to Sigmar for his soul, knowing that his life was about to end here in the Chaos Wastes. Then suddenly Gotrek was beside him, lending his massive strength to the struggle with the lever. And still it did not move.

Gotrek's beard bristled. The veins stood out on his forehead, and then something gave way. At first Felix feared that they had simply bent the stick out of shape but no, it was moving slowly, surely, inexorably backwards. As it did so, the nose of airship tilted skywards. Then it seemed like the airship was being thrown backwards like a galleon caught by a huge breaker. The deck rocked and he and Gotrek lost their footing, sent tumbling backwards towards the rear cabin wall. There was a sickening sensation in Felix's churning innards as the airship began to leap uncontrollably skyward and then was dashed downwards again.

'Hold on tight!' bellowed Makaisson. 'This is gannae be rough!'

LURK SQUIRTED the musk of fear. He felt his glands void until they were empty and still they tried to keep on spurting. The wind tugged at his pelt, riffling it with a thousand demon fingers. Glittering warpstone dust filled his mouth and threatened to choke him. He had already swallowed a fair amount of the stuff and a warm glow filled his stomach. His fur stood on end. The roar of thunder almost deafened him. Tears filled his eyes from fear and constant irritation of the onrushing wind. He clutched the rails of the crow's nest with all four paws; his tail was looped round the rails to anchor him in place. He fought to keep himself low within the observation post, yet still the wind threatened to tear him from his place and send him tumbling to his doom. It was almost too much to be borne.

He cursed the day he had ever left his nice warm burrow in Skavenblight. He cursed Grey Seer Thanquol for his stupid orders. He cursed the stupid dwarfs and their stupid airship and their stupid journey. He cursed everyone and everything he could think of – except the Horned Rat, towards whom he remembered to send the occasional prayer for his deliverance.

Only a few minutes ago it had all seemed so quiet. He had climbed from his hiding place in the hold up to the crow's nest to make his daily report to Grey Seer Thanquol. The ship had been vibrating a little but Lurk had become used to its little motions and had paid no attention. But by the time he had reached the observation deck, the movements had become larger, the whole ship was bucking in the air like a crazed horse. But it was only when he had poked his snout through the upper hatch into the crow's nest proper that he noticed that the ship was surrounded by the strangely glowing cloud and its bizarre, multi-coloured lightning flashes.

Sound skaven prudence had told him that he should retreat below but he had been held in place by one thing: the tingling taste of warpstone dust on his tongue. It held him in place, fascinated. It was the source of much of the grey seer's much-feared power, and quite possibly the source of all magic. He had thought that maybe if he tasted some he, too, might acquire magical powers, but so far there had been no sign of them. By the time he had tried to return below, the accursed dwarfs had sealed the hatches and there was no way he could open them from above. They were locked.

In frantic fear he had scrambled around inside the gasbag but the strangely shifting balloons had spooked him and he had grown tired of hanging from the ladder. So he had clambered back up to the crow's nest and there the wind had grabbed him. He had only just been able to save himself by seizing the railings and now there was nothing he could do except wait and pray while the airship rocked below him like a raft in a typhoon.

Another series of thunderclaps made Lurk look up. He saw a series of lightning flashes marching across the sky, coming ever closer. Their unholy brilliance dazzled him. He shut his eyes firmly but he knew beyond a shadow of a doubt that they were about to hit the airship.

He remembered to send a final curse in the general direction of Grey Seer Thanquol.

FELIX, TOO, SAW the line of lightning bolts exploding directly in front of the airship. Makaisson twisted the wheel instinctively trying to avoid being hit, but it was too late. The greenish bolts pummelled the airship. In the instant before the tremendous glare blinded him, Felix had time to notice that the gems on the ship's figurehead blazed bright as the sun. Then the ship shook as if it was about to fly apart and for a long moment Felix saw no more. For a heartbeat the terrible fear that he had been blinded filled him but it passed as his vision slowly returned, and he noticed that everything in the command deck was surrounded by a swiftly fading halo of green.

The amulet on his chest felt almost hot enough to burn and he felt like ripping it off until the thought struck him that this might not be wise, and that perhaps it was protecting him from the magic of Chaos which had so obviously been contained within the lightning. He saw that the amulet on Gotrek's bare chest was glowing a furious green as it absorbed the halo about him. Then suddenly the ship stopped shaking and the sky around them was clear.

Felix picked himself up and limped over to window of the command deck. He could still see the green-black clouds of the warpstorm boiling below them. Occasionally the clouds would flash brightly with a glow of witch-light as the lightning sparked again and again. It was like looking down on a peculiar chaotic sea and Felix half-expected to see some enormous monster rise up out of its depths and try and swallow the airship in its jaws.

It took him a few moments to realise that the drone of the engines had changed. The sound slowly died away, until they made no noise at all. The clouds slowly passed beyond the airship. It began to gently rotate this way and that in the breeze.

'We've lost power,' Makaisson muttered. 'This isnae guid.'

Snorri chose that moment to appear in the cabin. He was yawning widely. 'What was all the noise?' he asked. 'It woke Snorri up.'

FOURTEEN
THE RUINED CITY

FELIX LISTENED unhappily as the engineers reported back to the command deck in turn, each bearing a tale of woe. It appeared that the warpstorm had caused a great deal of damage. There were rips in the gasbag, the engines had stopped working properly, the rotor blades were bent out of shape and there was some structural damage besides.

'We'll joost hae tae stop fur repairs,' Makaisson announced calmly. Looking down through the windows Felix wished he shared the dwarf's confidence. The storm had finally cleared and the sky was its usual overcast mixture of strangely coloured clouds. Below them lay the ruins of an enormous city, with not a soul visible in the streets. Such desolation was eerie. The wind whistled mournfully as it stirred the shifting sands which drifted through the abandoned buildings.

Then Felix heard a much more cheering sound: somebody, somewhere had managed to get one of the engines working. Gleefully Makaisson took control of his craft again. He nursed the airship down until it was only a hundred strides above the buildings.

'We'll moor here. Draup they lines.'

Mooring lines dropped. Felix saw the grapnel hooks on the end of one snag on a tumbled stone wall. It was enough to hold the drifting airship in place.

'Right, get doon there and secure they hooks! I'll try tae haud her steady up here.'

'Wait,' Felix said. 'It might be dangerous.'

'Och, yer right, laddie. Gotrek, Snorri, Felix, off ye go and make sure that there's nae wee beastmen lurkin' aboot doon there.'

Felix wished that he hadn't opened his mouth.

FROM THE GROUND the ruins looked even more vast and forbidding than they had from the air. The buildings seemed immeasurably ancient. Huge blocks of stone had been placed atop of each other without the use of mortar. Originally their weight and the precision with which they had been positioned held them in place. It was a style that Felix had seen only once before – in the ruins he had seen above the ancient underground dwarfhold of Karak Eight Peaks. He said this out loud.

'This isn't dwarfish workmanship, manling,' Gotrek sneered. His voice was muffled by the scarf he had wrapped round the lower part of his face to keep out any warpstone dust that might be in the air. Both Snorri and Felix had done the same thing. It seemed descending into madness and mutation did not fit in with the Slayer ideal of a heroic doom. 'Looks like it. Maybe it was copied or perhaps the builders had dwarf advisors but this was not dwarfish work. Stonework is shoddy. The alignment is less than perfect.'

Felix shrugged. His mail shirt felt heavy on his shoulders but he was glad it was there. In this strange place, the more armour he had the better. Right now he wouldn't have minded a complete suit of plate mail. He glanced around him. The street on which they stood was paved with huge flagstones. On each stone was inscribed an outlandish rune. The wind whispered eerily through the desolation. It was cold and he had the uncanny feeling of being watched.

'I have never heard of any human cities this far north, and it does not look like elvish work.'

'Elvish work!' Gotrek said contemptuously. 'A contradiction in terms: elves don't work.'

'I doubt this was built by beastmen or the warriors of Chaos. It seems too sophisticated for them, and it looks very ancient.'

'Looks can be deceiving here in the Chaos Wastes.'

'What do you mean?'

'There are all manner of illusions and mirages, and it is said that deep in the Wastes, the Great Powers of Chaos can create and destroy things at their whim.'

'Then we'd best hope that we are not so deep in the Wastes.'

'Aye.'

An eerie wailing call echoed through the ruins, like the shriek of a soul in torment or the cry of a mad thing wandering lost and forlorn through an endless wilderness. Felix span around and ripped his sword from its scabbard.

'What was that?' he asked.

'I do not know, manling, but doubtless we will find out if it comes closer.'

'Snorri hopes it does!' said the Slayer almost cheerily.

Felix glanced at the rope ladder hanging from the airship's side. He had not enjoyed clambering down it, and he did not look forward to the prospect of climbing up it again, but it was good to know that it was there, just in case they needed to beat a swift retreat. The bizarre call sounded again, closer now, but it was hard to tell exactly.

With the echoes in these ruins it could be coming from leagues away. Felix consoled himself with the thought that at least it had not been answered. He fingered the amulet on his chest, but it gave no sense of warmth. Perhaps there was no Dark Magic at work here; perhaps it had become overloaded in the warpstorm. He had noticed that none of the gems on the airship's sides were glowing now. That might mean something good or it might mean something bad. Felix did not know enough about magic to be able to tell.

Varek was gesturing them from the opening above. He seemed to want to know whether they were about to secure the airship. Felix shook his head, trying to indicate that the folk above should do nothing till they had ascertained what was making this hideous racket.

'Should we investigate the shrieking?' Felix asked.

'Good idea, manling,' Gotrek said nastily. 'Let's go wandering through these ruins and see how far we can get from the airship. Maybe we should split up too. That way we can cover more ground!'

'It was just a suggestion,' Felix said. 'There's no need to be sarcastic.'

'It sounded like a good plan to Snorri,' the other Slayer said.

Just then, from amidst the ruins, a figure limped into view. It looked like a human but it was so filthy, ragged and unkempt that Felix wasn't sure if this was the case. Around him he sensed a change in the attitude of Snorri and Gotrek. Without them visibly changing position, they seemed to become more wary, ready to strike out in any direction at a moment's notice.

Felix heard a clinking from behind them, and turned his head momentarily – to see that the grapnel at the end of mooring line had come loose. The airship was drifting free on the breeze. The vessel's engines chose that moment to sputter and die. He cursed silently to himself as the rope ladder rose out of his reach, then he turned his head and forced himself to concentrate once more on the advancing figure.

He could see that it was indeed a man. He walked in a shuffling crouch. His hair was so long that it reached his waist. His beard was filthy and dragged almost to the ground. Weeping sores covered his hands and arms where they were exposed. He limped wearily up to where they stood and let out another long wail. He was leaning on a staff that looked like it had been made by lashing together a number of human bones with sinew. A blank-eyed skull glared from its tip.

Felix stared at the man, and met a gaze full of melancholy madness.

'Begone from my city or I will feed you to my beasts,' the stranger said eventually. He fingered one of the many verdigrised copper amulets which hung from a chain around his neck. Felix could see that it had been carved into the likeness of a screaming skull.

'What beasts?' said Gotrek.

'Snorri thinks you're a nutter,' Snorri said.

Listen to who's talking, thought Felix.

'The beasts which fear and worship me,' the man said. 'The creatures to whom I am a god.'

Felix looked at the man and felt a surge of fear, knowing that he was mad. On the other hand, he did not want to simply slay the man out of hand just because he was mad. He had obviously been here for some time and it occurred to Felix that the man might have useful knowledge. He thought he had nothing to lose by humouring this lunatic.

'What is your name, oh mighty one?' Felix asked, hoping the others would have wit enough to play along with him. It was, he knew, most likely a forlorn hope but he thought he might as well try. The stranger appeared to consider this for a moment.

'Hans, Hans Muller – but you can call me the divine one.'

'And what are you doing here, Divine One?' Felix asked softly. 'You're a long way from anywhere.'

'I got lost.'

'Take a wrong turning back in Kislev, did you?' Gotrek asked sarcastically. Felix saw that the Slayer's axe was held ready to strike. There was a faint glow along the runes of the blade. This was usually a very bad sign.

'No, short one. I am a magician. I was experimenting with certain spells of translocation and something went wrong. I ended up here.'

'Short one?' Gotrek said, a note of menace in his voice.

'Translocation?' Felix asked hastily. The fact that the man was a wizard was not making him feel any easier. He had never much cared for sorcerers, having had several bad experiences with them.

'A method of moving between two points without traversing the lands in between. My theories were at least partially correct. I moved. Fortunately I moved too far and ended up here where the natives recognise my godhood.'

'Tell us, oh Divine One, what do you know of Karag Dum?' Felix asked.

'The great daemon has returned there,' Muller said instantly.

At the mention of daemons, Felix shuddered. In the Chaos Wastes it seemed all too likely that such sinister entities could be present.

'Daemon?'

'The daemon told of in the Prophesy. The Great Destroyer. It awaits only the coming of the Axe Bearer to fulfil its prophesy and its destiny!'

'Tell us more,' Felix said, shuddering.

Seeing Felix's reaction, a strange, furtive look came into the mage's eye. He licked his lips with the tip of a thin pinkish tongue. He looked twisted and cunning and suddenly Felix did not trust him at all.

'My beasts must be fed,' the mage said, then made a strange gesture. His hand moved through the air and seemed to gather oddly glowing energies to it. A shimmering sphere of light suddenly surrounded his hand. Even as he made to cast it, Gotrek's axe flashed and severed the hand at the wrist. The sphere of light fell from Muller's outstretched fingers and hit the ground. There was an explosion. A blast of warm air passed over Felix. His flesh tingled and he felt an odd dizziness.

In a moment he had recovered and the flashing before his eyes calmed down. He was grateful to see that Gotrek and Snorri were still there too, although the wizard had vanished.

'That was not a very destructive spell,' Felix said. 'He could not exactly have been a powerful wizard.'

'I'm not so sure, manling,' Gotrek said.

'What do you mean?'

'Take a look around.'

Felix did so. The first thing he noticed was that the airship was gone. Then he noticed the roof, the walls, and the peculiar patterns arrayed on the flagstoned floor.

'Next time we meet a sorcerer, manling,' said Gotrek, 'let's kill him first and ask questions later.'

THEY STOOD IN an oddly shaped chamber, in the centre of a large pentagram. At each point of the pentagram was a human skull and within each skull something glowed. A greenish light leaked from the eye-socket of every skull. Overhead was a massive stone roof. The walls of the chamber were carved from the same stones as the rest of the city. Odd-looking luminous moss grew in the cracks between blocks.

'Where are we?' whispered Felix. There was something about the atmosphere of this place which made him want to be extremely quiet. An aura of watchfulness, a sense of something old and evil waiting for something to happen. His words echoed away. Under the shadows of the roof something rustled and stirred and Felix sincerely hoped that it was only bats.

'Snorri has no idea,' said Snorri loudly. 'Somewhere underground, maybe.'

'Let us go and find out,' said Gotrek, striding towards the edge of the pentagram. As he did so, the chalked lines on the floor began to gleam brightly. The hair on the back of Felix's neck stood on end.

'No! Wait!' he shouted.

Gotrek strode blithely on. As his foot touched the edge of the pentacle, sparks flew up and he was surrounded by the brilliant glow. The smell of ozone filled the air. In an instant the Slayer was thrown backwards into the centre of the pentagram. It did not even slow him down. He threw himself at the barrier once more – and once again was tossed back.

As this happened, Felix watched closely what was happening. Each time the spell took effect, the eyes of the skulls blazed brighter; after Gotrek was thrown backwards, the illumination dimmed.

'You could try smashing one of those heads,' Felix suggested. Gotrek did not respond but stomped over to one of the points of the pentacle. His axe flashed downwards, the runes on the blade blazing. The skull smashed into a thousand fragments. A cloud of ectoplasmic vapour rose above it. There was a long, shrieking wail, as of a soul that had been set free after centuries of imprisonment. As the cry subsided, the remaining skulls went dark. Gotrek stepped outside the pentagram easily this time.

A quick inspection revealed that there was only one way out of the chamber. It led down a long ramp into a maze of gloomy corridors. The whole area was lit by glowing gems set in the ceiling. Felix had seen their like before, beneath Karak Eight Peaks.

'Those do look like dwarf work,' he said, as they marched down the shadowy corridors.

'Aye, manling, they do. Maybe the folk of Karag Dum traded with this city.'

'Or maybe Karag Dum was plundered by the people here.'

'That is an evil thought but it is also a possibility.'

Once more they fell silent. Gotrek led them easily through the maze, always moving with confidence, never having to retrace his steps. Felix was amazed by the certainty that the dwarfs showed here, for he knew that if he had been on his own, by now he would have been hopelessly lost.

The watchful stillness had once more settled over the labyrinth. Felix's flesh crawled. Every so often he stopped to glance back over his shoulder just to make sure that there was nothing coming up behind him. He felt as if a blade might be plunged into his unprotected back at any moment.

As they hurried on, Felix wondered where the other dwarfs were. He hoped that they had not left without them. The situation at the moment did not look good. The three of them were trapped in a huge maze, without food or water and with no knowledge of exactly where they were. If they made it to the surface, and they were still in the ruined city, then they might be able to attract the attention of the airship. But if it had already gone, then their prospects were bleak. Felix did not look forward to a long trek through the Chaos Wastes in an effort to get home. From what he had witnessed on the journey so far it seemed unlikely that they could survive.

He pushed these thoughts aside and forced himself to concentrate on his surroundings. The corridor had opened up into a long hallway. Light filtered in from high overhead. Glittering particles of dust shimmered in the beams. The hall itself was many storeys high. On each level was a gallery. A huge ornamental pool, filled with scummy water, took up most of the ground floor of the chamber. In the centre of the pool stood a fountain which had long since ceased to flow. It was a statue carved in the shape of armoured warrior. The warrior looked human enough, save for the fact that he had an additional arm in which he held some sort of staff.

Felix walked to the edge of the pool and looked in. The water was murky except where little flecks of green light glowed in, like trapped stars. He had seen this stuff before and knew it was warpstone.

'We won't be drinking this water,' he muttered, and the thought immediately made him thirsty. And as he thought this, he noticed a distorted reflection in the water. A huge winged shape which grew larger behind him even as he watched.

'Look out!' he shouted and threw himself backwards away from the pool. Razor-sharp talons slashed the air where he had stood mere moments before. Felix had the fleeting impression of a hideous winged humanoid, much like the ones he had seen flying over the battlefield earlier. Then there was a huge splash as the creature tumbled into the waters of the pool.

Felix had a moment to recover himself and look up. A horde of the winged creatures were emerging onto the galleries set into the walls high above them and throwing themselves into the air. He could hear the flap of their wings and the snapping of their pinions as they took flight. These creatures were not flying silently. The one which attacked him must have glided down from a long way above.

'Harpies!' Snorri shouted. 'Good!'

Gotrek looked grim as he brandished his axe. Snorri grinned like a maniac and capered on the spot at the prospect of impending violence. Felix glanced back over at the water where the winged fiend had vanished. There was a great splash and droplets of water soaked his face as the creature broke surface and flexed its water-logged wings. As it attempted to take to the air, it gave an unearthly shriek as a huge tentacle, as thick as a cable and covered in suckers, enfolded the mutant thing and dragged it back below the water. Felix was suddenly very glad that he had not disturbed the water, and then he had no more time for thinking.

The hellish flock descended. Felix was surrounded by flapping limbs. Their wingbeats drove the awful charnel stench of the creatures everywhere. He ducked a slashing talon, lopped off the attached hand with his counterstroke and caught a quick glimpse of a hideously contorted shrieking face. Quickly he slashed all around him, clearing an area in which he could fight. The dwarfs' battle cries rang in his ears along with the infernal croaking of the harpies.

He twisted his head trying to see where the Slayers had got to, intending to fight his way towards them. As he did so, he felt a sharp piercing pain in his shoulders. The whole world performed a cartwheel. The thunder of wings filled his ears and the smell of rotten meat filled his nostrils. He had been grabbed by a harpy and was being born aloft, like a field-mouse being taken back to an owl's nest to feed its fledglings.

The thing's acceleration was awful. He glanced down and caught a quick glimpse of the battle below. Snorri and Gotrek stood in the eye of a storm of wings. All around them lay the mutilated bodies of dead harpies, but many more came on. Gotrek reached up and grabbed one by its leg, pulled it down and crushed its head with the blade of his axe. Next to him Snorri smashed another's shoulder blade with his hammer. As the crippled beast flopped to the ground, the Slayer beheaded it with his axe.

In the pool, the water boiled and churned as something truly huge rose to the surface. The thrashings of the entangled harpy died away as more and more tentacles enshrouded it and crushed its life out. An enormous head broke surface. The sight of a circular leech-like maw filled with needle-sharp teeth distracted Felix from his predicament. He had been about to stab upwards at the Harpy and hope that the water below broke his fall – but now it seemed like that would simply be a case of jumping out of the cookpot and into the fire.

Snorri, seeing what was happening to Felix, cast his hammer straight up at the harpy. Felix flinched as it flew straight and true. There was sickening crunch as the weapon impacted and suddenly Felix was tumbling downwards towards the pool.

'No! You idiot!' he shouted as the turbulent waters grew beneath him and the air whistled past his ears. The thing in the pool looked up with huge, almost human eyes. In that moment it occurred to Felix that the creature might once have been a man warped by the hideous mutating power of Chaos. Then he saw the head turn upwards and the leech like mouth gape wide and in that instant he realised that he was going to die. If the fall didn't kill him then he would be grabbed by those hideous slimy tentacles and dragged into that vast mouth.

He knew a brief flicker of despair and then an eruption of something like a berserker's fury. If he was going to die, he was going to take the monster with him! He twisted his body to get his feet below him and as he impacted on the monster he drove his sword downward into the creature's rubbery flesh. All the force of his long fall, all of the weight of his body and all the strength of his arms powered the enchanted Templar's blade home. It cut through flesh and speared right into the creature's brain. The tentacles went limp instantly

The impact drove all the breath from Felix but he did not feel anything break. The beast's rubbery mass and enormous soft bulk had broken his fall. He swiftly sprang upright and leapt from the thing's head to the edge of the pool, taking great care not to touch the water. Even as he did so, he noticed that Gotrek and Snorri had routed the harpies. The majority of the surviving flock had taken to the air and were swiftly flapping their way out of the Slayers' reach. A glance behind him confirmed that the thing in the pool was already slipping back beneath the surface of the fetid waters.

Snorri bent down and picked up his fallen hammer. He looked up at Felix and grinned. 'Good throw, huh?' he said.

Felix restrained himself from striking the dwarf with his blade.

'Let's get moving,' Gotrek said. 'We don't have all day to waste.'

FELIX STOPPED and rubbed his shoulder. The bruising was painful and the area was tender. Fortunately for him the harpy's claws had not penetrated his flesh, although they had burst some of the chain links and driven the points through the armour's leather under-jerkin and into his arm. They were more like scratches than real wounds. Normally he would have paused to wash and dress them but here in the midst of these Chaos haunted ruins he had no desire to stop – and even less desire to remove his armoured shirt. To tell the truth, he had not seen any water he would trust here either.

While Felix had paused, Gotrek and Snorri had continued onwards up the seemingly endless stairs. He rushed to catch them up, not wanting to be left on his own. The brooding stillness of the place had only intensified since the harpies' attack and he wondered what wicked thing they could possibly encounter next.

His legs were aching from the constant climbing of steep stairs. They had risen about ten levels. The pool was still visible below them. He stumbled suddenly. A warped skull, humanoid but with goat horns, rattled away from his foot. It had been stripped of all flesh. Felix stooped and picked it up. It was light and cold, dry in his hands. Looking inside he saw score marks along the crown. An image flickered through his mind and he saw one of the harpies reaching inside the severed head to scoop out the brain and devour it. Hastily he tossed the skull away. It fell and clattered among the bones which lay strewn about the gallery.

They had obviously reached the area where the harpies nested, for there were bones everywhere, cracked for marrow and stripped of all flesh. The skeletons of beastmen, mutants and humans lay mingled with each other. Many of them were fouled with light brown excrement and the stink was awful. Even through the scarf wrapped over his mouth it made Felix want to gag. He wondered how much longer these galleries could go on for, and whether he could go through even one more without vomiting.

Why had Muller made his lair here, he wondered? And how had he survived among all these ferocious monsters? Had his magic prevented them from attacking him? Or had he come to some arrangement with the creatures? Felix was forced to acknowledge the fact that he would never know, and in truth, he was not sure he really wanted to. The pacts and alliances that must be needed to survive in a place like this did not bear thinking about – and that was before you came to consider the question of food and drink.

Perhaps Muller had even been sane when he came here, but had been driven mad by a diet that must have consisted of tainted flesh and warpstone-corrupted water. Felix did not want to consider that this might be the only option open to him and his companions too, if they did not find a way out of here soon. At the moment, death seemed preferable to such an existence but who could tell? Perhaps it would become easier as your brain degenerated and warpstone-inspired madness consumed the mind. Perhaps you might even come to enjoy it. Once more he forced the thought from his head – and as he did so he realised that the staircase had finally come to an end.

Up ahead Gotrek stood in front of a massive archway. The lintel was covered in a mass of carved daemon heads. They smiled mockingly, bared monstrous fangs, stuck out their tongues. Their expressions were crazed and debauched and full of madness and Felix wondered at the minds which could have carved such things. The archway itself was sealed by an enormous slab of stone inscribed with the twisted characters that Felix had come to associate with the followers of the Dark Powers of Chaos. It was becoming increasingly obvious that this part of the ruined city, at least, had long been home to the slaves of Darkness.

Gotrek reached out and pushed the stone but nothing happened. The slab did not budge. Slowly the Slayer applied more and more pressure until the huge muscles swelled and rippled all along his back and arms. Sweat beaded his forehead and his breathing came in ragged gasps. Snorri joined him but even their combined strengths had no effect on the archway. Felix did not even bother to try and help them. There was not enough room for him to squeeze in between them, and anyway he doubted that his efforts would count for much compared to the amount of force the two dwarfs were bringing to bear.

Eventually Gotrek gave up. He stood back and scratched his head with one massive hand. He picked up his axe and looked as if he was considering swinging it at the door but then he simply grinned and reached out to touch one of the leering daemon heads carved on the lintel. He pushed down on the tongue. It moved and as it did so the archway swung open, sending the still-straining Snorri sprawling through it to land flat on his face on the dusty flagstones beyond.

'No damage done. He landed on his head,' Gotrek muttered and strode through. With a last glance at the galleries behind them, Felix hastily followed.

THEY EMERGED ONTO a wide flat space open to the sky. Ahead of them was a walled barrier like a battlement. Behind them was a massive wall. Felix strode forward to the barrier and looked down. At once he realised that they were on the penultimate level almost at the very top of a massive ziggurat, for below them were all the lower steps. Close by was a flight of monstrous stairs leading all the way back down to the ground. The stairs also led up to a peak of the pyramid, and Felix hastily climbed them. At the top was a great open ledge. It was old and crumbling and it extended out over a wide expanse of empty air. Felix gingerly walked to the edge and looked down.

A long way below him was the pool in which the monstrous thing had dwelled and all the galleries in which the Chaos harpies had nested. There were chains and manacles along the walled edges of the ledge, and a slow realisation of the platform's function came to him. This was a place of sacrifice. Living victims had once been brought here and then thrown screaming from the ledge to tumble into the pool below, where the dweller in the murky water devoured them. It must have been an unpleasant fate, and Felix wondered about the sanity of those who had devised it.

Had this whole vast ziggurat been built purely with this function in mind? Or it had it once served a different purpose and become corrupted as the foul power of Chaos spread across this ancient land? Was it even possible, as Gotrek had suggested earlier, that this whole structure had been created by whim of one of the Dark Gods or their daemonic servitors?

None of his thinking was going any way towards finding salvation, Felix decided. They had found the open air but they had no idea where the airship was or how they could locate it. And if they failed to do that they were doomed.

He turned back from the vertiginous drop and scanned the horizon. Surely, he thought, if the airship was still over the city, it would be visible. He squinted in the strange light filtering through the clouds and tried to concentrate, wishing all the while that he still had the telescope that he had left on the ship. All he could see was the cloud of harpies circling high above them.

Then, to his amazement, far off in the distance, he saw a small dark speck that seemed to be moving in their direction. He prayed fervently to Sigmar that it was the *Spirit of Grungni*. Then he raced over to the outside edge of the ziggurat's uppermost level and shouted for the dwarfs to come and join him. But even as he did so, he noticed that an enormous horde of beastmen had emerged from the nearby buildings far below and were racing along the streets towards the ziggurat. Over their heads fluttered two harpies, screaming in their foul tongue.

Doubtless they were the things which had attracted the beastmen's attention. Before he could throw himself flat, one of the bestial Chaos worshippers noticed him, for it brandished its spear in the air and pointed with one outstretched arm towards Felix. The whole disgusting horde let out a howl of triumph and began to hurry up the long stairway towards them. Felix cursed his luck and went to join Snorri and Gotrek.

The two Slayers seemed profoundly indifferent to the fact that several thousand beastmen were racing towards them, too many for even such formidable warriors as themselves to slay.

'The stairway is a good point to make our stand,' observed Gotrek. 'Narrow. Not too many of them can get to us at once. Good killing.'

'Hardly seems fair,' Snorri said. 'They'll be tired by the time they get to us. All that running and then all those stairs. Maybe we should go down and meet them halfway.'

'They're spawn of Chaos. I will do nothing to oblige them.'

'Fair enough. Snorri sees your point.'

Felix shook his head in despair. He was going to die, and he was going to die in the company of two maniacs. It was too much. He had survived evil magic, the attacks of a tentacled monster and a flock of mutant harpies only to be brought down at the last by a horde of shambling, misshapen monsters, beasts that wore the shape of men.

He turned his head to the heavens to ask blessed Sigmar to simply smite him down and get it over with when he noticed that the dot in the distance had swollen into the definite outline of the airship. It was heading directly in their direction. Felix looked down the ziggurat again. The beastmen were almost halfway up it. He glanced back at the airship. It was much further away than the beastmen, but it was moving much faster. He hardly dared hope that it would reach them in time.

The beastmen were well up the stairs now, an onrushing tide of twisted flesh, brandishing spears and howling war cries. Felix could distinctly hear the clatter of hooves on the stone stairs. His heart raced. His mouth felt dry. This was almost worse than certain death. Now there was a faint hope that they might get away.

The airship swept low over the beastmen. Felix could see that the outside had been cleaned and all the engines were working. The rips in the gasbag had been repaired. He would not have believed that it was possible for so much work to be done in so short a time. The dwarfs had certainly been busy. He could see now that the doorways in the side of the ship were open as was the hatch in the bottom. Someone had thrown open the portholes as well, and a rain of black spheres was descending on the onrushing horde. One of them burst in the air sending shrapnel everywhere. Beastmen howled in agony. Felix realised that the dwarfs on the ship were dropping bombs!

More and more fell tearing great holes in the ranks of the beastmen. The foul Chaos things stopped and howled and shook their weapons at the sky. One or two threw their spears but they fell short, then dropped back into the tightly pressed mass of beastmen, impaling their comrades. For a moment Felix dared to hope that they would be routed by their fear of this awesome apparition above their heads. Then a larger leader-type emerged from the milling throng and shouted at the rest of its force to advance, and the beastmen came on once more. Still, the precious moments of confusion had given the airship time to sail forward until it was almost overhead. Felix could see Varek in the hatchway above him, uncoiling the craft's beloved rope ladder. He let out a long sigh of relief, knowing that he was safe.

Then the airship passed on by him, taking the rope ladder with it. What were they playing at, thought Felix, risking a glance down at the oncoming ranks of beastmen? This was no time for stupid jokes! Then he realised what had happened. The airship still had momentum from its rush to save them. The howling of the engines above him revealed that Makaisson had thrown the craft into reverse and was killing his vessel's speed expertly.

The *Spirit of Grungni* now hovered directly over the well in the centre of the ziggurat. Felix turned to the Slayers and bellowed; 'Come on! We must find Karag Dum! That is your destiny!'

The Slayers looked at him as if he were mad. He realised that they did actually want to throw away their lives in this pointless battle against superior numbers. Inspiration struck him. 'There is a daemon at Karag Dum! It pollutes sacred dwarf soil. It is your duty to kill it!'

Well, he thought, he'd done his best to talk the Slayers out of their folly. Now it was time to go. Without looking behind him, he raced up the stairway and out onto the ramp from which sacrifices had been thrown. The ladder dangled right out in the middle of the great central well – far too far for him to jump out and reach it. Behind him he could hear the roaring of the beastmen. They seemed to be almost upon him. He risked a glance over his shoulder and saw Snorri and Gotrek brandishing their weapons defiantly. He knew that it could only be a matter of moments before the horde was upon him.

He glanced back and saw that the rope ladder was coming back in his direction. Instantly he made his decision. He sheathed his sword, took a flying leap and made a grasp for the ladder. For a moment, he had a dizzying sense of the enormous drop beneath him, then his fingers were clutching the rope. The impact felt like it was going to tear his arm from its socket, and sent a surge of agony shooting through the shoulder that the harpy had bruised earlier. Somehow, he managed to hold on and then to grasp the swaying ladder with his other hand and begin to pull himself up.

He risked a glance down and saw that they were running in the direction of the ramp's edge.

'Snorri! Gotrek!' he shouted to encourage them.

Just beyond and below them he could see the first of the onrushing beastmen come into view. The Slayers looked up and almost as one reached up and made a grab for the ladder. Both managed to catch hold of it as it went flying by and were pulled off into the ziggurat and into the air. Felix caught a view of the great mass of bestial faces glaring up at him as they went soaring past. A rain of stuff was dropping from the ship now, and Felix realised that Makaisson was jettisoning ballast to enable them to gain height quickly. The sludge and pebbles dropped on the Chaos worshippers. They responded by casting their spears. Reflexively he closed his eyes as the missiles whizzed past his ears, then the beastmen were left far behind on the sacrificial ziggurat and the airship was gaining altitude fast.

Looking back to where they had been he saw an awful thing was happening. Before they had realised their danger, the leaders of the charging beastmen had gone running right off the edge of the ramp and were tumbling out into space. A few of their followers had time to realise what was happening and to give out roars of horror and fear. However, pushed on by the press of bodies behind them, they were being forced off the edge of the ramp and out into the abyss beneath them.

Felix offered up a prayer of thanks to Sigmar for his deliverance and began to pull himself, hand over hand up the ladder and into the *Spirit of Grungni*. Once safely there, he turned to reach down and helped pull the pair of Slayers up into the airship.

'Missed a good fight there,' Snorri said. 'Pity they got the drop on us.'

Felix gave Snorri a penetrating look. Was it actually possible that the idiot was making a joke, he wondered. In the distance he could still hear the screams of the falling beastmen.

'How did you find us?' Felix asked Varek as the ruined city faded into the gloom behind them.

'After you vanished, we finished the repairs and all the crew we could spare manned the telescopes,' Varek said. 'We were lucky. We saw a great flock of those winged things rising over the ziggurat in the centre of the city and decided that something must have attracted their attention. We thought even if all we found was your corpses it was worth the effort.'

Felix realised exactly how lucky they had been. The same thing that had attracted the horde of beastmen had also brought the attention of the airship's crew. He shuddered to think of what might have happened if they had fought with the creatures during the night. They would never have been found.

FIFTEEN
THE HORDES OF CHAOS

LURK FELT PECULIAR. His skin tingled. His fur itched. He was hungry all the time. Ever since he had been exposed to the warpstone dust during the storm, an odd sickness had convulsed him. He had taken to stealing more and more of the dwarfs' supplies away, and he devoured them all in great orgies of consumption where he simply could not stop himself until all the food was gone. He was just thankful that someone had eventually opened the hatch back into the ship before he started to eat his own tail.

The effects of all this consumption were starting to show. His muscles had swollen, his tail had grown thicker and he was getting bigger. His head hurt a lot and he found it difficult to think straight. He prayed to the Horned Rat that he had not caught some sort of plague. He remembered his fear when he had fallen sick in Nuln and how that had almost ended his life. If the plague returned now, he had none of the herbal medicines Vilebroth Null had used to preserve his life.

Slowly he pulled himself up the ladder to the crow's nest so that he could make his daily communion with that wretched Thanquol. He was heartily sick of that nagging voice within his head, babbling foolish orders and telling him what to do. Part of his mind knew that he should not be thinking this way, that it was most unwise but he could not bring himself to care. His body ached all over. His vision was blurring and his fur was beginning to fall out in places where monstrous boils were erupting. He decided not to bother about contacting the grey seer. He would return to his burrow and sleep. First though, he would need to eat. He was starting to feel a hankering for a nice bit of plump dwarf flesh.

FELIX KNOCKED ON the door of Borek's cabin. The metal echoed beneath his knuckles.

'Come in,' the dwarf said. Felix opened the door and went in. Borek's cabin was larger than his. The walls were lined with crystal-fronted cabinets containing many books. A table was bolted to the floor in the centre and on it was laid out an ancient map, held in place by four strange looking paper-weights of black metal.

Noticing Felix's curiosity, Borek said, 'Magnets.'

'What?'

'Those paperweights are magnets. They stick to iron and steel. It's some odd philosophical principle, akin to the one that keeps compass needles pointing northwards. Go ahead: try to pick one up.'

Felix did as he was told, and felt a resistance that he had not expected. He let go of the metal and it seemed to leap from his hand and adhered to the table with a click. It was typical of the dwarf's attention to detail, he thought, that they had managed to find a way of keeping maps in place even on such an unstable platform as this airship. He mentioned this fact.

'It's a power that has been known for a long time. It's used by our navigators on the steamships out of Barak Varr.' He smiled. 'But I suspect that you are not here to discuss the finer points of furnishing a vessel's cabin...'

Felix agreed that he was not and he began to speak, telling Borek about what had happened with the sorcerer and his mention of the daemon. The encounter with Muller had made him think. For the first time, he had really begun began to take seriously the dreadful possibility that such a thing might exist at Karag Dum. The old dwarf listened, nodding occasionally. When Felix finished, there was a short silence while Borek filled his pipe.

'How can this be?' Felix asked. 'How can daemons exist here and not outside the Wastes?'

Borek looked at him long and hard. 'They can and do exist outside the Wastes. According to our records, many have fought against the armies of the dwarfs.'

'Then where are they now?'

'Vanished. Who knows why? Who can truly explain the workings of Chaos?'

'But surely you have a theory?'

'There are many theories, Herr Jaeger. As far as we know, raw magical energy flows much more strongly through the Wastes. It seems most likely that daemons feed on this energy and need it to exist. Beyond the Wastes they can manifest for only a short time before vanishing because magic is weaker. Here in the Realm of Chaos they can manifest themselves for much longer periods because there is more power for them to draw on.'

'Why is that?'

'Schreiber believes there is some sort of disturbance at the very centre of the Wastes which is the source of all magic. According to him, it also warps time and distance in some manner. Many scholars claim that time flows in different rates in different parts of the Wastes, you know. And that the further you go into the Wastes, the more pronounced this effect becomes.'

'Why are the fiends not swarming all over us now then?'

'Perhaps because we have not gone far enough. I doubt that it is possible for a daemon to exist for long out here, so close to the edge of the Wastes, but I do not know for certain that this is the case. There is a lot I do not know about these matters.

'But you think a daemon still dwells in Karag Dum?'

Borek laughed grimly. 'It is all too possible. Even as I left there were dire rumours that some dread thing had been summoned and King Thangrim Firebeard and his runemasters marched to meet it. It may be it was trapped there or never left. I do not know. I and my kin escaped the city before those final battles.'

'It is not exactly a pleasant thought.'

'No, but it is one that we will soon know the answer to. We should reach Karag Dum within the next day or so.'

'What then?'

'Then we will see.'

* * *

'FASTER! QUICK-QUICK!' Grey Seer Thanquol chittered. He was tired and restless from being constantly cooped up inside his palanquin. Such confinement went against all his skaven instincts to get up and scuttle about, but he really had no choice. For the past few days he had done nothing but use communications spells and ride relays of palanquins through the subterranean roadways of the Under-Empire, stopping only long enough to change bearers and palanquins, eating all his meals as he moved on. He had blisters on his rump from sitting so long and he felt like his back was going to be permanently curved.

His bearers whined their complaints and Thanquol considered blasting one or two apart just to make an example of them, but he knew it would be counter-productive. All he would achieve would be to slow himself down until they reached the next way-station, where he could acquire a change of slaves. Still, he promised himself, once they were there, these whinging lackeys would suffer!

That is, if he could find the strength. The grey seer felt drained by the strain of having to expend so much power to communicate with Lurk over so long a distance. And now the buffoon was not even responding to his calls. It was so frustrating! He had no idea what had happened? Was Lurk dead? Had the airship crashed in some hideous accident? Was this long chase all for nothing? Surely it could not be, but ever since he had seen that accursed Jaeger, Thanquol had felt a sinking feeling. Where the human and his wretched dwarf companion were concerned, Thanquol was always prepared for the worst. The two of them seemed to have been born only to thwart him.

He cursed the engineers of Clan Skryre. Why could they not bend their accursed ingenuity to building some improved means of transport through the tunnels of the Under-Empire? Surely they could think of something more effective than simple relays of slave-born litters! Did they always have to spend their days working out bigger and better weapons? Why not warpstone-powered chariots or traction engines, Thanquol wondered? Or some long-range version of the doomwheel? Surely such things could not be beyond them? If he remembered, he would mention his ideas to the Council of Thirteen in his next report.

'Faster! Quick! Go-go!' he urged, his throat hoarse. He needed to get to the northlands soon, he knew, and find out what had happened to that wonderful airship. If only he could get his paws on that, he would never again lack for swift transportation.

And when he got there, he vowed, someone was really going to pay for the discomfort he had endured.

FELIX LAY ON the bed in his cabin, staring at the metal ceiling. His head spun with all the things he had learned this day concerning the Realm of Chaos. The world was a great deal more complex than he would ever have thought possible, and it was increasingly obvious to him that his own people still had a lot to learn from the Elder Races.

He closed his eyes but sleep would not come. He felt tired but also restless. His shoulder still pained him, despite the healing salves which Varek had applied. He knew the area was going to be tender for some time to come. Still, his mail had been repaired by one of Makaisson's apprentices, and it looked better than new.

Cursing his lot, he rose from the bed and pulled on his boots. Leaving his chamber, he walked to the airship's rear observation turret. The rearmost bubble of the turret was small and housed an organ gun mounted on a swivel platform. Felix slumped down into its seat and worked the foot pedals that sent it turning first to the left and then to the right. He found the motion oddly relaxing, reminiscent of swinging in a hammock or being in his grandfather's rocking chair.

He reached up and grasped the handles of the organ gun. This was another of Makaisson's unusual designs. It had grips like a pistol and was fired by pulling a trigger. The whole mechanism of the gun was balanced on a gimbal and could be swivelled up or down, left or right, almost without effort. Felix did not know what the dwarfs expected to attack them flying at such an altitude, but they were obviously taking no chances.

He gazed out over the land over which they had passed. The sky had darkened into some semblance of night. At least, the clouds were darker above them and there was no suggestion of a sun above. Felix wondered about that. They had reached an area where it seemed no matter how high they climbed the sky was always obscured. He had decided that it was either some form of potent magic or simply that somewhere in the distance, great masses of warpstone dust were being thrown high into the air and driven upwards by powerful winds. The only illumination came from huge fire-pits set in the rough terrain below, craters resembling the bubbling mouths of volcanoes around whose glowing mouths twisted figures capered.

As the airship passed over the fire-pits, it shuddered slightly, caught by the rising current of warm air. This did not frighten Felix as it once had. He had come to find gentle turbulence actually rather soothing. It was strange. The more he flew, the more he had come to regard the sky as being something akin to the sea. The winds were its currents, the clouds something like the waves. He wondered if the sea, too, had currents at different levels, the way the winds appeared to move at different speeds at different heights. There was much here for a philosopher to study, he thought yawning, and slipped gently into sleep.

LURK PULLED HIMSELF slowly and stealthily down the corridors of the ship. The hunger in his stomach was like a living thing clawing and trying to escape. It caused him actual physical pain. Ahead of him, he sensed prey. It did not have the scent of dwarf but of humanity. Lurk did not care. He simply wanted to feel hot red blood gush into his mouth and gorge on chunks of raw, warm meat and a human would suit his purposes just as well as a dwarf.

He entered the rear chamber and heard the snoring of the figure in front of him. Good! His foolish prey was completely unaware, lost in a swinish slumber the like of which no skaven would ever allow itself to fall into, even if there were no obvious threat of danger. The human's blond-furred head was thrown back, and his neck was bared, as if inviting Lurk's fangs. Lurk tip-toed forward and loomed over the human's sleeping form. Saliva filled his mouth at the prospect of fresh meat. All it would take would be one bite to sever the artery! He would lock his jaws on the human's neck to smother his screams. Another few paces and he would be in a position to strike.

Suddenly Lurk heard footsteps on the ladder leading down from the deck above. Someone was coming! He cursed quietly, knowing that if he attacked now, he would be discovered before he could consume his prey, and that the alarm would be given. Some spark of self-preservation buried deep in his mind told him that this would not be a good idea, so he padded swiftly back down the corridor, returning the way he had come.

FELIX WOKE SUDDENLY at the sound of wary footsteps on the ladder. He was glad to be woken, for he had been having a nightmare in which a giant rat-like thing stalked ever closer to him down a dark, mist-shrouded tunnel. Doubtless it was a bad dream inspired by the beastmen he had seen today. Sigmar knew, they had been monstrous enough to inspire a lifetime of nightmares.

He looked up to see Varek lowering himself onto the observation deck. He carried his book in one hand and his pen in the other, and he looked a little disappointed to find someone else present, as if he had desired to be alone here.

'Good evening, Felix,' he said, forcing a smile.

'Is it evening?'

'Who can tell,' the dwarf shrugged. 'It's as good a term for it as any in this foul place. The sky is darker and the land is obscured so I suppose it might as well be.'

'Then good evening to you, Varek,' said Felix. 'What are you doing here?'

'I came here to write up my notes. It's difficult to do when you're sharing a cabin with Gotrek and Snorri.'

'I can imagine.' Felix was suddenly glad that his height and the fact that he was a human had qualified him for his own cabin. It was one of only three single rooms on the entire airship, and Borek and Makaisson had the others. 'What were they doing?'

'Gotrek claimed that Snorri had beaten him on a technicality in their last head-butting contest. They were having quite an argument about it. Snorri wanted to have another contest right there and then to settle the matter but I talked them out of it.'

'How?' Felix couldn't imagine this soft-spoken young dwarf talking the pair of Trollslayers out of anything at all.

'I reminded them that it usually takes about three days for the loser to recover from a head-butting bout and that's assuming nothing serious is broken – and if that happened one of them would miss out on our arrival in Karag Dum. Assuming that we would arrive on time, of course. That seemed to do the trick. When I left them they were having a vodka drinking contest instead. Hopefully by the time I get back they'll have knocked themselves out with that instead.'

'I wouldn't bet on it,' Felix said.

Varek smiled sadly.

'Nor would I.'

'Don't mind me,' said Felix. 'I was just taking a nap.' He made to settle back once more.

'Before you do, could I just ask you to go over all the details of today's events. I want to make sure I get it all exactly right.'

'Of course,' Felix said, and began to go over the story once more, with only slight exaggerations.

FELIX WOKE LATER, still in the gunnery chair of the organ gun to find one of the engineers sweeping the decks around him. Yawning and stretching, he pulled himself up and decided to go get some breakfast. As he rose he noticed that there was a small band of mounted warriors directly below them, apparently riding in the same direction as the airship was flying.

'Are they following us?' he asked, knowing it was a foolish question even as he asked it. While he watched, the black-armoured riders had fallen far behind the swiftly-moving airship.

'No,' replied the dwarf, 'but something is surely up. All morning we've been passing over war-bands moving in the same direction. It's almost as if they know where we are going and are moving to intercept us.'

'That isn't possible,' said Felix, but in his secret heart he was unsure. After all who knew what the forces of Chaos were really capable of.

'IT'S GETTING WORSE,' Varek said, continuing to focus the telescope out the window of the command deck. 'There are hundreds more. Now there seems to be more of them ahead of us than there is behind.'

Felix was forced to agree; even with the naked eye it was obvious. All day they had been passing over bands of beastmen, Chaos warriors and other wicked things. The further they travelled, the more frequent the sightings had become. And all of the followers of Darkness were streaming in the same direction the airship was moving in. It was as if a secret signal had been given and an army was being gathered.

'I don't like this at all,' said Felix. 'Can they really know what we're doing? Are they waiting for us?'

'I don't think that is very likely,' Borek said, a little testily. He had slumped back into one of the padded leather command chairs and sat there, stroking his beard meditatively with the fingers of one gnarled hand. 'There is no way they could be aware of our coming. We have no traitors aboard this ship. No one could have known our plans until we set out, and even if they did, they surely could not have sent word faster than we have travelled.'

The old dwarf sounded as if he was trying to convince himself. Felix had no difficulty finding flaws in any of his arguments. Schreiber had known about their goal, as had Straghov and any number of his followers. Sorcery could transmit a message even faster than the airship could fly. More simply still, perhaps the Chaos followers had visionaries in their midst who could foresee the future. It sometimes appalled Felix how quickly and easily he could find the dark side of things.

'And we're assuming they are concerned with us,' Borek continued. 'There is no proof of that either. Perhaps they have their own reasons for gathering along this route.'

'And what could those be?'

'I don't know but I'm sure that if it's the case we will find out soon enough.'

AS THE AIRSHIP flew on, the warbands became larger, as many of the smaller mobs of Chaos worshippers met and banded together to form larger units. In some bands up to a dozen banners could be seen fluttering in the wind.

Grotesque creatures were becoming more common among the creatures below. Felix saw strange warriors, part man, part woman with enormous crab-like claws. They were mounted on loping two-legged creatures with long protruding tongues. As he watched through a telescope from high above, this troop of daemonic cavalry chased down a scattered band of mutants. Their foul steeds shot out their long sticky tongues, grasped their victims and reeled them into their masters' – or mistresses' – claws the way certain jungle lizards were supposed to capture flies.

Odd, brightly coloured creatures whose hideously exaggerated faces appeared to emerge directly from the middle of their torsos capered through the bright desert sands. They waved up at the passing airship as if greeting a long lost kinsman and then clutched their sides, rolling around in insane daemonic mirth.

One enormous black-armoured rider led a pack of twisted hounds across the rocks. His animals had enormous reptilian crests and their skins glowed a bright metallic red. At times Felix felt like he was looking down into scenes dragged from some madman's nightmares, but he could not stop himself from watching all the same.

Ahead of them a range of hills rose out of the desert. As they approached, Felix saw that the foothills were merely outriders of a much larger range of towering peaks, tall as anything in the World's Edge Mountains. These hills shimmered with unnatural colours. And for the first time Felix saw something in the Wastes that resembled vegetation.

A forest of monstrous slimy fungi bloomed on the hillsides. Each of the mighty mushrooms was as large as the tallest tree and its canopy was huge enough to shelter a small village. Each was a slightly different sickly shade – jaundiced yellow, bone white, nausea green – and each rose towards the sky as if fighting with its fellows for every scrap of light and every inch of space. Some of the fungi had multiple caps, each branching from a central stalk. A vile mucous enshrouded the flesh of the fungal trees and dripped poisonously onto the ground below. All suggested something unnatural and evil, a life that should not exist in any sane world.

Here and there one of the mighty fungal trees had fallen – or been deliberately felled – and beastmen and mutants crawled over it, like ants on a rotted log. They consumed the corrupt flesh of the fallen giant and drank its slime. After they ate it, they shouted and fought and engaged in orgies of unspeakable activities, as if the dead thing's substance contained some strange and intoxicating drug.

As the hills rose before Felix's rapt gaze, they became cleaner and devoid of the unnatural vegetation. Instead more ruins became evident. He spied small forts made from little more than accumulated boulders. Intricately crafted castles with walls shod in steel and brass. Palaces carved from the living rock of the hills. There was no rhyme or reason to it. Near every structure lay skeletons and unburied corpses or gallows from which dangled dead beastmen. The smell of burning and death rose from the hillside. This was an area that had obviously seen a lot of fighting but was now deserted, and as they flew on, it became obvious why.

Over the hills warriors moved en masse, flowing like a turbulent stream down into the roads which passed through the valleys, joining the torrent of Chaos worshippers who travelled on the dusty roads. They rode, they limped, they marched, they crawled, they hopped, they flopped obscenely but they all moved – and they all had one destination in mind. There could be no doubt now that all the worshippers of Chaos were heading in the same direction that they were themselves – the distant mountains.

HOURS WENT BY. The airship passed over a flat plain in the shadow of the hills and still the endless flow moved beneath them. In the centre of the plain, Felix could see that four enormous boulders had been carved into monstrous parodies of the human form. At first he had thought it was a trick of the light, a mirage brought on by the odd shape of the rocks and his own tired eyes but after a while he had realised that this was not true. Each of the mighty stones really had been carved into the shape of what he assumed was one of the Dark Gods of Chaos.

As he came closer he began to get some idea of the scale of these monumental statues. Each was loftier than the mooring mast at the Lonely Tower. He had heard that some of the peaks on the elves' Islands of Ulthuan had been carved into enormous statues but this was work that must surely dwarf even that. Some awesome magic had been used to reshape the very bones of the earth into these mocking images, and in a moment of wonder and terror Felix came to some understanding of the true might of the Powers of Chaos.

One of the statues was a huge squatting thing, its sides blotched with boils and cankers. Its leering image spoke of a million years of pestilence and death. Somewhere in the back of his mind, a voice whispered to Felix the name of Nurgle, Daemon God of Plague.

Another was shaped into something bird-headed, with enormous wings enfolded round its body. Eerie and unnatural light played around the head, a crown of mystical energy that transmitted the thought that here was an object sacred to Tzeentch, the Architect of Fate, the Changer of Ways.

The third statue was carved in the shape of a creature not quite man and not quite woman, posed in an attitude at once both lascivious and mocking. Huge caves made blank empty eye sockets. Felix shivered, for somehow he knew this to be a depiction of one of the many aspects of Slaanesh, Lord of Unspeakable Pleasures. He had encountered this Daemon-God's worshippers many times in the past.

The last took the shape of a massive warrior, bat-winged, armed with sword and whip, face masked by a helmet that obscured all features. There was something in the stance that suggested a creature at once shambling and ape-like, but possessed of enormous physical power. This must be Khorne, the Blood God, Lord of the Throne of Skulls. Felix shivered. Khorne's was a name which had inspired terror since the dawn of time.

Around the feet of these titanic effigies a few worshipers prostrated themselves and threw down offerings but most simply saluted and moved on. Felix had given up on any attempt to count the Chaos worshippers. They numbered in the thousands now. It was like watching an army of ants on the march, and the motives of the horde seemed just as incomprehensible and just as threatening. He was only glad that they were marching away from the lands of men, deeper into the Wastes, although he realised that it would take only one order to turn this great army around and send it scything southward, if a powerful enough leader were to arise.

The command deck behind Felix was silent save for the throb of the engines, and Felix knew that all the dwarfs present were thinking the same thoughts as he was. All of them had been overcome by the terrible majesty of the army gathered below them.

The foothills climbed beneath them and now ahead of the airship loomed the true peaks of the range. Beneath them the land looked almost normal, with streams and trees and what might have been goats leaping along the ridges. Was it possible that some parts of the Waste had remained untouched by the warping influence of Chaos? Did some counter-balancing force still strive against its effects? Or was this some trick of the Dark Powers, an innocuous veil drawn over a secret thing even darker and more terrible than anything they had yet witnessed?

Makaisson let out his breath in a long, slow whistle as he pulled levers and turned the great wheel. sending the airship soaring through a long valley which sliced between the brooding black peaks. He had to make constant small adjustments to the controls as he fought against crosswinds and turbulence while threading a path through the winding valley.

The airship turned almost ninety degrees to the right and ahead of them lay a long vale teeming with the followers of Chaos. Wisps of smoke rose from their cooking fires to form a dark cloud that threatened to obscure their vision. Tens of thousands of beastmen looked up at them curiously. Thousands of Chaos warriors were drawn up within a crazy maze of earthworks. The airship droned steadily down the valley towards the deepening darkness that filled its far end.

Enormous chariots pulled by hideous mutant beasts larger than elephants rose above the mass. Here and there some had tumbled down, some had melted, some had simply been smashed as if by a superior force. Huge t-shaped crosses had been placed among the ranks of tents and blockhouses, and each bore a crucified figure. Some were fresh; others had been reduced to skeletons by the carrion birds.

Ahead of them loomed a singularly enormous mountain. Its huge bulk blocked the end of the valley. Its sides were covered in row upon row of broken fortifications. The ground on the mountain's lower slopes was covered by a white plain of bones. The fortifications rose to a citadel atop the mountain's very peak, and it was obvious that a battle had been fought here – and recently, for smoke still rose from burning buildings and black-armoured warriors moved among the corpses of the recently dead.

A tense silence filled the command deck of the *Spirit of Grungni*. All of the dwarfs appeared to be holding their breath in amazement and horror. Eventually Borek spoke and his voice came out in a harsh croak.

'Behold the peak of Karag Dum,' he said.

SIXTEEN
KARAG DUM

'LOOK OUT!' Felix shouted. From amidst the teeming hordes below them, one of the Chaos worshippers – a tall, lean figure robed in black, covered in amulets and wearing a silver helm with curved goat's horns – had raised an ornate staff to point at them. Sizzling energies crackled around the staff's tip and a bolt of blood red lightning leapt from the ground to the airship. His fellow sorcerers gathered to add their power to the attack, and the fury of the assault intensified until the blaze hurt the eye and the roar of the thunder threatened to deafen Felix.

Lightning flashed and crackled all around the *Spirit of Grungni*. The burnt tin stench of ozone filled the air. It was as if they were trapped in the centre of a thunderstorm all of their own. The gondola trembled and shook. The gemmed eyes of the figurehead blazed and Felix felt the amulet on his chest grow warm. Makaisson wrenched the wheel and tugged the altitude lever and they headed skywards towards the low, overhanging clouds.

The airship shivered and bucked like a frightened horse, and Felix feared that their magical protection was going to be overcome. Then, as suddenly as the attack had started, it ceased.

Not a moment too soon, as far as Felix was concerned. He looked down on the encamped Chaos army. It seemed that they had crossed some boundary, come too close and so had been attacked. It seemed possible, therefore, that as long as they kept their distance, they would be allowed to fly above the army unmolested. Perhaps the Chaos worshippers had feared an attack from above, thought Felix. Or, just as likely, they were simply mad.

An appalled silence filled the control room. The dwarfs exchanged shocked glances. Felix crouched down by the window and watched them. Eventually Borek spoke in a low croak.

'This is not what I expected,' he said, and the weight of his years showed in his voice. He shook his head. 'This is not possible.'

Gotrek was pale, though whether with fury or some other suppressed emotion Felix could not tell. 'Does the citadel still stand? Are our people still down there?'

Borek looked up at him with one rheumy eye and shook his head. 'Nothing could withstand the forces of Chaos for two centuries. There can be no one left alive down there.'

Gotrek's knuckles whitened as his grip on his axe tightened. 'Then why is that huge army down there? Why do they lay siege to the dwarfhold? Who are they fighting, if not our kinsfolk?'

'I do not know,' Borek said. 'You saw that army. You saw the devastation in the vale. The dwarfhold could not have withstood such an attack for so long.'

'What if they have? What if there are still dwarfs alive down there? It means we have abandoned our kinfolk to the mercies of Chaos for well nigh two centuries. It means we have forsaken our old treaties of alliance with them. It means our nations have not kept faith.'

Borek picked up his walking stick and tapped its tip on the steel floor. It was the only sound audible save for the hum of the engines. Felix considered their argument. He had to agree with Borek. It seemed hugely unlikely that any citadel could have held out for nearly two hundred years against a siege by the ravaging armies of Chaos, even one held by such tenacious defenders as the dwarfs. Another possible explanation struck him.

'Isn't it possible,' he ventured, 'that Karag Dum fell to the forces of Chaos and some warlord of the Dark Powers took it over and used it as his citadel? Perhaps the Chaos worshippers fight among themselves for possession.'

He saw that all eyes were upon him. On some faces was written understanding, on some disappointment. It struck him that some of the dwarfs had hoped to find their lost kinsfolk down there, Gotrek included.

'That seems the most likely explanation,' Borek said. 'And, if it is true, then there is very little for us to do here. We would be as well to turn this airship around and go home.'

Again Felix sensed disappointment in the control room, this time greater than before. These dwarfs had come a long way, made great sacrifices in order to get here, and now their leader was telling them it might all have been in vain. Even so, the dwarfs all nodded their agreement. Except Gotrek.

'But it is not the only explanation,' the Slayer said. 'We do not know it is the case for certain.'

'True, Gotrek, but what would you have us do?'

'Land someone in the citadel! Conduct the expedition into the depths we came to mount. Find out if any of our people yet live down there.'

'I take it you are volunteering to do this.'

'I am. We can wait until it's dark and then descend on the peak. If I remember your maps there is a secret passage down from the cliff face. I can enter there and make my way down to the Underhalls.'

'Snorri will go too,' said Snorri. 'Can't let Gotrek grab all the glory. Good chance to smash some Chaos warriors as well.'

'I will go too, uncle,' Varek said suddenly. 'I would like to look upon the home of my ancestors.'

'I suppose I'd better go as well. You'll need someone with half a brain down there,' said another voice. Felix was shocked when he recognised it was his own.

'Before we do anything, let us take another look at what is going on below,' said Borek. 'Perhaps then we will have a clearer idea of what is happening.'

THEY TOOK THE airship down to just below cloud level and moved in a wide sweep round the mountain. As they did so, it became obvious that it was surrounded by not just one but four enormous armed camps.

Each camp was dedicated to one of the great Powers of Chaos. Over the nearest fluttered the blood red pennants of Khorne. Over another hung the luminous banners of Tzeentch.

Over the third, the polychromatic flags of Slaanesh pulsed and changed hue. The slime-dripping flags of Nurgle erupted from the pestilent horde at the fourth camp.

As they watched it became obvious that the followers of the powers were wary of each other. Each camp was surrounded by a ditch, not just facing the peak but all around, as if the armies feared attack by each other. Here and there, along the boundaries Felix was sure that he saw sporadic skirmishes being fought between some warriors.

He also saw that these camps were the final destination of all the Chaos worshippers which they had seen out in the deserts. They were arriving from all points of the compass and found their way to one or other of the camps. Felix was willing to bet that they were each seeking the camp of their own faction, and going to swell its ranks.

He supposed there was a certain warped logic to it all – if the four powers were all rivals and fought with each other as much as they did with anyone else. Given the friction that must exist between their followers it made sense to segregate them and minimise tension. Somehow, though, he could not help but feel that he was missing something.

Then, even as he watched from the safety of the airship, he saw the army of Khorne muster along its border with the army of Slaanesh, and, with a mighty roar, fling itself into battle. It was plain these armies were here to fight with each other, as much as they were to besiege Karag Dum.

'We will wait for you for as long as we have food and then we will go,' Borek said solemnly. 'We'll fly high and watch the peak through our telescopes. If you discover anything, make your way back up and fire one of Makaisson's green flares. We will come and get you as quickly as we can.'

Felix nodded and not for the first time checked the flares he had stuck in his belt. They were still there, along with the other equipment the dwarfs had given him: a compass, an ever-burning lantern that used one of their precious glowstones for illumination, several flasks of water, and another of vodka. He had a small sackful of provisions over his shoulder. He wore his mail coat once more and was glad of it.

And not for the first time, too, he asked himself why he was doing this, and once more he discovered that he could not quite formulate a reason. It made much more sense to stick with the airship. At least that way, he could get home even if Gotrek and the others failed. Yet there was more to this than common sense. He and Gotrek had faced countless perils together, and despite the Slayer's quest for death they had always survived. Felix suspected that there was more than luck involved, some kind of destiny even, and that he would have a better chance of escaping alive from the Chaos Wastes in the company of the Slayer than on his own. At least he was trying to convince himself that this was the case.

And at the end of the day there was his oath. He had sworn to follow the Slayer and record his doom, and he suspected that enough of dwarfish culture had rubbed off on him for him to take his promise very seriously. He glanced out of the window. Below them he could see the fires of the Chaos camps, and the shadowy figures which moved around them. Occasionally, too, he could hear the sounds of weapon on weapon as a brawl broke out.

It was night, or what passed for it here in the Wastes. They had waited many hours for the sky to darken and eventually their patience had been rewarded. The airship too was dark, all the lights having been extinguished so as not to give away their position. The engines were being run with minimum power so as to make as little noise as possible. Ahead of them loomed the shadow bulk of the peak. He hoped that Makaisson knew what he was doing, and that they weren't going to smash into the mountain. Intellectually he knew that dwarfs could see much better in the dark than humans, but there was a difference between possessing that knowledge and believing it with all his heart, particularly at a moment like this, when his life was at stake.

'If you discover people still alive and want us to come for you, fire a red flare,' Borek said. 'Understand?'

'I understand,' Felix said. It would have been difficult not to have. Borek had explained it all to them a dozen times during the long wait. The flares were another of Makaisson's inventions, a variant of the basic rocket which would leave a brilliant trail of a chosen hue behind itself.

The airship juddered to a halt. Felix knew that this was their signal to go. Gotrek led the way, swinging himself out of the hatch and down the ladder. Snorri followed him, humming happily to himself. Next came Varek. He paused in the opening and gave Felix a nervous grin and then he, too, vanished through the hatch. He had a sack of bombs strapped to his chest and Makaisson's strange gun slung over his shoulder. Felix wished he owned one of the weapons and knew how to use it, but it was too late to learn now. He took a deep breath, exhaled and let himself out onto the ladder.

The night wind bit into his flesh. It was cold in a way that he would never have expected in the middle of a desert. He told himself to be sensible. They were somewhere far to the north of Kislev. It was bound to be chilly. The ladder swung a little under the weight of the climbers and Felix's stomach lurched.

Sigmar, what am I doing here, he asked himself? How did I end up dangling from a flying machine designed by a maniac, hovering over the sides of a mountain on the slopes of which are camped a great army of thousands of Chaos warriors. Well, if nothing else, he told himself, it will be an interesting death. Then he gathered all his courage and continued the descent.

THE FOUR OF THEM stood on a ledge close to the peak, under the shadow of a protective wall. Felix glanced up to see the ladder being rolled back into the airship, and the vessel lifting skyward once more out of range of the Chaos horde's sorcerers. He strained his ears to see if he could pick up the sound of any sentries giving the alarm. All he could hear was Snorri humming.

'Stop that, please,' he whispered.

'Sure,' Snorri said loudly.

Felix fought down the urge to hit him with his sword.

'This pathway should lead us to the Gate of Eagles,' Varek murmured.

'Then let's get going,' Gotrek said. 'We don't have all night.'

THEY STOPPED by a monstrous statue of an eagle carved in the face of the rock. Gotrek reached down between the talons of its right claw and depressed a hidden switch. A small opening, just large enough for a dwarf to scramble through, opened in its base. They hurried through. Felix heard another switch click and the dim light of outside vanished behind them.

He felt Varek tug at his sleeve. They had already agreed that they would not shine any lights until they knew their way was safe. That way there would be nothing to give them away in the darkness. It was all right for the dwarfs, Felix realised, for they really could see in the dark but this plan left him blind and utterly reliant on them for guidance. Perhaps this had not been such a great plan after all. He reached out with his left hand to feel the cold stone of the wall, and then he followed where Varek led.

'There are many such secret escape routes out,' Varek whispered. 'They were used as sally ports during sieges.'

'What if traitors used them to break into the city,' Felix asked.

'No dwarf would ever do such a thing,' Varek said. Felix could hear genuine shock in the young dwarf's voice that anyone could even suggest such a thing.

'Quiet back there,' Gotrek said. 'You want to attract the attention of every beastman and Chaos thing on the mountain?'

'That's not a bad idea,' said Snorri. There was a noise that sounded suspiciously like Gotrek's fist connecting with Snorri's head, then there was silence.

LURK GRINNED. The pain was over. The long days of sweating and writhing in his makeshift burrow had ended. He no longer felt the pulsing ache in his skull and the wracking agony of every bone in his body being stretched. He had been purified by pain, reshaped by agony. He had been chosen by the Horned Rat, blessed by the Lurker in Unknowable Darkness, the Scurrying Lord of the Pit.

He knew instinctively that he had changed and that these changes were a sign of his master's favour. The warpstone dust had been merely a catalyst, an agent of change that carried the blessing of his god. He was bigger now, too big to fit into his crate, so large he had to hunker down to squeeze through the corridors. And he was strong. His shoulders were as broad as a rat-ogre's. His chest had become a barrel of muscle. His arms were now thicker than his legs once had been and his legs were pillars of pulsing power. He felt like he could bend steel bars with his bare paws and rip through granite with his fangs.

His teeth were much longer and sharper now. His lower canines protruded like tusks and made it difficult for him to keep his mouth properly closed. Saliva dribbled constantly from the corners of his mouth.

His skull was heavier and it felt like the bones had erupted through his cheeks to create a mask of hard armour. Large, ram-like horns had emerged from his forehead. At the time they had caused him a splitting headache but now he could see that it was a mark of the Horned Rat's favour, a sign that he had truly been chosen, a blessing that marked him as different, special, superior. All his life he had known he was better than other Skaven, and now, at last, was the proof.

Look at his tail so long, so sleek, so supple and crowned with four spikes, a veritable mace of bone. Look at his claws – so much longer, so much sharper, each the size of a poniard. He had become a living engine of destruction fuelled by the hatred and hunger burning in his heart. He had nothing to fear from a non-entity like Thanquol. When he returned to Skavenblight it would be in absolute triumph. The Council of Thirteen itself would grovel at his feet. He would lead the assembled armies of skavenkind and crush everything that got in his way. The whole world would tremble and be conquered by the invincible, omnipotent Lurk.

But now he was hungry, and it was time to hunt. He could hear dwarf feet approaching. After listening for a moment, he realised that there was more than one of them. A deep rooted instinct told him that superior numbers were only a good thing when they were on your side. It was not sensible to attack a group of foes. Perhaps, he decided, he would wait a little longer, until there was just the one, and then... then he would reveal his awesome power.

FELIX HEARD THE deep rumble of stone on stone as Gotrek pushed another switch. A gust of foul air passed his face and he guessed that the dwarf had opened another secret door. They moved swiftly forward and Felix heard the opening shift back into place behind them. He was not sure how it was done. He had not heard a second switch being thrown. Perhaps the mechanism was timed. Perhaps there was a pressure plate underfoot. He knew he should wait to ask another time. He might have to find his way back this way on his own, if he became separated from the others.

There was light up ahead, a dim and distant glow. It was subdued and occasionally it faded, only to return to brightness once more. It was not like the light of a torch, more like that of glowstone or a spell. By its faint illumination, he could now see the squat outlines of the dwarfs ahead of him. Gotrek held up a hand to indicate that they should remain where they were and then moved forward silently alone, with a stealth that Felix would not have guessed he was capable of.

He was glad that the Slayer seemed to be taking their mission so seriously. It appeared that his need to learn the fate of the inhabitants of Karag Dum was overriding even his desire for a heroic death. And why not, Felix asked himself? The two were not mutually exclusive. If Gotrek wished to be remembered in dwarfish history, surely there would be no better way than being recalled as the saviour of these lost kinsfolk? Or did he have another, more personal motive? Felix knew he would never dare to ask.

He took another deep breath to calm himself. The air smelled fusty, and there was a hint of rot and something else in it. It was the same sort of scent he remembered in the harpy's lair back in the ziggurat, the rank odour of Chaos beasts. He heard Snorri sniffing and knew that the hammer-wielding Slayer had noticed it too.

Gotrek had reached the junction ahead and beckoned for them to follow. They hastened forward until they reached the opening and emerged into another long corridor. The flickering light came from glowgems set in the ceiling. Some had been smashed, others removed. Those which had been left behind were cracked and worked only intermittently, sending shadows skittering away into the gloom.

The stonework reminded Felix of the dwarf architecture he had marvelled at in Karak Eight Peaks. The walls were supported by hewn blocks of basalt. Massive arches supported the high, arching roof. Each was a work of art. The nearest were carved with the likeness of two kneeling dwarfs, facing each other across the corridor, lifting the roof on their backs.

They must have been beautiful when they were made but they had been vandalised. The faces had been chipped off and parts of the stonework had been scored with blades. It angered Felix that someone could have defaced something into which an artist had placed so much labour. As they crept down the corridor, he saw that the destruction was no isolated incident. Every last arch had been ruined in some way. Many had been blackened by fire or scorched by spells. Some looked as if they had been eaten away by acid.

Slowly it dawned on Felix that he was not looking at mere wanton vandalism, but rather the evidence of a battle. A bitter conflict had been fought out in this corridor using all manner of weapons, natural and supernatural. They started to pass skeletons, still clad in armour and clutching weapons in their bony fingers. Some belonged to dwarfs, some to hideously mutated beastmen.

'Well, we know that the followers of Chaos got in,' Varek murmured.

'Aye, and were met with cold steel by stout-hearted dwarfs,' said Gotrek.

'But are any of them left alive now?' Felix muttered.

THE CORRIDORS carried them deeper and deeper into the depths. Some sloped downwards. Others brought them to steep stairwells. Everywhere there were signs of old battles. Mummified corpses lay everywhere. An aura of evil brooded over everything. Somewhere in the depths lurked a terrible presence. Felix fought hard to control the fear which had started to gnaw at him, the certainty that – round the next bend or at the bottom of the next flight of stairs – they were going to encounter something malign, supernatural and terrible.

Gotrek paused in one long hall, lined by titanic statues. Bodies were strewn everywhere but none of them belonged to dwarfs. All were of beastmen or Chaos warriors. One pair of bodies lay with swords through each other's ribs. They had killed each other with simultaneous strokes.

Gotrek gazed down on them thoughtfully. 'Here there was a blood-letting between the foul ones.'

'Perhaps they fell out over the division of spoils.'

'So where is the treasure, Felix?' Varek asked.

'Carried away by the victors?' Felix replied. He looked closer at the corpses and noticed that their insignia were different.

'Perhaps they followed different powers or rival warlords. Perhaps there was some kind of squabble between the victors.'

'Perhaps,' said Gotrek.

'Why is it so quiet here?' Felix asked. 'There was an entire army outside, but we have seen no evidence of anyone since we got in here.'

Gotrek laughed. 'This is one of the ancient dwarfholds, manling. It extends for leagues under the earth. There are hundreds of levels. The total length of the corridors and halls must come to thousands of leagues. You could lose an army the size of the one outside in a small corner of this city.'

'Then how are we going to find any survivors which might be here?'

'If any dwarf lives on down here, there are certain places where they will be, and we are heading there,' Varek said.

With that, they pushed on into the darkness.

IN MANY MORE places it was clear that the battles had not been fought between dwarfs and Chaos worshippers but amongst the followers of the Dark Powers themselves. Only occasionally did they come across signs that dwarfs had been involved in any of the warfare. It became increasingly evident from the bodies they found that there had been a war between the forces of Chaos. Here they found signs that the warriors of Slaanesh had fought against the berserk followers of Khorne. There they found evidence that the worshipers of Tzeentch had struggled with the plague-ridden servants of Nurgle. In one large hall, they came across a place where the followers of all four powers had fallen out and slaughtered each other.

Felix found the gloom oppressive. It was depressing to wander through these endless, battle-scarred corridors and find the remains of old battles. He thought of that vast army camped outside. Who did they represent? What were they waiting for? It seemed senseless. He shrugged. Then again, why did that surprise him? The followers of Chaos were not sane as he measured sanity. Perhaps they fought for the unknowable amusement of their Dark Gods. Perhaps they fought for the amusement of the evil thing he sensed down here. Perhaps they, too, were only being allowed to proceed by some whim of whatever thing lurked down here. He wondered if the others felt this same uneasy sense of presence. He could not find the courage to ask them.

As they passed through gallery after echoing gallery, and chamber after high-ceilinged chamber, it became obvious that Gotrek was right. There was certainly room enough in here to house a dozen armies even if they were all the size of the forces gathered outside. He wondered what it must have been like to dwell here in an underground city like this in its heyday. Even before the followers of Chaos came, it must have been near-empty, for he knew the dwarfs were a dying race and had been so for millennia. Still, there must have been a time when these streets were filled with dwarfs buying and selling, laughing and crying, loving and living and going about their daily business. Now it seemed like a tomb, and the dead bodies of interlopers everywhere seemed like a desecration.

GOTREK KNELT BESIDE the goat-headed corpse before which he had suddenly paused. It was not like the others they had seen – it was still warm! Flesh still clung to its bones. Warm black blood formed a pool under it. Nearby lay other beastmen, all just as dead.

Felix squatted for a better look. In life the beastman had not been pretty, and death had not improved its looks. It had the great head of a goat and the body of a man. Its furry legs ended in hooves. Its brow had been branded with mark of Khorne. Its strange liquid eyes were glazed in death. They stared blankly up at the towering ceiling high overhead. A crossbow shaft protruded from its chest; another stuck out from its gut. One hand still clutched at the missiles which had killed it. The hand was beautifully formed, more like that of a monk than a monster, and Felix thought of how incongruous it looked on that bestial form. The beast stank of wet fur and the excrement and urine that it had released when it died.

Gotrek tugged at one of the crossbow bolts. It came free with a hideous sucking sound and a thin trickle of black blood oozed forth from where it had been. Gotrek turned the missile back and forth in his hand, studying it closely with his one good eye. Felix could not see what fascinated him so much about it. It looked well made but hardly any different from any other crossbow bolt he had seen.

'This is a dwarf weapon,' Gotrek said eventually, and there was something which might even have been triumph in his voice.

'How can you tell?' Felix asked.

'Look at the manufacture, manling. No human ever made a point that fitted so well, or feathered a bolt so perfectly. Also, there are dwarf runes on the tip.'

'So you're saying that these beastmen were killed by dwarfs?'

Gotrek shrugged and looked away. 'Maybe.'

'Perhaps the beastmen found one of the armouries,' Varek suggested tentatively. He plainly didn't want to contradict Gotrek, and Felix could see that he hoped he was wrong. He wanted for there to be dwarfs down here and still fighting.

'When have you ever seen a beastman armed with a crossbow?' Gotrek asked.

'It might have been a dark warrior.'

'Or such a warrior armed that way, for that matter?'

It was a fair point. In all of his encounters with the followers of the Dark Powers, Felix had never met one which used such a sophisticated weapon. Of course, that didn't mean there couldn't be a first time. He decided to keep that thought to himself. Instead he asked: 'How will we find these dwarfs then?'

'Maybe Snorri should ask those beastmen,' Snorri suggested from behind them.

Felix's heart skipped a beat when he heard Snorri's words. He turned to look in the direction that the Slayer had indicated. Sure enough there stood a band of at least twenty beastmen. For a moment, they looked just as surprised as Felix but then they recovered from their shock and raised their spears for the attack.

'Or maybe we should just kill them,' Gotrek said, lowering his head and charging.

'No! Don't!' shouted Felix – but already it was too late. Varek had started to turn the crank on his strange looking gun. A hail of bullets tore into the beastmen, killing two and dropping another pair. Howling with rage and frothing with berserk fury, the beastmen charged forward. Felix knew there was nothing for it now but to fight and most likely die in a futile skirmish with the Chaos worshippers. Snorri had obviously decided the same, for he had raised his weapons and begun to move forward as well. With the two Slayers blocking his line of sight, Varek started to move to a new position, hoping to out-flank the beastmen and pour fire into the side of their formation.

Felix drew his blade and raced forward to aid Gotrek and Snorri. Before he could get into action, before the two sides had closed to within twenty strides of each other, a new hail of crossbow bolts hurtled out of the dark and scythed into the beastmen. The missiles fell like a dark rain. Felix saw one dog-headed monstrosity tumble with a bolt through its eye, tears of blood running down its cheek. Its chest was pin-cushioned with bolts even as it dropped. Another clutched its heart and fell, to be trampled below the hooves of its brethren. The beastmen's rush faltered as more and more of them fell. The survivors halted and looked around, desperately trying to see where the attack was coming from.

Gotrek, Snorri and Felix crashed into them and went through their line like an axe through rotting wood. Felix felt a shock run up his arm from the impact, then something warm and sticky was running over his hands. He pulled his blade free, kicked his chosen beastman to the ground and stabbed another. His sword took the surprised beastman in the shoulder, glanced up and lopped off an ear. Not waiting to draw his weapon back, he smashed the pommel into his foe's face and felt teeth break in its mouth. The beastman bellowed in pain, before Felix clubbed it down and stabbed it through the heart.

Almost before it had begun, the fight was over. Overwhelmed by the fury of their foes, the last surviving beastmen turned and fled. Felix could see that Gotrek had slaughtered four of them; their sliced remains lay at his feet. Snorri was jumping up and down on a corpse, happy as a child playing in a sandpit. A burst from Varek's gun chopped down the surviving beastmen even as they fled.

Felix looked around, panting more with reaction to the sudden short combat than from the effort. He wanted to see whoever it was who had aided them and thank them.

'Be very still!' said a deep, guttural voice. 'You are inches away from death.'

SEVENTEEN
THE LAST DWARFS

FELIX FROZE. He tried not even to blink his eyes, let alone breathe. He had no doubts that whoever was lurking in the shadows meant what they said, and he had no desire to find his body bristling with crossbow bolts.

'Are you dwarfs?' Varek asked, with what Felix thought was more curiosity than common sense.

'Aye, that we are. The question is: what are you?'

A massively broad-shouldered dwarf strode into view in front of them. He was garbed in leather armour, huge metal shoulder pads protected his upper torso. A winged helm with cheekguards shielded his face. Slung over his shoulder he carried a crossbow. A heavy warhammer dangled from a loop on his belt. He removed the helmet to peer at them and Felix could see that his face was craggy and his eyes were feverishly bright. His beard was long and black shot through with silver. There was an unnatural leanness about his face such as Felix had never seen in a dwarf before.

He sauntered around the four of them and inspected them with a casual air that was almost insulting. Felix could tell that Gotrek and Snorri had their tempers barely under control and if something was not done soon, murderous violence would ensue.

'Two of you look like Slayers,' the newcomer said. 'One of you has the look of Grungni's folk. The other, the human, must die.'

Almost before Felix realised that the dwarf meant him, the newcomer had unslung his crossbow and pointed it directly at his chest. Felix found himself staring at the glittering point of a crossbow bolt. As if in slow motion he saw the stranger's finger begin to squeeze the trigger. He knew he could never throw himself aside in time but his muscles tensed for the attempt.

'Wait,' Gotrek said softly and there was such a note of command in his voice that the newcomer froze. 'If you harm the manling, you will surely die.'

The other dwarf laughed harshly. 'Those are brave words for one who is no position to back them up. Tell me why should I spare him?'

'Because he is a Dwarf Friend and a Rememberer, and if you kill him your name will live long in infamy and will be recorded in the Book of Grudges as a fool and a coward.'

'Who are you to speak of the Great Book?'

'I am Gotrek, son of Gurni, and if you cross me in this matter I will be your death.' There was cold certainty in the Slayer's voice that commanded belief. Gotrek added something in dwarfish, which caused the newcomer's face to flush and his eyes to widen.

'So you speak the Old Tongue,' he said.

Felix heard a shocked murmur from around the hall, and suddenly realised how many other dwarfs were watching them. It seemed inconceivable that such a large force could have moved through the tunnels with such stealth. He risked glancing around and saw that several score of lean, weary looking dwarfs had emerged from the gloom. All of them had weapons pointed at the party, and seemed prepared to use them. He could see that their wargear all had the same look, as of something that had been patched and reused many times over.

A brief spirited debate followed in dwarfish between Gotrek and the newcomers. Felix looked over at Varek. 'What is being said?'

'These dwarfs think that we are agents of Chaos. They wanted to kill us. Gotrek has told them that we come from outside and that we can help them. Some of them don't believe it and say it is a trick. Their leader says that he cannot risk killing us and that it is a matter for his father, the king himself, to decide.'

To Felix this seemed like a very bald summary of what was obviously an impassioned debate. Voices were being raised. Harsh guttural oaths were being sworn. Both Gotrek and the dwarfish leader had spat on the ground in front of each other's feet. It was an odd sensation to know that his very life hung in the balance and that he could neither say nor do anything to influence the decision. He was reminded of being on the airship during the great warpstorm. All he could do now was remind himself that they had survived that, and might survive this.

Varek continued to mutter: 'It is only the fact that we speak the Old Tongue which keeps them from killing us out of hand. They do not want to believe that any follower of Chaos could have learned it. Certainly no dwarf would teach them.'

'That's reassuring to know,' said Felix.

The argument ended. The dwarf leader turned and spoke to Felix in strongly-accented Reikspiel.

'I do not know if this tale of flying ships and other wonders is true. I only know that this is too grave a matter for me to decide. Your fate is in the hands of the king, and he will pass judgement on you.'

'I still say it's a trick, Hargrim,' said one of the other dwarfs, an old, miserable-looking fellow with deep set eyes and a beard of pure grey. 'We know that the world outside is ruled by Chaos. There are no other dwarfholds left. We should kill these interlopers, not lead them deeper into our realm.'

'You have had your say, Torvald, and my decision stands until the king himself overturns it. If the world has not been overrun by the forces of Chaos, this is indeed momentous news. It may be that we are not the last dwarfs.'

'Aye, Hargrim, and it may be that we are fools and dupes of the Dark Powers. But as you say, you are our captain and on your head be it. There will be time enough to kill these outsiders soon, if they prove false.'

'The king will know,' Hargrim said. 'Come! Let us go. We have wasted enough time and I would not want to be caught in these halls if the Terror comes. Bind them and take their weapons.'

A group of dwarfs broke away from the main body and moved towards them. As they did so, Gotrek stepped forward menacingly.

'You will take this axe from my cold, dead hands,' he said softly and with such menace in his voice that the dwarfs froze on the spot.

'That can be arranged, stranger,' Hargrim said just as quietly. Gotrek raised his axe and the runes on the blade flashed in the dim light. The closest dwarfs gasped.

'He bears the weapon of power!' Torvald gasped, and his voice held horror and wonder. 'It is the Prophesy. Those are the Great Runes. The Terror has returned and the axe of our ancestors has come back to us. The Last Days are upon us.'

A look of shock once more passed over Hargrim's face and he advanced towards Gotrek, his eyes fixed on the blade of the axe. As he read them, a great look of wonder appeared in his eyes.

'Where did you get this blade?' the dwarfish captain asked, then added something in dwarfish.

'I found it in a cave in the Chaos Wastes many years ago,' Gotrek replied slowly in Reikspiel. He appeared to be considering whether he should say more, then thought better of it.

'If you are truly a dwarf then you are favoured by the Ancestor Gods,' Hargrim said. 'For that is a mighty weapon.'

Gotrek grinned nastily and scratched one of the Trollslayer tattoos on his shaven head meaningfully. 'If the gods favour me, they have shown no great sign of it,' he said dryly.

'Be that as it may, such a weapon does not find its way into anyone's hands by chance. You may keep your weapons for now, until the king declares differently.'

Hargrim looked at Gotrek for a long time, and what might have been a thin smile creased his lips. 'It may be as Torvald says, Gotrek Gurnisson. It may be your coming was foretold. The king and his priests will know.'

He turned to his troops. 'Come. We have far to go before we can rest, and we do not want to be caught abroad while the Terror stalks the Underhalls.'

He glanced back at them over his shoulder. 'Come with us,' he said. The four comrades moved into place behind him and marched off into the gloom.

'We will rest here,' Hargrim said, holding up his hand to indicate that they should halt. At first Felix had no idea why the dwarf captain had chosen this spot. It seemed to be just another ruined hallway, like so many others they had passed through. Eventually, though, he noticed that there was a rune carved low in the corner of the wall, and a jet of water sprayed from the wall into a large cistern. This, at least, would be a place where they could drink.

Hargrim barked an order to one of his warriors and the dwarf moved forward. He produced a stone from his leather satchel and dipped it in the water. For a few moments, he stared into the cup and then nodded his head.

'The water is clear, captain,' he said.

Hargrim noticed Felix's curious glance. 'Sometimes the outsiders poison the wells. Sometimes it contains Chaos stuff that causes madness and mutation. Mikal's runestone contains old enchantments that warn of such things.'

'A useful thing to have,' Felix said.

'No. An essential thing to have. Without it, sooner or later, we would all die.'

'What is this Prophesy of which you spoke?' Felix asked, determined to at least try and get an answer.

'It does not concern you,' Hargrim said bluntly. 'It is for the king to test its truth. Best get some rest while you still may.'

Wearily, the dwarfs threw themselves down to rest, except for four sentries who took up positions at each entrance to the room. Felix noted with approval the four exits from this chamber, so hopefully if danger threatened from any direction they would always have a line of retreat. He walked over and sat down beside Gotrek, Snorri and Varek.

All three of his companions seemed strangely elated. Felix thought he understood why – they had found their lost kinsfolk. There were still dwarfs alive in the Underhalls of Karag Dum. In defiance of all probability, a few still lived, even after two hundred years of isolation in the Chaos Wastes.

He lay on his back and stared at the ceiling, thinking of the journey they had made to get to this isolated place. It had not been easy. They had made their way further and further into the labyrinth of tunnels beneath Karag Dum. During the trip Felix had counted the number of dwarfs around him; there were nearly fifty. All of them wore leather armour and were lightly armed and armoured, very unlike the traditional dwarfish warriors he knew of. It seemed they travelled light and quickly through the halls of what once had been their city, and relied more on stealth and surprise for victory than on the strength of their arms. Tunnel fighters, Varek had called them.

As they travelled further, Felix came to understand why they were so lightly armoured. They passed through areas where the presence of Chaos was evident and signs of open war between the powers were visible all around. It looked like an insane and ferocious struggle was being fought here in the ruins of the dwarf city. He had asked Hargrim about this, but the dwarf had not replied. There were mysteries here that was clear. He just needed to find someone who could explain them to him.

Well, there was little sense in worrying about it now. He lay back and stared at the ceiling, wondering what Ulrika was doing now. In moments, he was asleep. the last thing he heard was the scratching of a pen, as Varek recorded the day's events in his book.

AN EERIE HOWLING woke Felix from his sleep. It echoed down the great hallways and had penetrated his dreams, jerking him awake. There was something unnatural about the noise, something that evoked primal terrors. The mere sound of it sent shivers of fear running down his spine, and made his legs feel weak.

All around him the dwarfs had come awake. He could hear the clamour as they reached for their weapons. He glanced around and saw his fear was echoed on every face, save Gotrek and Snorri's.

'What is it?' he asked. 'The Terror?'

'No,' Hargrim said. 'It is the hounds.'

'What are they?' Varek asked.

'You will soon see,' Hargrim said. He turned and spoke to his followers. 'I want ten volunteers to hold the hounds off, while the rest of us try to win clear.'

It was obvious from the expressions on their faces that the dwarfs thought he was asking for volunteers for a suicide mission. Still, more than twenty of them stepped forward.

'I will stay,' Gotrek said.

'Snorri too,' said Snorri.

'You cannot. I must get you away. King Thangrim must hear your story.'

'It might be too late for that,' Felix said glancing over his shoulder at the northernmost entrance. An enormous beast had leapt through the entrance. Before anyone could react, it ripped off the nearest sentry's arm with a single snap of its jaws and pulled another to the ground and disembowelled him with its claws. The beast moved so swiftly, with almost supernatural grace, that Felix was barely able to follow its actions.

Through the doorway several more huge beasts bounded. They resembled monstrous dogs with strange reptilian ruffles around their heads and great iron collars around their necks. Their flesh glistened, the colour of blood. Each was bigger than a man. One of them opened its mouth and bayed. As it did so, its mouth distended widely like that of a snake. It looked like it could take off a man's head with a single bite. Something about the daemonic creature made Felix want to turn and flee, screaming for help. He forced himself to stand his ground. He knew that if he ran the beast would simply overtake him and rend his flesh as it had the sentries'.

'Flesh hounds of Khorne,' he heard Varek gasp. 'I thought they were only legends.'

'Fire at will,' Hargrim ordered. A hail of crossbow bolts hurtled towards the ravenous beasts. They opened their mouths and bayed mockingly. Most of the bolts simply ricocheted off their flesh and fell to the floor. As far as Felix could see only one had bit home. Varek fired and his bullets had no more effect than the crossbows. The hounds bounded forward, loping with a deceptively long easy stride which covered the ground faster than a horse could run.

'Stand back,' Gotrek said and paced out to meet them. None of the dwarfs disobeyed. Felix could tell that they were just as affected by the creatures' supernatural aura as he was. Only Gotrek showed no sign of dismay. Felix noticed that the runes along his axe blade were glowing brighter than he had ever seen them do before. Even so, Felix wondered whether the Slayer would survive. The creatures were so fast and strong. They were upon him almost before he had a chance to realise it. Their huge jaws widened. Their metallic teeth glistened. Their triumphant baying reached a crescendo loud enough to wake the dead.

Gotrek's axe flashed forward like a thunderbolt. The first hound's armoured skin smoked and burned where the blade touched. The beast seemed almost to explode as the axe swept though it, cutting it in two, sending innards erupting all over the floor. The Slayer's next stroke impacted on a second hound's collar. Sparks flew as metal met metal. There was a hideous grating screech. The runes on Gotrek's axe glowed as bright as red-hot coals and the collar gave way. The flesh hound's head and neck parted company. The corpse flopped to the ground, molten ichor spilling out onto the floor. Another stroke cleaved a third flesh hound down the middle lengthwise, revealing skeleton and spine and ruptured organs.

Surprised by the fury of the Slayer's attack, the remaining pack pulled back, snarling like wolves at bay. Then, with an eerie intelligence, they returned to the fray. Two flesh hounds attacked the Slayer simultaneously, one from each side. Gotrek dashed one's brains out with the axe and caught the other by the throat even as it leapt. Almost without effort the dwarf held the monstrous creature at arm's length, then he lifted it so high that its hind limbs scrabbled for purchase on empty air. He dropped it. Before it had touched the ground he has smashed through its ribs with the axe.

The last beast had circled right behind the Slayer and was about to leap on his back. 'Look out!' yelled Felix but Snorri had already tossed his axe. It bounced from the creature's shoulder but the force of the blow distracted the flesh hound. It gathered its legs beneath it for the spring but even as it took to the air, Gotrek half turned and sent his axe slashing through a bloody arc which crunched through the creature's ribcage and ended in its stomach. The force of the blow flattened the flesh hound into the ground. Gotrek stomped on its neck. There was a hideous sound of grinding vertebrae and then the axe fell once more, ending the monster's unnatural life.

The corpses of the Chaos creatures started to bubble where they lay. For a moment flesh and bone melted and ran, evaporating like boiling water. Even as Felix watched, they turned into wisps of foul looking vapour which rose towards the ceiling, then disappeared. It was like they had never been there.

For a moment there was silence, and then the dwarfs burst into cheering and applause. After a few moments they seemed to remember who they were applauding and fell silent.

'If ever I doubted that was the Axe of Valek, I do so no longer. That was a fight worthy of King Thangrim himself,' Hargrim said.

'It was easy,' Gotrek said and spat upon the floor.

'We'd best be moving,' Hargrim said. 'If the hounds were here, their foul master may be near, and however mighty you are, Gotrek Gurnisson, against that you cannot prevail.'

'Bring it on and we'll see.'

'No! Now more than ever I must bring you before the king. He must hear your tale.'

After the fight with the flesh hounds, Felix noticed a change in the dwarfs' attitude. They seemed to be more accepting of the four comrades, and less suspicious. Even old Torvald contented himself with only an occasional suspicious glance in their direction. They marched on through the endless silent corridors and even Felix could tell that they were descending all the time now. He wondered how long this could continue. After several more hours it seemed to him that they would keep going down until they reached the world's fiery heart but it was not to be.

Instead they stopped in the middle of a long and seemingly featureless corridor. While his troops shielded him from view Hargrim manipulated a hidden switch which opened a small secret doorway. An opening appeared in the wall where none had been before. The dwarf gestured for four comrades to enter, his face stern.

'Tread very carefully now. You are on sacred ground and we will kill you at the first sign of treachery.'

EIGHTEEN
FIREBEARD

WARILY, FELIX STEPPED through the entrance. This corridor seemed no different from the rest, save that the glowstones all functioned and the air smelled slightly cleaner. The rest of the war-band hastily pushed in behind and the door swung shut behind them. Felix noticed that the dwarfs of Karag Dum relaxed visibly; conversely, Gotrek, Snorri and Varek appeared more excited. He could not tell why. Perhaps because they felt they were getting closer to their goal. It was not a feeling he shared. The long trek through the Underhalls had made him tense and nervous and he just wanted to find a place to lie down and rest.

This new corridor led into a winding maze of passageways. Every now and again Hargrim stopped and pressed a panel in the wall. He gave no explanation as to why, he simply did it and moved on. Felix looked at Varek to see if the young dwarf could tell him what was happening.

'Deadfalls. Pit traps. Defensive works of some sort, most likely,' the dwarf said quietly, but was silenced by a nasty look from their guardians.

They passed maybe a dozen sentries at their posts, all of whom looked amazed at the sight of strangers from the outside world. Eventually they entered a monstrously long hall which was plainly inhabited by the dwarfs. This was a huge place with many exits. A well had been sunk deep into the floor in the far end of the chamber. The ceiling was low, with none of the vaulting of the magnificent halls they had passed through en route. A forest of enormous squat pillars propped up the roof. On each pillar was inscribed a strange symbol which hurt Felix's eye when he tried to read it.

'Runes of Concealment,' Varek breathed from beside him. 'No wonder this place has survived so long.'

'What's that?' Felix said.

'These runes protect the halls from magical seekings, just as the concealed entrances protect it from normal sight. This place would be all but impossible for one who was not a dwarf to find unaided.'

Felix could see hooded and cowled dwarf women working at their chores. A few priests strode backwards and forwards, speaking words of comfort and reassurance, patting heads, invoking blessings. There were many warriors, a good number of whom were crippled. Some had hooks. Some stumped around on the wooden legs. Some had bandages over their eyes indicating that they were blind. Felix had never seen so many maimed people together in one place before, not even on the beggar-filled streets of Altdorf. It certainly looked like these people had come out on the losing end of a war. Nowhere did he see any children in evidence.

'So few,' Varek muttered. 'This was once a great city.'

'Welcome to the Hall of the Well. Wait here,' Hargrim said. 'I will bring news of your coming to the king.'

The captain strode off through a huge archway and vanished somewhere into the recesses of the city. Many of those who had been working stopped and stared frankly at them. A few of the crippled beggars came over. One reached out and touched Felix disbelievingly.

'You are the first human ever to set foot in this citadel,' he croaked.

'I am honoured.'

'Ha! You may soon be dead,' the crippled warrior said and turned away. The rest of the crowd moved in. One of the cowled women asked a question in dwarfish. Varek responded. The crowd emitted a collective gasp. One of the women burst into tears.

'They asked where we had come from,' said Varek in answer to Felix's unspoken question. 'I told them we had come from across the Wastes, from the kingdom of the dwarfs.'

'I don't believe you,' said another greybeard, and turned and stalked away. It looked like there were tears in his eyes. As they waited, the crowd did not disperse. It surrounded them and stared until Hargrim returned, accompanied by a group of fully armoured warriors, each of whom carried a rune-engraved weapon. The eldritch symbols burned with a mystic light. Felix knew enough about dwarfs by now to tell that these were powerful magical weapons. These longbeards were the best equipped dwarfs Felix had seen since entering Karag Dum. They marched with a precision that would have shamed the Imperial Guard in Altdorf. Their armour gleamed, and they moved with pride and discipline.

'The king will see you,' Hargrim said. 'Now you will be judged.'

'So we are to meet the legendary Thangrim Firebeard after all,' Varek said. 'Who would have thought it?'

Gotrek laughed nastily.

'I have never seen so many rune weapons,' Varek murmured to Felix. 'Every one of those warriors carries one.'

'We collected them from the dead,' Hargrim said coldly. 'There have been so many dead heroes here.'

King Thangrim's hall was vast. Huge statues of dwarf kings stood like sentries against each wall. More of the heavily armoured dwarf warriors stood immobile between the statues. The four newcomers were surrounded by an escort of the king's guard. They were taking no chances of this being an assassination attempt. Their weapons were drawn, and they looked as if they knew how to use them.

A raised dais dominated the far end of the chamber. On the dais was a throne bearing a powerful and majestic figure wearing long robes over heavy armour. Two priests flanked the king. One was a priestess of Valaya. Felix could tell that by the fact that she carried a sacred book. The other was armoured and carried an axe, and Felix wondered if he was a priest of Grimnir, the warrior god.

As they came closer to the dais Felix got a better look at the dwarfish king. He was old, as old as Borek, but there was nothing feeble about him. He looked like an aged oak, gnarled but still strong. The flesh had fallen from his arms but still there were massive knots of muscle there, and his shoulders were broader even than Snorri's. His hair was long and red, although striped through with white. His beard reached almost to the floor and it, too, was white in places. Piercing eyes glittered in deep-set sockets. Felix knew that this dwarf might be ancient but his mind was still keen.

The weapon that sat upon the king's knees drew Felix's attention. It was a massive hammer, with a short handle. Runes had been cut into the head and something about them compelled the eye to look. He knew without being told that this was a weapon of awesome power, the legendary Hammer of Fate, which they had come all this way to find.

The guard parted in front of them to leave a path leading only to the throne. The four comrades advanced. Varek went down on one knee, making florid and elaborate gestures with his right hand. Gotrek and Snorri lounged arrogantly beside him, making no sign of obeisance. Felix decided to err on the side of caution; he bowed low, then knelt beside Varek.

'You are certainly impertinent enough to be Slayers,' said the king. His voice was rich and deep and surprisingly youthful coming from that ancient throat. He laughed and his mirth boomed out through the chamber. 'I can almost believe that the cock and bull story you told Hargrim is true.'

'No one calls me a liar and lives,' Gotrek said. The flat menace in his voice caused the guards to raise their weapons in readiness.

The king raised a mocking eyebrow. 'And few indeed threaten me in my own throne room and live. Still I ask your forgiveness, Slayer, if that is what you be. We are surrounded by the servants of the Dark Powers. Suspicion is only wisdom under such circumstances. And you must admit that we have cause to be suspicious.'

'That you have,' Gotrek admitted.

'You have come to us claiming that you have voyaged here from the world beyond our walls. I would hear your tale from your own lips before I pass judgement. Tell it to me.'

'I claim more than that,' Varek said suddenly. 'I claim kinship with the folk of Karag Dum. My father was Varig. My uncle was Borek, whom you sent out into the world to seek aid.'

King Thangrim smiled cynically. 'If what you say is true it took a long time for Borek to send aid, and you do not represent much of an army. Still, tell your tale.'

The king listened attentively while Varek spoke, stopping occasionally to ask confirmation from Gotrek. He told the tale simply and well, and Felix was astonished at the power of his memory. He also noticed that as the dwarfs spoke the priestess of Valaya's eyes never left them, and he remembered that the priestesses were supposed to have the gift of knowing the truth. At the end of the tale, the king turned to the priestess.

'Well,' he said.

'They speak true,' she replied. There was an audible gasp from the warriors in the chamber. The king raised his hand and scratched his chin through his fine long beard. He considered them for a moment and then smiled grimly.

'Now tell me, Slayer, how you came by the Axe of Valek,' said the king.

Gotrek's answering smile was as grim as Thangrim's. 'Its owner had no use for it, being dead, so I took it. Do you have a claim upon it?'

'The person who carried that blade from here was my son, Morekai. He sought to cross the Wastes and find out if anyone still lived there.'

'Then he is dead, Thangrim Firebeard. His corpse lay in a cave on the edges of the Wastes. It lay surrounded by the bodies of twenty slain beastmen.'

'There was no one with him? He left here with twenty sworn companions.'

'There was only one dwarf. I buried him according to the ancient rites, and being in need of a weapon at the time, I took this one. If it is yours, I will return it to you.'

The old king looked down and grief entered his eyes. When he spoke again he sounded as old as he looked. 'So he died alone at the end.'

'He died a hero's death,' Gotrek said. 'He paved his road to the Iron Halls with the bones of his foes.'

Thangrim looked up once more and his smile was almost grateful. 'Keep the blade, Slayer. Such a weapon is not owned. It has its own doom, and it shapes the destiny of its wielder. If it is in your hands now, it is there for a reason.'

'As you say,' Gotrek said.

'And you have given me much to think on,' Thangrim said wearily. 'And my apologies for doubting you. Go now. Rest. We will talk again later.'

'Prepare apartments for our guests,' he shouted. 'And feed them of our finest.'

Felix could not help but notice that there was a note of bitter irony in the king's voice.

FELIX STARED AT the fish suspiciously. It was large and it looked well-cooked, yet there was something odd about it. After a few moment's consideration he realised that it had no eyes. The meat smelled good and everyone else was eating it, yet he kept thinking of the things he had seen in the Wastes, of the mutants and beastmen, and of all the things he had been told about warpstone dust. He just could not bring himself to eat a mutant fish, and he knew there was good reason for this.

By all accounts it was possible for mutation to be passed on through eating mutated food. It was said that the worst mutants were always cannibals who fed on other mutants. He had no desire to put this theory of mutation being contagious to the test.

'It's blindfish, manling,' said Gotrek from across the table. Felix realised that the Slayer must have seen the look on his face and understood what was going through his mind. 'It is naturally this way. Dwarfs have feasted on it since long before the coming of the Darkness. You can eat it.'

'It's a delicacy, actually,' Varek added. 'In the dwarfholds we breed them. They dwell in the deep cisterns. We feed them on mushrooms and insects.'

Somehow this knowledge did not make the fish seem any more appetising. Unaware of the effect he was having, Varek continued to speak. 'They live in darkness. Some loremasters think that is why they have no eyes. They don't need them. Try some.'

Felix speared some on his knife and lifted the flesh up for examination. It was white and tender looking and when he tried it, it was delicious. He said so.

'It can be monotonous,' said Hargrim, who was sat on the other side of him. 'We live on mushrooms and bugs and blind-fish. There are times when I wish I could have something different.'

Felix dug into his pack and produced a strip of beef jerky. Hargrim looked at it just as suspiciously as Felix had inspected the fish. 'Try some,' Felix said.

Hargrim took some and began to chew. Eventually he managed to swallow. 'Interesting,' he pronounced carefully.

Snorri laughed. 'Now the blindfish doesn't taste so bad after all, does it? Here try some of this to wash it down.'

Snorri handed over a flask of Kislevite vodka. Hargrim swigged it down. For a moment, he looked like he might actually cough but then he recovered and smacked his lips and took some more. 'That's better,' he said.

Felix emptied his pack onto the table. There was waybread and cheese and more jerky. It added to the mushrooms cooked in blindfish oil, the blindfish itself and the jugs of water. 'Help yourself,' he said.

Hargrim did so. With the speed the provisions disappeared Felix was glad that Hargrim was the only one of the local dwarfs who had joined them at their table.

Felix looked around the room. It was richly furnished with thick but worn carpets and drapes, fine dwarfish statuary and a merchant's ransom in silver and gold. It was one of the royal apartments. Each of the comrades had been given a similar one. Felix supposed that was one good thing about the casualties the dwarfs had suffered: there was plenty of room. He pushed the thought aside as unworthy and realised that he was getting drunk.

'I still cannot believe that we have strangers here,' Hargrim said. From the flush on his face, Felix could tell that the captain was inebriated as well. 'It astonishes me. For so long we thought we were the last dwarfs in the world. We thought Chaos had overrun everywhere else. We sent out messengers and scouts into the wilderness but they never returned. It all seemed so hopeless and now you arrive and tell us that there is a whole world beyond the Wastes, that Chaos was thrown back, that the Empire and Bretonnia and all those other places of legend still exist. It hardly seems possible that others have survived these past twenty years without us knowing it!'

'Twenty years?' spluttered Felix and Varek almost simultaneously.

'Aye! Why do you look at me that way?'

'It has been two hundred years since the last incursion of Chaos!' Felix said.

Hargrim looked at him in astonishment. 'That cannot be!'

'Time flows strangely in the Chaos Wastes,' Varek reminded them.

'Strangely indeed,' said Felix, remembering what Borek had told him of the odd powers of the place. Could the Dark Powers warp even the flow of time, he wondered, or was this some strange property that the Wastes themselves possessed?

'Believe me,' Varek said to Hargrim, 'Here in Karag Dum only twenty years may have passed but beyond the Wastes it has been centuries, and there Chaos was thrown back.'

'How did it happen?'

'Magnus the Pious rallied men and dwarfs to his cause, and broke the hordes of Chaos at the Siege of Praag, in Kislev. Eventually the followers of the Dark Ones were driven back to beyond Blackblood Pass.'

'And yet no one ever came to relieve us,' said Hargrim, and he sounded almost bitter.

Felix did not know what to say. 'Everyone thought Karag Dum had fallen. The last reports were of the city being overrun by the hordes of Chaos.'

Gotrek surprised him by speaking. 'No one knew what had happened. The Chaos Wastes had retreated but they had still advanced beyond where they once had been. They always do. Karag Dum was cut off. No one could find a way through. It was tried, believe me. Borek sought long and hard for a way to return.'

'I do believe you, Gotrek, son of Gurni, for I have seen the Wastes, looked out from our highest towers, and I know they stretch as far as the eye can see. I have fought the warriors of Chaos and know they are as uncountable as flakes of snow in a blizzard. We have so few warriors that we soon stopped trying to get messengers out. Many were captured and hideously tortured.'

'How have you survived?' Varek asked – somewhat tactlessly, Felix thought. Still he was glad the young dwarf had asked the question. He wanted to know the answer himself. Hargrim shook his head.

'With great difficulty,' he said at last and smiled wearily, 'But that is not a fair answer my friends. The answer is that our foes are divided and we hide and fight them as we may.'

'What do you mean?' Gotrek asked.

'Tell Snorri about the fighting,' said Snorri.

'After the last great siege, when the forces of the Enemy used terrible sorcery to break our walls, we retreated deeper and deeper into the mines, determined to sell our lives dearly and make them pay for every inch of dwarfish territory with blood. Our people divided up into their clans and hosts and made their way to the secret fastnesses we had prepared against such a day.'

'Like this one,' Felix said.

'Precisely. We retreated under the earth, to places shielded by runes of power, and we emerged into the debated halls to raid and fight and we discovered a strange thing...'

'What was that?' Gotrek asked.

'We found that the forces of Chaos had fallen out with each other. We did not know then but we found out from captured prisoners that their supreme leader, Skathlok Ironclaw, had been drawn away to a battle in the south, and that his lieutenants, each of whom followed a different power, had fallen into dispute over the spoils.'

'When was this?' asked Varek.

Hargrim gave a date in dwarfish which meant nothing to Felix.

'It was the Imperial Year 2302,' Varek translated. 'At about the time of the Siege of Praag.'

'If this was the case, why did you not drive them from the city?' asked Gotrek. Hargrim laughed and there was no mirth to his laughter.

'Because there were still so few of us left, son of Gurni. After the Great Siege we numbered less than five thousand warriors, and those were split between five hidden citadels. Even with the majority of their warriors gone, our foes numbered ten times that and divided though they were, we knew they would unite to fight against us if we emerged in strength. So, over the years, we learned to sally forth in small groups and pick away at our enemies. It was not a good strategy, as we later learned.'

'Why?' asked Felix.

'Because for every one of their warriors who fell, another one would appear. For every war-band we destroyed, two more would come in from the Wastes. But when we lost a warrior we could never replace him. We may have killed twenty for every stout-hearted dwarf we lost, but in the end we had no way of replacing our losses, and they did.'

'I can understand this,' said Felix. 'There are many warriors out in the Wastes, and this is a worthy citadel and would provide them with shelter.'

Hargrim shook his head sadly. 'You do not understand the followers of Chaos at all well, if that is what you think, Felix Jaeger. They came here because there was treasure here – gold and dwarf-made weapons, and most of all the black steel they covet for the making of their armour and the forging of their foul weapons. They came here because they knew they would find others to fight of their own kind, and thus win glory in the eyes of their insane gods. This place has become a kind of testing ground for the warriors of Chaos, where they can find others to slaughter in order to advance themselves.'

Hargrim's words made sense to Felix. He had occasionally wondered where the Chaos warriors got their weapons. He had seen no sign of foundries or factories or any kind of manufacturing since they entered the Wastes, yet the followers of the Dark Powers must get their gear from somewhere. He had simply assumed that it was the product of sorcery or bartered from renegade human smiths but now he saw another answer. Here at Karag Dum was ore and all the equipment produced by dwarfish industry. If some of the things he had heard were true, this one hold could produce more steel than the whole Empire. He voiced his suspicions at once.

'You are correct, Felix Jaeger. We tried to destroy all the forges and furnaces and anvils we could not dismantle and carry into the hidden places, but we did not have enough time to get rid of them all. Some were seized by the followers of the Ruinous Powers. Some were repaired using black and incomprehensible magics. Now the mines are worked by hordes of beastmen and mutant slaves, and mage-priests oversee the manufacture of weapons and armour.'

'If this place could be retaken, it would be a terrible blow to the powers of Chaos. For where else would they get their weapons?' Felix said in drunken excitement.

'Perhaps. Perhaps not,' Hargrim said. 'The Chaos worshippers must have other mines and other foundries now and empty as Karag Dum now seems it is still well held.'

'What do you mean?'

'It is not now as was in the early days. Many warriors of Chaos have come here and hold their own small fiefdoms. There are entire towns in the Underhalls now which are dedicated to the worship of one of the four Powers of Darkness. They each have their own liege lords and armies. They trade ore, weapons and armour to those outside. They exchange swords for slaves, spearpoints and arrowheads for their disgusting food, armour for magical devices.'

'You said there were other dwarf fastnesses in Karag Dum,' Varek said.

'Gone now,' Hargrim said. 'Over the years, they have been wiped out. Those of their people that survived made their way here. Most did not. Many have been hunted down by the Hounds of Khorne as they fled. Others would not come here lest they led the followers of the Terror to our last haven.'

'The Terror?' Felix said.

'Of that it is best not to speak,' said Hargrim. 'For it is our doom. When first it came it took the lives of hundreds of stout warriors. Our runemaster gave his life to drive it off. Now that it has returned I doubt that anything can stop it – although your axe gives me some hope, Gotrek Gurnisson.'

Felix's heart sank as he saw Gotrek and Snorri exchange glances. He knew that Hargrim had aroused the Slayer's professional interest. Hargrim saw this too and shook his head.

'Tell me: what do you think King Thangrim is thinking about?' Felix asked, just to change the subject. 'Do you think it likely that he will send messengers to the outside world.'

'I do not know, Felix Jaeger. I think it likely that we will all die here.'

After that there was silence for a minute, and then Gotrek spoke: 'I wish to know more of this creature known as the Terror.'

'This does not surprise me,' Hargrim said, looking up and inspecting the dwarf's tattoos. 'You wish to hunt it?'

'I do.'

'That would not be wise.'

'It is not a question of wisdom. It is a question of my doom.'

'And Snorri's,' said Snorri.

'Spoken like true Slayers,' Hargrim said. 'Very well. I will tell what I know of this fell creature. It is a daemon of Chaos, potent and deadly. It was summoned by Skathlok in the last days of the siege and he treated with it not as a master treats a servant but as a warrior treats his king. It came upon us at the south-west gate after that was thrown down and none of us could stand against it. It slew a dozen heroes armed with potent rune weapons. It almost slew King Thangrim himself when he faced it in the Hall of Shadows. They exchanged blows for mere moments but it had the mastery. He could not believe its strength.'

Gotrek reached down and grabbed his axe. A gleam had come into his eye. 'It must be strong indeed to withstand the Hammer of Fate.'

'Stronger than anything it is, Gotrek Gurnisson. More fell by far than the three orc chieftains of the Red Fang. More dangerous than the three ogre mages of Ventragh Heath. Deadlier even than the dragon Glaugir, for all its poison breath. I speak without boasting when I say have stood beside my liege as he measured himself against mighty foes, but this vile thing was by far the mightiest. I doubt that in the full pride of his youth, even so great a warrior as Thangrim Firebeard could have overcome it.'

'How then was it beaten?' asked Felix, licking his lips nervously. 'How did you survive to tell us this tale.'

'It was not beaten, it was driven off when one of our high Runesmith Valek smote it with the sacred axe you carry, then invoked the Rune of Unbinding. Such a wound it was that anything but a creature so great would have died instantly. This thing merely withdrew into the deepest depths of the mountain, near its fiery heart. It must have brooded down there for many years, recovering its strength, for now it has returned. As it prophesied.'

'Prophesied?'

'Even as it disappeared, it told us it would return to be our doom. It told the king that one day it would return and tear out his heart with its claws and devour it before his still-living eyes, and he told Thangrim that this was his doom. And all of us who heard it believed this prophesy, for there was a flat truth in its voice.'

'It was a daemon,' Felix said softly. 'Daemons have been known to lie.'

'Aye, but this one gloated as it spoke and we knew that it intended to work our ruin in its own time and way. Some of the warriors even suspect that this is why we have been allowed to survive for so long. And our Runesmith Valek also spoke a prophesy before he died. He told us to fear not, for his axe also would return to us when the Last Days came. Many of us wondered about this prophesy, for how could the axe return to us when it was destined to remain hidden in our fortresses. Then the king's son took the axe and we thought it lost. And lo, you have returned it to us but a score of days after the Terror returned.'

He looked meaningfully at Gotrek's axe. 'You can see why your coming has disturbed the king.'

'How did Valek invoke this Rune of Unbinding?' Gotrek asked.

'I know not. He was a runesmith and knew many secrets. I only know that he summoned its power and it killed him, consuming his life even as it banished the daemon. The axe you bear is old and potent beyond all reckoning. It passed from runesmith to runesmith from the most ancient times. Its full history was passed only from bearer to bearer, but with Valek's death the tale was lost. His son and apprentice fell before him in that final battle. The king's son, Morekai, took it from the runesmith's smouldering corpse and bore it away with him when he tried to cross the Wastes.'

'Then without the Rune of Unbinding this creature cannot be beaten?' Felix asked.

'Who can say. That weapon is potent indeed even without the Rune of Unbinding. Perhaps in the hands of a warrior sufficiently strong...'

'Describe this daemon,' Gotrek said.

Hargrim leaned forward drunkenly and rested his chin on his fist. For a moment, he smiled a smile empty of all humour. Then he sank into reverie and gazed off into the distance, as if looking once more on a sight he would rather not see.'

'Huge it was,' he said eventually. 'More than twice the height of a tall man. Vast were its wings. Vast and bat-like, and when it unfurled them there was a crack like thunder. In one hand it bore a terrible whip. In the other an axe emblazoned with evil and eldritch runes that hurt the eye to look upon. Its eyes burned with infernal fire. Horns crowned its bestial head. On its brow was the mark of the Blood God.'

As Hargrim spoke, a silence and a chill spread across the chamber. Felix began to have a terrible suspicion that he knew what the dwarf was describing. It was a creature that was hinted at in the old books he had read about the time of Chaos. It was indeed a creature worthy to be known as the Terror.

'A Blutdrengrik,' said Gotrek quietly.

'The Bane of Grung,' Varek mumbled, tugging nervously at his beard.

'A Bloodthirster of Khorne,' Felix whispered, and felt the cold hand of fear touch his spine. He had just named the deadliest, most violent and implacable creature ever to emerge from the nethermost pits of Hell. A daemon second only to the Dark God it served in its mythical powers of destruction. A being which even the mightiest would fear to face.

'Let's go and kill it,' said Snorri.

'Let's have another drink first,' Felix said, hoping to dissuade the Slayers from this foolish quest for as long as possible.

FELIX AWOKE with that same feeling of disorientation which he had become quite familiar with over the years. He was in a strange place, looking at a strange ceiling and he felt somewhat nauseous. It took him a few moments to get his rebellious mind and stomach under control and to work out where he was. When he managed to do so, he wished he had not.

He was deep underground in a chamber in a ruined dwarf citadel, somewhere deep in the Chaos Wastes. And he had a hangover. Surely there were few worse fates that could befall a mortal man, he told himself. He pulled himself up off the sumptuous but rather fusty smelling and too short bed, pulled on his boots and strode out into the corridor to find something that would settle his stomach. As he did so, he was greeted by one of the king's armoured guards who informed him that his presence was required in the throne room. Immediately.

Felix realised that he had indeed found a worse fate. Not only was he stuck in this terrible place but he had to face an old and irascible dwarfish tyrant on an empty stomach. Stifling a groan he followed the guard.

'WE CANNOT LEAVE this place,' said King Thangrim Firebeard. 'There are too many of us. According to what you have told me there is not enough room in your ship for more than an extra dozen people at most. There are several hundred of my people here. It would be unfair to chose some to go and some to stay.'

Felix had to admit the old dwarf had a point. He had arrived in the ruler's chamber only to find the others already being grilled by the old despot. Apparently Varek had suggested that the people of Karag Dum should leave their ancestral home. Thangrim had raised a few cogent objections.

'It would only be a temporary measure, your majesty,' Varek said. 'Once we had flown those people back to the Lonely Tower we could return with a skeleton crew and take more. We could continue to ferry them back until we had taken everyone. It is possible.'

'Maybe. But you have told me that even flying across the Chaos Wastes is perilous. Perhaps your ship will crash.'

'Surely, your majesty remaining here, with the forces of Chaos pounding upon your doors is more perilous. It is only a matter of time before you are hunted down and destroyed.' Varek was becoming impassioned and flustered. His eyes were large and round behind the lenses of his glasses.

'You do not understand, youngling. We have here wives and wounded. We cannot simply abandon them or send them away with but a small escort. You know how perilous the halls are. You have seen them. It would take many warriors to guard them, and there is not enough room on your ship for them and the escort.'

'The escort could return to your halls,' Varek said. 'They are warriors. They have done this before.'

'Your point is a fair one but eventually we would have to move our ancestral hordes. These are no small treasures, and not a gold piece or trinket will I leave behind for the despoilers.'

Felix spoke up for the first time. 'But surely gold means nothing when the lives of your people are concerned, your majesty.'

Every dwarf present looked at him as if he was either deranged or profoundly stupid. No one even bothered to answer him. Felix wished the floor would open up and swallow him. He should have known better than to try and make such a rational argument to dwarfs when gold was being discussed.

'Could we carry away our father's treasures on your one small ship?' Thangrim asked.

'From what I have heard about your horde, may it ever grow and prosper, I doubt it.'

'Then how can you expect us to leave this place while we have blood left in our veins?'

'Perhaps we could return with more than one airship, great king,' Varek said. 'Perhaps we could return with enough craft to carry all your people and all your horde.'

'If you could, I would see that you were suitably rewarded. Let me think on what you have said. You may go.'

Varek rose to go and Felix moved to join him. He felt a vague sense of relief at being about to leave the king's presence – and at the prospect of getting some food.

'Thangrim Firebeard,' Gotrek said. 'I crave a boon.'

'Tell me what it is, Gotrek Gurnisson.'

'I wish to seek out this creature you call the Terror, and either slay it or find my doom.'

King Thangrim smiled down at Gotrek and appeared to consider his request.

At that moment, however, a distant horn sounded. A few heartbeats later a dwarf raced through the entrance of the throne room and advanced at once to the king. Thangrim gestured for the messenger to come closer and then listened to his whispered words. When the new arrival had finished speaking, his face looked grim indeed.

'It appears it will not be necessary for you to seek the monster out, Gotrek Gurnisson. It is coming here now – and it brings with it an army.'

Wonderful, thought Felix, and I haven't even had a chance to grab my last meal.

NINETEEN
BLOODTHIRSTER

'THE HORDES OF Chaos come again,' King Thangrim said. 'Sound the war-horns. We muster for battle.'

The king raised himself from his throne and lifted his great warhammer up high. In that moment Felix could see a glittering aura like lightning playing around the head of the weapon. The air was filled with the smell of ozone. The king's guard cheered heartily but Felix sensed a deep uneasiness behind their show of courage.

'This is good,' Gotrek said.

This is very bad, thought Felix, contemplating the oncoming hordes of Chaos, led by a daemon of unspeakable power. He wondered how he could ever have thought things were bad when he got up this morning. All he had to worry about then was a hangover. Now he had much worse things to concern himself with.

The king strode down the steps accompanied by his priests, and made his way out into the hall. His guards fell into step behind him. Outside in the Hall of the Well, dwarf folk were hastily assembling. Warriors rushed out of every entrance. Some buckled on shields and weapons. Others had breastplates half-strapped to their chests and were hastily tightening fastenings as they assembled. As Felix watched, he saw one old warrior jam a helmet onto his head, spit on the floor and make a few practice swipes with his axe. Seeing Felix looking at him, he gave him a thumbs-up sign.

Out of the corner of his eye, Felix saw Hargrim assembling his tunnel fighters. They too were strapping on heavier dwarfish armour. It seemed that the time for stealth was over and now they wanted the heaviest protection they could get. Felix did not blame them. His own chainmail shirt suddenly seemed woefully inadequate when he remembered the vast mass of bestial warriors he had seen during the approach to Karag Dum, and when he thought of the legendary deadliness of the Bloodthirster.

But what else was there to do but fight? He drew his own enchanted blade from the scabbard and strode over to where Hargrim stood. 'How did they find us?' he shouted to make himself heard over the din of dwarfs preparing for battle.

'I know not. Perhaps they found the place where we killed its hounds. Mayhap others of his foul pack found out scent. What does it matter? It is the Prophesy. The Last Day is upon us.'

'Try not to be so cheerful,' Felix said, and glanced around to see where Gotrek, Snorri and Varek were. He could see the Slayers standing near the king. Varek was nowhere to be seen. Felix wondered where he had gone. He realised that whatever happened in this battle, his place was beside his companions. If nothing else, he knew he had no chance of finding his way out of these halls on his own. Any of the others could probably manage it blindfolded.

On the other hand, he was probably being far too optimistic imagining there would be any chance of escape whatsoever. Snorri and Gotrek would never leave while the Bloodthirster was present, but he doubted that even those two formidable warriors could prevail over so mighty a daemon.

'Good luck!' he shouted to Hargrim and raced over to where the Slayers stood.

'May Grungni, Grimnir and Valaya watch over you, Felix Jaeger,' Hargrim said and returned to bellowing orders to his troops.

NOW FROM OUT of the access tunnels came the sounds of battle: the brash echo of horns, the clash of weapons, and the bellowing of something hideous echoed down the corridors.

The dwarfs had finished their dispositions and their line of battle was drawn up across the Well Hall. There were certainly more dwarfs here than had defended the Lonely Tower, but that was not a reassuring thought. Compared to the numbers their attackers could summon, they were pitifully few.

Felix looked up to where King Thangrim stood carried on a shield held by four bearers. 'They have breached the outer gate,' said the king. 'Our sentries will hold them for a while.'

Looking beyond Thangrim, Felix could see that the women and those too aged and wounded to fight were disappearing through an entrance he had not seen before. Once the last one had gone through the doorway was sealed behind them, and it was done so cunningly that no sign of the hidden exit remained.

'They go to the vaults with our hoard, to wait out the final battle,' Thangrim said. 'If we are victorious they will be freed. If not, they die.'

'What do you mean?'

'The vaults can only be opened from the outside,' Gotrek said. Felix was suddenly glad he had not tried to flee through those doors. He could think of nothing worse than huddling in the gloomy vaults, waiting to die of suffocation or starvation while the battle raged outside. At least out here, he would have some control over his fate, and when death came it would be quick. He hoped.

He could see Varek returning now. The young dwarf had Makaisson's gun strapped to his chest and carried a bag full of bombs. He moved with a purposefulness that Felix had never seen in him before as he raced up and came to a stop beside Felix.

'Hold this for a moment,' Varek said to Felix and handed him the gun. Felix sheathed his sword and took it, surprised by how heavy it was, and by the ease with which Varek had handled it. Varek produced his book and pen, and began to inscribe a few notes on its pages. Seeing Felix's astonished look, he said: 'Just a last explanation. In case someone comes upon this later. Well, we can but hope, eh?'

Felix forced himself to smile, but it came out shakily. 'I suppose so.'

In the distance the clamour reached a peak and then there was a bestial roar of triumph. Felix guessed things had not gone well for the dwarf sentries.

Thangrim had started to shout in dwarfish. Felix could not understand a word he was bellowing but the dwarfs seemed to like it. They cheered him mightily, even Gotrek and Snorri. Only Varek did not add his voice to the resounding chorus, for he was too busy writing.

Felix kept his eyes glued to the doorway through which he knew their foes would come. He knew that several hundred crossbow-toting dwarfs were doing the same thing. But still this did not reassure him. He had an oppressive sense of approaching doom. Fear gripped his heart. A shadow lay on his soul. He knew that something terrible was approaching.

'Bet Snorri kills more beastmen than you, Gotrek,' said Snorri.

Gotrek grunted derisively. 'The manling will kill more beastmen than you,' Gotrek replied.

'Want to bet on that, Felix?' Snorri asked.

Felix shook his head. His mouth was too dry for him to form a response. Terror had started to take root in his mind, a paralysing fear that shook the foundations of his sanity and made him want to find a dark corner in which to hide himself and whimper. Part of his mind told him that this was unnatural, that he should not feel such fear, but it was still hard to fight against it. There was something in that hideous roaring that turned his blood to water.

'Just remember, Snorri,' Gotrek said. 'The daemon is mine.'

'Depends if Snorri gets to it first,' said Snorri with a grin.

Felix found he could not bear to look at the entrance anymore so he glanced at Gotrek and Snorri. Even the Slayers were tense, he could tell. Gotrek's knuckles were white from gripping the haft of his axe so tightly. Snorri's hand trembled a little where he clutched his axe. Seeing Felix looking at him, he grinned. He appeared to make an effort to calm himself, and the trembling stopped.

'Snorri's not worried,' Snorri said. 'Much.'

Felix grinned back, knowing how unnatural he must look. He felt like the skin of his face was too tight and as if all his hair was trying to stand on end like a Trollslayer's crest. He was probably pale as death too, he thought.

Suddenly, just for a moment, everything fell silent. In the eerie stillness all Felix could hear was the scratching of Varek's pen. Then even that stopped and Felix felt a tug on his arm and realised that Varek was asking for his gun back. Felix gave it to him, and unsheathed his sword once more.

The roar which shattered the silence was so loud and so terrifying that Felix almost dropped his blade. He looked up and fought down the urge to soil his britches. The most frightening thing he had ever seen had entered the hall and behind it he could see the leering heads of hundreds of beastmen.

As he gazed on the creature in wonder and in terror, Felix thought: this is what a daemon looks like. This is the incarnate nightmare which had bedevilled my people since time began.

He knew now that there was something magical about the terror the thing inspired. It was the unnatural aura of something which had crept forth from the nethermost pits and which no mortal being could help but sense and respond to. In some ways it hurt the eyes simply to look upon the Bloodthirster. Its very appearance told you it was made from no natural substance. The charnel stink of the thing was worse than anything he could have imagined. It reeked of rotting meat and congealed blood and other less describable and far more loathsome things.

It looked as Hargrim had described it. It was far taller and far heavier than Felix. Vast bat-like wings flexed on its shoulders. It was as muscular as a minotaur. In one hand it held a great coiled whip, in the other a terrifying axe larger than a man's body. Its skin was ruddy red and its face was savage and bestial. And yet of all the Bloodthirster's features, it was its eyes which Felix knew he would never forget.

They were like pools of infinite darkness out of which a malign and ageless intelligence gazed. Somewhere in those unknowable depths flickered red fires of savage hatred, an insane ferocity that would overthrow the order of the entire Universe if it could, in order to try and sate a bloodlust that could never be satisfied. Here was a creature that had looked upon the birth and death of worlds, and might look out on the death of everything. Compared to its life, his own existence was less than the life of a mayfly. Compared to its strength and savagery and cunning, he was less than nothing.

And yet looking on, Felix felt his fear start to drain away. After all, embodied terror that it might be, it really was not as bad as he had imagined it would be. It could never be as fearful than the nightmare thing his own brain had been conjuring up mere heartbeats before. It was awe-inspiring, mystical and potent to be sure but he felt now that he had seen it, he could fight it, and glancing at the others he knew that they felt the same. In a way, he was not too sorry to look upon the thing, even if it caused his death. He knew he had now seen something that few men ever would, and there was a certain satisfaction in that. He knew also that he could confront this ultimately fearsome thing and in the end, not be completely daunted.

Then it spoke and the fear returned, redoubled: 'I have come to claim my blood debt, King Thangrim, as I said I would.'

Its voice was like a brazen horn, and yet there was something in it that suggested the void, and a cold so chilly that it burned. It was as loud as thunder and yet so perfectly pitched that every word carried exactly the minutely calculated freight of hatred that the daemon intended it to. It was the voice of an angry and vengeful demi-god. Felix could tell that the daemon was not speaking in Reikspiel and yet he could still somehow understand its meaning perfectly, and not for a moment did he doubt that the same was true for the dwarfs.

'You have come to be cast into the pit once more,' King Thangrim said. His voice was clear and deep and resonant but, compared to the Bloodthirster, he sounded like a rebellious child shrieking defiance at an adult.

'I will tear out your heart and eat it before your still-living eyes, just as I promised,' the thing replied. 'And not all your little warriors will save you. For every moment of every hour of every day of every year of my waiting I have looked forward to this day, and now it has arrived.'

As the daemon spoke more and more beastmen and black-armoured warriors filtered into the room behind it, yet not a single dwarf fired a bolt or raised a weapon. There was something hypnotic about the creature and something unbearably fascinating about its confrontation with the ancient dwarf king. Felix wanted to shout a warning, to tell the dwarfs to attack, yet he did not. He was held enthralled by the same spell as held them all, while more and more followers of Chaos flowed in. Thangrim looked as if he wanted to reply, but could not. He looked old and weary and beaten before he started.

'You have lost none of your arrogance, little one, but you are old and feeble now and I... I am stronger than ever I was.'

'You certainly smell that way!' Gotrek roared suddenly.

The daemon's burning gaze shot towards the Slayer and Felix quailed as for a moment the thing's eyes rested upon him. It was as if Death itself had looked on him from out of its bony sockets. Felix was astonished that the Slayer managed to hold the daemon's gaze but somehow he did. After a moment he even managed a feral grin and brandished his axe. The runes along the blade blazed brighter than ever Felix had seen them. Gotrek took his thumb and ran it along the blade. A single bead of blood appeared and the Trollslayer flicked it contemptuously in the direction of the daemon.

'Thirsty?' he inquired. 'Try that. It will be all you get today.'

'I will drink every drop of your blood, and I will crack your skull and devour your few brains, and as I do I will consume your soul. You will learn the true meaning of terror.'

'I am learning the true meaning of tedium,' Gotrek said and laughed a grating laugh. 'Do you intend to bore me to death with your speeches or do you want to come over here and die?'

Felix was amazed that the Slayer could say anything with that soul-blasting gaze upon him, but somehow Gotrek had managed to speak. And in doing so he had heartened the whole dwarf army. Felix could sense the dwarfs throwing off the influence of the daemon's presence and readying their weapons to fight. Thangrim straightened and raised his hammer and as he did so lightning crackled once more about its head.

Amazingly the daemon smiled, revealing long fangs and a mouth that looked like it could swallow a horse. 'A moment of defiance earns you an eternity of torment. You will have aeons to reflect on your folly. And before you die, consider this. It was you who led me to this secret place.'

Seeing that Gotrek refused to rise to the bait, the daemon continued: 'That axe and I are linked. Since it wounded me I have always been able to sense its presence, no matter how well it was hidden. I followed its spoor to this place. I thank you for the service you have done me, slave.'

Felix looked at Gotrek to see how he was taking this. No emotion save implacable hatred showed on the Slayer's face. Felix wondered how Gotrek managed it. His own mind whirled. It seemed that their whole long quest, all the ingenuity which Borek had expended to bring them here, all the dangers they had overcome, had served only to lead this daemon to its final goal. It was a maddening thought that all their efforts had come to this, that they had been caught up in an intricate web of prophesy and doom of which they had known nothing, that they were simply pawns in an aeons-long game played by the Ruinous Powers.

Looking across the narrow gap which separated the two armies, Felix once more felt the sick certainty of defeat. Ranks upon ranks of crooked horned beastmen were drawn up beside the daemon. Row upon row of Chaos warriors stood ready to attack, awesome mystical blades held read for slaughter. Packs of their terrible hounds bayed hungrily, as if demanding the souls of their prey.

Ranked against them was a dwarf host which looked pitifully weak. Around the king's fluttering banner was his guard, all finely decked in the best armour and armed with potent weapons. Between King Thangrim and the daemon stood a line of mighty warriors, each armed with glittering rune-carved blades. Beyond the king, the army's right flank was hidden from him but Felix knew it was made up of units of crossbows and hammer wielders. Here on the left flank were rank upon rank of long-bearded veterans armed with hammers and axes. Among them stood Gotrek, Snorri, Varek and himself. Felix offered up a prayer to Sigmar of the Hammer. If the deity heard he gave no sign.

Instead the daemon raised its blade and gave the signal to advance. In a cacophony of drums and braying, brazen horns the Chaos Horde began to advance. The lean hounds loped ahead of the foot troops ready to rend and tear. The daemon watched with an expression of hideous satisfaction. As the beastmen came on, the dwarfs opened fire with their crossbows, carving a bloody swathe through their inhuman foes.

Felix was almost deafened as Varek opened fire with his gun. The blaze of the rotating muzzles underlit the young dwarf's face as he sent a stream of hot lead out to mow down the oncoming brutes. In the flashes, Varek's twisted face looked no less demonic and hate-filled than the creatures they faced.

King Thangrim raised his hammer, lightning bolts flickered around it, gigantic shadows flickered away to the edge of the chamber. He whirled it around his head and it seemed to gather power and light as it did so. The runes blazed dazzlingly.

Blue sparks rained down all around it. The smell of ozone cut through the stench of the daemonic host.

The dwarf king released the Hammer of Fate. It hurtled towards the Bloodthirster like a comet, trailing sparks and streams of lightning. Where these fell beastmen fell also, their skin blackened, their fur standing on end. The great warhammer flew straight and true and impacted on the daemon with a sound like a thunderclap. The Bloodthirster bellowed in anguish and stumbled. The dwarf host roared mightily. To Felix's amazement the weapon hurtled back across the chamber, causing beastmen to flinch and duck. The king stretched out his hand and his weapon flew back, like a hawk returning to a falconer's glove after hunting.

For a moment Felix hoped that the awesome and terrible weapon might have downed the Bloodthirster. But when he dared look his hopes were dashed. Drops of blazing ichor dripped from a wound in the daemon's side and vanished into puffs of poisonous looking smoke where they hit the floor, but it still stood, immensely strong and immensely terrible gazing mockingly at the dwarfs. Its fiery glance silenced their cheers in a moment.

'If it will not come to us, we will just have to go to it,' Gotrek said and charged forward to meet the onrushing Chaos horde.

'Snorri thinks this is a good idea!' said Snorri, racing after the other Slayer.

'Wait for me,' Felix said and loped along cursing beside them. With his longer stride it was easy for him to keep up with the running dwarfs and still have some time to glance around at what was happening. Around them, he could see the whole dwarf army was advancing to meet their oncoming foe.

Tactically Felix knew that this was a mistake. The dwarfs should have kept their distance and hammered their foes with crossbow bolts until the last moment. Now they seemed caught up in the general madness of the daemon's presence, overwhelmed by a lust to get to grips with their enemy, hand to hand, breast to breast, to rend and tear and kill at close range. Felix could not blame them. After so many years of being hunted through what had once had been their home, they were filled with blazing hatred. In gratifying that hatred, Felix saw they were throwing away their one small tactical advantage.

Still, perhaps, it did not matter. They were going to die anyway, and so it might just be best to get it all over with. He gripped his sword with both hands as the first wave of beastmen swept over them, and then there was no more time for thought, only for killing.

A shock passed up Felix's arm as his blade embedded itself in the chest of a dog-headed beastmen. The sickening stench of blood and wet fur filled his nostrils as the creature fell against him. He kicked it away and chopped out at another of the foul creatures, severing an artery in its throat. As the thing reached up to try to press the wound shut, Felix worked his blade under its ribcage and up into its heart.

Around him Gotrek and Snorri hacked and chopped and slew. Every time Gotrek smashed down with his axe, a mangled foe fell clutching the bloody ruin of its chest, the amputated stump of its limbs, or tried to staunch the flow of blood that simply could not be stopped. From the corner of his eye, Felix saw Snorri smash forward with a simultaneous blow of both axe and hammer that caught a beastman's head between them. The top of the creature's skull came away, sheared off by the axe and its brains erupted forth in a pulpy grey jelly driven out by the force of the hammer blow.

A deafening bang followed by howls of bestial agony told Felix that Varek had lobbed one of his bombs. A moment later a cloud of acrid smoke filled his field of vision and brought tears to his eyes. He coughed and the sound attracted the attention of another beastman. A monstrous axe shrieked towards him from out of the smoke and he had only just time to raise his blade and parry before it hit. The shock sent tingles of agony shooting up into his shoulder. A moment later a huge hand came out of the gloom and grabbed him by the throat. Sharp nails driven by iron-sinewed fingers bit into his neck. Beads of blood ran down his windpipe.

As the smoke cleared he saw he had been grabbed by a monstrously muscular beastman. From the corner of his eye, he saw one of the beastman's disgusting brothers running closer with spear levelled. Everything started to happen in slow motion. He knew that he was about to die. Frantically, he tried to pull himself clear but the beastman was too strong, and was already drawing back his axe for the killing blow. The tip of its comrade's spear glittered as it came closer. With those awful fingers round his neck Felix could not even call for help from Gotrek or Snorri.

Any second he expected the spear to burst through his ribs or for the axe to descend with skull-smashing force. Knowing he had only moments to live filled Felix with desperate strength and ferocious cunning. Instead of trying to pull away, he suddenly relaxed and stepped forward. His unexpected movement threw his captor momentarily off-balance. Taking advantage of this, Felix swivelled on the spot and threw all his weight into the move, swinging the beastman round and to the side. The Chaos worshipper grunted as the spear which had been aimed at Felix drove right into his back. His muscles spasmed in agony and his fingers loosened around Felix's neck. Felix stepped back, took careful aim and lopped off its bestial head with one swing.

The sightless goat's head rolled onto the floor. Black blood gouted towards the ceiling from the stump of the neck rising in powerful spurts which weakened even as the body tumbled forward onto the floor. The second beastman stood there, holding its newly freed spear, blinking in stupid astonishment as if he could not quite believe that he had just killed its companion. Felix took advantage of his momentary confusion to stab it in the groin and then send his blade ripping upwards, slicing the belly and sending ropy entrails looping to the ground.

For a moment, he stood in the eye of the storm, surrounded by a swirling vortex of incredible violence. dwarf fought with beastman. Axe smashed against spear and club. Over to his right he could see Gotrek engaged in combat with two Chaos warriors. The black-armoured giants raced forward, hoping to take the Slayer from either side so that one could strike him while the other held his attention. Gotrek raced towards them, striking the first as he passed, caving in the warrior's breastplate with a blow of astonishing power. The armour did not quite give way, but the blood leaking through the armpits and joins at the waist told of a fatal blow. Instead of halting, the Slayer swept on past, leaving the second warrior to strike uselessly at the spot where he had been. As he did so, Gotrek struck downwards and backwards at his attacker taking his foe through the back of the leg, hamstringing him. As the warrior toppled Gotrek caved in his head and glanced around for more prey without a second thought.

The Slayer was covered in blood and looked as if he had been working in some hellish butcher's shop. Felix realised that he looked no better. His hands were red and slimy stuff covered his boots. He shook his head and noticed that the Slayer was gesturing a warning to him. Just in time he turned and ducked beneath the blow of a monstrous black armoured figure. His new opponent's sword was enormous and odd runes blazed redly along its length. Felix brought his own blade smashing forward but it rebounded off the man's armour. Demented laughter peeled forth from inside the man's face-concealing helmet. It was as if Felix had merely tickled him. The man slashed forward once more and Felix sprang backwards, out of reach of his blade. Seeing an opening, he hit the man's blade as it passed, adding to its momentum and sending his foe spinning round. As he did so, Felix leapt forward in a shoulder charge, sending his off-balance opponent tumbling to the floor. Before the man could rise, Felix pulled back his helmeted head and ran his blade along the man's leathery throat, severing an artery and leaving the dying Chaos Warrior flopping on the ground like a fish stranded on dry land.

He had no time to enjoy his triumph. He sensed rather than saw a blow descending on his own exposed skull and tried to leap to one side. His foot slipped on the blood-slick stone and he was only partially successful. A massive club clipped his head and sent him sprawling to the ground. Stars danced before his eyes. Even that glancing blow had come close to driving consciousness from his head. He tried to pull himself to his feet but he suddenly had no control over his limbs. They flopped wildly instead of obeying him. He was vaguely aware of a misshapen figure towering above him and a huge club being raised to dash his brains out.

A sudden weariness overcame Felix. All sound seemed to die away. He was too tired to care and he was not afraid to die. There was nothing he could do now. The club would descend and his life would be over. There was no sense in struggling. Best just to lie back and surrender to the inevitable.

For a moment only, he felt so helpless. Then he gathered all of his willpower to make one final futile attempt at movement. He knew it was impossible, that in his weakened state he could never get out of the way in time. His shoulders tensed and at any moment he expected to feel agony smash through his brain as the fatal blow connected.

It never came. Instead, his foe toppled away from him, blood exploding from his back. Gotrek bent over, gripped him by his chain mail vest and hauled him to his feet.

'Get up, manling. There's still killing to be done!' The Slayer swung his axe and dropped a beastman with one blow. 'You cannot die till you have witnessed me kill a daemon!'

'Where is it?' Felix asked, still dazed.

'Over there,' Gotrek said and pointed with one blood-covered finger.

Felix looked in the direction he had indicated and through a gap in the fury of battle witnessed a scene of momentous courage. Snorri steamed headlong at the daemon and lashed out at it with his axe and hammer. The daemon looked down and laughed mockingly as Snorri's attacks bounced off its hide.

'Snorri, you idiot!' Gotrek bellowed. 'Only rune weapons will affect the accursed thing!'

If Snorri heard, he gave no sign. He continued to lash ineffectually at the mighty monster, launching a whirlwind of blows that would have dropped a dozen oxen, yet left the daemon unscathed. At last, as if tiring of watching the antics of a jester, the Bloodthirster lashed out almost languidly with its axe. Snorri tried to block, crossing both weapons in front of him, but he had no chance. The haft of his axe and his hammer splintered, and the sheer force of the daemon's blow sent him hurtling across the chamber like a stone launched from a catapult. He went tumbling through the air to land at the feet of King Thangrim, splashing the old dwarf's beard with blood.

The Bloodthirster ploughed on through the warriors of King Thangrim's elite guard. Its weapons flickered almost too fast for the eye to follow and every time one struck a dwarf warrior fell. It seemed like no armour could resist those hell-forged weapons. In mere moments, brave warriors were reduced to mewling, dying piles of ragged flesh. Proud armour was rent asunder. Even as Felix watched, the Bloodthirster smashed through a row of dwarfs with its axe, leaving only mangled corpses in its wake. Yet the great daemon was not having things all its own way. The rune weapons of the dwarfs had bitten its flesh in a few places. Smoking ichor dribbled onto the floor as it advanced.

Rage blazed in King Thangrim's eyes. His beard bristled. He raised his hammer once more as if in answer to the daemon's challenge and cast it to smash on the daemon's breast. Once more the ancient weapon bit home. Once more daemonic blood spurted forth. Once more the hideous thing staggered – then grinned and came on with redoubled fury.

Nothing could stand in its way. It ploughed through the dwarf king's guards like a battering ram through a rotting doorway. Felix saw that one warrior managed to ram a runic blade into its back before it was aware of him. The blade stuck fast, protruding out from the Bloodthirster's shoulder blades before it turned and lashed out with its whip. Felix had no idea what that infernal lash was made from but they cut through dwarf-forged armour with ease and flayed its targets to the bone. Felix saw skin and muscle part as if slashed with a cleaver, white bone and yellow cartilage suddenly exposed in the dim, guttering light. The whip lashed forward again, spinning its shrieking victim like a top and tugging more flesh from his carcass. Another dwarf strode forward and smote the daemon with a rune-etched hammer. The impact caused the daemon some discomfort, but the swing of its axe decapitated its attacker. All the while it kept lashing its victim. In heartbeats, a bloody, skinned carcass that was not recognisable as a dwarf lay at its feet.

'How much longer will you hide behind your warriors, little king?' asked the daemon, and such was the dreadful magic of its voice that the words were audible where Felix stood even above the clamour of battle. The king threw his hammer once more but this time the daemon threw down his whip and caught it with one outstretched claw. The runes blazed along the hammer's head and where it held the weapon the daemon's hand blackened but it reversed the weapon and sent it hurtling back towards the king.

There was a crack like thunder and the hammer flew too fast for the eye to follow. It crashed into the dwarf king and sent him sprawling to the ground. A groan came from the dwarf army as they saw their leader tumble and fall. The daemon bellowed in triumph. Insane laughter rumbled above the fray and echoed through the hall. The host of Chaos fought on with redoubled fury and everywhere seemed to gain the upper hand over the dwarfs.

The Bloodthirster strode through the dismayed throng, slaying right and left as it went. The priest of Grimnir went forth to meet it and was disembowelled with a slash of its claw even as his warhammer buried itself in the daemon's flesh. The old priestess of Valaya stood before it. She raised her book as if it were a shield. A glow leapt from the pages and for a moment the daemon paused. Then it laughed once more and brought its axe arcing down, cleaving through the book and the priestess both. Her bisected form fell in two pieces to the floor and the daemon strode forward in triumph to stand above the dying king.

'Come, manling. Now is the hour of my doom,' Gotrek said, and made to stride towards the daemon. Nothing could stand in the Slayer's way. Anything that tried to do so died. He was now as much an engine of destruction as the daemon had been. As he moved towards his goal he struck left and right and everywhere he struck beastmen and Chaos warriors fell, cloven by the power of the axe and the arm that drove it.

With a shrug, Felix strode along behind, resolved to his fate. His head still rang from the glancing blow he had taken, and the scenes of nightmarish carnage all around had taken on a unreal quality. There now seemed nothing unlikely about the Slayer's mission. It did indeed seem inevitable that Gotrek would fight with the daemon, and die his heroic death, and that Felix would witness it and die in turn himself. There was no other possibility. Looking around the hall Felix could see that the dwarfs were beaten. Their foes had the upper hand, and the fall of King Thangrim had demoralised them utterly. There was no sign of Snorri or Varek. Felix knew that he was not going to leave this battlefield alive. He might as well do as the Trollslayer wished. He owed the dwarf his life once more, and this was the way to pay the debt.

The Bloodthirster stood over the recumbent form of the old dwarf king. It drove its axe blade deep into the ancient flagstones so that the weapon stood there quivering. Then it reached down and picked up Thangrim Firebeard with both its claws, as gently as a man might pick up a small child.

Felix ducked the swing of a beastman's axe, lopped his attacker's hand off at the wrist and kept running, leaving the amputee falling to his knees and clutching a bleeding stump. Three Chaos warriors came between Gotrek and the daemon.

His axe smashed through the neck of one, opened the stomach of another and buried itself in the groin of a third. The backward swing of the axe toppled them to the floor and left Felix with a clear view of what happened next between the king and his tormentor.

The Bloodthirster peeled away Thangrim's armour like a man might strip away the peel from an orange. The dwarf managed to lean forward and spat in his tormentor's face. The spittle mingled with the ichor that ran down the daemon's brow and evaporated with a sizzle. Grinning widely, the Bloodthirster pushed its claws into the king's exposed flesh and began to pull outwards. The dwarf's ribcage cracked and flew open like the shell of an oyster, revealing the exposed innards. Blood sprayed across the Bloodthirster as it kept at its unholy work.

It raised the body to the level of its eyes, holding him easily with one hand. With the other it reached out and tore Thangrim's still-beating heart from his chest, raised it so that the king's wide eyes could see what it was doing. It squeezed the heart. The meat was crushed with an audible squelch. Blood gushed forth and sprayed down into the monster's mouth. Then, like a Bretonnian epicure devouring the flesh of an opened shellfish, it threw back its head and let the heart slid down into its open mouth. All this the king watched with wide, appalled eyes.

The daemon's throat swelled as it swallowed the whole heart and then it opened its mouth and gave an enormous belch of satisfaction. It let the heartless, now dead thing which had once been the proud king of Karag Dum flop to the floor and turned to bellow its triumph to its assembled followers. Felix had a perfect view of the whole thing, for at that moment he and Gotrek had almost reached the Bloodthirster.

'I hope you enjoyed your last meal, daemon,' Gotrek said. 'Now you die.'

The daemon looked down at him and smiled. 'Your brain will be my desert,' it said with terrible certainty.

For a moment the Slayer and the daemon stood frozen facing each other. Gotrek held his blazing axe poised to strike. A look of near-berserk fury transformed his face into something almost as terrifying as the daemon. The Bloodthirster flexed its wings with an audible snap and gestured mockingly for Gotrek to advance. Felix looked from Gotrek to the daemon to the corpse of Thangrim. He had heard that the brain could still live for moments after the heart ceased to beat. He knew that in Thangrim's case this was true, for it was what the daemon had willed in order to fulfil its unholy oath. Suddenly he was very angry, at the senseless cruelty of the daemon and the insane malignity of all of Chaos. He wanted to take his sword and plunge it into the daemon's breast.

The long frozen moment ended. Gotrek bellowed his war cry and charged. His axe flashed forward and down and buried itself in the daemon's chest. Blazing ichor belched forth, scorching the dwarf and sending him reeling backward for a moment. He recovered himself well and launched another blow. The Bloodthirster raised its claw to block it and another huge gash appeared in its arm. For a moment, Felix thought that in his fury Gotrek might overwhelm it, but the Bloodthirster stepped back out of the Slayer's reach and made a grasping gesture.

Its huge axe sprang up out of the ground and flew into the daemon's hand in the time it took to blink. For a moment the daemon stood there. Felix could see that it had taken damage. The dwarf guard's sword still protruded from its back. Thangrim's hammer had left deep welts in its flesh, through which broken bones showed. Gotrek's axe had left two gaping wounds from which ichor dripped, smouldering to the floor. From its entire body rose a foul vapour like smoke. At times its outline seemed to waver and go out of focus as if it were not quite there. Then it snapped into being once again, becoming hard-edged and distinct.

And it launched itself at the Slayer.

There was a flurry of blows much too fast for the mortal eye to follow. Felix had no idea how Gotrek survived the encounter but he did, reeling backwards with a great gash across his forehead and claw marks all across his chest. The Bloodthirster bore another great rent on its arm but appeared less damaged than the Slayer.

'I see you've had enough,' Gotrek gasped defiantly.

The daemon laughed and prepared to spring forward once again. Felix steeled himself, knowing now that what he was about to do was suicide. He was going to die. It did not matter, Felix knew that, if the Slayer fell, the daemon would overpower him in heartbeats, so he decided to get in his blow while he could. He sprang forward and struck with all his might at the daemon. The Templar Aldred's enchanted blade bit deep into the daemon's flesh. Felix pulled back the sword and tried for a second blow. The daemon turned to face him at the last second and sent him sprawling backwards with a mere buffet of its arm that nearly knocked the life from Felix.

As its claw made contact, something exploded against Felix's chest, sending a surge of pain flickering right through him. The Templar's blade was sent spinning from his hand. As he fell, he landed on something hard and heavy, and the wind was knocked from his lungs. He could hear what might have been a howl of unearthly agony coming from the Bloodthirster.

Gotrek took advantage of the distraction to spring forward and for a moment Felix thought the Slayer was going to be able to take the Bloodthirster. His axe flashed through a ferocious arc and almost connected but the Slayer's wounds slowed him and the daemon leapt aside and avoided the stroke which otherwise would have beheaded it. There followed another flurry of blows that were too fast for the eye to follow. They ended with Gotrek's axe being knocked from his hand. As the dwarf stood there, staggering, barely upright, the Bloodthirster smashed down with a mighty fist, slamming the Slayer to the ground. Gotrek fell prostrate at the daemon's feet. All hope fled from Felix's heart.

He reached down and tried to push himself upright. Looking down he could see the smouldering remains of Schreiber's amulet on his chest. The daemon's fist must have caught it when it struck him. The amulet had exploded, overloaded by the daemon's sheer power. Still, thought Felix, perhaps it had saved his life. Something had robbed the Bloodthirster's blow of much of its force. He was certain that it should have killed him – yet it had not.

He could not find his sword but his fingers clutched something hard and heavy. He realised that it was the Hammer of Fate. He tried to lift it but it would not move. It was not simply that it was too heavy, it was that some force kept it locked in place on the ground like the magnet which held maps in place on the airship.

Felix cursed. They had come so close. The daemon was moving slowly now, breathing hard, ichor dripping from great rents in its flesh, barely able to maintain its form. One more blow would finish the thing, of that he was certain. He heaved until he thought his muscles would crack and still the accursed hammer would not move. It was a magic artefact, intended to be wielded only by dwarf heroes, and it was beyond the strength of mortal man to overcome its magic.

The Bloodthirster had bent down now over Gotrek, as it had over Thangrim. It reached down and enveloped the fallen Slayer's head with one might hand. Slowly it lifted him upwards.

Felix knew what was coming next. The daemon would squeeze the dwarf's head until his skull shattered like a melon, then it would consume his brain and eat his immortal soul. Behind the triumphant daemon he could see the beastmen were crushing the last of the dwarfs' resistance. Varek stood at one of the pillars. The scholar had armed himself with a hammer from somewhere. A wave of frenzied beastmen closed in.

'Help me, Sigmar of the Hammer,' Felix howled with a fervour which he had not felt since he was a frightened child. 'Help me, Grungni! Help me Grimnir! Help me, Valaya! Help me! Help me, damn you!'

At the invocation of the gods' names, the runes on the hammer flickered and fire leapt back into them. Felix felt the weapon begin to come free of the ground. It was heavy at first but weighed progressively less as he lifted it, as if some other force was lending him the strength to overcome its vast weight. A burning pain shot through Felix's hand where he held the warhammer. He felt sparks scorching his sleeve. The taint of ozone filled his nostrils. The pain made almost made him drop the thing. He fought to keep a grip on it while every nerve ending in his hand shrieked with agony. Somehow, he managed to maintain his hold.

Felix knew he would only get one chance. He drew the hammer back for the cast. The daemon sensed the gathering of energies behind it and turned to face him, the Slayer held negligently in one hand, the way a man might hold a broken doll. The terrible eyes rested on Felix and for a moment he felt another surge of that familiar terror. He knew the daemon was about to spring, to rend him limb from limb and he would not be quick enough to stop it. He wrestled down his fear, smiled shyly and decided to try anyway.

The Bloodthirster dropped Gotrek and sprang, both claws outstretched, its mouth wide open, its fangs bared. Eyes through which hell looked out upon the world glared directly into Felix's soul. Its hideous odour filled his nostrils. The heat of its body radiated across the closing gap. Felix flung the sacred warhammer forward and released it. It hurtled forward like a falling meteor, trailing a comet tail of blazing lightning. It smashed directly into the daemon's head with a noise like a clap of thunder. The force of the impact stopped its headlong rush. It toppled over backwards but only for a moment. The Hammer of Fate glanced off it and flew into the gloom.

Slowly the daemon pulled itself upright. Felix knew now that there was nothing he could do to stop it. Its victory was inevitable. He had done his best, and it had not been enough. He barely had the energy to stand, let alone flee from the creature. His chest was scorched. His hand felt like the flesh was peeling off the bone.

The Bloodthirster staggered forward, grinning evilly. The look in its ancient eyes told him that it knew what he was thinking and that it mocked his despair. Its enormous shadow fell across him. It flexed its wings, pulling the rune-carved blade free from its back and sending it flying across the chamber. It drew back its claws for the killing blow.

'Oi! You! I haven't finished with you yet!' roared Gotrek's voice from behind it.

The monstrous head of his great, ancient axe suddenly protruded through the Bloodthirster's chest. As it did so, the daemon began to come apart, in a shower of red and gold sparks which transformed into stinking vapour. The thing started to vanish, like a fire burning down before their eyes. Through the fading mist Felix could see the bruised and battered form of the Slayer, barely able to stand upright. Slowly the Bloodthirster faded from view.

But Felix could still see the daemon's blazing eyes and its last words still echoed inside his head: *I will remember you, mortals, and I have all eternity in which to take my vengeance.*

Wonderful, thought Felix, that's all I need. The enmity of the favoured of Khorne! Still, his heart had lifted. The daemon was gone and the terrible fear that its presence had inflicted had vanished like morning mist in the light of the rising sun. Felix felt a weight fall from his shoulders that he had not even known was there, and a vast sense of relief filled him.

Gotrek reeled over to where the Hammer of Fate lay and picked it up. This time the weapon lifted easily and as it did so something strange started to happen. Bolts of lightning flickered between the hammer and the axe, creating a searing electrical arc. As they did so, the Slayer seemed to swell with barely contained power. His crest stood on end above his head. His beard bristled. His eyes blazed with an odd blue light.

'The gods mock me, manling!' he roared in a voice that was as audible as a thunderclap. Bitterness twisted his face. 'I came here seeking my doom, and instead brought doom upon this place. Now, someone is going to pay.'

He turned and walked back into the fray. The Hammer of Fate left an blurred trail of light behind it as it struck. His ancient, daemon-slaying axe smashed through a Chaos warrior and took a huge chunk out of the one of the pillars behind him. An aura of fear surrounded him now, like the one that had surrounded the daemon, and the Chaos worshippers began to back away. Gotrek let out a mighty battle cry and leapt into their midst, and a terrible slaying began. Filled with god-like power by the awesome weapons he held, the Slayer was invincible. His axe sheered through armour and flesh effortlessly; no weapon could stand against it. The hammer sent bolt after bolt of terrifying power out to lash the Chaos warriors like a daemon's whip.

Felix watched appalled at the carnage the Slayer wrought until he saw his blade lying on the floor, forced his hand to grip it, and rushed down into the fray himself. In moments it was over, dismayed by the fall of their leader. Unable to withstand the invincible power of the angry Slayer, the remnants of the Chaos horde turned tail and fled.

TWENTY
AFTERMATH

FELIX SURVEYED the Hall of the Well wearily. Corpses lay everywhere, evidence of a battle fought with insane ferocity on one side and unyielding dwarfish determination on the other. Dried blood carpeted the floor. The stench of death filled his nostrils.

He looked down at where Gotrek lay, pale and still, propped up against one of the pillars which supported the ceiling's roof. His entire chest was swathed in bandages and one arm was held immobile in a sling. Bruises covered the Slayer's head, evident even beneath his tattoos. The grip of the daemon had not been gentle. The fight with the Bloodthirster had come very near to killing the Slayer and the combat afterwards had not helped any. The Slayer's chest barely moved, as he struggled on the borderland between life and death. Not even Varek could say whether he would live or die.

The young dwarf looked up uncertainly. 'I have done my best for him. The rest is in the lap of the gods. It is a wonder he lives at all. I suspect only the power of the Hammer of Fate kept him alive as long as he was fighting.'

Felix wondered whether the time had finally arrived when he would have to record the Slayer's doom. It had certainly been an epic battle, all that Gotrek could have wanted for his end.

The dwarfs had rallied at the sight of the daemon's banishment. The Chaos horde had lost all heart for the fight as the berserk Slayer ploughed through their midst, armed with his invincible weaponry, violent and deadly as some ancient divinity of war. Such was the slaughter Gotrek had wrought, it must have seemed to the Chaos worshippers that their vile gods had turned against them. In the end, demoralised and panicking, they had turned and fled the hall, leaving the dwarfs triumphant. Only then had Gotrek collapsed.

Such a victory had been bought at a hideous cost. Felix doubted that more than a score of the dwarfs survived and most of those had been hidden in the Vault when the fighting was on. If not for the power of the hammer and Gotrek's skill with the axe, he doubted that any of them would have lived. And it seemed that the Slayer might yet pay the ultimate price for their victory.

Snorri limped through the dead, favouring his right leg. He did not look much better than Gotrek. His chest had been stitched together with whipcord. It was probably testimony to his awesome dwarfish toughness that he was still alive at all. No human could have survived the Bloodthirster's blow or the loss of blood which followed. A makeshift turban of bandages wrapped round his head made him look like a very short, very broad, and very stupid native of Araby. He whistled happily to himself as he surveyed the red ruin all around. But even he lost some of his cheerfulness when he looked down at Gotrek's recumbent form.

'Good fight,' he said softly to no one in particular. Felix was about to disagree. He wanted to say that, in his opinion, there was no such thing as a good fight, there were only those you won and those you lost. Fighting was a dirty, messy, painful and dangerous business, and on the whole he had decided it was something that he would rather avoid.

Yet even as he thought this, Felix knew that he was trying to deceive himself. There was a bizarre elation in survival and awful joy to be found in victory, and he was not immune to it. And when he considered the alternatives to victory he found he was forced to agree with Snorri.

'Yes, it was a good fight,' he said, though he wondered whether any of those lying dead on the cold stone floor would agree, were they able to speak.

The effort of talking made his own body ache. He inspected his hand. It was stiff and scorched from where he had held the Hammer of Fate as it discharged its lightning bolts. Even the opiate salves that Varek had applied could not dull the pain entirely. He wasn't entirely sure what magic had protected Thangrim from this sort of thing, but it obviously did not work for humans. Still, it had done its work and he shouldn't really complain about the sloppy way in which the gods had answered his prayers.

Looking at the bandages which bound his hand, he now wondered how he had ever managed to keep fighting – but really he knew the answer. In the heat of battle, a man could endure pain that would floor him under normal circumstances. He had once seen a man continue to fight for some minutes after taking a wound that eventually killed him. Looking at his hand, he wondered if he would ever be able to wield a blade again. Or even the pen that would be needed to record the Slayer's death.

Varek had assured him that he would, in time, but right now he was not so sure. Still, he supposed, he could always learn to wield a blade left-handed. He tried to draw the Templar's sword from the scabbard with his left hand but it felt all wrong. Still, there was time enough to learn.

His whole body ached and he wanted simply to lie down and sleep, but there was still much to do. Hargrim and the other dwarfs finished their discussion and strode over to him. Hargrim held the Hammer of Fate in his right hand. Felix noticed somewhat sourly that it had not burned him.

'We owe you a debt we can never pay, Felix Jaeger,' Hargrim started. 'You have saved the honour of our people and prevented the sacred warhammer of our ancestors from falling into the hands of our foes.'

Felix smiled at the dwarf. 'You owe me nothing, Hargrim. The Hammer of Fate saved my life. There is no debt.'

'Nobly spoken. Nevertheless, what we have is yours.'

'Thank you, but I just want to go home,' Felix said, hoping he did not sound ungrateful.

'We will leave together,' Hargrim said. Felix raised an eyebrow.

'There are too few of us now to defend this place, and the Dark Ones surely now know of its location. It is only a matter of time before they return. It is time to take our Book of Grudges and the hammer and what we can carry of our hoard, and leave.'

'I believe there is enough room on the *Spirit of Grungni*, Felix,' said Varek. He looked on Felix respectfully, as if seeking his approval for the decision. Obviously wielding the Hammer of Fate had given him some status among the dwarfs. 'There are only twenty-two dwarfs of Karag Dum now and if we clear the hold and double up in the cabins there will be space enough.'

'I am sure you are correct,' Felix said.

'It is imperative that we get the sacred warhammer away from here. And as much of the dwarfhoard as we can carry.'

'Of course it is,' Felix said, looking at the chests the dwarfs were bearing out of the hidden vault. 'But I worry about how we are going to get everything out. We have to find our way through the Chaos worshippers. And we are too weak and too few to fight.'

Hargrim grinned. 'Do not worry about that, Felix Jaeger. There are still many secret paths through Karag Dum which are known only to the dwarfs.'

Felix looked over at the recumbent Gotrek, who looked far too pale and feeble to be moved. 'What about Gotrek and the other wounded?' he said. Perhaps they should wait for the Slayer to die and bury him here in the vault along with the other heroes of the battle.

'When I'm too weak to walk, manling, I will be too weak to live,' came a voice from the Trollslayer. Gotrek's one good eye slowly opened. They all hurried over as he forced himself upright.

'Then, by all means, let us get going,' Felix said happily.

The Slayer looked around at the field of battle. 'It seems my doom has eluded me yet again,' he said sourly.

'Don't worry,' Felix said. 'I'm sure some other doom awaits!'

THANQUOL PULLED back the curtain of his palanquin and blinked as the unaccustomed light crashed into his retina. He had just emerged from the Underways into the day. The bright summer sun of northern Kislev glared down on him like the watching eye of some pitiless god.

He looked out into the awesome crater of Hell Pit. Beneath him he could see the enormous fortress of Clan Moulder. A sense of satisfaction filled him. He had driven his exhausted bearers for days to reach his goal.

'Move quick-quick!' he ordered the panting slaves. 'We still have a great distance to go!'

Slowly the bearers stumbled down the slope.

Eerie echoes erupted from the oddly sculpted towers. Great beasts roared. The smell of monsters and warpstone made Thanquol's nostrils twitch.

Here he knew he would find the allies he needed to capture the airship and take his inevitable revenge on Gurnisson and Jaeger. Already he could see skaven warriors accompanied by misshapen shambling beasts coming to greet him.

Now, if only he could re-establish contact with his minion Lurk Snitchtongue, things would be well. He wondered what Lurk was up to right now.

LURK WAS NOT quite sure what those stupid dwarfs were up to, but he knew that soon the time would be right for him to act. He felt strong and certain that the Horned Rat was with him. Now, he waited only for his opportunity to strike. If the situation called for action, he would not wait. Oh no. He would spring out and overwhelm his foes.

Maybe.

Provided there weren't too many of them.

William King will return with *SPACE WOLF*, coming soon from the Black Library.

Here is a short preview.

CHAPTER ONE
THE SEA OF DRAGONS

'WE'RE ALL GOING to die!' Yorvik the Harpooner screamed, glaring round, his eyes wide with fear. Lightning slashed through the sky of Fenris, illuminating the man's tormented face. Sheer terror made his shout audible even above the roar of the wind and the thunder of the waves against the ship. The driving rain running down his face looked uncannily like tears.

'Be silent!' Ragnar shouted and slapped the terrified man across the cheek. Shocked at being hit by a youth barely old enough to have the down of manhood on his cheeks, Yorvik reached for his axe, his fear momentarily forgotten. Ragnar shook his head and glared at the older man with his cold grey eyes. Yorvik stopped, as if realising where he was and what he was doing. They stood in full view of all the warriors on the prow of the ship. Attacking the son of his captain would gain him no credit in the eyes of the gods or the crew. The flush of shame came to Yorvik's cheeks and Ragnar looked away so as not to embarrass the man further.

Ragnar tossed his head to get his mane of long black hair from his eyes. Squinting through the lash of the wind and the salt-spray of the storm-tossed sea, Ragnar silently agreed with Yorvik. They were going to die unless a miracle occurred. He had been going to sea since he was old enough to walk, and never had he seen a storm this bad.

Sullen dark clouds scudded across the sky. It was dark as night even though it was noon. Spray billowed as the prow of the ship cleaved through another enormous wave. The dragonhide of the deck echoed like an enormous drum with the force of the impact. He struggled to keep his balance on the constantly moving deck. Even over the wind's daemon shriek, he could hear the creak of the ship's bones. It was only a matter of time, he decided, before the sea killed the vessel. It was a race to see whether the force of the waves smashed the *Spear of Russ* into a thousand pieces, or whether it simply stripped the cured dragonhide from the ship's skeleton and left them to founder and drown.

Ragnar shuddered and not just from the chill, sodden wetness of his clothing. For him, as for all his people, drowning represented the worst of all possible deaths. It meant simply sinking into the clutches of the sea daemons, where his soul would be bound in an eternity of servitude. There would be no chance of earning his place among the Chosen. He would not die with spear or axe in hand. He would not find himself a glorious death or swift passage to the Hall of Heroes in the Mountains of the Gods.

Looking back along the rain-lashed deck Ragnar saw that all the massive warriors were as frightened as he, though they hid it well. Tension was written on every pallid face, and visible in every blue eye. Rain matted their long blond hair and gave them a hopeless bedraggled look. They sat huddled at their benches, useless oars held at the ready, massive dragonskin rain-cloaks thrown around their shoulders or flapping in the wind like the wings of bats. Each man's weapons lay beside him on the soaking deck, impotent against the foe that now threatened their lives.

The wind howled, hungry as the great wolves of Asaheim. The ship plunged down the far side of another enormous wave. The dragon tooth on its prow smashed through the foaming water like a spear. Overhead, the sails struggled and flexed. Ragnar was glad that they were made from the purest dragongut; nothing else would have survived the storm's rending claws. Ahead another massive mountain of water loomed. Somehow it did not seem possible that the ship could survive it crashing down on them.

Ragnar cursed in fury and frustration. It seemed that his short life was over almost before it started. He would not live even to see his entry into manhood next season. His voice had barely broken and now he was doomed to be lost at sea. He shielded his eyes and gazed out into the storm, hoping to catch sight of the longship of his kinfolk. They were nowhere to be seen. Most had likely gone to the bottom. Their bodies would become food for the dragons and the kraken, their souls would provide thralls for the daemons.

He turned and aimed an angry glance at the stranger who had brought them to this. There was some satisfaction in knowing that if they died, he would too. That is if he were not a sorcerer, or some sea daemon in disguise sent to lure the Thunderfist folk to their doom. Watching the way the old man stood on the water-covered deck, fearless and unafraid, that seemed all too possible at the present moment.

There was something supernatural about this gnarled ancient. He looked strong as a warrior in his prime despite all the furrows age had ploughed in his brow and he held his balance better than many a seafarer half his age despite the white in his hair. Ragnar knew that he was a sorcerer. Who but a sorcerer would wear the pelts of those enormous wolves around his shoulders and that strange metal armour encasing his entire body, so unlike the leather tunics of the sea folk? Who but a sorcerer would carry all those strange amulets and charms around his person? Who but a sorcerer could offer his father and their kin enough ingots of precious iron to attempt the near suicidal passage of the Sea of Dragons in this, the Season of Storms?

Ragnar saw that the stranger was pointing at something. Was this some sorcerer's trick, he wondered, or was the stranger casting a spell? Ragnar turned to see and felt his mouth go dry with fear. Lightning flared once again. In the flash Ragnar saw a huge head had broken from the waves next to the ship, almost as if the stranger had summoned it. A nightmare face filled with teeth the size of daggers loomed above them. The long neck flexed and the head descended searching for prey. It was a sea dragon, and no mere hatchling but a full-sized monstrosity, large as the ship, stirred from the sea bottom by the fury of the storm.

The thunder spoke its angry words. Death struck an arm's length from Ragnar. He felt the wind of its passage as the huge jaws of the dragon closed on Yorvik. Great fangs pierced the tough leather of Yorvik's armour as if it were paper. Bone gave way. Blood gouted. The screaming man was lifted into the air, arms flailing, the harpoon dropping from his fist. A sneer curled Ragnar's lips. He had always known Yorvik was a coward and now he had proof. He would find himself a place in the cold hells of Frostheim. The dragon bit down and gulped and part of Yorvik disappeared down its throat. The other part splattered down on the deck near Ragnar. The rushing waves cleansed him of blood and bile.

The warriors swarmed from their benches, raising their axes and their spears in defiance. Ragnar could tell that in their hearts they were glad. Here was a quick death and a heroic one, fighting a monster from the depths. To many it must seem as if Russ had answered their prayers, and sent them this beast to grant a great doom.

The enormous head began to descend once more. At the sight of it, several of the warriors froze. As if it had been sent to weed out cowards, the beast struck them down, biting them in two with its rending fangs. Other Thunderfist warriors lashed out at it with their weapons. Axes bounced futilely from the heavy armoured scales. A few spears bit deep into flesh but the creature paid as much attention to them as a man might pay to a pinprick. The pain merely goaded it to greater fury.

It opened its maw and let out a terrifying bellow, audible even over the thunder of the waves. The sheer volume of it paralysed all the warriors. They froze as if overwhelmed by a sorcerer's spell. Ragnar could see that the creature had reared half out of the water. Its enormous length towered over the boat. It had merely to fall forward and its huge bulk would break the ship in two.

Something snapped within Ragnar. His anger at the storm, at the gods, at this enormous beast and his cowardly kinsman bubbled over. He reached down and picked up the harpoon Yorvik had dropped. Not pausing to think, not pausing to aim lest fear of those enormous dripping jaws should freeze him, he threw the harpoon directly into the creature's eye. It was a good cast. The bone-tipped spear flew true and buried itself up to the shaft in the dragon's eye.

The monster pulled itself up still further, screaming in rage and pain. Ragnar thought he would be deafened by the chill evil of its cries. He was certain now that he was going to die, that the entire ship was going to be smashed to flinders by the enraged beast. Then he heard another sound, a stuttering roar that came from the back of the ship. He risked a glance at the stranger and saw that he was the source of the noise.

The ancient had drawn some kind of massive iron icon from his side, which he held aloft and pointed at the beast. A searing blast of fire spurted from the end of the holy charm along with the roaring sound. Looking back at the dragon Ragnar could see that huge gaping wounds were stitched across its torso – testimony to the strength of the stranger's magic. It opened its mouth to scream in pain and the stranger raised his talisman still further. A hole appeared in the roof of the dragon's mouth and the top of its head exploded. The creature tumbled backwards to vanish beneath the waves.

The stranger threw back his head and laughed. His booming mirth drowned out the sound of the storm. Ragnar felt a shiver of superstitious fear. He could see that two enormous fangs jutted downwards from the stranger's mouth. He bore the mark of Russ! In him flowed the blood of the gods. Truly, he was a sorcerer or something more.

Crouching low on the deck, keeping his balance easily despite the motion of the ship, Ragnar turned and moved back towards the helm. Spray ran down his face like tears. When he licked his lips he tasted salt. As he moved past the stranger, a huge wave broke over the ship. He felt the pressure of tons of water and floundered. The force of the wave lifted him clear of the deck and send him tumbling. In the waves' fury he could get no clear view of where he was. He simply knew he was going to be swept overboard and carried to his doom.

He growled with rage and restrained fear. It seemed that he had survived the dragon's jaws only to be taken by the sea daemons. Then iron-strong fingers clamped on his wrist. Enormous strength fought against the power of the sea. Then the water was gone. In a moment Ragnar floundered on the deck, saved by the stranger who had banished the dragon.

'Be still, boy,' the sorcerer said. 'It is not my destiny to die here. Nor is it yours, I think.'

So saying the stranger turned and strode away to the prow of the ship. He stood there gazing forward like some elder god. Filled with fear and a strange superstitious reverence, Ragnar made his way to the place where his father stood. Looking up he saw understanding there.

'I saw it, my son,' his father shouted. Ragnar knew no further explanation was necessary.

The saga continues in SPACE WOLF, to be published by the Black Library in July 2000.

Also from the Black Library

TROLLSLAYER

A Gotrek & Felix novel
by William King

HIGH ON THE HILL the scorched walled castle stood, a stone spider clutching the hilltop with blasted stone feet. Before the gaping maw of its broken gate hanged men dangled on gibbets, flies caught in its single-strand web.

'Time for some bloodletting,' Gotrek said. He ran his left hand through the massive red crest of hair that rose above his shaven tattooed skull. His nose chain tinkled gently, a strange counterpoint to his mad rumbling laughter.

'I am a slayer, manling. Born to die in battle. Fear has no place in my life.'

TROLLSLAYER IS THE first part of the death saga of Gotrek Gurnisson, as retold by his travelling companion Felix Jaeger. Set in the darkly gothic world of Warhammer, Trollslayer is an episodic novel featuring some of the most extraordinary adventures of this deadly pair of heroes. Monsters, daemons, sorcerers, mutants, orcs, beastmen and worse are to be found as Gotrek strives to achieve a noble death in battle. Felix, of course, only has to survive to tell the tale.

ISBN 0-671-78373-4 • March 2000

Also from the Black Library

SKAVENSLAYER

A Gotrek & Felix novel
by William King

'BEWARE! SKAVEN!' Felix shouted and saw them all reach for their weapons. In moments, swords glittered in the half-light of the burning city. From inside the tavern a number of armoured figures spilled out into the gloom. Felix was relieved to see the massive squat figure of Gotrek among them. There was something enormously reassuring about the immense axe clutched in the dwarf's hands.

'I see you found our scuttling little friends, manling,' Gotrek said, running his thumb along the blade of his axe until a bright red bead of blood appeared.

'Yes,' Felix gasped, struggling to get his breath back before the combat began.

'Good. Let's get killing then!'

SET IN THE MIGHTY city of Nuln, Gotrek and Felix are back in SKAVENSLAYER, the second novel in this epic saga. Seeking to undermine the very fabric of the Empire with their arcane warp-sorcery, the skaven, twisted chaos rat-men, are at large in the reeking sewers beneath the ancient city. Led by Grey Seer Thanquol, the servants of the Horned Rat are determined to overthrow this bastion of humanity. Against such forces, what possible threat can just two hard-bitten adventurers pose?

ISBN 0-671-78385-8 • April 2000

Also from the Black Library

FIRST & ONLY

A Gaunt's Ghosts novel
by Dan Abnett

'THE TANITH ARE strong fighters, general, so I have heard.' The scar tissue of his cheek pinched and twitched slightly, as it often did when he was tense. 'Gaunt is said to be a resourceful leader.'

'You know him?' The general looked up, questioningly

'I know *of* him sir. In the main by reputation.'

GAUNT GOT TO his feet, wet with blood and Chaos pus. His Ghosts were moving up the ramp to secure the position. Above them, at the top of the elevator shaft, were over a million Shriven, secure in their bunker batteries. Gaunt's expeditionary force was inside, right at the heart of the enemy stronghold. Commissar Ibram Gaunt smiled.

IT IS THE nightmare future of Warhammer 40,000, and mankind teeters on the brink of extinction. The galaxy-spanning Imperium is riven with dangers, and in the Chaos-infested Sabbat system, Imperial Commissar Gaunt must lead his men through as much in-fighting amongst rival regiments as against the forces of Chaos. FIRST AND ONLY is an epic saga of planetary conquest, grand ambition, treachery and honour.

ISBN 0-671-78375-0 • March 2000

Also from the Black Library

INTO THE MAELSTROM

An anthology of Warhammer 40,000 stories, edited by Marc Gascoigne & Andy Jones

'THE CHAOS ARMY had travelled from every continent, every shattered city, every ruined sector of Illium to gather on this patch of desert that had once been the control centre of the Imperial Garrison. The sand beneath their feet had been scorched, melted and fused by a final, futile act of suicidal defiance: the detonation of the garrison's remaining nuclear stockpile.' – **Hell in a Bottle** *by Simon Jowett*

'HOARSE SCREAMS and the screech of tortured hot metal filled the air. Massive laser blasts were punching into the spaceship. They superheated the air that men breathed, set fire to everything that could burn and sent fireballs exploding through the crowded passageways.' – **Children of the Emperor** *by Barrington J. Bayley*

IN THE GRIM and gothic nightmare future of Warhammer 40,000, mankind teeters on the brink of extinction. INTO THE MAELSTROM is a storming collection of a dozen action-packed science fiction short stories set in this dark and brooding universe.

ISBN 0-671-78386-6 • April 2000

Also from the Black Library

EYE OF TERROR

A Warhammer 40,000 novel by Barrington J. Bayley

Tell the truth only if a lie will not serve

'WHAT I HAVE to tell you,' Abaddas said, in slow measured tones, 'will be hard for you to accept or even comprehend. The rebellion led by Warmaster Horus succeeded. The Emperor is dead, killed by Horus himself in single combat, though Horus too died of his injuries.'

Magron groaned. He cursed himself for having gone into suspended animation. To be revived in a galaxy without the Emperor! Horrible! Unbelievable! Impossible to bear! Stricken, he looked into Abaddas's flinty grey eyes. 'Who is Emperor now?'

The first hint of an emotional reaction flickered on Abaddas's face. 'What need have we of an Emperor?' he roared. 'We have the Chaos gods!'

IN THE DARK and gothic future of Warhammer 40,000, mankind teeters on the brink of extinction. As the war-fleets of the Imperium prepare to launch themselves on a crusade into the very heart of Chaos, Rogue Trader Maynard Rugolo seeks power and riches on the fringe worlds of this insane and terrifying realm.

ISBN 0-671-78390-4 • June 2000